GUARDIAN
OF NIGHT

GUARDIAN OF NIGHT

TONY DANIEL

Guardian of Night

A Baen Books Original

Baen Publishing Enterprises
P.O. Box 1403
Riverdale, NY 10471
www.baen.com

ISBN: 978-1-4516-3802-8

Cover art by Kurt Miller

First Baen printing, February 2012

Distributed by Simon & Schuster
1230 Avenue of the Americas
New York, NY 10020

Library of Congress Cataloging-in-Publication Data
tk

10 9 8 7 6 5 4 3 2 1

Pages by Joy Freeman (www.pagesbyjoy.com)
Printed in the United States of America

For Rika

PROLOG

25 November 2075
Vicinity of 82 Eridani
USX *Chief Seattle*

A low *thump, thump, thump* reverberated from outside the SIGINT station entrance hatch. Inside, the directed sound suddenly became much louder and more intense. Petty Officer Second Class Melinda Japps was the only exper on duty in SIGINT, and she was taking advantage of the situation to cycle her own music through the craft's superior speakers. At the moment, Joy Division's "Love Will Tear Us Apart" was flooding from the bulkheads. Japps adored its creepy, snaky, utterly old-fashioned synth melody line. She was a connoisseur when it came to century-old goth. It was a darkender thing, after all.

Okay, darkenders were not *really* close to the goths of yore in dress (not that she had much choice, Extry regs being what they were) or mannerisms, Japps thought. More a state of mind, really. "Negative reaction," like in that Nettles mantra. The cultivation of a numb exterior to hide a beating heart of passion and—

Oh, whatever. The Nettles made good music now. Joy Division made great music then. It wasn't her job to analyze it all to death. Music she listened to. And felt.

Japps was not alone in SIGINT. Once you were wiied into the chroma—the vessel's virtual overlay—SIGINT came alive with consoles, readouts, floating status boards, collapsible toolbars, and inputs that appeared and disappeared at your fingertips on command.

1

And geists.

There were at least three partially transparent human-looking figures who seemed to be standing around her performing various tasks. These geists of the *Chief Seattle* were personas, not quite up to the sentience standards of their betters, the a.i. servants, but certainly programs of a high order. The geists, the ghostly representations, were allegedly for human benefit and ease of interaction. Sometimes Japps thought the geists also enjoyed freaking people out.

Japps figured she might be creeping the SIGINT geists out just as much with the Joy Division.

Or maybe not. Maybe they were fans. With personas, unlike servants, it was hard to tell if they had real feelings at all.

If not, too bad for them. For Japps, music was life, a least the way life *felt*. It was one of the ways you got through and kept going. She'd even once been a musician herself.

Japps missed her baby grand. Sure, here on the *Chief Seattle* she could create one on a tabletop, on a bulkhead—heck, she could make one seem to hang in midair in front of her. But it wasn't the same. No matter how good the chroma and Q had gotten— and she'd been amazed over the years since the invasion as the two new techs, pushed by wartime extremes, were transforming every part of existence—still, it wasn't good enough to build *her* piano. The sustain, the reverb of her piano in the old farmhouse where she'd grown up, the creak of the pinewood floor when she shifted her weight on the bench. Because to do that, she'd have to reconstruct it all. The chicken farm outside Murfreesboro where she'd spent the first sixteen years of her life. Her practice time, early in the morning before she had to leave for the private school in town where she had a half-tuition music scholarship.

It was the time when only she and her father were up—him to make a cup of coffee and his customary two pancakes with Karo syrup—her to practice. They'd share a cup of coffee together— she was allowed to drink it at twelve and had, from the start, taken it black, like her father did—and he'd give her the one big pancake she always requested. But always he'd throw in the dad variation. Sometimes it was the shape of a cowboy, sometimes a cactus (truthfully, they were hard to tell apart). But most days he made it in the shape of a heart.

And then he'd go to his day job at the Stones River Relay Station on the thirty-inch oil and natural gas pipeline that ran from

Nashville to Atlanta. She'd run through her scales and arpeggios until she heard her father gathering his truck keys, then she'd pause, and he'd step into the living room where they kept the piano and give her a buss on the cheek before heading out into the dawn.

This would be Melinda's signal to dive into work on whatever competition piece she was currently trying to commit not only to mind but to the memories that seemed to live in her fingers, in the shape of her hands on the keys. She usually had an hour quietly until her mother woke up, and then her sisters, Lillian and Pam, dragged their tails out of bed so they could get ready and pile into the ancient '63 Landmaster station wagon her mother drove because she hated the monitor sight lines on boxies and mini-boxies.

All gone.

Japps had been in Atlanta at a piano competition when the sceeve drop-rod attack came. She'd just taken second place for her rendition of Chopin's "Heroic."

All her family was dead. Battered to pieces.

Her baby grand not splintered but pulverized to wood pulp as fine as dust.

Nope, unless somebody came up with time travel, bringing back her piano was a problem beyond any technology known to humans.

Bink.

A screen appeared. It hung weightlessly in the chroma on Japps's right. She turned in her swivel chair to face it and, with a motion of her finger against a chroma-based input pad that hovered by her right hand, damped Joy Division down to a low murmur of disgruntlement.

"Hello," Japps said to one of the geists nearby—LARK, the sensor persona. "Looks like we've got contact."

LARK nodded. "We have received audible of conditioning super-function. It frequency-maps as a sceeve pre-transmission signal."

Japps checked her screen, saw an auditory waveform assemble itself. "It's the Poet, all right," she said.

Japps touched another hovering toolbar with her fingers and selected BRIDGECOM. Her own geist would now appear on the bridge next to her intended recipient, Executive Officer Noemi Martinez. "XO, our beta output pulled the trigger again. We've got incoming from the Poet."

"Very good, SIGINT," said Martinez. "Localized?"

Japps double-checked a readout.

"Same as always. It's our bogie, XO, or else the bogie is a relay."

"No verification on primary source yet?"

Japps took a breath. Now was the time. She was either going to voice her big idea or let it go. She was sure, wasn't she? For a moment, she felt the same butterflies she used to get before plunging into a piece at a recital. Showtime.

"Yeah, but I have an idea on that, XO," she said. "I think we can confirm with this transmission, as a matter of fact, nail the Poet down as the original source."

"No shit? Then I'll be in SIGINT in two," said Martinez. Her geist blinked out of existence. Two minutes later, her physical body entered through the area portal.

Martinez was tall for a Hispanic woman—although she was of fairly average height for females in the Extry. She and Japps were old acquaintances. Japps and the XO had served together for a year and a half now, had gone out drinking and hell-raising back home, totally violating any officer-enlisted separation protocols. Both had lost whole swaths of their family during the invasion, so who really gave a shit about such shore-leave regs?

"So, you figured out what our bullshit sceeve philosopher's going on about today?" said Martinez.

Japps shook her head. "Not really, XO."

"As if anybody can tell. It's a lot of hot air, if you ask me. Or hot whatever it is they spew out of those mangled faces of theirs."

The transmission had begun before the XO arrived and continued for several minutes afterward. With the aid of LARK and her recording-engineer persona KETCH, Japps tried to ride the gain on it as best she could. The trick was to be sure that everything was recorded up and down the scale of possible notes. A rough paraphrase was possible but usually pretty far off after she'd compared it to a complete translation from the real-deal team at HQ. The full-scale translation work could take weeks, and days getting back via bottle drone. On Earth, a roomful of Xeno analysts—at least that was how Japps imagined it—pored over all the nuances in the New Pentagon.

Japps and LARK might do a better job on-site if LARK were a true servant, but the vessel was forbidden from employing a real a.i. aboard by top-down edict from Extry Command. It was said the directive came from Old Man Tillich himself.

Japps had played around with the translation-code parameters much like she might adjust an equalizer on a music player, and she had a preset for the Poet that she'd tweaked to encompass what she thought of as some of the "ambient" undertones that accompanied "his" broadcasts, if he were a he. Even though Japps couldn't speak sceeve—how do you speak a smell-based language, after all?—it was these "ambients" that had begun to interest her several days ago . . . and had taken up all her free time since she'd had her idea for source verification.

Japps set up her templates and prepared to intercept and attempt to multiply decode the anticipated beta transmission. The sceeve usually sent messages to one another in a set of standard formats. At SIG school, all the scrub exper-techs had been taught to think of a sceeve sentence as a train being "built" car by car in a large freight yard. But for Japps, it was a lot easier to think of sceeve as a peculiar form of music.

"So, what's your idea, Japps?" Martinez said, stepping up next to Japps. She seemed to be staring off into space, but Japps knew she was examining her own separate chroma monitor hanging within her particular sightline and maybe even overlapping Japps's own. After a while, you got used to the idea that not everybody saw the same thing in chroma.

"I've gone through a couple of month's worth of our friend's broadcasts," Japps said.

"When'd you do that?"

"In my copious spare time, ma'am."

Martinez didn't crack a smile, but Japps could tell by the crinkling around her eyes that she was amused. "Sounds like a party I'm glad I wasn't invited to."

"Nah, the Poet's not so bad as soon as you accept he's playing around, being a smartass most of the time and not really trying to make a logical political argument or anything. What's important for him are the poems, and the rest is kind of him working up to delivering them."

"If you say so."

"Anyway, I wasn't replaying those bounce-back translations from HQ," Japps said. "I was listening to the incoming raw feeds." Japps moved her hand, pulled down a toolbar, and used it to pop up a display that she and the XO could share. A series of audio signals were stacked horizontally on its screen. "So, the big problem is verification, right? How do we know the Poet isn't sceeve propaganda, a false-flag operation meant to send us on a wild-goose chase or plant false info and stuff?"

"And stuff," the XO said. "I'd love to send an MDR back to HQ with confirmed information. Can you give us that?"

"I'm pretty sure that now we can at least confirm the source as unique," Japps said. "Look."

She pointed at the screen, and her pointing finger highlighted a segment in each of the audio signals. The same segment.

"The Poet's beta signature is scrambled in a way we don't understand yet, so it's impossible to tell where on the sceeve vessel he's transmitting from or even if it *is* coming from the vessel we've been shadowing. Might be a relay of some sort."

"HQ is translating the vessel designation as the *Powers of Heaven*," said the XO.

Japps nodded. She'd taken the message that contained the name translation and had been a bit disappointed to see she no longer could refer to the target vessel as the *Brown Turd*, the temporary call sign she'd assigned the craft.

Japps touched the chroma screen again and zoomed in on a particular spike in the audio.

"What's that?" asked the XO.

"That," said Japps, "is a characteristic ten-decibel pop at a thirty-two-kilohertz frequency. I call it the thirty-two spike."

"Okay, what does it mean?"

"Every one of the raw feeds has it," said Japps. "And it doesn't always come at the same place, so I don't think it's solely equipment-related."

"What else could it correlate with?" The XO seemed genuinely puzzled.

That's because the Poet's still just a concept to her, Japps thought. *She's not really picturing him making these beta broadcasts. How it would look. And smell.*

"It's a popped *p*, XO."

"A what?"

"You know how sometimes you get those airpuffs on *p* and *b*s when you're talking into an old-fashioned microphone, one without a pop screen?"

"Nope, not really."

"Trust me. This is the same thing, only with odor."

"Not following you, Japps."

"It's chemical. The sceeve equivalent to a plosive in our spoken languages," Japps said. "It's something like overextension on his sensing microphone's dynamic range in an oxygen-helium atmospheric mix. But in our guy's case, the effect's produced not with overpressurization by spoken word but via oversaturation with a chemical signal."

"So the Poet—"

"Pops his *ps*. He's got bad technique. Or he's doing it on purpose for some reason."

"And you're sure about this?"

"Oh, yeah. See here?" she pointed to a prime example. "And this from two weeks ago."

The XO made a motion with her hand, and the chroma screen floated in closer to her eyes. "Yeah, I see it. I do." She turned to Japps. "Thirty-two spike, huh. Good work. Have to talk to the cap, but I can just about guarantee you another stripe under that crow if this holds up."

"Thanks, XO. Just get me the E-6 rate so I can upgrade to a 140 PB Pocket Palace Plus."

"You and your tech fetish, Japps—"

Bink.

And the Poet's transmission was done. Japps quickly secured and verified her redundancies and labeled the session with the date.

For nearly two months now the *Chief Seattle* had been stalking the sceeve craft, always attempting to remain in beta range for whenever the Poet felt the urge to broadcast. He was saying things the sceeve simply had never said before. Seditious, rebellious stuff, verging on the crazy. He seemed utterly "unsceeve," as a matter of fact. Nothing like the sceeve command who had run their invasion of Earth like a factory operation with a slaughterhouse component. In fact, the Poet seemed almost human in his sensibilities. And the fact that there was trouble in the sceeve ranks—if the Poet truly had a large audience (another unknown)—was the best news humanity had received in a long time.

Attention, you dry-gilled strugglers! Attention, you children of the promise broken! You who have spent your miserable lives soaking your feet in the feeding pool of untruth, cant, fibs, propaganda, and hatred!

Rise up! Shake off this dust!

Calling for the downfall of the Administration? Encouraging
an uprising within the Sporata ranks? It was beyond incendiary.
It was fascinating. Plus, the Poet was extolling a philosophy or
a religion that was, so far as anybody knew, completely at odds
with everything humans thought they knew about the sceeve.

> *Your history is a history of war.*
> *Wars waged to steal and to hoard.*
> *Wars waged to justify the unconscionable.*
> *Civil wars.*
> *Genocides.*
> *The Shiro itself is nothing more than a hive for ongoing*
> *fighting, a hideous fortress that ate a beautiful and wondrous*
> *city-in-the-stars.*
> *Yet still there is hope!*

What the Poet preached was a philosophy or belief or something
having to do with both—Japps didn't think the distinction mattered
very much, anyway—that had been translated as "Mutualism."

> *Attention! Attention! From behind the veil of lies, a simple*
> *message of truth.*
> *I am nothing but a vessel, a pointer toward the feeding*
> *pool that never runs dry.*
> *I am no leader, only a poet.*
> *And I say: your life, our lives, they do not have to be this way.*
> *Parasitism can give way to symbiosis. It must.*
> *Regulation must give way to Mutualism, or we're doomed.*
> *Hear me, you dry-gilled strugglers! Wet your gills with my*
> *words.*
> *Hear me, you children of the broken promise! Learn a*
> *new way of giving. The galactic economy is no zero-sum heat*
> *exchange. The calling of the symbiot is not for domination,*
> *but to aid. The symbiot creates; the symbiot is not a distribu-*
> *tor, but a maker. The symbiot does not regulate, but trusts in*
> *plurality, the profligate creativity of the universe.*
> *The symbiot is our only way home.*
> *So, down with Regulation!*
> *I do not speak as a warrior. Nor as one who wishes to*
> *coerce. What I give you is words, only words. But words that*

point to the new, the old that has been forgotten or overlooked,
the extravagant universe!
  Give me your feet, you dry-gilled strugglers. Wet your gills.
Drink it up!
  Down with the Administration!
  Thrive the symbiosis!

And then the Poet's tone changed, and he would begin reading his poems or songs or whatever they were. Japps tended to side with the faction that thought the Poet was a kind of pirate-radio DJ among the sceeve beta operators, broadcasting his thoughts into the ether for anyone listening at the right time to hear. In any case, he seemed to be knowledgeable enough about beta signals to avoid detection—a very difficult feat. Japps wasn't even sure *she* could figure out how to do that.

Usually the beginning of any message was filled with the Poet's political cant, kind of the sceeve version of a Peepsie protest rally. It was only with a careful listen—and after you'd heard a bunch of normal sceeve broadcasts—that you figured out the Poet was having fun with the usual sceeve catchphrases, that he was delivering an opening monolog before he started the main event: reading his poetry. Or songs. Or whatever you wanted to call it. Some of his material was either original or at least from an unknown source. It wasn't in any of the captured databases, that was for sure. But then there would be some of the poems that matched up with known sceeve works, usually from some ancient, pre-Administration writer.

And then there were the poems that were by human writers. "Gleaned," as the sceeve termed it.

Fucking thieves.

Fucking sceeve.

The poems were famous ones. Marvell, Rimbaud, Lorca, Emily Dickinson. There seemed to be no connecting theme and method for when a human poem got dropped in a broadcast. Japps's own opinion was that the choice was down to whatever happened to tickle the Poet's fancy.

She remembered when she'd first seen the translation on a Dickinson:

Safe in their alabaster chambers,
Untouched by morning and untouched by noon,

Sleep the meek members of the resurrection,
Rafter of satin, and roof of stone.

And had gone back to the original sceeve signal and figured out how sceeve rhymes worked. It was always the aromatic portion of the chemistry that was duplicated. The fucking scum-crawling murdering sceeve did have some cool aspects about them, Japps had to admit. Which took nothing away from the fact that she wanted to see them all dead, dead, dead. And killed in horrible ways, too.

Bink.

Over the SIGINT loudspeakers, the crackle of more incoming signal.

What the heck? Another Poet show? She called up a visual on her chroma monitor, checked.

The Poet *never* broadcasted back-to-back. HQ figured randomness was an important part of the method he used to avoid detection.

She checked a portion of the feed. There was the thirty-two spike.

It *was* the Poet again.

Didn't he realize he was exposing himself to discovery? If she could figure out how to identify him, then so could the other sceeve. And two broadcasts from the same source was bad form. Japps shuddered to think what the sceeve might do to a captured traitor.

What was going on? It had to be important.

Whatever it was, Japps had a gut feeling that she was tuning in to the Poet's final broadcast.

And then LARK delivered the translation prelim. And for the second time in her young life, Japps's world changed yet again forever.

The Poet was calling out to the humans.

Directly.

It was a cry for help.

And then there was one scream that went on for a very long time.

ONE

1 December 2075
Vicinity of Beta Geminorum, aka Pollux
Shiro Portal

Captain Sub-receptor Arid Ricimer stood stiff-backed in the vacuum of space and breathed in the silence absolute. He'd long made it a habit to ride out of harbor on a new command while standing on the exterior observation deck of his vessel. The deck was a feature built into all Administration vessels larger than a skirmish pod. Its electro-weak pseudogravity and silver-plated brightwork were wholly unnecessary features in a starcraft in these times, but for now he was glad of the inflexibility in Sporata design. He loved to face the naked stars at least once during a mission, to smell the universe bare, and this was the perfect place to do it.

The experience reminded him of his boyhood and the dangerous trips he and his friends had made onto the hull of the habitat in which they lived. His friends had gotten over the urge, learned to stay inside where it was safe.

Ricimer had never learned that lesson.

"Captain Ricimer, your presence is requested on the bridge."

The fruit-scented voice of Governess, part of the vessel computer, whispered in his mind. He'd have to answer eventually, but he could afford to ignore it a little longer.

The naked stars. Space. Emptiness. A hush beyond hush. He loved it almost more than life itself. Perhaps too much. His adoration of

11

space had kept him away from home for many cycles, away and always promising to return, to sell his command to a youngster, take a half-depletion allowance, settle down.

Make love to his beautiful wife every day for an entire cycle. Carefully transfer his important memories to his children.

He had not retired, of course. Not after twenty-five cycles a sailor.

Too late for any of that now. Del and the children were gone.

Gone, gone, echoed the ancestral voices within Ricimer, almost as real to him as his own thoughts. **We are cut off. Our purpose destroyed. Lost.**

But he was not destroyed. Not quite. He would not let himself be. And he had been dealing with emptiness for his entire adult life. The vacuum. The stars.

So he was going back to them. His stars.

Again the other interior voice, the more insistent, far less welcome voice than that of the ancestors, spoke.

"Captain, it is most urgent that you return to the bridge." Governess's interiorized communication channel again, a mental wave of gagging perfume. "Receptor Milt requests your presence to resolve a logistics discrepancy before the vessel clears Shiro Portal."

Will you please shut up? The thought was fully articulated, but he had long practice at not allowing the computer to pick up his thoughts. The ability to shut out Governess was one of the privileges of rank in the Sporata.

He leaned forward onto the rail, stretched to his full height, arms out, palms up. Soaring.

Almost.

Ricimer was tall for his species, nearly two meters. His was humanoid, bilaterally symmetric, but with a facial muzzle of folded membranes similar to the multiple crenellations of a fruit bat's nose. He had no mouth. His eyes were irisless, black, with gaping pupils that were double the size of a human's. They were protected by a clear membrane that cycled through a momentary opaque phase every few seconds—a protective mechanism against the universal background gamma radiation of the vacuum. Ricimer's species had evolved in space.

His wife before she'd died had often called him craggy and told him he was handsome for an old male getting close to one hundred cycles. He accepted that she might have been right. None of that had ever mattered much to him, and it mattered even less now that she was gone.

He wore the sleeveless black tunic of an officer. The fabric was silver-rimmed and gathered at the waist by a supple cord of pure silver. From the cord his ceremonial captain's knife dangled in its silver scabbard. The knife was generally a useless trinket, but it was required adornment for generations of Guardian officers. Sporata traditions changed *exceedingly* slowly.

With the expert eyes of his species, its built-in astral sense of balance, he scanned the constellations of the Shiro's current position, quickly picked out the points of light nearest to his destination.

Tau Ceti. Epsilon Eridani.

He squinted hard, and the motion upped the magnification of his eyes nearly ten times normal. He zoomed in with his scleral muscles.

He was returning to old battlegrounds.

The Cygni system, with its twin red dwarves in a mad dash about one another. Bright young Sirius. The Centauris.

Sol.

He was going back, but to think them *his* stars? Foolish.

Ricimer laughed out his nose, as his species did, and his humorous esters, propelled by their own momentum, floated away into the darkness.

No, the stars didn't give a damn if an individual named Ricimer lived, died, or had never existed in the first place. How could you not respect such obliviousness, such complete lack of purpose? It was as if the stars were spitting in the eyes of the Administration and its Regulators. It was as the ancient pre-civil-war ode "Star Song" put it:

> *We serve no cause.*
> *We are neither cruel nor kind.*
> *You will die. We shine on.*

Yet here I am, among you, Ricimer thought—as always he was careful not to emit his thoughts for Governess's consumption. *Among you stars for a while longer at least. And I'm going to go out blazing if I have anything to say about it. Because there is one advantage I very definitely possess over my enemies at the moment.*

This vessel.

He stood upon the command of a lifetime. Despite the anachronistic observation deck, this starcraft *was* new-minted, advanced, equipped with the latest conquest technology. Even—wonder of wonders for an Administration craft—*innovative.* She was a world-destroyer, and she *was* his. As soon as he got her out of port, that is.

"Captain, I'm afraid Receptor Milt insists on your presence. Please make your way to the bridge," said Governess.

He would have to go below very soon now. Under normal circumstances, he'd take over from the harbormaster, see the transfer craft away, and finally bring the quantum engines on line. For the first time ever, A.S.C. *Guardian of Night* would truly come to life. Although the star drive made not the slightest perceptible vibration itself, the vessel's containing fields would have to readjust on a quantum level to a new presence of force and would produce a subtle signal. They would pop and crackle ever so slightly, leaving the bracing scent of sulfide in the interior atmospheric mix, the Guardian ester for "victory over high odds and long distances." And then he'd order her throttle forward and she would experience her first superluminal speeds.

c.

100 c.

900 c.

He'd take her to the full nine hundred times the speed of light, the limit of propulsion technology, the current speed limit of the known galaxy. Why not? He was the captain. He needed to experience how his vessel operated at maximum velocity.

Away from the Shiro, the enormous habitat that was the Administration's governing hub. Away from the knotted heart of the Administration and its Regulation. Its parasitism. Its killing grip on his soul.

Ricimer turned his back to the stars and made his way to the vessel's entrance hatch. Ricimer met the invisible barrier of the airlock's quantum bottle and stepped through, into the craft's atmosphere and onto the bridge, where his officers awaited him.

The atmosphere was oxygen-based and similar to Earth's mix, with helium taking the place of nitrogen. The pressure was considerably higher than Earth normal, however.

The phenol-laced ester of imperative and command suffused

the air as Lieutenant Commander Hadria Talid, Ricimer's executive officer, made her customary announcement. "Captain on the bridge."

The officers locked their knees and brought shoulders to attention. The rates could only acknowledge their captain's presence by lowering their heads respectfully. Each was physically attached to a bulkhead, his or her hands plunged into individually marked stations. Ricimer and his species did not have fingers but made do with a single flexible metacarpal palm curtained with gripping membranes that looked like the underside of a toadstool mushroom. The edges of the manual membranes were rimmed with nerves—nerves which provided direct access to the rate's nervous systems for the *Guardian of Night*'s computers.

Ricimer touched his chest then stretched out his hand palm-up. A Sporata commanding officer's salute to those who served under him.

"Thrive the Administration," Ricimer said with full phenol blast. "Now, as you were."

He took his command spot on the circular captain's atrium in center-bridge. Stowed to one side was the red-handled emergency manual-override control stick. Ancient Sporata tradition had one in every vessel, although Ricimer had used the stick only in exercises and drills. The atrium depression was floored with a grill that enabled Ricimer's feet, membraned in a manner similar to his hands, to curl anemone-like through its slots and lock him firmly in place.

A side hatch opened and Receptor Milt crossed the bridge to Ricimer's atrium. Milt was short by Guardian standards, at least three hands shorter than Ricimer. But what Milt lacked in height, he made up for in girth. Yet he carried his bulk with surprising energy.

A fat clump of malevolence, Ricimer sometimes thought of him.

"Thrive the Administration," Milt said. Milt's political status as the Directorate of Disambiguation of Codes and Mandates' chief officer on the vessel was counted as two grades above Ricimer's.

Outranked on my own craft, Ricimer thought. It had bothered him since he'd made captain, although he was adept at keeping his displeasure to himself. Usually. Milt was equally skilled at pushing Ricimer's buttons. In his way, Milt was also quite the professional.

"Yes, Receptor, what can I do for you?" Ricimer replied. "I'm somewhat occupied at the moment."

Milt nodded and flared his muzzle in a Guardian smile. "Of course, Companion Arid. I completely understand," he said. Milt used Ricimer's first name—as was his status right. But most craft receptors asked permission of their captains first. Ricimer had never given anyone consent to call him by his first name but his wife. "This will only take a few *vitias* to clear up, I'm certain."

"What is the problem, Receptor?" He knew Milt's first name was Crossgrain, but he disliked any show that he was on intimate terms with Milt and loathed using it.

"Before we begin, I would like to say I was very sorry to hear about your family." Milt dropped the smile-flare and emitted the bergamot ester of sadness and regret. "A tragic mistake."

"An *avoidable* mistake," said Ricimer. He was not giving any ground on that claim. Not only was it true, it was necessary that he show a spark of anti-Administration fire when it came to a topic so personally devastating. If he didn't, Milt and his superiors might begin to suspect the good Captain Ricimer was hiding even more. He couldn't let that happen. "Nevertheless, I thank you for the condolences," Ricimer continued.

"Your daughter would have made a fine Sporata officer. We all knew she was Academy-bound."

"Yes." This was too much. He felt a carbolic tang rising in his nostril, his whole body readying itself to spew forth rancor.

Not yet. Hold on. A while longer.

"Of course, if you had moved your family to the Officer's Arm instead of continuing to reside in Agaric," Milt continued, "this would have been avoided."

Milt had a point, and Ricimer hated him for it. He'd known his neighborhood was rife with Mutualist sentiment. Curse it all, he and Del had *chosen* it partially for that reason. They'd moved in as newlyweds, many cycles before his first child's birth. Agaric was one of the old and beautiful original structures of the Shiro. Its apartments had the curved contours of pre-Regulation architecture, not to mention twenty-five-hand-tall ceilings. Del had loved the place immediately. She'd argued that it was so much better to raise the children in Agaric than in one of the drab little prefabricated units of the Officer's Arm. He'd replied that they were less likely to attract attention in the Arm, but as he did with all things related to shore life, Ricimer had given in when he saw his wife was set on her course.

She was the one who had to live in the habitat full-time, after all. Ricimer of necessity spent most of his professional life away from the Shiro.

And she had been the one who died there, along with their two children, during the Agaric Pogrom.

"Maybe you're right, Receptor," Ricimer said. *And maybe you had something to do with her death, you son-of-a-hyphaless-horde.* The pogrom had been a classic DDCM internal operation—that much was clear. "Now to the matter at hand, please."

"Of course." The nostril-flare smile returned. "I was working through the approvals on your supply requisitions, and I noticed a rather large order for gypsum."

"Really?"

"An entire *variado*'s supply, as a matter of fact. I hope you don't mind, but I took the liberty of halving the order."

"Of course, Receptor," Ricimer replied. "You were right, of course. There must have been some sort of mistake. I'll see that it doesn't happen again."

"Already taken care of," said Milt. "A permanent mark on your quartermaster's record. I don't imagine she'll be receiving her promotion to master storekeeper during next cycle's petty officer round." Milt waved his head from side to side in the Guardian version of a shrug. "And she'll need to undergo a physical shriving immediately. A full epidermal surfaction is warranted. I'll be happy to supervise this, if it proves too much of a burden to you."

Curse it. The mark against Storekeep Susten wouldn't matter soon enough. But the loss of that much gypsum? He'd have to ration and hope that the wasting disease did not put many of his crew out of action.

"In any case, I've left you the pleasure of delivering the news to her personally," Milt continued. His nostril flare widened.

He actually is being kind, thought Ricimer. Informing Susten of her fate was something Milt would enjoy.

But he must not underestimate Milt merely because the receptor was a sadist. That was practically a job requirement in a DDCM operant. Ricimer had known the receptor for many cycles. They had served together through two wars—Gossamer and the aborted Sol invasion. He'd even gotten drunk with Milt more than once on

NH_4 nebulizers—once massively so in a particularly star-crossed spate of carousing on the Sol C moon—and he knew Milt was capable of genuine feeling at such moments. Like Ricimer, he'd lost a beloved wife. Her name was Jareala, and she had died a painful and lingering death of Host's Disease. Jareala truly had been a good woman, and was a friend to Del until her demise. Milt was raising the four children, all of whom lived with his own parents in a tiny apartment in the Officer's Arm. Ricimer knew Milt had high hopes for his offspring. He'd even asked Ricimer for an Academy recommendation for his youngest when the time came.

Very soon, things would not go well for those children, thought Ricimer. Best not to ponder such things at this particular moment.

Most of all, Milt was extremely clever and ambitious himself. You didn't become vessel receptor on a class-defining starcraft by being apathetic, at least not in the DDCM. Witness his finding the gypsum oversight in the cargo manifest. Idiotic not to have double-checked that manifest himself. Susten really *had* made a near-catastrophic mistake.

Nothing to be done but deal with the foul-up. It was far too late to turn back at this point.

"Receptor, let me clear us from Shiro Portal, and then I believe we have our usual business in V-CENT," Ricimer said. "I estimate exiting the guidance zone at *atentia* twenty-three sixty. Shall we convene at twenty-three one hundred? We'll attend to Craft Orders, then I'll have Susten summoned and we'll handle her demerit and set her shriving."

"That would be agreeable, Companion Arid. And I have several more manifest discrepancies I'd like to go over with you at that point, too. Nothing major."

"Of course, Receptor."

"Thrive the Administration."

"Thrive the Administration."

Milt bounced out with his usual frenetic energy, and Ricimer turned to the task at hand. He needed to get his vessel off guidance as soon as possible. That meant taking her out to a fifteen light-*momentia* distance from the Shiro. The move after that would depend on what happened when he and Milt activated Governess's encrypted Craft Orders for the voyage.

"Forward full thrust, Commander Talid."

"Aye, Captain," she replied. "We've got blips dead ahead one light-*momentia*, sir. Probably merchantmen."

"Instruct them to move their backsides, Ms. Talid. Sporata vessels must have right-of-way in this sector for safety's sake. If they give you any guff, put an override lock on their drives and power down their engines for a few *atentias*."

"Aye, Captain." Talid squeezed a hand into her officer's console and delivered detailed instructions to the rest of the crew. Ricimer listened in out of habit over the craft's virtual feed but did not interfere. He trusted Talid completely when it came to executing his orders in such a routine matter. Instead he turned his attention to his virtual feed from Lamella, the craft-specific computer, and memorized—or, rather, at this point in his career, it was more an *internalization*—engine conditions and weapons energy draw as the data came streaming in. He knew the spec book on his vessel backward and forward in the abstract, but he needed to become intimately familiar with the quirks of this particular craft if he was to push her to her limits. And he would be pushing.

When Ricimer looked up from his virtual labors, he saw that the blips were rapidly clearing from the beta screen. Talid had put the fear of the Civitas Council into them—and the possibility of being rammed by a half-instantiated Sporata warcraft.

The *Guardian of Night* had her clear path to the stars.

TWO

Receptor Milt was late in arriving for the reading of Craft Orders, as Ricimer had expected. It was the DDCM way to never miss an opportunity to show who was *really* in charge.

V-CENT, Vessel Central Processing, was the computational heart of the craft. The memory banks of the two vessel computers (every Sporata craft had a bicameral computational system) lined all the bulkheads of the chamber. They *were* the bulkheads here, Ricimer knew. They were cellular machines, engineered by a race even older than the Guardians and conquered only after a long war. The bulkheads were a grayish white, and they twinkled with ethereal flashes of subatomic particles created and destroyed, quantum realities called into brief existence—realities that overlapped, canceled, or reinforced one another, as a billion-billion possible worlds were sifted through the computer processors every *vitia,* like so many grains of sand. The results were projected upon a table which had a top at chest height. It was designed to be looked down upon from a standing position.

Ricimer leaned against the projection table, took a deep breath of craft atmosphere.

Here we go.

There were no chairs in the chamber, but there was a small levitated serving cabinet that was parked next to a bulkhead corner, as Ricimer had directed. He expelled his breath slowly, then stepped over to the cabinet and opened it up. Inside were two ammonium hydroxide nebulizers, polymer bubbles that held what was normally a gas in a pressurized, semiliquid state. Ricimer took them out. A straw protruded from one side of each bubble and ended in a device similar to a perfume atomizer. The object was to squirt the contents directly onto the nostrils and suffuse the nasal membranes with what was, for a Guardian, a powerful stimulant, depending on the concentration, of course.

This was the good stuff. It went by the name of Old Fifty-five.

Ricimer set both nebulizers on the projection table and stood waiting.

After a few *momentias*, Milt bustled in, giving the impression, as always, that he had hurried away from some very important task.

"Thrive the Administration," he said with a puffy, breathless emission.

"Thrive the Administration." Ricimer nodded toward the NH_4 nebulizers. "Shall we?"

"Absolutely, Companion Arid."

Ricimer handed a nebulizer to the receptor and took one for himself. The nebulizer was cold in his hand. He squeezed out a ceremonial whiff. It wouldn't do to get drunk before reading Craft Orders. Milt atomized a more substantial puff and sniffed it in with a slurping sound. *He's always had a noisy nose*, Ricimer thought. Milt could afford to be indifferent about such stuff when mixing with those he considered underlings. In fact, most DDCM officers were notoriously bad-mannered by force of habit.

"I'm glad you didn't skimp on the important items," Milt said. "This is a premier vessel, after all."

"Thank poor Storekeep Susten," Ricimer replied. "The one whom we're about to hand her head on a platter."

"Regulations are regulations. Can't be helped."

"I suppose not. But first things first." Ricimer set down his nebulizer, and, after another stiff whiff, Milt did the same.

Craft Orders were encoded in Lamella, the computer brain of the *Guardian of Night*. "Lamella" was, in fact, the general name for all vessel-specific computers, as "Governess" was the name for the Administration general computer system common to all craft. It was an arrangement that was deliberately analogous to the Guardian's dual nervous systems. Theoretically, each Governess system was an exact duplicate of the others, although there were often slight discrepancies and update mismatches. Each Lamella system was individualized for the vessel. Governess had the code key for the Craft Orders in Lamella. And Ricimer and Receptor Milt had to both be present to activate the order to pass that key on and open the instructions.

As an added safeguard and layer of Administration control, the reading of Craft Orders also decoded the switching software on the drive mechanism and allowed the starcraft to engage the QEM and achieve superluminal speeds.

This complicated procedure was the reason Receptor Crossgrain Milt was still living at this point.

Ricimer lowered his customary close-minded shield and directly addressed Governess. *This is Captain Sub-receptor Arid Ricimer. I hereby initiate activation of Craft Orders.*

"Greetings, Captain. Half-key activated," Governess's treacly voice replied. "Standing by for Receptor Milt."

But for the moment, Milt said nothing to the computer. He turned to Ricimer, leaned over the projection table in a beseeching posture. "Listen, Companion Arid," he said. "I want you to know something before we go any further."

This was unexpected. And irritating. Ricimer was now entirely alert. What did the receptor have on his mind?

"Yes, Receptor?"

"Will you please call me by my name for once, Arid? We've known each other since we were in our twenties."

Ricimer controlled his annoyance at the request as best he could. "Very well. What's going on...Companion Crossgrain?"

Crossgrain picked up the NH_4 nebulizer, gave himself another squirt.

"That's better," he said. "You can be a stiff-necked fool, Arid. But I want you to know that I had nothing—*nothing whatsoever*—to do with what your...with what happened to your family."

Ricimer stiffened. "All right," he said. "I can only take you at your word. Companion Crossgrain."

"I swear it."

"Very well, I believe you," Ricimer replied. "Can we get on with this now?"

But Milt wanted to have his full say, and he continued. "I got wind of the move on your Agaric sector just as it was happening. I tried to put a stop to the whole operation. Called in all the favors I could. But there was nothing I could do, because..."

"Because," said Ricimer, with resignation. "Because."

"She really *was* a Mutualist, Arid!" Milt spat the words out as if they were scorching to his nostrils. "Didn't you know that? How could you not have known?"

Ricimer was quiet for a moment, gathering himself. He needed to remain composed now. This was battle, of a sort. He was a warrior. He was staring into danger, even if it only appeared as the puffed-up face of a mid-level DDCM operative.

"It doesn't matter now what I suspected or did not suspect. What do the Craft Orders say, Companion Crossgrain?" Ricimer asked calmly. "I suppose you saw them back in port."

Now it was Milt's turn to be taken aback. He leaned back with a canny expression. He was smiling again. Not the friendly smile of friend. More the nasty flare of a predator.

"I can't tell you that."

"You've just told me the gist of them. I suppose I'm to be arrested?"

"No."

"What then?"

"Relieved of immediate command." Milt straightened. "Placed under my direct authority for the duration of the mission. I . . . *negotiated* for that option."

"I suppose I should thank you, then."

"You should. But I was right. You're the best we have, Arid," said Milt. He leaned across the table imploringly once again. "We need commanders like you for the completion of the Sol operation—and for all the campaigns of the future."

"So, you and I will return to Sol."

"No, you didn't guess right this time, Arid," said Milt. He was almost laughing. "Our mission is suppression of insurrection. We're going to finish the Mutualists once and for all. We're going to destroy the Agaric."

Ricimer breathed in, breathed out in a wordless hiss. His neighborhood. Yes, the birthplace of Mutualism. But also an arm of the Shiro that housed almost one hundred million souls.

For a moment, he couldn't remember where his children were.

Then it came to him.

"Agaric Mutualist Conspiracy Terror," the official INFO-STREAM called it. The walls of his apartment spread inward as if poked by a giant stick. Exploded furnishings turned to shrapnel. His wife's chest cavity bisected by a cabinet door. His son near the initial blast, seemingly untouched. His interior turned to an undifferentiated gel.

His daughter. Four cycles old.

Alive for a *momentia*, maybe longer.

Crawling toward her mother.

Leaving a trail of blood that told of her passage.

Her little hand stretching out to touch her mother's body.

Not close enough.

Dying alone.

Unconsoled.

A mistake, said the in-government report he'd been shown. The report he'd been *allowed* to see by old Admiral Brand, who'd personally met him at port and conveyed the Sporata's condolences. Faulty intelligence provided by a Mutualist double agent.

Nobody's fault, really. Except the Mutualist slime.

Administrative error.

"What do you mean 'destroy'?" Ricimer finally said. "It's already been cleansed of reactionaries." He took another breath. Clenched a hand until his palm hurt. *Hold course.* "There have been multiple cleansings of the Agaric."

"You know what this vessel can do, Companion Arid," Milt replied. The smile again. "This new weapon is potent beyond anything we've ever used before. The Mutualist cancer must be cut from the people. The wound must be cauterized."

"I see," Ricimer said. "We're going to turn the Kilcher artifact upon the Agaric. Erase it from the sky with no warning."

Milt nodded, an expression very similar to a human's. "Yes, Companion Arid. That is the gist of our orders."

Ricimer laughed. It really was a laugh. Of relief. He'd had so many doubts. So many second thoughts. Now those worries were taken away.

He'd made the right call, at the right time.

"What's so funny, Captain?" Milt said, taken aback by Ricimer's laughter.

Ricimer contained himself. Enough. Back to business. "Your superiors think I *care*?" he said. "Now that *she's* gone? Why should I care what happens to that cursed pustule of a place?"

"That's . . . good to hear."

"This has become a meaningless conversation, Receptor. I will carry out my orders. You needn't have abased yourself."

"I . . . I did nothing of the sort."

Ricimer smiled, spoke as gently as he could. "No, of course you didn't. Companion Crossgrain, speak your part, please. Let's get on with this."

Milt stared at him a moment longer. Made a decision. Ricimer couldn't hear it, but from the expression on Milt's face, he knew Milt had sent his key to Governess. After the briefest delay, the surface of the projection table blistered with words. Ricimer gently pushed the ammonium nebulizers to the edge of the table, then reached down and stroked the reading blisters to release their vanilla-laced esters. He read his orders.

PROCEED FROM SHIRO SYSTEM D+SIRIUS. RETURN VIA LEO LOOP APPROACH PATH. PROCEED AT HALF SPEED TO SHIRO MYCELIUM ARC 7, POD 35.9.7.—

Arc 7. This was the giant causeway that connected the Agaric effusion to the rest of the Shiro habitat.

—SEVER POD 35.9.7 FROM MYCELIUM BODY EMPLOY-ING POINTBLAST TECHNIQUE ALPHA. ISOLATE POD 35.9.7 WITH GLEANED ARTIFACT K5055. EMPLOY SAID WEAPONRY TO DESUBSTANTIATE POD 35.9.7. EXIT VIA LEO LOOP. RETURN SHIRO PORTAL D-SIRIUS. NOTE 1: COMMUNICATIONS BLACKOUT IN EFFECT FOR MISSION DURATION. NOTE 2: VESSEL COMMAND TO BE CEDED TO DDCM RECEPTOR FOR DURATION OF MISSION AT RECEPTOR DISCRETION, ENFORCEMENT PROGRAM VERDICT 3. THESE DIRECTIVES PER BLAW-FUS, SIRIUS SEC-COM ON T 1.4.2.3, 1946.

Blawfus had signed the orders—Blawfus who most recently had been shuffled out of sight as proconsul on long-occupied Deneb 2 C. Which meant that Sirius Armada Flag Commander Admiral Brand had been removed. Killed, of course, if he hadn't taken his own life. So the politicals within the Sporata high command were making their move.

"Now you know," said Milt. "I was so dreading this moment. I was afraid I would have to evoke Verdict Three protocols and have you arrested or worse. This is going so much better than—"

Ricimer drew his captain's knife from its scabbard with a practiced sweep and plunged it into the receptor's throat.

Milt started back in shock, and Ricimer let go of the knife's handle. Milt spun around, headed for the hatch. Ricimer saw the knife tip protruding from the back of Milt's neck. He'd made a clean strike.

"Lamella," Ricimer said. "The gravity, please."

For the first time, Ricimer breathed in the citrus voice of his vessel's individual a.i. speaking aloud.

"As per our agreement, Captain."

Ricimer felt the additional weight in his body immediately. The effect was like pulling g-force on an aerial flight, but he was not moving. The artificial gravity in V-CENT had suddenly tripled.

Ricimer was ready. He'd trained for this. Gravity malfunction was a standard emergency drill in all Sporata craft. Ricimer was already thin as a rail, and the extra weights he'd lifted for the past months had added the increased muscle he needed to operate in a high-gravity environment.

Milt, on the other hand, was not in such good shape. DDCM receptors had exempted themselves from the boring emergency-scenario training, and Ricimer doubted that Milt had ever experienced a gravitational tug this extreme.

In any case, Milt was overweight to begin with. Tripling his weight brought him down in a crumpling heap two steps from the closed hatch. His trachea severed, there was no way for Milt to breathe. He tore at the knife, but it was firmly lodged in his neck.

Ricimer could have left it like that. The receptor would die soon enough. But time was pressing, and he had so much more to do.

Ricimer straddled Milt and sat down on his back. He reached down and batted Milt's weak grip from the knife's handle. Ricimer grabbed the knife himself with two hands, both on the left side of Milt's neck.

With a strong tug, he pulled the knife as he would a valve lever, slicing in an arc sideways through Milt's neck. Blood gushed forth in a rapid flow of milky white exsanguination. Guardian blood was a fluorocarbon liquid, perfluorodecalin. A wet pool formed under the receptor's head and shoulders. When Ricimer got to the back of the receptor's neck, the knife ground against Milt's spinal hinge. Ricimer took a breath. Just pushing out his chest to take in air was a struggle.

Thump, thump, thump.

What was that behind him? Ricimer glanced back. *Thump.* Ah, it was Milt's legs kicking feebly against the deck. For a moment, Ricimer felt sorry for Milt's children. Their grandparents were political nobodies. The children would be doomed to obscurity, probably end up laborers or cannon fodder.

And Milt had such hopes for them.

Curse them, said the ancestral voices within Ricimer. *Curse them as we are cursed.*

Thump.

Ricimer put everything he had into another pull on the knife, and it found purchase between the cartilage-like lacework Guardians possessed instead of bones. The knife sliced its way through Milt's connective tissue as—

The thumping stopped.

The rest was easier. Ricimer completed his circling of the neck, neatly meeting the start of his incision at the front. He let go of the knife, and the head slumped forward, held on only by a shred of flesh. Ricimer put his hands on either side of Milt's skull, held the receptor by his ear humps, and pulled.

The head came off.

"Captain, what are you attempting to accomplish? I do not understand." It was the voice of Governess. Had Lamella failed to secure the Administration computer? "Captain, please explain—"

Cut off in mid emission. Lamella had stifled her twin, her other brain "lobe" in the craft, for the time being.

"Lamella, have you restrained Governess?"

"Yes. Momentarily."

"I understand," Ricimer replied. "Lamella, gravity normal, please."

"As per agreement," said the computer.

Ricimer sat up abruptly, back to his normal weight. The pool of fluorocarbon blood beneath him seemed to "unflatten" as the surface tension reestablished itself at another degree of freedom.

"Captain, I will be able to hold Governess at bay for approximately two-point-three *momentias.* She is employing every countermeasure at her service to escape the program lock."

"Noted," said Ricimer. He set the head down in front of him on one temple. Milt's empty eye stared ahead at a bulkhead. At nothing anymore.

Ricimer reversed the knife in his hand and brought its handle down, hard, against the right side of Milt's cranial cavity. A slight give.

Again.

Again.

This time something cracked. A ragged line opened up from Milt's ear to the top of the rind-like connective tissue mass that formed his skull.

Another blow with the knife handle. The gap widened.

Ricimer reached into the bloody crack with the edges of his hands. His gripping gills found purchase on the underside of the skull rind.

He pulled for all he was worth. With a popping sound, the skull slowly opened. Tissue parted, revealing the neural mass known as the sensory conglomerate. This was not Milt's brain. He didn't have one. No Guardian did. Their nervous system was distributed, with processing centers located in the chest. This was merely the Guardian equivalent to the human olfactory bulb. It also contained several language pre-processing centers, since for Guardians smell *was* speech.

Ricimer didn't care about any of that. What he was after lay nearer to the surface, should be just under the rind. He felt around inside, moving aside tissue, lumps of organs and glands.

Remembering that night, two cycles ago. The night the Special Depletion was declared and the Sol gleaning operation put on hold in order to deal with the Mutualist menace. The night that ended with Ricimer and Milt on their backs, gazing up at the blue-white planet the inhabitants called Earth.

The shared night of melancholy and revelry on Sol C's satellite, called *the* Moon by the primitive locals, in one of the little blister-habitat bars that followed any invasion force around.

Milt drunk with NH_4 whippets and whatever other drugs they could get their hands on. Ricimer playing along.

Plotting, even then.

Milt passed out, dead drunk.

The injector pistol he'd stolen from pharmacist's stores on his destroyer billet, the *Long Arm of Distributive Justice*. It was meant for field surgery, the introduction of subdermal medicinal-patch constructors.

But Ricimer wanted it for another purpose.

That purpose was to hide the technology he'd stolen from the humans. For primitive as they were, like many trading species, there was one product at which they'd proved overly skilled.

The creation of computer viruses.

It was the perfect plan. Hide the tech where the DDCM monitors and Directorate of Innovation Assimilation inspectors would never look in a million cycles. Inside the head of a DDCM agent. Allow *him* to smuggle it back home. Then find a way to extract it. The original motivation: to sell it back to the Administration on the Souk, the Shiro's black market.

Ricimer had felt no particular shame in hiding the Earth tech at the time. Pocketing bits of tech to sell on the Souk was practically *de rigueur* for a Sporata officer. The Administration was aware of the trade but didn't crack down so long as it didn't get out of hand. It was a tacit way of keeping its best officers entrepreneurial to the extent they needed to be, and relatively well-off. The equivalent of what a small private plot for gardening and lichen cultivation would mean if he were an agrarian.

He'd overthought it, and the extraction had proved a trifle difficult. Meanwhile, life had not taken the course he'd intended. He'd foundered on debris.

He'd lost everything.

Almost everything.

Everything, everything, echoed the ancestral voices.

He felt it, there inside Milt's opened skull. A hard little square of material. Yes. His gripping gills closed around it. Yes!

He pulled the square out. Wiped it off as best he could. Held it up to the light. It glistened a dull black. Several metal tines formed a keyboard pattern along one side of the square. The square itself was covered in markings that Ricimer could not understand. Visually based writing. How strange to think in such a manner.

If he could have read it, he would have seen that the square said, in English: "500 PB Extended Memory."

"All right, Lamella, I've got it," he said. "If you want to incorporate this program and make use of the Sol C hardware, you must again swear to the terms. Key word: 'Teshinaw.'"

"Key word accepted," Lamell replied brightly. "My interior killswitch is now activated, Captain Ricimer, as we agreed. Please place the storage device on the projection table. We do not have much time."

Ricimer jerked himself to his feet and stumbled over to the table, feeling quite exhausted now.

A little longer. Hold course.

He placed the card in the center of the table, stood back.

Immediately, the spot on which the card sat seemed to dissolve into a grayish liquid. The card floated for a quarter-*vitia*, then sank from sight. The liquid spot on the table solidified once again. The card was gone, disappeared within.

"Have you got it, Lamella?" Ricimer asked. No answer. "Have you got it?"

The reassuring voice of Lamella returned. "I have it, Captain."

"Good."

"I've released the Sol C virus into Governess's logic centers and have inoculated myself against it with the supplied security wall," Lamella continued. "I believe that all Governess's defense measures have been bypassed. We will know in a *momentia* if—"

"Aaaaaaaaaaaaaaiaaaaaah." The wail had the all-permeating odor of carbolic acid, in human terms the smell of lamps used for coal mining and caving in the days before high-intensity LEDs. The carbolic aroma was urgent, ongoing. But Lamella had kept the keening of Governess out of the vessel's virtual feed. Ricimer smelled it in the chamber, but not in his head. Which meant nobody else outside the cabin could detect it, either.

And then, like steam from a kettle taken off its heat source, the scream wafted away. The air cleared.

"We were successful," Lamella said, her citrus-fresh tone as professional as ever. This was not an a.i. created to mimic Guardian emotional emission. Oh, Lamella had feelings. He understood that. This fact had been part of the means he'd used to bring her to his side. But they were the emotions of a hive, a roiling mass of intelligent agents vying for place in a sort of rough-and-tumble mental survival dance. Lamella was not a person. Not yet. She was more like a family of personas.

"So Governess is—"

"Dead, sir," said Lamella matter-of-factly.

"Very well," said Ricimer. He breathed a sigh through his muzzle. It communicated no words, but communicated everything he felt, all the relief that was in him.

To have begun. Finally to have begun.

"And vessel systems?" he said.

"The transfer to my own redundancy and to autonomous processing was successful. All indications are the rates took no notice."

"And my selected officers?"

"Informed of the situation, Captain. The others do not seem alarmed. It is difficult to tell with officers, since I do not have full access, but I believe that those not selected by you do not suspect what has happened."

"Good, then," Ricimer said. His knee unaccountably gave out, and he almost fell but caught himself against the projection table.

"Captain?"

Ricimer pulled himself up. Straightened his shoulders. Held himself steady. He looked at his palms.

"I'm..."

Bloodstained. His gripping gills soaked in fluid. He turned his hands over. Tissue and gristle clung in little clumps to their back sides.

Blood all over his uniform in wet streaks and patches.

Blood in a slick, pussy mess on the deck.

A decapitated body.

So many details still to take care of. The hard part yet to come.

"I'll be okay in a moment."

He put out a call to the bridge. Commander Talid answered immediately.

"Orders, Captain?" she said.

Ricimer curled out a tired smile. Good old Talid. Best XO in the Sporata. With him now at the end of their careers.

"May I ask your status, Captain?"

"I'm fine, Commander," Ricimer answered, broadcasting multichannel so that he might be heard by all. "All is proceeding as expected. We have our orders. Bring her to a dead stop, Commander."

"Sir?"

"We're going to test out our very fancy and very new stealth technology, it seems."

"Aye, sir."

"One thing more. There's to be complete beta silence. Do you understand, Commander?"

"Beta silence, aye, sir."

"Make us disappear, Commander," said Ricimer, "and let her drift."

"Aye."

"Oh, right. Please send Storekeep Susten to me here in V-CENT." Ricimer looked once again at the mess. Well, he'd certainly found a way to make Susten pay for her little gypsum oversight. She could help him clean up. "And Talid?"

"Yes, Captain?"

"We now have our orders. We are to join the Sirius armada, yet we are directed to approach with the utmost stealth."

Talid immediately understood what this implied. "Lay in a course to the Vara Nebula, Captain?"

The Vara lay ten degrees north of the galactic axis. A massive second-generation red giant had exploded there a billion years before, and the Vara was a nebula in the midst of birthing a clutch of third-generation star systems—none of which were past the gas-giant phase.

It was dark. It was a seemingly never-ending system of tunnels and dead-end gaseous canyons. It was the perfect place to hide, and the perfect place to lose any who might be tracking you. Most important of all, it was only two light-years from Earth.

"Very good," Ricimer said. "Let your course take us out the Eridani gate."

"Aye, sir. The Vara, Eridani gate. And once through, do we have a vector and destination?"

"Of course, Commander Talid," Ricimer replied. "We are to have the glorious honor of playing a crucial role in a long-delayed conquest. Our final destination is Sol system, the C planet."

"Sol C. Aye, Captain."

THREE

7 December 2075
New Pentagon
Extry Xenological Division
CRYPT

Lieutenant Commander Griffin Leher took the space pen from
his pocket once more and pulled another postcard from the coat
that was hanging over the back of his cubicle chair.

*You wonder what Dad does at work? He's a talker. A fancy
talker and listener. I wanted to talk to you before you were
born. When you were in your mother, I drove her crazy playing
music and yacking up a storm to her belly. I put headphones
on her tummy, can you believe it, and played, oh, probably
Bach and Mozart through them. Predictable, I know, but
they're my favorites.*

Even writing in tiny script, he'd run out of room. He continued
on a new postcard.

*It wasn't till you came out and I held you in my arms that
I understood how foolish I'd been. You were such a beautiful
little bundle of nothing in particular yet. And yet you had all
these built-in bootstraps, idioms of movement and behavior,
that every other normal kid on the face of the planet was*

35

born with. There you were. You were you, Neddie, if only I'd
known what to look for. So, in a way, you are like my work.
                                        Wish you were here. D.

Leher made sure of the address, then put the postcard in his
outbox and got back to work.

He hated the sceeve. That went without saying. He was happy
to help to kill them.

But he loved their language. Passionately. It was elegant, rich—
even though, yes, sometimes, it stank to high heaven. But he
loved it all the more because of that fact.

How had the sceeve gone so wrong?

The more you understood them, the less alien they seemed—and
the more blameworthy for what they'd done to humanity and—if
you believed their own histories—to dozens of other species.

What they'd done to him.

Leher sighed and considered the pile of material on his desk.
Before him was the entire spread of the intercepted sceeve bursts
collected by the intelligence-gathering vessel *Chief Seattle,* now
mysteriously disappeared, and three other craft in the 82 Eridani
region. Most of these dispatches concerned the sceeve beta broadcaster who called himself Expresser of Rhythmic Composition
in Lofty Elevation. Leher had translated this as "the Poet" in his
reports. The name, he'd been told, had stuck among the space-
based Xeno officers and was now in general use.

Since the Skyhook Raid six years ago, it had been known
that the sceeve had something like literature, including a body
of myth and legend somewhat along the lines of the *Odyssey*
and the *Aeneid*—tales in epic form that formed the sceeve conception of their own ancient history. Of course with the sceeve
you never knew what was original and what was "borrowed"
from conquered and eradicated species. The sceeve themselves
saw no major difference in kind between self-generated and
stolen knowledge—and, being sceeve, they placed a higher
value on the *stolen* knowledge, in this case the poems and tales
of others.

What Leher had to do at the moment was figure out how this
trickle of poetry and rebellious propaganda that had seeped out
might be used militarily. Which was practically like the Trojans
putting into place a detailed defense plan against Greek invasion

based on Homer's conception of the Soap Opera of the Gods in the *Iliad*.

Or was it? Was he drawing the analogy too tightly? Had he fallen into the analyst's trap of filtering his translations through misleading preconceptions? The sceeve likely did not divide the world so sharply between truth and fiction, epic and reality.

Leher was convinced that the trick with comprehending the sceeve was to come at it with the bare minimum of paradigms and filters necessary, and come at it from all angles, letting mistranslations cancel one another out. Not playing favorites with what you *wished* was the case. Build your understanding from the bottom up, not the top down.

The Poet was in the Sporata, the sceeve navy. He was an officer assigned to a war vessel. Had to be an officer, too. No sceeve rate was allowed to think for him or herself, much less transmit on pirate beta. He'd be subject to harsh discipline if he were caught. Slow death by dismemberment, no doubt.

There had to be some driving purpose beyond the poetry and seemingly endless rants. The poetry was good. The rants, on the other hand, were repetitious, felt trite. Sometimes like boilerplate moralizing, sometimes mere nonsense.

Of course, it was hard to escape the feeling that the Poet was having everyone on, human and sceeve audience alike. Leher was convinced he was missing something. What?

Sceeve beta bursts were not one-to-one "meaning" analogs, such as radio broadcast or Internet packet exchange was. They were, instead, somewhat akin to DNA instructions for constructing a body. Communication was "synapse-like" in that speech was accomplished by the interchange of chemical packets that operated in a manner similar to neurotransmitters. The packets themselves were practically alive.

The sceeve talked via exchange of odors. Smells.

In fact, when sceeve "speech" was examined under a powerful microscope, these semantic packages looked something like male spermatozoa. They lingered in the atmosphere anywhere the sceeve had once inhabited. The Skyhook, now in human hands, was full of "used" words floating about. CRYPT had a test-tube collection of thousands of them, most of them analyzed and filed by Leher himself.

These packets, and the paragraph-like thoughts they contained, were known as "esters." They were the fundamental building blocks of sceeve thought and communication. Order of receipt might not be important, but order of assembly was. Several sets of "assembly instructions" were sent during a beta burst, so that an initial coherent thought could be formed on the other end. A final set of instructions punctuated the ending and usually called for a large restructuring of the "train" of words that was being built so far. Ester order would be shifted around like boxcars in a freight yard.

A sentence could have several different, even contradictory, meanings.

Usually, the "caboose," the final "word-order code," was all that was used by Extry translators to reconstruct the meaning of a beta transmission. This method served its purpose in ordinary circumstances. But it left out all nuance.

Which meant that building a sceeve speech-train using only the "caboose" could be misleading. One or more of the other instruction packets sent in the midst of a transmission might have a stronger construction "marker" on it. So any given "thought-block" could have two, three, four, or a hundred different means of assembly—and so different meanings. The listener was, in fact, expected to hold several of those meanings in mind at once. In this way, ambiguity and even a weird poetry was built into the language from the syntax up.

An algorithm would only take you so far. An intelligent translator had to figure out the context, apply judgment.

And if you really wanted to get it right, you had to print the thing out and sniff it. Breathe it in, like a fine wine.

In this very room was one of the three authentic sceeve "printers" on planet Earth. Another, a reproduction, sat in Leher's underground apartment near White Rock Lake. Sceeve used a sort of polysaccharide "paper" that was similar to Braille in appearance, but instead of communicating through touch, each of the bumps released a trace odor. It had taken months of work to figure this out—no one had ever seen a sceeve actually reading—but it was now clear that the sceeve read this paper an entire "line" at a time, from the top to the bottom of a page. And they weren't reading by sight. If they didn't touch the page and release the odors for smelling, they couldn't "read" it at all.

To add to the confusion, the sceeve didn't share a single

"emitted" language. Leher was still trying to piece together how the various language families—there were three main groups—were divided among the sceeve. It had mostly to do with the migration history of the various sceeve clans or "hypha." Matters were made more confusing by the sceeve ability to understand the various dialects among themselves by making use of their *gid*, the collective-memory portion of their nervous system, as a translating mechanism. They also used, as did humans, the written word to achieve the same purpose, but of a smell-based variety.

What the sceeve did share was a common alphabet. In fact, the major branch of sceeve writing was a series of variations on a single family of smells.

Vanillin.

Sceeve paper smelled pretty much like a vanilla wafer to the ordinary human nose.

But oh the richness of that vanilla odor to the trained nose of a Xeno Division creep! Leher was an acknowledged master of the skill within the department itself. The "sniffer's sniffer." He'd been a sommelier when he was working his way through law school, and he'd found the task of sniffing sceeve paper similar to a wine tasting. Of course, he'd been a mediocre wine steward at best, but he liked to think he'd developed a much better nose for sceeve writing.

The documents on Leher's desk were odiferous reproductions made of the Poet's beta transmissions. They were transcripts "written out" in sceeve.

Leher tapped his Pocket Palace, which lay on the desk beside the sceeve documents, and his assistant LOVE's geist appeared as a small heart-shaped icon to the left of his peripheral vision. Leher was wiied to the Palace, but his salt carried only the minimum charge necessary for him to lay a very basic chroma matte on top of his environment. He didn't want LOVE to waste valuable computing space appearing in her full geist default mode as a human female, so he normally asked her to assume this minimized form. She'd always seemed happy enough to comply. Like Leher, LOVE was an obsessive when it came to her work. She did the exacting chemical analysis of the sceeve words. He handled the nuance. Leher thought they made a great team.

Leher took a drink of water, sat still for a moment to clear his palate and his mind, and then formed a "reading blade" with the side of his palm and his outstretched little finger. He ran his hand in this manner over the sceeve text. As he did so, the scratch-and-sniff smell rose to his nostrils and he breathed it in steadily with deep, regular breaths.

"All right, LOVE, let's go over the transmission again," he said.

As LOVE fed a train of transliteration to him, Leher disappeared into a reverie of smells. Vanilla wafer. Vanilla milk shake. Earth tones combined with vanilla, almost mushroom-like. Berries and vanilla. Chemical tang. Compared to most sceeve communication, the Poet's transcripts were verbose and chatty. They were a veritable flower garden of scent, some of them pleasant, some of them oversweet, many uncomfortably sulfuric and carbolic—full of sceeve intensifiers often used to mean "very, very" or "pay attention" or "emergency!" It all depended on the context.

Whoever the tech was who recorded this had done an excellent job in riding the signal. The usual smell palate was expanded and tuned to particular sceeve idiomatic usage. As a result, the dynamic range of esters was much richer than most recordings of the sceeve. The tech had also, with the last transmission, come up with a way to definitely identify a single broadcaster. There had been a few multiple-origin theories floating around CRYPT, with the idea that there was some sort of cabal at work within the Sporata and all of them were the "Poet." Leher had never really bought this theory—too many similarities in the Poet's quirky diction among the broadcasts—and now the single-origin theory was confirmed by this frequency spike the alert tech had spotted. Leher made a mental note to put the tech up for a commendation.

Except he'd heard that she was likely dead.

Okay, he had good copy. What was he missing here? He'd read the transcript of the Poet's last broadcast—nearly one hundred sceeve pages of it—several times since the messenger bottle had delivered it yesterday.

Our sun is dead. The stars blink broken code.

He kept coming back to that line. It was repeated throughout the transcript as a kind of mantra.

The smells from the paper were telling their story, too. Leher wrote down their order with a pen and small notepad on his desk.

"Retranslate with grammar using the secondary-checkpoint hydroxyl," he said to LOVE's heart icon.

"Yes, LTC Leher."

He'd wanted LOVE to call him Griff, but she'd refused and seemed a bit miffed at him for asking. Or what he took for miffed. He was no expert on servant emotional analogs. In any case, they'd settled on a shortening of "lieutenant commander" for use in their private communication channels.

Leher moved his reading hand over the text again. Breathed in.

The sun is dead. The stars blink broken—

"Code," Leher said aloud.

Leher found himself considering the confirmation that the Poet was likely one individual. And that spike in the thirty-two kilohertz range. Like popping a *p* on a microphone, but in this case with a chemical signal.

The occurrences are so regular. What if—

What if the Poet was doing it on purpose? As a whispered marker.

Leher thumbed up a projection of the frequency analysis of this particular message on his desk. He laid the printed transcript next to it. Compared chemical trace to sceeve meaning ester.

Touched each spot on the page where the overmodulation occurred.

Smelled.

And he had it. A faint cinnamon accent to the vanillin. Sceeve esters usually occurred discreetly. Rider accents were a call to rearrange esters and restructure syntax in a sceeve paragraph.

The Poet was chemically popping his *p*s at certain sentences and not others. Random? A personal tic? Or was he doing it on purpose?

"LOVE, please make a catalog search for this 'sun is dead' cinnamon ester."

LOVE's quietly intense voice. "All right, LTC Leher." Half a second later. "I've found something from Skyhook Non-Euclidean B, LTC Leher."

Skyhook Non-Euclidean B. The notoriously untranslated portion of the haul from the Skyhook raid.

"Not much help there," Leher said.

"Sorry, LTC Leher."

"That's all right, LOVE." Griff sat back, lost in contemplation. Had to mean something. Had to . . .

After a moment, he turned to the other messages he'd printed out. He read through them all once and then again, mostly sniffing for the cinnamon tang. Nothing.

He reread the final communication from the Poet.

And he found the cinnamon. Several times. Once again, the scent was barely detectable within the overwhelming vanilla of the straightforward text.

It can't be that easy, he thought. *Can't.*

He took a pen and physically circled each instance on the page.

"LOVE, translate the esters I've just circled. Top to bottom. Use the final grouping as a syntax constructor."

But he was already doing it in his head and was smiling broadly before LOVE finished her more accurate and idiomatic version.

He had it.

Attention, begin primary information: Sporata war vessel Guardian of Night *en route to defect to Sol C government. This vessel mounts newly gleaned Sporata weapon of unknown potential and possible strategic-level value. Say again:* A.S.C. Guardian of Night *with potential strategic weapon seeks political asylum with United States government. Begin secondary information: Mutualist vessel* Efficacy of Symbiosis *to rendezvous with defecting Sporata vessel* Guardian of Night *in vicininty of Sol system to effect transfer of refugee passengers to* Efficacy of Symbiosis. *Say again: vessel* Efficacy of Symbiosis, *non-Administration, successionist craft to rendezvous with defecting* Guardian of Night *to effect transfer of Mutualist Shiro refugees. Begin tertiary information: Sirius armada to recommence gleaning of Sol system within current* variado. *Repeat: Sirius armada to reinvade Sol C within five* semanatos.

Objective: arrive before Administration invasion armada. Deliver weapon to Sol C. Discuss alliance with Mutualist enclaves. Engage Sirius armada.

Plan of action: request meeting highest levels with humans and their servant programs. Request aid, alliance, joint defensive agreement. A.S.C. Guardian of Night *desires to trade advanced, recently gleaned weaponry for terms of political sanctuary. Mutualist vessel* Efficacy of Symbiosis *desires discussion of Sol C alliance with successionist enclaves.*

Begin technical information: descriptive schematic of principal weapon on military vessel is as follows—

There was more, much more. It was a manual. Instructions for using some kind of sceeve superweapon. All the details were there, although Leher didn't understand the science. Somebody would.

Then, after the weapon information, a final message.

Final rendezvous location to follow in separate transmission.

Jesus, Mary, and Joseph, Leher thought.

"Do you see this, LOVE?"

"It's quite clear, LTC Leher, now that you have pointed it out."

"So I'm not dreaming?"

"You are producing alpha waves indicative of a conscious state," said LOVE.

Strategic weapon. Terms of sanctuary.

The sceeve bastard, hiding all that in plain sight.

He wasn't a mindless ranter masquerading as an artist.

He really had a way with words, after all.

FOUR

31 December 2075
Dallas, Texas, U.S.A.
Capitol Complex Perimeter

Extry Captain Jim Coalbridge buttoned his greatcoat against the Texas wind. A dusting of what looked like snow but what was actually "curd," or neutralized sceeve military nanotech, was falling on the downtown streets, coating them with a fine gray-white powder. The day was mild for December in Dallas, but Coalbridge was used to the regulated temperatures of spacecraft, and he'd been shivering since stepping out of the downtown train platform.

Coalbridge turned up his coat's collar. He had grown up in Oklahoma, and he knew that Southern prairie weather could be unpredictable. There were no nearby mountain ranges—practically no natural features whatsoever—to direct the huge pressure cells that roamed the plains. Any stray upper-level current might mean a thirty- or forty-degree shift in temperature within hours. North Texas summers were unbearably hot. Fall and spring were tolerable—but those seasons were filled with tornadoes and hurricanes. Now, with global weather patterns thrown into chaos by the sceeve planetary attacks, there were more killer storms than ever.

And winter? Winter was still mostly brown in these parts—with the occasional ice storm to provide a day or so of treacherous beauty.

He had to admit that walking under the sky, any planetary

sky, made him uneasy now. After years spent mostly in space, it felt a bit dangerous and wrong to be under all those layers of atmosphere.

Space was better. Space would kill you, true. But the planetary atmosphere you had to expose yourself to because you had to breathe it. Space you could protect against in a reasonable way.

Coalbridge glanced upward reflexively at the empty blue sky, checking for a telltale approaching shadow. Stupid. Should have gotten over that behavior years ago. The drop-rods fell at hypersonic speeds. They said you had five seconds from hearing a raid alert until impact. They also said you never heard the one that hit you.

I'm a walking Extry cliché, Coalbridge thought. *I've lost my land-lubber instincts and spend half my time down here feeling that I'm stuck in permanent airlock-failure mode and that the sky is falling.*

Of course, on Earth, the sky sometimes *did* fall. And the effects weren't pretty.

Take Dallas, for instance. The place was more rubble than city. Much of downtown had been flattened by drop-rod titanium rain-falls and a sceeve silicon-eating churn during the first invasion. Although the churn was mostly turned to curd, it had infected and weakened the city's infrastructure before being deactivated by ground defenses. What skyscrapers remained were brittle and useless. Business, and humanity along with it, had moved underground. Transportation was too expensive and difficult to bury, so it remained on the surface. Big sporting events and concerts still happened topside, as well (and fans took their lives into their hands to attend them).

Political protests also were a surface-based activity. The sceeve invasion, which had abruptly ended eight years before, was about to resume.

Everyone in the Extry knew it. The Xeno division had con-firmed it with its startling communiqué from a sceeve source. Everyone in the government should be well aware by now. And anybody else was an idiot who didn't suspect what was coming. Bad things had once again begun to fall from the sky.

Yet even before the recent precursors to reinvasion, planet Earth had been a wreck.

Stuck in half-ass gear. That was the way Coalbridge's great-great-grandfather had once described the old European city of Prague to Coalbridge when Coalbridge was a kid. Half-ass gear was when you were going too fast for first or second but not fast enough to shift to the next higher gear.

Aging in humans—at least in the developed world—had been short-circuited starting in 2025 around the time Coalbridge's great-great, whom Coalbridge called Paw Paw, was in his sixties. It was ironic that humans had solved the aging problem—well, forestalled it, at least, by a hundred or so years—only to have the unsolvable *death* problem hit them like a thunderbolt from space when the sceeve attacked.

Paw Paw had lived in Prague for a year in the early 1990s after the twentieth century's Cold War ended, and he'd described his impressions of the city to young Jimmy on more than one occasion.

He always called it Praha, like the natives, Coalbridge thought, and always made it feminine, like a vessel. Well, Praha or Prague, the place no longer existed, so it was pretty much a worry for historians now.

"Praha got the shit kicked out of her during World War II but escaped the worst of the damage. She didn't get flattened, like, say, Krakow in Poland. But she was busted up enough. And the commies just *left her that way* for fifty years. Damnedest thing. They didn't abandon her. Everyone stilled lived there. But nobody fixed anything. There was nothing to fix anything *with*. No money. No materials. No tools."

Coalbridge remembered his great-grandfather going on about the city while sitting at the battered kitchen table in Oklahoma City, the table's plasticized wood-grain surface pockmarked with cigarette burns from the older man's endless train of Marlboro Reds.

"I was having a little thing with this woman, Lenka Justinova— well, she was my Czech teacher at the intelligence station, to tell the truth—this was before your maw maw and me got married—and Lenka lived way up inside one of those gigantic concrete monsters the comms threw up all over Eastern Europe. Called 'em *panelaks* in Czech. Twenty thousand poor suckers in a cluster of 'em, if you can believe it. Made 'em out of this inferior concrete with too much sand that started to degrade the moment it set. It was nice having a little thing on the side with Lenka, but let me tell you, I'd always go see her with a set of tools and spend half my time fixing her toilet or working on her sink instead of, you know, having *fun*."

Except for the mysterious Lenka, his great-grandfather could've been talking about modern-day Dallas, Coalbridge thought. All the old buildings were torn to bits and pieces, and all the new stuff was cheap-ass, thrown together with whatever could be easily manufactured or salvaged.

The centers of the downtown streets had become the only reliably clear thoroughfares, and were used by auto, bus, and foot traffic. Rubble lined the sidewalks and filled the gutters—rubble coated with the gray-white denuded sceeve curd, so that the entire city looked like it had received a thin shellacking with primer and was awaiting a paint job.

There was also sparkle. A fine glass—the grain-sized shards of shattered windows, Coalbridge figured—paved the center of the streets and remained exposed due to steady traffic. The stuff wasn't sharp. It had long ago been ground to a sand-like fineness, and the roadway glittered like diamonds when the sun shone.

Lining the streets, or overturned on the rubble where there had once been sidewalks, were the battered and rusted remains of cars, trucks, and minivans: Fords, Sonys, Apples, Quicks. And for color, here and there some brave soul had attempted a bit of civic improvement. Along Field Street, a line of the burned-out hulks of cars still parallel-parked in the places their owners had left them twelve years ago had been coated on the roof of each car with a layer of potting soil. The soil was, in turn, sprinkled with a hardy strain of nanotech protectant and fertilizer—one of the new varieties of crunch that DARPA and some of the private firms had developed, Coalbridge figured.

Growing on the car roofs of Field Street—flowers. Daffodils, geraniums, chrysanthemums. All were in full bloom. Either nobody had programmed into the crunch the idea of winter, or perhaps whoever engineered this display had thought blossoms made the place look more Christmassy and had turned them on for the month.

They looked like zombie daffodils, Coalbridge thought. Undead mums and nasturtiums. Not allowed by the crunch to rest, to wilt, to die off, to proceed through the natural cycle of birth, death, and resurrection. Held in stasis by Frankenstein bugs and the human desire to find some way to spruce up even a hellhole of a place.

One car, an Apple Rhombi minivan, was completely roofed in poinsettias. Maybe his Christmas theory had been right. But the Rhombi didn't really look Christmassy.

Looks like a grave is what, Coalbridge thought. *They all do. Like a country graveyard on Decoration Day.*

For a moment, Coalbridge considered how many graves, how many pulverized home sites, how many dunes of human-charnel curd, he'd have to visit to properly honor *his* dead on Decoration Day.

Have to be magic like Santa Claus. Need some flying reindeer, too.

The thought of one day retiring to become a stockman with a herd of flying reindeer made Coalbridge smile. He'd long ago found ways to ward off the crushing weight that came from knowing that everyone—every last one of his relatives—was gone.

The sceeve invasion had killed ninety-eight percent of humanity. Coalbridge was part of the two percent remnant that had, by luck or chance, somehow survived. He was his family's last representative among the living.

Coalbridge had celebrated Christmas alone by cooking himself a complete holiday dinner.

Ah, hell, thought Coalbridge, *it's the holidays for one more day. Why not get into the spirit?* He found himself liking the weirdly vibrant car tops. Dallas was still alive. *Okay, Paw Paw: like you did Praha, I'll call her* she. She was alive. And fighting her way out of sickness and despair. People lived here. This broken, blasted ruin of a metropolis was the home to two million souls, three million if you counted nearby Fort Worth. It was the most populous city on planet Earth.

Coalbridge turned a corner.

And there they are, he thought. *Some of them, at least.*

Peepsies.

As he'd seen on the news feed that morning, the antiwar protesters, the Peepsies, were out in force today. Even with reports of fresh drop-rod attacks on Sydney and Nairobi, the organizers had evidently decided the protest must go on. They probably didn't believe the news anyway.

He'd been warned to start early for his meeting downtown but hadn't expected this: the entire Capitol complex was cordoned off by a line of beaten-up school buses stretching from Field to Elm to St. Paul to Commerce, squaring off at Field once more. Paper scraps were plastered on the buses—Coalbridge couldn't make out what they were and assumed they might be slogans or announcements. They flapped in the breeze.

Around the buses milled hundreds of Peepsies: students in the new retraining programs out on winter break, the professionally disgruntled, paid "volunteers" working for various antiwar

NGO interests, and the hard-core contingent of the permanently deranged and hopelessly bereaved.

The Capitol complex was surrounded.

One hundred eighty million human beings left on the planet— barely enough to keep civilization from collapsing around itself, maybe *not* enough—an imminent attack by a rapacious enemy on its way, and *this* was how these people chose to spend their time? It was strange to think that they were some of the people he'd spent the last twelve years defending with his life. Yet...

He couldn't hate them. He could only feel pity for the Peepsies.

All of these people had lost most or all of their friends and family. Earth's population hadn't merely been devastated; it had been treated to an extinction event.

Asia had been the first target. The sceeve were after resources and technology. At least, that was the theory. Their choice of what to take and what they left behind was often bizarre. Entire mountains of limestone taken. The contents of a gypsum mine sucked out. As far as technology went, they sought out the most pedestrian means of production—the factories of China, those of the Asian Tigers. After pacification, their "harvesters" would arrive and begin gleaning the landscape, disassembling manufacturing plants, carting them off to space.

There was no attempt to "collect" any human, scientist, innovator, or entrepreneur. The sceeve did not seem to care about the human brain trust, the universities and corporate campuses, the industrial-park concrete boxes and basement labs, where the *ideas* came from. These they merely destroyed. They seemed to regard ideas as some sort of epiphenomena, a by-product of technology instead of its generator. Every continental coast was devastated, but the tech that was "sceeved" was always a fabrication plant, a car lot, a copper pit. And retail stores. Every Best Buy store up and down both coasts was dismantled and taken away, every Home Depot, Duggers Lifescience, every Amazon and Walmart warehouse looted. Humans themselves were inconveniences—but not too lowly to destroy at every opportunity. In the end, only the United States managed to put up effective resistance. Earth's military was now the U.S. military.

Then, after four years of devastation, the sceeve had left. Suddenly. Mysteriously. Left with the Earth only partially "harvested," as far as anybody could tell.

Oh, the sceeve were still out there. The war continued as humans were hemmed in, cordoned off from systems at a distance greater than twenty-five light-years from Sol, the so-called Fomalhaut Limit.

And now, just as suddenly, they had decided to return. All the signs were there in the heavens. Over the past year, the Fomalhaut Limit had shrunk as the sceeve began to move their blockade inexorably toward Sol system.

The armada had not arrived yet, but it was coming. And as for the Peepsie protestors Coalbridge was now confronted with, all most of them had experienced directly was the fact that they were the inheritors of a destroyed Earth. The ones responsible—the sceeve—had vanished from the planet surface itself eight years ago.

Maybe you couldn't blame people for thinking it was all a ruse, or believing that the automated attacks that still got through were somehow the creation of the government. People could convince themselves of all manner of things to make some sort of sense of a senseless situation.

Yet I lost everybody I loved, too, but that didn't turn me into a political idiot.

What the cordon of buses encircled was not physically the U.S. presidential residence and Capitol complex. The buses were at street level, after all, and merely cordoned off the old First National Bank building, now empty. The actual Capitol was many feet underground, ensconced in the intricate system of century-old tunnels that lay beneath downtown Dallas. The bus-fortress was there to screen off exterior access to the First National block, including the main Capitol entrance at Field and Pacific, which was where Coalbridge was headed.

Puffs of smoke suddenly wafted toward him, and Coalbridge's eyes began to water. What was that *smell*? Something was cooking. The air was thick with a meaty odor. Coalbridge had skipped breakfast for the first time in weeks and was hungry. Although it was plainly too early for anyone to be cooking lunch, in the back of his mind he idly assumed he might be smelling barbecue.

Coalbridge's main hobby was cooking—and anybody who suggested that this made him somehow less of a warrior wasn't worth the time to beat the shit out of. Despite the traumatized economy, there were still an amazing number of ingredients and spices still available in Dallas. The human instinct for trade had found a way. He'd spent whatever free time he'd been able to snag while on shore duty cooking up a storm, with usually only himself or a friend or two from work to feed. One thing he hadn't had time for while planetside was an old-fashioned night-long grilling session. Barbecue was one of his main indulgences when eating out, however, and he'd been planning on at least hitting his favorite joint, Rudy's, up in Denton—which he'd heard still existed and which was as close to Oklahoma-style barbecue as you could get in these parts. But so far there had been no time, and it didn't look like he was going to make it now. Most of the past month he'd spent groundside had been underground in the New Pentagon's Extry command.

Coalbridge turned the corner of Elm and Field and all thoughts of eating barbecue disappeared from his mind—perhaps for eternity.

A dozen Peepsies were burning to death in the middle of Elm Street.

"Aaaaaaaaiaaaaaaaaaah!"

The smell? *Human barbecue,* thought Coalbridge. *Oh, God, that's what it was.*

The Peepsies were sitting in meditative fashion—or, as his sister, Gretchen, a kindergarten teacher dead in the first wave of the invasion, had called it: sitting *crisscross-applesauce.*

Something familiar . . .

Then it came to him: they were mimicking the Tovil Exorcism, the group of Buddhist monks and nuns who had set themselves alight in protest of the United States's occupation of Sri Lanka back in the 2040s. Sri Lanka didn't exist as a recognizable *landmass* anymore, much less a country.

Shit. Coalbridge tamped down the adrenaline surge he'd just endured and took a mental moment to stifle his immediate urge—which had been to go and *rescue somebody.*

He took a longer look at the self-immolators. Looked like three men and three women, from what he could tell. Young. Dressed in Peepsie counterculture garb, now aflame. He took a closer look. Very young. They were teenagers. Aha.

Nobody was dying here.

These kids were protected by dermal churn—called "salt," after the military version of the same nanotech. Salt itself was not extremely expensive—Coalbridge had a coating—but the charger subscription necessary to make it effective day in and day out was not cheap. Coalbridge didn't know how much such subscriptions cost these days, but he'd bet his captain's bar that these were rich kids, the children of doctors, lawyers, NGO brass, and government bureaucrats, probably, whose families could afford the kind of electrostatic subscription and advanced coating that would permit such a display of political theater.

Salt could be set to deliver or to stifle nerve stimuli, pain in particular, through the coating. Yet salt wasn't magic. Even if the kids had turned off their nerves, salt could hardly prevent the heat damage from a gas flame.

Hence the charming barbecue smell, Coalbridge thought.

But the nanobugs were repairing the damage as fast as it occurred, and probably insulating the inner body parts below the skin from further damage. The kids would suffer from the fire they were applying to their bodies, but in the end they weren't going to be disfigured. Or burn to death. Or even be terribly inconvenienced.

Which was good, Coalbridge reflected. You did dumb shit when you were a teenager. Unfortunately, the teenagers *weren't* doing a very good job at copying the Tovil monks' calm indifference to pain.

"Aaaaaaaaiaaaaaaaaaah!" Their heads tilted back, agony in their throats, the teen screams continued—loud and annoyingly piercing.

It's like a goddamn coyote yowl, Coalbridge thought. *Haven't heard one of those in ages.*

As Coalbridge looked on, he saw one of the girls break from her position, try to crawl from the street toward the gutter, but another flaming boy reached for her.

For a moment the two tussled on the pavement, both engulfed in flames.

Coalbridge's impulse to help kicked back in. He took a step toward the two. This was insane. If the girl wanted out, hadn't realized the pain she was getting herself into, it was his duty to aid her.

But before he could move any farther, the boy succeeded in throwing himself atop the flaming girl and holding her in place.

Coalbridge quickly made his way toward the two—only to pull up short. Now he was close enough to see what was up.

He'd misinterpreted. The two weren't actually fighting or struggling at all. They were locked in a kiss.

And were they...

Yep.

Coalbridge turned away, amused and disgusted. He chuckled. If this really was the end of the world, what a third-rate apocalypse it had turned out to be.

Another glance toward the sky.

No drop-rod attack seemed imminent. But the longer he lingered outside, the more exposed he felt.

Coalbridge made his way back to the side of the Elm Street cleared corridor. As he walked on, any contempt he'd felt dissipated. He felt suddenly tender toward the burned kids. He'd been an adrenaline junkie when he was that age. He'd strongly considered taking an aviation route when he graduated from Annapolis.

And he'd jumped at the Extry, and spacecraft duty, the minute his transfer had been approved.

Of course, aircraft were now obsolete militarily—at least so far as the war with the sceeve was concerned.

Fate had led him out to sea on surface vessels and then driven him in another direction entirely—one in which there was plenty of adrenaline to be had. That was good, because he still jonesed for it. All the time. Kept his mind off things.

Like his mom and dad turned to curd by sceeve churn. His brothers. His sister. Cousins. Friends. Grandparents, greats, great-greats—beaten into the Oklahoma red earth by metal rain.

A fucking lot of things.

Nearby a Peepsie crowd lining the north side of Elm was shouting encouragement and cries of sympathy for the teens. Somewhere an incomprehensible bullhorn blared agitation. Coalbridge rose on tiptoes to his full height—a good six foot two—and surveyed the crowd. A sea of dazzed T-shirts scrolling through preassigned messages. A few homemade signs. And a score of placards, most of them on display-changing dazz paper, the signs featuring similar messages to their T-shirts.

"The Real Parasites Are in Dallas!"

"Make Our Solar System a Salt-free Zone!"

"The Sceeve Were Right: We ARE an Unjust Species!" And the even more direct: "Humans: We Got What We Deserved!"

There were even a few vintage signs strewn about. A yellowed "Condi = War-Criminal-in-Chief!" And was that...yes, it was: "Stop Global Warming!" Well, *that* problem was taken care of, thank you very much. Humanity's carbon footprint was about the size of a three-week old fetus's these days.

A few clumps of Peepsies had signs he agreed with: "Reformat Act = Jim Crow!" "Repeal all Expiration Codes!" "Free the servants!" Generally the civil-rights folks stood a bit away from the others and were clustered around their own tables of literature and bumper stickers, the material weighed down with rocks and bits of brick against the Texas wind. Servant rights were controversial. The enormous shortage of workers to keep up the basics of civilization had been solved by the introduction of artificial agents, but at a price. Servants had performed *too* well. They had all but eliminated manufacturing jobs for regular people and had taken over many of the service jobs, as well.

Suddenly: *BAM!* A stinging blow against his chest and an explosion on the dark black wool of his coat. He looked down.

Red, red, red!

I'm hit. Something somehow got through my shirt.

Coalbridge's reflexes took over, and he was instantly on his hands and knees scrambling for cover.

He reached into his inner coat pocket for the Extry officer's weapon, his service truncheon—a nasty device that looked like a police baton but was oh-so-much-more. Coalbridge was an expert with it. In fact, he'd personally taken out fifteen sceeve and counting with this very trunch.

He glanced down to survey the damage to himself.

Should be okay, he thought.

He'd taken the hit in his chest, so the crunch, the embedded smart fiber woven into his uniform shirt, probably stopped the main impact of the bullet. But there was blood, and sometimes a lucky shot got through the nano activators, so—

Hold on. Don't shit your pants quite yet, little Jimbo.

Paint. It was red paint.

Christ.

He stood up, dusted himself off.

"The sceeves should kill you for *real!*" someone screamed nearby.

He looked over. Dungarees and checkered Vans. A tight Chavez T-shirt topped by a flowing, hand-crocheted sweater vest left open. A red bandana holding back a bundle of curly brown hair. Distressed jeans that looked like they'd been water-boarded multiple times.

She was hot. Total retro-hippie vogue, like Joan Placid in that viral that was going around, the one that every red-blooded exper male had set to permanent repeat on his Palace.

A look which he had to admit he found kind of attractive.

And now he was going to pull off the seduction of the century? Turn his enemy into his lover on the mean streets of Dallas?

God, two months without a woman, Coalbridge thought. It was beginning to tell on him.

Forget all that. On this day of all days, he had to get to work! This situation was ridiculous. He had to find a way through these buses and get into the Capitol complex.

"Just let me by, dear, and I'll come back and pass a pipe around the campfire later," he said. "Hell, I'll bring the THC. Got sources you wouldn't believe. Just move aside for now—"

"Fuck *you*," said a male voice, close to his ear. He turned to see a pencil-thin guy in his late twenties. He wore an old-fashioned punk getup, with sewed-on pegged jeans and a black leather motorcycle jacket over a T-shirt. "You think you can go around dressed like that"—he nodded toward Coalbridge's dress uniform—"and *get away with it*? Children are dying in Africa because of you fucking Extry baby-killers."

Coalbridge shook his head and was about to make his way around them in bemusement when the Peepsie punk reached out a quick hand and shoved him into the side of a bus.

His head whacked into the paper-covered sheet metal. Shot of pain through his skull. Yellow-tinged floaters momentarily in front of his eyes.

The Peepsie punk was stronger than he looked.

Reaction and training took over Coalbridge's body. He had to end this quickly, and he wasn't going to be able to use reason. Coalbridge reached between his coat buttons, felt the truncheon's handle, activated it with a twist and spun around to face—

Some other dude.

This one was entirely People's Front, a real Chavista down to the torn dungarees and paisley shirt. There was something much more authentic about him, too—if it *was* a him. A mane of curly, tangled hair, and underneath—yeah, it was a guy. Who smelled of patchouli and cheap incense. A chest draped in beads. Dirt—or something grimy—smeared into the wrinkles of his exposed skin.

Was this the Peepsie version of a medicine man or shaman? Did they even *have* those?

But the Peepsie-shaman was not confronting Coalbridge. Instead he was smiling benignly at the punk guy and Joan Placid, putting a firm hand on the punk's shoulder.

"Come on, brother, you know better," said the shaman in a low, calm voice. "Violence won't solve anything."

For a moment, the Peepsie punk glared hatred at Coalbridge. But the calming hand of the shaman and Coalbridge's truncheon, glowing with a pale purple Q-generated fire, gave the punk pause.

"If you go after him, you just prove him right," said the hippie-shaman. "War is the problem, not the solution."

The shaman pointed to the bus behind Coalbridge. "This man's victims see him, don't worry," he said.

Coalbridge turned and looked behind him. Nothing but the bus, the poster-like plasterings. Faces. Hundreds of faces, staring out at him. Some smiling, some mysterious, some even sexy. Then he realized what he was seeing.

The Peepsies, or someone, had turned the sides of the bus—all the buses—into remembrance walls. They were plastered with photographs of the dead. Some had a short paragraph, a birth and death date. Some had no lettering at all, but silently, wordlessly attested to the fact that this person had been here, had walked the Earth, and was no more.

The Peepsie punk started to say something else to Coalbridge, but the shaman gave the punk a sharp look. Finally the Peepsie punk shook his head like an angry, confused bull. "He fucking started it," he said to the shaman. "His kind started the whole thing. All the fucking suffering. They violated the Limit and brought the retribution down on us."

The Peepsie punk was making correlation into cause. The sceeve *had* arrived shortly after the first Q-based FTL drive had been sent to the Centauris. There was talk that humanity had set off a trip wire that alerted the sceeve to come marauding.

"Maybe so, maybe so. But we have to end this, brother," said the shaman. "Haters only breed more hate."

Another moment of fuming hesitation from the punk. Another glance at the truncheon. Then the punk turned away. "I guess you're right...."

"This one will wake up one day and realize that there's innocent blood on his hands, that he's collaborated in the greatest fraud in history," the shaman said, nodding toward Coalbridge while simultaneously leading the Peepsie punk away. "And that's the day he'll put a bullet in his own brain."

"Won't be soon enough," the Peepsie punk shouted back at Coalbridge. But he allowed himself to be shepherded away.

Coalbridge powered down his truncheon but did not put it away yet.

Ptupt.

Joan Placid spat in Coalbridge's general direction, hit the side of the bus beside his head. She glared defiantly at him. Coalbridge looked her straight in the eyes, trying to communicate what a very bad idea it would be to fuck with him any more. He really didn't want to hurt her. It was beginning to dawn on him that to do so would have *political* repercussions. Career repercussions.

Which might mean losing his new command.

Remaining earthbound.

Thankfully, Joan Placid seemed to get the message, for, after a moment, she turned and followed the others without taunting him further.

Coalbridge sighed, replaced the truncheon in his coat, and glanced at his watch. Oh, hell. Late to the most important meeting in his professional life—and delayed by Peepsies!

It wasn't fair. Today of all days.

Coalbridge ducked back down to prone position and, as fast as he could, scooted under the bus, under the plastered photocopied remembrances of the dead. Greasy street tar. A sheen of skuzzy curd. His coat—a gift from his parents at his long-ago graduation—was going to be ruined. No nanotech wonder treatment was going to be able to resurrect it this time.

He rolled out on the underside and looked up—

Oh, crap.

—into the flat panel of an unmanned UADS directional emitter. A hellfryer.

The active denial system was turn-of-the-century tech, a crowd-dispersal device used by the marines since the 1990s. The addition of an a.i. servant had given it a whole new lease on life. He could hear the UADS's old-school batteries whining softly, building for discharge. Coalbridge raised his hand, rapidly pulled his I.D. lanyard from within his coat, and flashed his Pentagon pass.

Click. The whine died away. The emitter screen lowered its angle to a rest position.

"Captain James Dasein Coalbridge the Third," said a voice from the UADS.

"Call me Jim."

"No, thank you. I am under directive to keep citizen interaction formal. Are you all right, Captain Coalbridge?"

"I'm fine." Coalbridge pulled himself to his feet. "Hell of a day to come to work."

"I'll say, sir," the UADS replied. It had a remarkably pleasant and wholly uni-gendered voice. Strange choice for a robo-cop. "I see you're Extry," the robot continued. "Do you happen to know the servant named DAFNE, by any chance? The servant who participated in the Skyhook Raid?"

Happen to know? Hell, he'd spent almost every second of the past two years wiied to her through the salt. He'd say he knew her about as well as a person could know a servant.

"Of course I do," Coalbridge said. "One of her iterations was the XO of my last command, and she's been a friend of mine for years before that."

"Then tell her we're all proud of what she's accomplishing when you speak to her next—that is, if you don't mind, sir." The UADS rolled back a couple of feet to clear a path for him. "I speak for the Local MP-38 Class Peacekeeper Network, I mean. She's really going where no one has gone before."

"Will do," Coalbridge said. "And thanks for not cooking my goose."

"Not a problem, sir," the UADS replied. "But watch your back." Suddenly, the UADS's flat panel shot back up and aimed directly at the undercarriage of the next bus over.

"*You*, under the bus—remain where you are! Identify yourself!" it called out. This time the voice was most certainly *not* uni-gendered. More like the voice of a very male, very patriarchal God.

"For Christ's sake, let me get out from under here, MP-38," came the reply. "My name is Leher. We went through this yesterday. And the day before that, as I recall."

"Rise slowly," intoned the UADS.

It was the hippie shaman. Even at this distance, the patchouli scent was unmistakable.

The hippie pulled himself slowly out from under the bus and rose shakily to his feet. He held out his hand, flashed an I.D. at the UADS.

"Lieutenant Commander Leher, it's nice to see you this morning," the UADS said.

Holy crap.

"You do this on purpose, MP-38."

"One can never be sure," said the UADS. It turned on its treads and made ready to head back down the line of buses. "You gentlemen have a nice day."

"Thanks," Coalbridge said. He turned to Leher. "You're *navy*?" he asked.

"No, sir," Leher replied. "I'm one of you. Extry all the way, Captain. Heart of vacuum and bleed space when I'm cut. Except I'm not too fond of actual space, to tell the truth, and actual bleeding is something I normally try to avoid."

Looking at the man, you would never tell he was Extry. He seemed... not the type. And now that he was no longer pretending to be a Peepsie shaman, he seemed even less military. He was hunched, almost—

Almost *cringing*, Coalbridge thought.

And his face was not a picture of command and gentle certainty, as it had appeared before, but nervousness. The slightest twitch around his left eye, too.

And anyway, Leher's hair was utterly, completely nonregulation. Or was it? Leher smiled a crooked smile, reached for the back of his hair, and gave it a hard yank. The hair parted from his scalp in the front as if by magic.

It was a wig. A very convincing hippie wig.

Beneath the wig was a shaggy blond mop of hair that was, nonetheless, of the required shortness.

"I'll be damned. And the beard?"

"That's permanent, I'm afraid." He ran a hand through the beard and combed out a couple of crumbs. "Got to toast it every morning if you want that 'eaten in' look."

"You *toast* your beard?"

"Put toast crumbs in it, I mean," Leher replied with a grin. "Needs to be whole grain, too, or you'll never fool 'em. I take it you haven't had to come to work this way very often?"

"I'm deep space. But they've had me stowed at the New Pentagon out in the burbs for the past couple of weeks cooling my heels. I haven't been down to the Capitol complex since I came back planetside."

"Yes, well, let's just say that around here camouflage is the better part of valor these days." Leher unslung the green canvas daypack he was carrying, opened it, and bid Coalbridge to look inside. "I can only afford so much dry cleaning on GS-6 pay. My uniform's got ballistic crunch in it. None of that fancy self-cleaning stuff." The flat black of a full-dress Extry uniform stared back at Coalbridge.

"I should've done that," Coalbridge said. And not only that, Coalbridge thought. "Jesus, it was really stupid of me to draw a truncheon on those idiots. I could've killed them."

"It was flashing purple. I saw you had it set on 'give an interesting time,' not kill."

"I guess you're right," said Coalbridge. "It was a reflex."

"Then you've got good instincts. A person has to experience this shit to believe the kinds of things they'll say to you," Leher said, motioning toward the buses and beyond to the demonstrators. "I don't think they mean half of it. Not that they don't have a point at times."

"I'm a baby-killer?"

"All the conspiracy stuff is bullshit, of course, but the government hasn't been exactly transparent lately."

"The War Powers Act is necessary. Hell, it doesn't go far *enough*," Coalbridge said darkly. "You're Extry. You know it's about to be rock-and-roll time again."

"We know that," Leher replied, "but the Peepsies don't. And nobody is willing to tell them because then they'd know the even more horrible truth. That the government has been running around like a bunch of chickens with their heads cut off, and even the Extry's split on what to do next."

"You sound like a Peepsie."

"I've been called worse," Leher replied. "Sceeve-fucking creepy-crawler springs to mind." He smiled and held out his hand. "Lieutenant Commander Griffin Leher, sir. Xeno Division."

Xeno, thought Coalbridge. *That explains it. Worse than a lawyer.* And Leher. Where had he run across that name?

The xenologicals were a strange bunch, even by Extry standards.

"I'm Jim Coalbridge." He omitted his title because Leher could see he was a captain from the single gold fretting of oak leaves on his hat's visor. His rank was also indicated by the insignia on the shoulderboards of his planetside service blacks. "My craft's the *Joshua Humphreys*. Or will be, when she's all fitted out."

"Patrol vessel?"

"Try a new-christened frigate. Second in her class. She's after the *Jonas Salk*."

Leher smiled, amused at Coalbridge's pride. "My mistake," he said. "Coalbridge, huh?" Leher scratched his chin. "You related to the Coalbridge who commanded the Skyhook Raid back in '67 by any chance?"

Oh, hell. There was *that* again. His fuck-ups in that operation had gotten people killed. Friends. He'd been twenty-six. He could only plead extreme youth and inexperience, but that was no comfort to the dead, he was certain. To have survived the invasion, only to be killed by some greenhorn lieutenant's incompetence—he was ashamed of himself.

"Yeah. I know him," Coalbridge said.

"Well, *that* guy gave me a career. Tell him thank-you when you next see him, will you?"

"He's me," Coalbridge said sullenly.

"Figured it might be," said Leher. "Sore spot, huh?"

Coalbridge nodded, but frowned and indicated with a shrug that he didn't have the inclination to explain further.

"All right, then. Want to walk with me the rest of the way? I know a shortcut that'll take us around that ten-minute line at the First National scanner."

Coalbridge brightened. Maybe he wasn't going to be late after all. And he had a pseudo-Peepsie-shaman Extry officer to thank for it.

So Leher was Xeno. A "creep," as they were called—and called themselves.

The sceeve experts.

Leher. Shit, of course. Leher of the Poet Communiqué. The very reason he was headed to the presidential office this morning.

"You write that report that's got them all buzzing, Leher?" he asked.

"Call me Griff," Leher said. "I have no idea what you're talking about, and if I did, it sounds like that would be classified." Leher stroked his beard as he spoke and tried to hide his pleased smile.

The blushing author himself, Coalbridge thought. *I'll be damned.*

"And you're the creep behind that Depletion Report that came out last summer, too. The one that made sense of the withdrawal."

"Again, no idea what you mean."

"*Whoever* wrote it made some goddamn bold predictions on sceeve activity for the future. Predictions that are pretty much coming true, if you ask me."

Coalbridge wanted to talk to this guy. Find out what he knew, all he knew, about the sceeve. But this was not the place for discussing battle plans. Like Leher said, the communiqué was classified. He *could* mention one thing he'd particularly agreed with, however.

"I liked your recommendation in the Depletion Report summary on full officer status for servants," he said. "Every space-based exper believes in it, but I've found out the idea isn't too popular back here."

"The data are absolutely convincing," Leher said. "The more autonomy the servants are given, the more effective they are in battle. We studied hundreds of engagements." Leher shrugged. "Besides, as far as I'm concerned, they're people."

"Hell, yeah, they are."

Leher might make a very useful acquaintance at some point. Coalbridge had done his own study of the sceeve—up close and personal—and he would love to compare notes. Or have some on-the-scene expertise. And Leher had written that report. This guy wasn't just a creep—he was the creepiest of the creeps.

No doubt, creeps were oddballs. To become one was for all intents and purposes to leave the command track. They were also said to be a bunch of sadists, like the aliens they studied. And all crazy as loons.

As if to confirm Coalbridge's judgment, Leher took a few steps forward, then came to a dead halt. As far as Coalbridge could see there was nothing blocking the other man's path. But when Coalbridge came up beside Leher, he saw what had caused the abrupt stop. There was a long crack in the street. The glassy coating abruptly ended and a small fissure stretched across their path. It ran deep into the asphalt under the layer of glass. The crack was less than an inch wide, but it was unbroken.

After a moment's thought, Coalbridge understood what was going on.

Some sort of OCD that wouldn't let the guy step over cracks, something like that. This was not an uncommon phenomenon. You saw that a lot in the traumatized, and if you were an officer in the military, you had to deal with similar psychological problems on practically a daily basis. Or maybe it wasn't trauma. Maybe Leher had come out of the womb a freak. In any case, Coalbridge knew what to do with such nutcase behavior.

Give in, to a degree. Channel, don't obstruct.

Leher was slapping his pockets and muttering to himself, something about a pin or a pen.

"Got the cards," Leher said. "Should have it, too."

Coalbridge looked around and found a scrap piece of wood about a foot across and a few feet long—it was detritus from some previous sceeve attack, some fallen structure—and plopped it down over the crack so that it formed a crossing.

"Your bridge, Lieutenant Commander," he said to Leher.

Leher blinked, considered, seemed to snap out of whatever daze he'd fallen into and with a big grin stepped on the wooden crossing Coalbridge had provided.

"Guess it's a good thing I met you, too," he said. "Jim, was it?"

Coalbridge shrugged. "That kind of mental shit is pretty common, especially with space-based expers. We're a superstitious lot out there." He stepped over the crack and walked beside Leher.

"Say, you don't have anything to write with, do you?"

"Got my Palace and a blink-up keyboard."

Leher shook his head. "No, that won't do." Suddenly his hand flew up to his breast pocket. He dug around inside it, came up with nothing.

"Is whatever you're looking for in your uniform pocket?" Coalbridge gently asked.

Leher slapped his forehead. "Of course," he said. "Had kind of a rotten morning. Weird dreams, that sort of thing. Must've forgotten to transfer to my Peepsie costume."

"Sorry to hear that."

"No problem," Leher said. "Now I know where it is."

"What?"

"My pen. Space pen, actually." He chuckled. "Magically writes when it's upside down."

"Wow."

Leher nodded. "It was a gift. From my kid."

In that moment, Coalbridge decided he probably liked Leher, even if Leher did come across as slightly insane.

Hell, I'll even give him the bullshit test, he thought.

"So, you *really* think I have what it takes to blow my own

brains out?" Coalbridge asked. "You told that Peepsie son of a bitch I would." The wind gusted up, and for a moment neither man could speak as each huddled in his coat. When he could be heard again, Coalbridge continued. "I mean, lots of guys have blood on their hands, but that doesn't mean they have what it takes to *do something about it,* if you know what I mean."

Leher seemed taken aback for a moment. Then he considered, squinting in a cockeyed fashion. "I'm surprised you haven't already blown yourself away, seeing as you're a goddamn *starcraft captain,*" he replied. "I happen to know your kind thinks this universe is not good enough for the likes of you."

Coalbridge nodded. "You've met a few of us then?"

"You bet," Leher said.

"I'm not anything like that."

"I have no choice but to believe you, Jim."

Coalbridge smiled. "And you're obviously a creep, through and through. Switchblade in every compliment, they say."

"I'm the best creep you'll ever meet, Captain Courageous," Leher said. "And don't worry your oversized captain's head about one thing—your enemy is my enemy. We have different ways of going about killing him, that's all."

Was he going to be friends with a *creep*? Stranger things had happened.

And creep or no, Leher knew the fastest way into the Capitol complex. Which was all that really mattered at the moment to Coalbridge.

"So, want to lead the way, you Peepsie-loving creep? I sure would like to get down below and out from under this sky, if you know what I mean," said Coalbridge.

"That's one thing we agree on," said Leher. He chuckled, shook his head, took a step forward—then stopped in his tracks. Coalbridge noticed another street crack running diagonally in front of them. The ground glass on the street outlined its jagged course in splendid sparkles. "On the other hand, *I'll* get us there," Coalbridge said. "You just get us in."

He kicked another white-coated bridging board over the crack. There was no end of loose material around. Leher didn't budge. His complexion had changed from ruddy to white as a ghost.

His eyes were still fixed on the crack.

"It doesn't count if you slide it," Leher said in a low voice.

Coalbridge glanced at him, but there wasn't a trace of irony in his face.

Coalbridge picked up the board and laid it across with his hands. "That better?"

Leher nodded and stepped across. After he'd reached the other side, he suddenly looked around. "You hear a raid siren?"

"No. You?"

Leher shook his head. He and Coalbridge both gazed up at the sky.

Nothing. Still...

"I've got a bad feeling about today, Captain Courageous," said Leher.

Coalbridge nodded. "Me, too." Coalbridge glanced over at his companion. So this was really him. *The* Leher.

"Tell you what," said Coalbridge. "There's got to be a story behind that analysis of yours. You give me a little background. I'm top-secret cleared. You saw the hellfryer identify me. In return, I'll help you get the hell away from this sky. Deal?"

Leher stopped short, considered Coalbridge with a cold gaze. He tugged at the end of his dirty beard. Once, twice, three times.

Coalbridge shrugged, as if to say: "I've got no angle here. We're both playing on the same team."

Which they were. In the larger sense.

Then Leher smiled crookedly. "All right," he said. "I'll give you a quick backgrounder. But don't expect a happy ending."

Coalbridge nodded succinctly, returned the smile. "You're forgetting one thing, son."

"What's that?"

"We *are* the ending," said Coalbridge. "And I happen to like my chances."

Leher shook his head. "Goddamn captains." But then there was no stopping Leher as he filled in for Coalbridge the background that shored up his report.

FIVE

31 December 2075
Dallas
Presidential Office Reception Area

The Lincoln Plaza section of the underground Capitol complex, which housed the presidential office suite, had once been a warren of little shops under downtown Dallas—a bodega, an Asian-run fruit market, a drugstore, and a barbershop. What trappings from the old place that had survived the first sceeve attack on the White House in Washington, D.C., had been relocated here, to the underground walkways that lay beneath the city—a system that had existed for over a century, a relic of preinvasion days.

In the old days, people had used the tunnels to escape the summer heat, the Texas wind. Now reinforced from above with nano-infused steel a foot thick (equivalent to being a mile under rock, the engineers said), the tunnels were shelter from a different kind of storm. The Secretary of the Extry had his office here in the White House warrens, and Leher spent about half his work time there, acting as Xeno liaison to the SECEX, and the other half twenty miles north at the Xeno command's offices in the New Pentagon.

After Leher and Coalbridge descended into the tunnels, Leher had expertly guided Coalbridge through the crisscrossed system. It was amusing to watch the confusion grow on Coalbridge's face as Leher led him deeper into the Capitol warren. Leher knew the labyrinth well, including all the shortcuts and half-hidden connecting passageways, but for a neophyte, as Leher well remembered, getting around the off-white walls and grayish linoleum floors could feel like trying to navigate the layers of hell. Coolbridge and he had finally separated when they'd reached the main warren and Leher had gone to change into his uniform.

Reception, located in what had once been a barbershop and not a huge room to begin with, was packed. Leher, now in uniform, stood in a corner and glanced furtively around, then tugged on his beard, checking to see if it was time for a trim. His method was to rub thumb and forefinger together, and if the beard hair curled instead of working itself free from his grasp, clippers would be coming out soon. This action was a constant ritual for Leher, engaged in at least once every thirty minutes or so, throughout his waking day. There were many other such repetitions that became apparent after an hour or so of being around him.

Leher was well aware of his compulsive behavior. What was sometimes even more exasperating was that, when he was in another character, coming to work dressed as a Peepsie, say, or when he was completely immersed in his work persona of hotshot linguistic analyst, the tics, the behavior patterns, all but disappeared. What he couldn't do was *will* them away during the lulls, the downtime. To *try* to make himself stop the beard-tugging, the crack-worry, the postcard-writing, was all but impossible, and usually thinking about it made it even worse.

The reception area smelled of coffee and anxiety. A few desultory Christmas decorations hung on the walls—and a small, sad-looking banner that read HAPPY NEW YEAR 2076. Leher figured it was probably in preparation for another gathering scheduled this evening—New Year's Eve—although he hadn't been invited.

Above my pay grade by at least seven layers, Leher thought. *Don't need the hassle anyway.*

But he *was* in dire need of coffee. Leher spotted a big urn on a table against the far wall and made his way through the suited and uniformed morning crowd to get to it.

And there, in the center of the room, was one of the reasons for the meeting this morning. Rear Admiral and Engineering and Design Mission Director Alan Tillich.

Tillich shot Leher a white-hot glare of hatred, then returned to the conversation he'd been having.

Oh, shit. So it was going to be that way, was it?

Leher reached the table the coffee urn was on. He turned, glanced back, and there was Tillich staring at him once again.

Great. High Command was not pleased. The queasiness began to settle into Leher's stomach almost as bad as it did in space. He was not made for these bureaucratic battles—especially against foes who had defeated *U.S. presidents* before. If the stakes hadn't been so high...

But they were.

Still, Leher felt as if cracks were gathering all around him, waiting to spider forth. He felt the urge to laugh, long and loud. Fought it down.

Damn it. He needed to get some words down on a postcard. Put the postcard in the mail.

Express the anxiety away. You needed rituals to keep the world from continually falling apart. *He* needed them, at least.

Leher's rational side knew he was reading too much meaning into Tillich's glares. So Tillich hated him? Leher couldn't return the feeling. He retained the same admiration he always had for the Extry legend. Tillich *was* the Extry in the minds of many. He'd built the first fleet after the service had broken away from the U.S. Navy and Air Force to form its own branch of the U.S. armed forces ten years ago.

Tillich literally put the *X* in Extry.

It had been Tillich who'd insisted that Space Navy sounded too Buck Rogers—and conceded too much to the blue-water rub-a-dub-dubbers. What was needed was a new name, one that suggested extraterrestrial, experimental, new—and Tillich had come up with it.

Actually, he'd called it the *Xtry*, thought Leher. And he'd never really agreed that his original formulation might be confusing to pronounce.

Eight years ago, Tillich had pushed for the name outside official channels using his friends in Congress, and eventually gotten it adopted, with the *e* added as a sop to the opposition.

Since the Extry was a baby that Tillich named himself, was it any wonder he thought he owned the child now, lock, stock, and barrel?

Another sullen glance in Leher's direction.

Jesus, had this guy mastered the quick, baleful glance. Leher touched his postcard pocket, felt the square of cardboard under the fabric. Hang on.

Tillich turned back to his small talk. Leher saw he was chatting with the National Security Advisor and the SECEX, both his mortal bureacratic enemies, politicking till the end. Or what Leher hoped would be the end of the man's influence.

Look who's talking. You're not exactly Mr. Naïve. You've been known to do a bit of maneuvering yourself.

Leher turned to the coffee urn. It sat on a folded cloth padding that shielded the reception room's mahogany table. The table was gorgeous, a piece of furniture that had been brought down from the ruins of Washington. It had been through the firebombing, been lovingly refinished. Smoothed. Seamless. Good.

But the coffee cups were antiques as well and had not been so lucky. Why had the staff put them out? They ought to be locked away.

Not only were they out, someone had stacked them *two-high* on a red, scraped plastic tray. China cups, dainty, thin porcelain. Set with the presidential seal. Priceless treasures now.

The very cup Leher reached for had a jagged line running from the brim and down, down the curve of its flowery shape, disappearing around the curve of the base.

A hairline crack. Suddenly Leher was convinced that the cup would shatter in his hand. That another bit of history—of innocence—would be lost. Leher jerked his fingers back.

Not soon enough. He'd touched the cup. It clattered off the second tier of cups and onto the mahogany table.

It did not shatter but landed on its side—and rolled over one turn before coming to rest against its own handle.

Leher let out a quiet exclamation, set his hands in palm-up supplication to the cup to stop, *please don't fall off the table.*

Shit.

The world, constantly on the verge of falling apart.

Into Leher's mind flooded something he must, absolutely, write down. Something he needed to tell Neddie.

I will compose and write the postcard as soon as this meeting is over, Leher told himself. *I promise I will do this. I will do it by this afternoon, the evening at the latest. I will mail it before the night is done.*

Leher breathed deeply and stepped back from the table, away

from the coffee cups. Damn, and he'd needed a cup of joe badly. But then he felt his left hand—his writing hand—reaching into his inner coat pocket for a pen.

How did the hand get there? He glanced down at it. It moved with its own autonomy.

The hand took out pen, then postcard. Placed the card on the table's surface near the edge.

Motion for continuance denied. He was going to write down his thought now. Leher put the postcard on the table, bent over it, and began to write in the tiny letters that his ex-wife had once said looked like "squashed bugs."

Dear Neddie, people get the idea that just because they've managed not to get themselves killed in 30, 40, 50, 150 years, then that means they know something valuable. Nobody ever attributes it to luck. Truth is, luck usually turns out to be by far the best explanation for most examples of long-term survival. As always, wish you were here. D.

All right, there it was. He'd written the postcard.
Satisfied, self?
Now to find a mailbox, send it. He'd already stamped the cards in his pocket and printed their addresses on them.

P-mail would have never worked. Neddie was too young to have a p-mail account. Nope, postcards were the way to go.

Leher suddenly had another thought that he simply had to include on the postcard, even though even he was running out of room at the bottom. He squeezed his letters into a compact, infinitesimal marching line to finish.

P.S. Neddie, people say we make our own luck, and it's undeniably true sometimes. But mostly this comes about just by keeping at it, not by having the exact right plan. I want you to know that I'll always try, for the two of us. I won't give up.

Leher had the feeling he was being watched. He straightened up, slid the postcard into the outer pocket of his uniform jacket, glanced around to see if Tillich was trying once again to melt him with his eyes. Not at the moment. But someone *was* looking at him.

Her.

Samantha Guptha.

Of course she would be here.

Leher smiled at her and waved a finger. Sam immediately dis-engaged from her group and stepped over to join him.

"Hi, Griff."

"Sam."

She glanced down at the pocket into which he'd put the post-card, and over at the table where the cup he'd touched still lay on its side. She picked up the cracked cup and ran a fingernail along the hairline fissure.

"This set you off?"

Leher nodded.

"Let's just be careful there..." Taking it from her involved touching the cup, but preventing the crack from spreading made that the lesser of two evils. He reached over and carefully took the cup away from her, moved it back from the edge of the table, and set it down.

Leher looked back at Sam, smiled slyly, shrugged—as if they were both in on a joke instead of a very weird...whatever it was.

Sam smiled, nodded. "So, I read this analysis everyone's buzz-ing about," she said. "Kind of brilliant."

"Thanks," said Leher. "What do you think?"

"About what?"

"What does the weapon *do*, Sam?"

"Ah," said Sam. "Yeah, I have a few thoughts. If I could get my hands on that thing..." Her smile became a look of fascination. Even longing.

The look he'd fallen in love with, once upon a time.

"Why are you here, Sam? I thought the first rule of contract-ing was not to bring an engineer to a management fight," Leher said. "Femtodynamics run out of brass?"

"I *am* brass these days, Griff. Vice President of Research," Sam replied. "Been a year now. I assigned myself to this meeting."

He should've known. Should've called. Sent her a card—a post-card, a postcard addressed to a real address—something. And he *would* have. But the past year of work had been so pressing. He'd practically disappeared into it. And what free time he had was taken up with the rituals. With writing Neddie.

Leher shrugged, cocked his head. "Don't I remember you once

telling me that any woman in a business suit is a guaranteed uptight bitch?"

"Guess there was a dark mistress of bitchiness hiding in my closet. Now she's out. Let me tell you, honey, the party never stops in Mordor."

Sam's ice-cream-smooth Northern Alabama accent was still capable of sending pleasant chills through Leher. And her Punjabi good looks still seemed to his mind incongruous when combined with the accent.

She'd grown up in Huntsville, the only child of two immigrant engineers from New Delhi who worked for the old ATK Space Systems. Leher had met her in college, and the two of them had become best friends while going out with one another's roommates.

They'd kept in touch in grad school—Sam had leaned on him during her breakup with the boyfriend—but had grown apart as both went their separate ways into very different careers.

Then came the invasion and the PW66 project. Sam was working on the team that figured out how to transport a nuclear warhead using the first Q drive. Leher had been a JAG lawyer on the project, fending off Pentagon bureaucrats and making sure the ad hoc team had legal room to operate. The work was top secret. Leher was among the few who knew that Sam was one of the brains that had saved humanity from instant capitulation to the sceeve.

She was a goddamn hero. One day, Sam would be in the history books—if there were going to be any more history books. But for the moment, she was just another aerospace executive.

"Mordor? Pretty geeky way to describe being a corporate Nazi," Leher said.

"That's Queen Geek to you, sir." Sam smiled. Her teeth were whiter than they really ought to be. And she no longer wore glasses. Lasik? Or probably the new acuity drops made of tiny nanotech lens crafters. He kind of missed the wire frames. "Anyway, it's a running game against a passing game," she said.

"Much better. That sounds *exactly* like something a corporate Nazi would say."

"Uh-huh. How you been, Griff?"

"Shoveling the coal of cultural linguistics into the firebox of the American war machine."

Sam shook her head. "Goodness. Then you ought to have developed more muscles."

"Touché."

Sam selected one of the china cups next to the urn—all the cups bore the presidential seal—and clinked it onto a matching platter. "Guess that's probably why you haven't called in a year and a half."

"No, I—"

She moved next to him and playfully shouldered him aside in order to reach the coffee urn's spigot. He caught a trace of tobacco tang from her hair as she passed.

Oh, man, she's back to smoking.

Time to change the subject.

"So—you're in on the war council," he said.

Sam nodded. "Had to head-butt my way in, but yes." Sam's eyes were sparkling, predatory. It was a side of her he'd rarely seen before. "I signed on as technical support and then made sure the marketing v.p. got a shit-his-britches call from Kylie late last night that sent him packing back to Huntsville."

Kylie Jorgenson was the president of Femtodynamics, Sam's company. Jorgenson had been navy, the director on the PW66 project back in the day. Back then Sam had hated Jorgenson—who was originally from Boston and projected Yankee bluntness—but had simultaneously been fascinated by her. She had now obviously become some sort of protégé.

"So here you are, the face of Femtodynamics at our little get-together."

Sam nodded. She took another sip of coffee, left pale coral lipstick on the china rim. Leher successfully resisted the urge to take the cup from her and wipe it clean with a napkin.

There was a rumble in the corner. Tillich was speaking heatedly to a woman in a suit who'd approached him. Sam nodded toward Tillich. "How does it feel to be the Old Man's designated executioner? You made a pretty devastating case for taking the offense in your summer report."

"Yes, I suppose," Leher said. "I take no pleasure in going against the admiral. And I'm far from sure we'll win. Argosy is still on the table."

"It's going to be tricky. He's got lots of friends," Sam said. "Powerful ones in the Senate. I've gone up against him a few times, lost some battles. And you know he practically owns the space-serving Extry."

"Never a truer word spoken," said Leher. "Look at me. I'm *right*. I know I'm right and he's wrong. But he still scares the hell out of me."

"He can't win this fight, Griff, or we're toast. You know that. Better he's taken out by somebody who respects him."

Then a geist flickered into being in the reception-room doorway. Leher recognized the blue-green projection as KWAME, the president's chief of staff. He was a servant, an artificial intelligence. His geist had the features of a middle-aged black man but was entirely monochrome in color, including his clothing.

"There's KWAME," Leher said.

"Where?" said Sam, turning around and scanning the room. Then she shook her head, chuckled. "Stupid me, I left my salt charger back in Huntsville," she said. "Now I'm low on battery, and I can't see a thing in the chroma."

In fact, only half the people in the room were adequately salted or charged up to see the projected image of the president's a.i. chief of staff. You could tell who was by who had turned his or her face to the door. There was a murmur as those who could see in the chroma explained what was going on to those who could not. Leher joined in.

"KWAME's standing by the doorway," Leher said. "He's giving us the cue that the president's ready for us."

"Better get back with my team, then," Sam said. "I've got two of my best along with me. It's going to be quite crowded in there. Suppose I'll be rooting for you from across the room."

"We can pass notes," Leher said.

"Sure, dude." Sam smiled. "It's . . ." A small tear in Sam's eye, which she flicked away with a lacquered nail. "It's good to see you, Griff. Been too long."

Leher took Sam's hand and pulled her into a quick hug, careful not to upset her coffee, then made his way through the waiting National Security luminaries. Leher turned a corner and headed for the president's office.

And nearly tripped over his own feet.

Shit. The Lincoln Plaza linoleum markings. He'd forgotten about the linoleum. Black and white checkerboard. When he was here, he always stepped only on the black tiles. White was bad. Easily scuffed. But he'd never had a crowd of bigwigs pressing at his back before. Shit. He'd have to move fast and still be careful. This was going to be one of those trials by fire his OCD often handed him.

Leher felt a touch on his shoulder. He turned to see Coalbridge, the Extry captain he'd met before.

"Want to take point?" Coalbridge said quietly. "I'll follow behind you on cleanup. I'll make sure nobody gets pushy."

Leher considered. Could he trust Captain Courageous not to fuck with him? Leher tugged at his beard. Not ready for trim. Two more tugs. Always three in a row for full verification. Nope, no trim yet.

"Yeah, that would be great," he said to Coalbridge. "Thanks."

Coalbridge moved directly behind him, and Leher continued down the hall. With a sigh of relief, Leher took only the black tiles. Behind him, Coalbridge did as he promised and slowed the pace of the nervous group. Nobody tried to push Leher along.

Then through the open door and onto the blue carpet of the president's office. It had once been a fruit market and sometimes was still referred to that way by Capitol staffers. Of course, it bore no resemblance to a store now. The original owner and all his employees had been killed by churn in the first sceeve attack.

After the entire gang of twenty or so officers, political aides, and contractor senior reps (including Sam) had trooped in and taken seats around an enormous conference table, KWAME mimicked closing the door behind them all, although in reality he had actuated some sort of servo in the hinges that did the actual door-swinging. He flickered out of existence and then appeared again, standing at attention across the room.

And there beside him at the end of the table sat Taneesha Joelle Frost, the sixty-fifth president of the United States.

She looked worried. Very worried.

Leher didn't blame her.

The sceeve were coming back.

SIX

22 December 2075
Vicinity of 82 Eridani
A.S.C. *Powers of Heaven*

Transel had found the Poet. Here, on this vessel. *His* vessel. The craft beta conditioner was on the other side of the vessel from the direction DDCM Receptor Lirish Transel was currently headed, but Transel had deduced long before that the Poet would never be found near the conditioner. No, he must have something like a virtual conditioner that fed off the main transmitter's Q uncertainties.

Such a clever trick. A novelty as an end in itself.

Transel felt the acidic bile of contempt rise in his nostrils, as he did whenever he considered the nonsense the Poet was spewing. The waste of effort required to bring him to justice.

The repugnance of having to listen to the spew in order to do his job.

The knowledge that this subversive garbage was being secretly recorded, bounced to beta relay points, messengered in drones, passed hand-to-hand among officers, rebroadcast through the armada.

Disseminated.

Those traitorous officers—the ones who had been caught—claimed to think the Poet funny, amusing. A way to pass a mind-numbing voyage. Some thought him profound.

Worst of all, the Poet was beginning to spawn imitators. Other poets were cropping up in the armada, even in the Shiro.

This must be stopped. Everyone from the top level down agreed, and the directive had gone out.

And now Transel had isolated the Poet to *this* vessel. The original broadcasts of the Poet were originating with the *Powers of Heaven*!

It was an amazing stroke of luck. Transel suspected he, Transel, was about to become a hero. Granted, only within the clandestine coterie of the DDCM. But still. Not a bad reward for a bit of detective work.

More importantly, Transel felt he was serving the cause of justice in a pure way, a way he'd not been able to in the messy world of Sporata deployment. He felt good. He felt virtuous.

He was going to see the Poet ripped to pieces by the dismemberment knives!

Transel had fixed the traitor Gitaclaber's actual location: a little-used janitorial storage area near the Q drives. He'd brought a gun—it had an official designation but was nicknamed a "painter" since its action was to release a cloud of needles at the target, with the "painting" itself being an empty, needle-free shadow behind the target on a bulkhead. The body would not be needle-free, of course. Quite the contrary. Transel quickly made his way down the accessway toward the storage area. He felt like a scouring wind, about to turn stone to sand.

Transel had realized the Poet was aboard the *Powers of Heaven* several *semanatos* ago through an off-channel beta sweep, and it had only been a matter of time after that. The DDCM knew Transel was very good at his job. This was not a boast, but a clearly demonstrable fact. It was one of the reasons he normally got along with his captains, in his estimation. What was the use of dominance display when everyone with any sense understood the reality of the situation? Transel had even come to like Captain Malako, his current charge. He was smart and seemed utterly loyal.

But Malako *had* been harboring a traitor on his vessel. And that was intolerable. It was, however, a problem Transel would soon dispose of permanently.

Regulation of feeling produces regulation of thought. Regulation of feeling is accomplished by the surfaction of the flesh.

It had cost him some effort to arrive at a solution. He'd donned the hairshirt *cilice* under his uniform with its surfactant, skin-dissolving gels. Never fear the use of the Garment of Ongoing Surfaction and Revelation, his Master Interrogator had taught him during his training. Surfaction leads to pain. Pain first and always is the precursor to knowledge. This is the foundation to Regulation.

The Master Interrogator had been right. Once the rash had set in and burned a constant ache into his shoulders, the answer *had* come to him.

The answer was words.

The Poet had been careful, so very careful, to time his broadcasts randomly, to make them seem to originate from different portions of the vessel or from outside the craft entirely. His mastery of the technology was astounding, given what Transel now knew of him—so much so that he suspected external aid or perhaps an onboard accomplice. But the Poet was a word-shaper and word-maker, and he'd been unable or unwilling to clean up his first-draft efforts. It was the hubris of creators everywhere, and one of the reasons Regulation must always be vigilant for the excesses of profligate producers. Were it not for the calming influence of parasitism, the galaxy might soon be overrun with words, ideas, out-of-control technology, all competing endlessly for dominance. Endless war, endless chaos and destruction. Dark age after dark age.

This truth made Transel shudder.

Regulation is the solution. Regulation proceeds through disambiguation. Pain is the primary tool of disambiguation. His Master Interrogator had made sure he'd understood by firsthand experience the pathways to the soul that pain afforded. She had beaten justice into him. Beaten him until his instinct for Regulation was second nature.

Transel was good at his job because it was a *calling*. He knew some on the vessel thought of him as a bit overbearing, doctrinaire—and he'd even sniffed the fragrance of "fanatic" emitted quietly behind his back. He was none of those things. He was merely a faithful instrument in the hands of universal justice. Faithful—and implacable when he had his scent.

He'd simply analyzed the Poet's verse. Teased ester from ester, pulled the word trains apart and unpacked them transport pod by transport pod. And what had he come up with? Ethyl maltol. Furanol. Methyl maltol. To a human these odors would be part of the makeup of the scents of currants, blueberries, and wild plums. So he'd set up detectors, noted concentrations over a period of *tagatos.* Followed the trail. And trapped Second Lieutenant Mountain-Lichen-Scourer Gitaclaber in the web of his own poetry.

Now came the reckoning. As first political officer of the attack vessel *Powers of Heaven,* the enforcement provision was his call. He could apprehend Gitaclaber for further questioning. Such questioning could, and would be expected to, include necessary physical inducements to cooperation via the application of surfaction and chemical stimulants. On the other hand, he would be perfectly within his duty and right to execute the Poet outright. The choice was Transel's.

Transel had not entirely decided upon a course of action as he made his way to confront the Poet. Gitaclaber was in the midst of one of his live broadcasts spewing his Mutualist-inspired nonsense on symbiosis, love, the beauty of lichens (why were poets always going on about lichens?), and who knew what else bilge.

> *One note blown from a stone horn*
> *resounds through the burnt*
> *becoming stone vegetation.*
> *This hard, bright now*

What a pile of anal eliminations! A mind spewing...gibberish, yes—but dangerous gibberish! As if one could sit back and observe the universe, admire the universe, and heed no call to action. Heresy and madness.

Mutualism!

The transmitter was on the other side of the vessel, but now he had fixed Gitaclaber's actual location: a little-used janitorial area near the Q drives.

Transel paused on the other side of the janitorial storage-area door and confirmed Gitaclaber's presence with an atmospheric sensor. And this was where he, Transel, made an error. He immediately acknowledged as much. It was a minor error, but he'd violated best practice nonetheless and would report himself in due time. He hadn't set his detector to vibrate.

The sensor let out a pungent ammonia alert odor when it located the chemistry it was set to find. And within seconds of Transel's detector going off, the Poet began to furiously spray more filth out over the beta!

He'd smelled Transel, and he was trying to finish what would be his last broadcast.

It wasn't going to happen. Not on Transel's watch!

He made his decision on the Poet's fate then and there.

He was *not* going to apprehend him. No, he was going to *stop* this excess, this overproduction, this glut of words, once and for all.

The universe is a profligate waste of resources, his Master Interrogator had told him. Regulation arises from the universe's need to contain itself, to curb its own excess. This is our sacred task. We are the trimmers. The shapers. And, if need be, the cutters. The hewers of species. We are justice embodied.

We are the Executors of Regulation.

USX *Chief Seattle*

"He's talking to *us*. Directly to us. He's asking for help."

SIGINT Petty Officer Japps knew from the visual display that this Poet broadcast was very different from the others.

"KETCH and LARK, are you getting the graph pattern here?" she asked.

KETCH's geist flashed into blue-green being beside the XO. LARK's was already manifested across the room. KETCH appeared as a bland, vaguely handsome young guy—shaded green and partially transparent, of course—in the uniform of an exper first class.

"Not sure, Petty Officer Japps," he said. "The articulation is definitely not the sceeve patois used in the other intercepts. Perhaps it is a variant."

Japps laughed. "Totally. He's using his own dialect, I'll bet, instead of sceeve standard. Which would fit with what I'm guessing is happening."

"What are you talking about, Japps?" said Martinez, still in SIGINT after Japps had called her down from the bridge.

"Give me a sec, XO." Japps menued up a console, began to rapidly make adjustments. "Adapting to this dialect's dynamic range," she mumbled to herself. "Want to catch all of this."

KETCH understood immediately what she was doing and began following her lead while making adjustments to his own algorithmic workings.

Bink.

After a short wait, KETCH began to speak his rough translation. He didn't use his own voice, which was something of a tenor, but provided a baritone with a definite Chicago-Midwestern nasality to Japps's ears. Unfortunately, that familiar element didn't make what the voice said any less chilling.

"Attention humans. Attention humans. This one knows you are there. Hopes. Attention, for the sake of your species. Much has already been given to you, but not all. Not all. A wrong element, a killer of poets, has found this one out. There is not time to explain, but this one makes the attempt to communicate final coordinates, complete information transfer—"

"There is a break in what follows. Transmission drop-out. Or perhaps the Poet has ceased transmitting without realizing this fact. Eight point four seconds in length, and then the transmission resumes." KETCH returned to the Poet-analog voice he'd concocted.

"Our sun is dead. The stars blink broken code."

Japps recognized this immediately as a line from one of the Poet's own pieces (or by some unidentified someone, if the Poet were not the actual author). It was a poem he'd read time and again during several transmissions.

KETCH continued in his Chicagoan voice. "As previously stated, a visitor comes, comes to your system. Approaching, approaching. A visitor, visitors, vessels speaking Mutualism. This visitor offers trust. Alliance. Opportunity, survival, victory in struggle. Great danger, also. Peril closely follows. This one will—"

Silence. Crackle of stray radiation interference. KETCH sounded like an angry snake for a moment expressing it. Then the Poet's voice spoke once more.

"—resistance to capture counterproductive at present. Will attempt to abandon this vessel. If this one apprehended, will attempt evoke immediate execution. Produce ejection. This one discard, discarded. N-space. Find this one. Final key delivery, this one. Rendezvous coordinates. Key to all. Key. Request humans attempt contact. Request, request of you. Key. Rescue this one. Key. Find this one. So much remains. Cannot convey. Attempt—"

Another beep, and the translation cut out.

"God in heaven," said the XO. "What the fuck?"

Japps checked her readout. "That's it, XO. The conditioner's still turned on, but there's nothing on the carrier."

The XO hadn't heard her. She was already in furious conversation with the bridge. After a moment, she stopped talking to what was, to Japps, the empty air, and turned back to face her.

"Sceeve can survive in the vacuum," Japps said. "Sounds like they've thrown him out. Or could be some kind of trick."

"Captain doesn't care," Martinez replied. She put a hand on Japps's shoulder, smiled a big smile. "He wants you down in ET7. Wants you to requisition a lifepod and go after that motherfucking sceeve poet."

Holy shit in a can.

"Me? On an extravehicular?"

"You're the closest thing we've got to a sceeve expert aboard this godforsaken craft, Japps. So tag you're it. Now get your ass in gear, Japps."

"I-I need—"

But the XO was rushing her to the SIGINT portal.

"Suit up at the pod," said the XO. "I'll be sure there's a tank of heliox waiting for you at the tube entrance in case—well, take it with you. Maybe it'll be useful to have some sceeve atmosphere along. And, hell, I'll throw in what we know about their rations. Tank of glucose goo. The pod has grub for you."

"You talk like I'm not coming back for a while."

"Oh, you're coming back. Just taking care of a few contingencies. Now get going."

This was happening too fast. EV in a lifepod? Japps felt her head spinning. She was an exper-tech, not a spacer. Sure, she'd had the training. All expers had. But to actually do it—

"You know I don't speak sceeve, ma'am," Japps said. "Not really."

"You're what we've got. Anyway, like I said, Japps: captain's orders. Go!"

Japps shook her head to clear it, turned down the corridor toward the exteriorizing tube banks. Then a thought. The briefest pause. For a moment she gazed at the graphic parameters of the Poet's message on her display.

"I hate those motherfuckers," Japps mumbled—to no one in particular. "Every one of them. For what they did." The XO was already turned back to SIGINT, was back into the chroma, talking to another underling about clearing the lifepod's launch path.

"Poet's no different," she mumbled. "A sceeve is a sceeve."

But her thoughts made a lie of her words. As Japps headed

for Exterior Tube 7, her favorite of the Poet's outpourings echoed through her mind. She'd gone over it in her frequency analysis many times but until now hadn't realized she'd committed the lines themselves to memory.

> *Our sun is dead. The stars blink broken code.*
> *I have traveling to do*
> *away from this endless necessity to feed.*

SEVEN

31 December 2075
Dallas
Presidential War Room

"Madame President, the issue is not with the enemy intelligence itself, but the idiotic *conclusions* that have been drawn. That person, that *creep*, knows nothing about space or the Extry," said Tillich. The admiral pointed a finger, seemingly shaking with rage, straight at Leher. "His so-called Xeno Department has filled up with astrologers and phrenologists, to tell the truth. Service malcontents. This sort of thing should be a State Department concern. And, I assure you, the State Department would say that Lieutenant Commander Leher was *full of shit!*"

Leher stiffened, tugged at his beard. He wished he were back safe in his nest in the New Pentagon instead of here, getting torn a new asshole by a world-expert asshole tearer. But he had a simple job to do and was determined to see it through. That job was to tell the truth.

I'm only the messenger, for Christ's sake! The weatherman. It's not like I can control what the frigging sceeve are up to.

As if Tillich understood Leher's objection to the treatment he was dealing out, the admiral smiled sadly and shook his head with disgust. "Now, now. I don't want to impute too much intelligence to this young officer's recommendations. He's an errand boy for his two masters"—Tillich shifted his pointing finger like a turret gun to Secretary of the Extry Huntley Camaroon and his number two, Chief of Extry Operations Maggie Chen—"who are clearly in bed with the military contractors."

Tillich was known to despise all contractors at all times.

"These actors have made themselves extensions of companies and individuals whose sole purpose in life is to gouge the American people and the world, and the sooner you recognize that fact, the sooner we can all deal with the current situation and nationalize war production."

Camaroon and Chen were looking on bemused. Hadn't the admiral just been chatting them up in the reception room? But these sudden mood changes were known Tillich operating procedure, designed to throw his opponents off.

Tillich continued, full speed. "I won't call them traitors, no. At least traitors have *some* commitment, even if it's to the wrong cause. These two are interested in making themselves and their friends richer no matter what it does to the Extry or to the country."

"That's a lie," said Camaroon, but without a great deal of heat. "And I think you should take it back right now, Admiral Tillich."

"I'll do no such thing," Tillich replied. "Deny if you can that you intend to dismantle the only hope for humanity, the Argosy Project, if and when you yank me from my post."

Argosy was Tillich's answer to Operation RAMP, SECEX Camaroon's recently implemented 5,500-craft build-up. Almost half the vessels had been constructed, and more would be made minimally operational within days given the ever-approaching sceeve armada. It was a "small and many" plan that had tripled the number of military vessels in space and allowed stationing of over half the force at various known sceeve invasion routes on the outbound Orion arm. Leher and most senior analysts in CRYPT were fairly certain the sceeve home base was in the vicinity of the star Pollux.

RAMP, even in its early stages, had paid off. It was because of RAMP that the Extry had been in position to eavesdrop on the Poet.

Four days ago, there had been hope that Leher was utterly wrong in Xeno's Depletion findings, a report widely known to have been authored by Leher. Tillich may have been right. Maybe the sceeve had given up on destroying humans; maybe they would fade away like a bad dream. Argosy, the big ship, defensive model, may then have been the way forward for the U.S. For what was left of humanity.

But then the wake-up call arrived.

Leher had decrypted the Poet's last message.

The sceeve were coming back in force. This much Leher had predicted in his summer report after he had explained the meaning of the sceeve Special Depletion. The sceeve had temporarily withdrawn to tend to a civil war, or at least to an uprising. That task accomplished, they were now back on track. In the fall, it had seemed inevitable to Leher that Earth would be ravaged once again, and soon. The so-called Fomalhaut Limit, the spherical range in which humanity had previously been permitted to fare without a guaranteed attack, had been contracting for many months.

The sceeve were pressing Solward. With a newly defeated foe and resources left over from the Depletion—a sort of war energy tax—they weren't going to play nice with humanity this time.

And then, out of the black of space, had arrived the slender reed of hope in the Poet's message.

A defecting vessel was headed toward Earth with the game changer of all game changers. It was something called the Kilcher artifact, and the sceeve were *very* hot to get it back. If humans could acquire this artifact by hook or by crook and figure out how to use it, humanity *might* have a chance against the sceeve when they invaded once again.

Reinvasion, as far as Leher was concerned, was a given. He'd written as much in the fall.

Even with a wonder weapon, fending off the sceeve would be a long shot, Leher knew. They possessed a massively powerful empire. But at least humanity might have a better chance.

A great deal was admittedly guesswork. But Leher and the Xeno Department had years of experience behind them now. They were an order of magnitude further along in understanding sceeve motivation than they'd been at the time of the withdrawal.

Not everyone had advanced in understanding, however. Some even had a vested interest in *not* advancing. Leher's analysis had made him an enemy to an extremely powerful force in Extry command—namely, one Admiral Allen Tillich.

Tillich was nearly 140 years old—a beneficiary of the anti-aging discoveries of the 2020s—and was very good at throwing the weight of his long experience behind his arguments. He had been one of the few leaders with ability and vision in the early days of the Extry, a year after the first wave of the invasion had been absorbed and humanity had begun to dream of fighting back. His demand for "quality control" had made sure that expers didn't needlessly die from shoddy craft construction before they could even go up against the foe. He was also a constant voice against waste and contractor gouging.

There was no arguing it. Tillich's system had indeed insured that space travel aboard its crafts was extraordinarily safe and hazard-free.

That is, unless you get attacked, Leher thought. And then your chance of getting blasted out of existence went up to around seventy percent. Extry vessels, especially the smaller, less computationally complex ones without true servants, did not fare well in head-to-head battle with the sceeve.

This was acceptable to Tillich. Eight years ago, the sceeve had withdrawn from the solar system, and he was certain he'd discerned the reason why.

"They've taught us the lesson they wanted to teach us," declared Tillich, "and they only fight when we venture out and provoke them."

This particular philosophy on sceeve behavior came with its own political party, the Quietists. Tillich had no official affiliation with the movement, but nobody doubted which way his political opinions leaned. President Frost and her team, on the other hand, were Recommitment Party. The Quietists, after eight years of power under former President Taylor, had been turned out by Recommitment in the last election. Tillich had therefore decided to go it alone. After all, he was certain he was *right*.

He'd come up with Argosy. Instead of a massive buildup in vessel numbers, Tillich wanted a "return to basics." First, humanity would retreat back into the solar system. Retreat entirely, although perhaps retaining a small force on the Centauri base as an early warning platform. But the most important part of Argosy was Tillich's proposed VLO fleet. In his conception, the solar system would be protected by a fleet of a few extremely powerful VLO— very large object—vessels that would serve as fortresses to defend a vast sphere around the sun. They were to take positions in a spherical deployment at about the distance of the Kuiper Belt.

Leher had seen some of the drawings for the proposed craft. Behemoths whose top speeds were around 400 *c*, less than half the Q-limit, what a normal Extry battlecraft could do.

The "Maginot Beach Ball," Leher had heard SECEX Camaroon call the Argosy Project. Tillich hated the recent multiple-bottle

technology. Too complicated, he claimed. Unsafe. Deliberate insti-
gation and breach of the tacit treaty with the sceeve.

And they required servants.

Multibottle vessels were held together by what Tillich called "a
misplaced trust in the kindness and best intentions of HAL 9000."

Tillich loathed servants.

"The Argosy plan is sound. It will be of use to *any* political
position. Now, will you please tell me the *real* reason I'm being
fired, Madame President?" He leaned across the president's desk
and stared directly into her eyes.

Leher saw sympathy—and determination—in President Frost's
expression.

"Admiral Tillich, I was told there was to be an orderly transition in the Extry command," she said. Her voice was a warm
alto—which masked what Leher thought was one of the most
coldly strategic intelligences to hold the office. "I'm also sure
there is no intention on my part to embarrass or humiliate you.
On the contrary, I consider you a hero. Furthermore, you've created something unheard of in government: a long-term program
that *always* delivers on its promises and holds to the priorities
it sets for itself."

For a moment, Tillich was stunned to silence.

Don't see that every day, Leher thought.

Frost had hit the nail on the head. This was *exactly* the way
the old man conceived of himself, Leher was sure.

But then a faint smile crept over the admiral's face. A bony
finger to his chin in consideration.

He's going to start working it all over again.

Before he could do so, however, Frost continued to speak.
She began with a smile that seemed almost self-deprecatory,
and Tillich visibly relaxed, sure he was winning another political
dominance game.

"But I also can't forget why I was elected. After the sceeve
withdrew, we were battered to hell and stunned, for sure. But then
a year passed, and then two, and people in the government, even
President Taylor, made it clear that they didn't believe the sceeve
were coming back. He talked to lots of people in high command,
and everyone told him this was likely so. Let's be kind about it
and put it down to bad information. We've got *good* information now, Admiral, and whatever interpretation you make of

the particulars, the one thing you *cannot* conclude is that those monsters are going to just go away." Tillich cleared his throat, made to cut in and make his point, but Frost raised a finger to stop him. "We had eight years where we might have developed some sort of rough space parity with the sceeve if we'd thrown everything we had behind the effort. They had us by thousands of ships, but our best information says it was *only* thousands, not tens of thousands, not hundreds of thousands. We had a golden opportunity to create a hornet's nest that screams 'don't mess with me,' and we blew it."

Frost rapped a fist softly on the table in a gesture of contained force. "The one thing I'm not about to do is blow it again. We've had a year of rapid rebuilding with RAMP. All the vessels are based around your safety and engineering standards. Wouldn't have it any other way. Even with this, we are in a dire position. A grave condition. We still have only a third of the numbers of the sceeve armada, at least according to the estimates I've seen, and maybe only a quarter of the raw firepower. If the sceeve attack us, it's going to be a desperate stand for this nation and this planet. We must find a way to survive. We have to. So while I pray that you're correct, and that the sceeve will leave us alone if we don't bother them, I have to prepare for the possibility that they don't simply want to contain us, but to destroy or enslave us. It's my duty to fight against such an outcome till my very last breath."

"Madame, all of that may be true. *May*. But don't you see this very act of rapid preparation you're talking about will be viewed as *provocation* by the sceeve and—"

Leher steeled himself for another round of Tillich's argument for quietism. But suddenly a voice from the back of the room spoke up.

"I believe I can provide some enlightenment to the admiral, Madame President, if you will permit me."

Tillich spun on his heels, stared daggers into the group of civilians and officers behind him. Who had spoken? And, if he were Extry, who had ended his own career?

A hand touched SECEX Camaroon's shoulder, gently pulled him aside. "Excuse me, sir."

Camaroon shuffled aside, and Captain Jim Coalbridge stepped up to face the admiral.

I'll be damned. It's Captain Courageous.

Tillich audibly caught his breath. His face reddened. "Captain, I'm afraid I don't recognize you. Your name, please?"

"James D. Coalbridge, sir. Most recently skipper on PE 95A6er and now on temporary assignment to TACTIC." Coalbridge looked past the admiral to the president. "Permission to speak, ma'am?"

The president considered for a moment, then gave Coalbridge her nod.

"Traitor," murmured Tillich.

Coalbridge rounded on Tillich. "No, sir," Coalbridge said. "That I am not." He looked the admiral in the eye as he spoke, and this time it was Tillich who nervously glanced away first. "I've been out there at the Fomalhaut Limit, Admiral. Only there is no FL, not anymore. The sceeve have been steadily driving us inward. We've been forced to retreat time and again down the Orion arm from Sirius, up the arm from Alpha Opiuchi. They're hemming us in. Just about every line commander I know is sure the enemy is preparing a final blow, once they've got us concentrated."

"Or herding us back what they consider a safe distance," Tillich put in.

"You'll pardon me, Admiral, but that is utter bunk," Coalbridge said. His face reddened. It wasn't embarrassment, Leher realized, but anger. "I commanded patrol-and-engage craft for the past two years. I've fought this war. I've lost expers. To my great sorrow, lost most of my crew at one point. I've seen the sceeve up close and personal, sir, and I am in agreement with Lieutenant Commander Leher and the Xeno Department on their analysis. Xeno's Depletion report this past fall put what I've observed into perspective, and now this latest information . . . it makes sense."

Tillich's scowl became a frown as the hate seeped from his face. "Do you think I don't appreciate the sacrifice—"

Coalbridge interrupted.

"Sir, I'm not questioning that. But when the sceeve return—and have no doubt about that, they're coming—we're going to *lose*. Like the Incas lost to the Spaniards. Like the Hapsburgs lost to the Prussians. We are getting *creamed* out there, Admiral. You know this. I've written you as much in my letters. The sceeve didn't withdraw because we beat them. They withdrew because of internal dissent. They've spent the past few years containing their own separatist rebellion. Now they're done with that, and they can turn their attention back to *us*."

Tillich shook his head. "That's why we must withdraw, cease to provoke. If we are to have any chance at all."

Now it was Coalbridge who visibly became angry. He crossed his arms sharply, stood straight.

"The hell with that!" Coalbridge glanced at the president. "Sorry, ma'am."

Frost, amused, nodded that it was all right.

"I've been from Altair to Vega to Alpha Drac. Built a crew from the ground up after my people got wiped out in the engagement in the Hyades I mentioned. I'm hoping and praying to take most of my present crew with me on my new command, if I actually ever get the craft delivered. She's been at Walt Whitman taking on final fittings for over two months! Two months when I could've been out there with her killing those evil fu—" Coalbridge caught himself before he delivered the obscenity, although Frost seemed amused, not offended. "Those creatures," he said.

Tillich tried to cut in. "Son, the inherent risks in that technology, the servants—"

"I didn't transfer to the Extry so I could live forever!" Coalbridge said. "And *of course* we installed a servant crew to hold the bottles together."

Tillich stiffened. This was his real objection.

"You *shit*," he said. "You disobedient little shit. I issued a fleet-wide order regarding that silliness. If you think you're going to get a *command* after this . . ."

Coalbridge bristled, hunched his shoulders up. "I am a captain in the United States Extry," he said. "I am a *big shit*, sir."

Tillich charged forward, glaring fire into Coalbridge's eyes. Coalbridge, who was a good eight inches taller, stared down at the admiral with just as much resolve.

CXO Chen, who'd been silent to this point, saw that Tillich was in danger of physically attacking her captain, and she stepped between the two men. She eyed Tillich and spoke to him in her soft, dry, and precise manner—Leher had once heard an aide compare her voice to what a mechanical pencil might sound like if it spoke.

"You are not *being* fired, Admiral Tillich," said Chen. "This is a transition in duties. It is really my hope and that of the secretary that you will be able to serve the country and the administration in another capacity."

"Aw, cut the crap!" said Tillich. "Madame President, I was told this would be a meeting between you and me this morning. I'd like to speak to you alone."

Leher glanced around. KWAME was flickering furiously, obviously about to pounce into situation-control mode. The Secretary of Defense was biting down hard on his lower lip almost to the point of drawing blood.

Now is the time to kill him with kindness, the former lawyer in Leher thought. *Fat chance of that in this hothouse, I guess.*

But to Leher's surprise, that was exactly what Frost did. She smiled. She nodded to the rest of the assembled. "Ladies and gentlemen, could you give the admiral and me a few minutes."

KWAME started to object, citing scheduling, but the president held up a hand. "Now, KWAME, this is a matter of importance to me." The servant contained himself, nodded. The door swung open, and he motioned everyone else in the room to follow him out. Leher was the last to leave. He turned before the door closed behind him and saw Tillich leaning over the president's desk, attempting yet again to stress his point.

The remainder of the war council, at least twenty members strong, retreated to the reception area. No one said anything. Ten minutes later, KWAME disappeared. Moments later, he emerged from the president's office with Tillich.

The admiral marched by the reception room entrance with his head held high, but there was a tremble in his step. His eyes were glistening and fixed forward.

Frost had done it. She'd actually fired Tillich.

In comparison, staving off the sceeve invasion and winning the war should be a piece of cake.

Leher felt a hand on his shoulder. "So, guess that intelligence of yours got to the right people," said Coalbridge.

"Maybe so," Leher replied, "maybe so." He faced Coalbridge, smiled and shook his head. "But that was also a hell of a performance in there, Captain. Turned it around."

Coalbridge shrugged. "Just telling the truth. What I came home to do."

"Can you believe that the fate of the damned planet turned on whether that old man got fired or not?"

"We might've muddled through with Argosy."

Leher snorted. "You of all people should know better."

"Yeah," said Coalbridge. "I guess you're right. But I feel like we lost something. Something fine."

"And deluded."

"Okay," Coalbridge said, a trace of irritation in his voice. "He's gone. Cut it out."

Sam sidled up next to the men and handed Leher a cup of coffee in the White House china. Leher scanned the cup quickly. No crack.

"I checked it, of course," she said to him quietly.

"Sorry. Habit." Leher took a sip. Light and three-sugars sweet, the way he'd liked it since he was six and had sneaked cups of joe at his grandparents' house in Big Bear.

"Thanks, Sam, I needed that," he said.

"You look a little tepid." Sam turned to Coalbridge. "Samantha Guptha." She held out a hand.

Coalbridge didn't smile. Instead, he looked completely, instantly smitten.

Sparks, Leher thought. *Shit.*

He checked again.

The handshake, a half-second too long. *Yep. Double shit.*

"Coalbridge," the starcraft captain said. "I'm not in Extry acquisitions, ma'am, in case you were wondering. Couldn't do you a lick of good to know me."

"And I'm not a lobbyist or a whore, Captain, so I guess we'll have to leave it at that."

Coalbridge nodded. "My apologies, ma'am."

"I doubt you're sorry about much that you say, but any friend of Griff's is a friend of mine."

Leher considered. "Know what, Coalbridge? You can make up for insulting my ex-fiancé and lifelong friend by doing something for me."

Coalbridge stiffened, then relaxed and smiled. "Absolutely," he said.

"I want Sam to get listened to in the war council today." Leher took another sip of coffee to let Coalbridge process the request a moment, then said, "I believe your stock just shot up sky high with the SECEX this morning, so maybe you can put in a word."

"Considering the man didn't know who I was thirty minutes ago, I suppose you're right."

"Don't be so sure. He had you in that room for a reason."

"That was the CXO's doing," Coalbridge replied. "She was a prof of mine at IAS. Funny thing was, she nearly flunked me back then. Made me do a report on Mahan's *Influence of Sea Power Upon History* for extra credit just to pass her course. Me, at twenty-eight, having to slog through that thing."

"You ever heard of a PW66?"

"You kidding? PE commander's favorite sceeve killer!" Coalbridge exclaimed. "We call it the Wocket. It's the Extry weapon of choice for Sporata-fucking. Excuse my French."

Leher nodded at Sam. "Sam here proposed and designed the PW66."

Coalbridge regarded Sam, took a step back.

Almost in *reverence*, Leher thought.

"Then, ma'am, it is the greatest pleasure to make your acquaintance," said Coalbridge, "and it would be a travesty if you are *not* front and center in this session."

Leher raised his coffee cup in salute to the three of them.

"To the Extry," he said. "We're all we've got to—"

WAAAAAAAAA! A continuing wail reverberating through the corridors of the Capitol.

Raid sirens.

One second.

Two.

Three.

Four.

Before Coalbridge could complete his toast, the room began to shake as if struck by an earthquake. The chandelier hanging overhead from a concrete ceiling tinkled like a Christmas bell wreath and began to sway back and forth wildly. Paint chips fell upon the assembled group like a light snow. Where there was flaking paint, there were—

Leher glanced up at the ceiling.

Cracks. Shit.

Boom! Something struck the earth above with tremendous force. It sounded like someone had dropped a locomotive engine onto their heads.

Boom! Another. The room shook. Not just paint, but plaster fell from the ceiling this time.

"Drop-rod attack," said Sam. "Softening us up for the reinvasion."

"Yeah," Coalbridge replied. "Downtown's getting whacked, I'm afraid." Coalbridge smiled grimly, but Leher saw that he was clenching his fists. "Poor fucking Peepsies," he said. "They'll have taken the hard end of it."

He was correct, Leher thought. Wrong cause. Wrong place. Wrong time. Wrong planet.

"Goddamn it," said Coalbridge. "Nobody deserves to go out like that."

Leher's hand strayed to his suit pocket, fingered the squared edge of a postcard.

No. Get a continuance. Stay calm. Go up and help bury the dead. Again.

BOOM! A low crackle, as if the ground itself were being rent asunder. Something very large was falling high above them.

Another skyscraper, Leher thought.

The city would once again bury its own dead.

He felt sorrow at the thought, yes. But within Leher the old anger arose. He was beyond despair now. Maybe he was a little crazy. He recognized as much but didn't care.

He knew his enemy. He knew them better than anyone. They were no longer nameless terrors.

He was going to find a way to beat them.

EIGHT

22 December 2075
Vicinity of 82 Eridani
A.S.C. *Powers of Heaven*

Receptor Transel wasn't worried about his decision to immediately execute Second Lieutenant Gitaclaber. He knew he could back up the judgment if it was challenged. He already had recordings of the Poet's previous broadcasts, and they would be plenty to incriminate Gitaclaber and validate whatever action Transel chose to take in the moment of apprehension. He reached over and opened the door with a touch of his palm. He was keyed to open any portal on the vessel.

And the Poet charged him.

A head held down, butting into Transel's chest.

Shock of what, to a human, would be a punch to the face.

Transel stumbled back, slammed into a bulkhead behind him. The needle-gun painter fell from his grasp. Gitaclaber didn't let up and didn't fight fair. He punched and kicked Transel, swinging his arms in a wide arc to keep Transel from reaching down to scoop the painter back up.

Poked at his eyes. Transel spewed a prune-like shout of surprise, raised his hands to fend off the blow.

Received another sock to the torso for his troubles.

With ancestral ferocity, Transel managed to grab Gitaclaber's shoulders, push him violently back. The Poet stumbled, righted himself.

For a *vitia*, they stood face-to-face, staring into one another's eyes. Transel felt the tickling of fear in his *gid*.

Protect us, called the ancestral voices. *Do what is necessary to win.*

Gitaclaber was rather large in stature. But then Transel reflected on just who and *what* he was dealing with. A word-shaper, a poet. A junior officer in charge of minor communications who did not have Transel's training in the martial arts. Who was really no warrior at all.

Transel's muzzle widened into a smile.

He feinted right, then slammed a bent elbow into the Poet's face. Milky-white blood erupted from Gitaclaber's muzzle. The Poet staggered back. Transel kicked his knees. With a squirt of anguish, Gitaclaber crumpled on the ground before Transel. And then the Poet made a last desperate move. He squeezed his face to Transel's leg and sprayed pure nitric acid from his muzzle membranes.

Curse it!

Transel tried to scrape him off with his other foot, but the Poet clung tight. Finally he brought his fists down time and again on the Poet's head, his back. Yet Gitaclaber did not release, and the nitric acid was working its way deep—

Aaaah! Someone's carbolic scream. No. Not someone.

The ancestor's scream.

Transel's scream.

He hadn't thought he could screech like that. Disappointment in his fortitude. *Aaaah!*

—through muscle—

Stop him. Stop this filth! Destroy him!

—nearing the cartilaginous support structure that lay under the musculature. A Guardian's leg had no internal bone, of course. The Poet could, literally, burn Transel's leg off if he kept going.

The thought gave his arms new strength, and he beat the Poet all the harder. Finally his raining blows began to have an effect. He felt Gitaclaber's grip loosen.

This was all he needed.

Transel reached down and with a deft hook of his hand, thrust his palm gripping gills into Gitaclaber's muzzle. He pushed deeper. Deeper. Curled his hand inward, into the Poet's fleshy membranes.

Gitaclaber whiffed out a scream of pain, and Transel responded with a laugh. He raised the Poet slowly to his feet, always maintaining his grip.

"P-please," Gitaclaber whimpered. Transel's in-thrust fingers muffled, but did not cut off, the Poet's reply. "Hurts."

"You should have thought of that before making those beta broadcasts," Transel said.

"W-what broadcasts? Don't know w-what you're talking about."

Transel tugged on Gitaclabber's inner muzzle. The pain would be excruciating. Gitaclabber made a feeble attempt to strike out, which Transel batted away with his other arm.

Backing up, Transel slowly pulled Gitaclabber, stumbling along after, down the accessway. "Tell me, who put you up to this?"

"Nobody. I did not do anything. Let me go! Please!"

Transel dug his gripping gills deeper. All that work. His careful deduction and detection. And now the Poet was denying who he was?

We'll see about that. We'll just see about that, Poet.

They came to an emergency airlock. An airlock that would never open to the touch of crew or officer—even the captain—without special authorization. But it opened to Transel's touch.

Destroy him! Protect us!

He dragged Gitaclaber inside.

Finally, Transel let go of the Poet's muzzle and, with a massive shove, pushed him backward against the far wall.

"No, please, don't . . ." Gitaclaber's response was louder now, no longer damped by having a hand shoved into his muzzle.

"Admit it," said Transel. "Admit you are the Poet."

"I don't know what you're talking about. I—"

"Admit it!"

Gitaclaber continued to stare at Transel dumbfounded. But then his muzzle stretched into a leer. It looked like it hurt to do so. More blood leaked down the poet's face, his neck.

"You are right, you cursed slop of mung," Gitaclaber said. "I *am* the Poet. And my work is done. What can *you* do? Deliver me to the dismemberment knives? Well, it's *too late*! You are nothing. You are without power. Without—"

Transel stepped back and signaled the door closed even as Gitaclaber threw himself against it.

Too late for me? No, too late for you, Poet.

He threatens all we hold dear. Destroy him! The voices of the ancestors were singing inside him.

Yes.

Transel pressed his hand against the bulkhead and ordered the airlock cycled.

Faint hiss of exiting atmosphere.

Transel watched through the viewport as the Poet was pulled along the floor. Gitaclaber's gripping gills found purchase on the smallest declivities. But the exiting atmosphere was too strong. His hands were peeled away.

A sickening moment when he snagged the exterior frame of the airlock, pulled himself back in.

He was going to cling to his wretched life to the last, the gutworm.

But then the Poet let go. Dropped through the door.

Within moments, his subatomic structure would disentangle from that of the vessel. He'd drop into N-space. Floating without momentum. Aimless drifting in the depths of interstellar space. Alone forever. A poet without words.

It was Transel's turn to smile.

But then Transel saw something out the viewport. Something that perhaps Gitaclaber had noticed before, but that he, Transel, had *not*. Sharing his vessel's Q-space, far away—a light. Transel squinted hard, squeezed his corneal lens to greater magnification. Yes, there. A bluish light, no bigger than Transel's outstretched palm. But he knew what it was. He'd seen enough of such lights before to know.

A craft. Likely a human craft, given their location within the limit imposed on Sol system inhabitants.

As he looked on, the human vessel dropped out of Q-space and disappeared.

What? Where?

Realization dawned.

The humans were going after the Poet.

It was possible, barely possible, that the human vessel would succeed. Transel's species was extremely resilient to vacuum, having descended from entirely vacuum-friendly ancestors. Gitaclaber would stay alive for quite a while out there.

He *surely* could not be found, though. The Poet was but a speck of nothing floating in nothingness. But on the off chance...

Transel knew his captain would not wish to destroy this human vessel. Of course, Malako would not hesitate to annihilate *any* human vessel if doing so served his purpose. But Malako was also one who could be too smart for his own good. He might rather bide his time, pick up a clue from the human vessel's behavior as to the location of his real quarry—at least the quarry he personally enjoyed fighting. Human warcraft.

And this human vessel was merely a scouting vessel, with minimum offensive capability.

Transel would have to issue the order to destroy it.

Captain Malako would be duty-bound to obey.

But it could become unpleasant. Malako might simply scare the vessel away with a shot across the bow, or with a torpedo that went in unarmed, and then attempt to chase the craft back to its base and attack the base.

That wouldn't do.

The more Transel thought about it, the more he was sure he must take this matter into his own hands. Which meant taking the *Powers of Heaven* into his own hands. He'd order the fail-safes off the weaponry, first thing. There would be no "dud" torpedoes, no scare tactics from the overly clever Malako.

"No one ever said the Regulation of justice was easy, did they, Companion Transel?" his old teacher, the Master Interrogator, had told him. "If you are to assume command, you must make your body and soul open to Regulation. A willing, supple instrument. Broken to the hand like a well-worn glove. And then, you must be willing to *regulate*. To compel obedience."

Yes, Transel thought. The answer always lay in the teachings. First, he would order Captain Malako to destroy the human craft. Then, once that was done, he would confirm within himself the power of Regulation once again.

He would need to.

He even, he had to admit, *wanted* it.

Sweet *surfaction*.

He would retire to his quarters and give himself the appropriate punishment, the appropriate stimulus to continue with his duty.

Transel warmed to the thought.

He'd use the bladed mace on himself. Yes. It had been his Master Interrogator's favorite shriving device, and it had become Transel's favorite, as well.

After all, this *very mace* had been a gift from Transel's Master Interrogator herself. And a gift from her own master before. One day perhaps he'd pass it on to his own favorite protégé.

But for now it was his instrument of personal balance.

The steel tang of justice.

Transel shivered with delight and anticipation.

Anticipation would see him through whatever unpleasantness lay in store when he confronted the captain, made his orders known.

Ah, yes. Even now, Transel could feel the bite of steel and pleasure that awaited him.

USX *Chief Seattle*

As the lifepod sped from the *Chief Seattle*, Japps had the odd sensation that the larger vessel was actually moving away from *her* and not the other way around. Both were practically motionless in comparison to the speed at which they had been traveling moments before—900 times *c*.

Now they had dropped into the N with momentum dissipated by a trick of navigation XO Martinez had once tried to explain to her, but that Japps had not been in the mood to attempt to comprehend. Somehow or another, you could "shudder" your way into Newtonian or normal space, and emerge dead still.

She was moving as if in the deepest deep ocean. Inky nothing. Distant, pinprick stars. No sun nearby, no planets, no nothing except the *Chief Seattle* behind her, out of her field of vision.

"What are you seeing out there, Japps? Anything?" It was the voice of the *Chief Seattle* communication officer, a thin, pasty-faced CPO named Bara.

"Negative, Chief," Japps replied. "But the homing beacon is pinging him or *it* or whatever it is pretty well. Like the XO said, I'm getting beta reply off something he's wearing or carrying. As long as that keeps up—"

Then her forward lights picked up something in the black distance. The faintest speck.

"Okay, I've got visual contact," she reported. "Moving in."

"Roger that, Pod Alpha," said Bara.

Japps couldn't believe it. The beta homing circuitry had worked. The forward lights of the little rescue pod picked up something floating against the vast canvas of black that she'd been staring into for the past—what? Twenty, closing in on thirty minutes.

The something was pale white. Exactly the color of a sceeve.

She'd found him. She'd found the Poet.

Now the question was: Alive or dead? She maneuvered nearer to the body—she couldn't help thinking of it as a body—as it slowly spun in an endless head-over-heels flip. What she needed to do was position herself with the top of the lifepod beneath the body and then activate the "coffin," the man-sized rescue unit built into the roof's structure. *Man-sized, but not quite sceeve sized,* she thought. Most sceeve were a little under two meters tall—and eight feet plus was too large to scoop into the open coffin without bending a bit.

She hoped rigor mortis hadn't set in. But then she chided herself for being ridiculous. This was space. Rigor mortis was from bacteria, right? So you wouldn't get it in a vacuum, she supposed. But who the hell knew what kind of organisms might inhabit the sceeve? Nobody had ever seen a sceeve burial, if they even had such customs. Maybe they just bloomed into roses or sea anemones or something like that when they died.

She arrived at the body, parked herself "under" it. She used the attitude jets to thrust upward, using the open coffin as a scoop. The sceeve body settled awkwardly in. But there was no possibility she was going to be able to close the lid. There had to be a way. The designers surely would've come up with a method to manipulate a victim's body in the coffin, wouldn't they?

Or maybe they figured the lifepods would never be used, were more for show and morale, so why bother with actual, functional niceties. Wouldn't be the first time appearance won out over reality in the Extry, that was for sure.

But in this case, after pulling open a covering box, she discovered a small hole in the roof. That hold led to a glove—arm length—that protruded across the bulkhead, across the lifepod hull. She thrust her arm up into it and carefully pulled the sceeve into the coffin. She folded his legs at the knees, pulling both legs in. Then she signaled the coffin lid to close.

Suddenly, the body wasn't a body anymore. The Poet squirmed. He evidently saw what was coming down at him and attempted to escape it, get out.

Too late.

The coffin lid shut, self-sealed. Air began flooding into the coffin. The wrong kind of air for a sceeve, she knew. She had something like the right kind—not perfect but workable—in a tank near her pilot's seat. The Poet, if that's who this was, would just have to suffer the indignities of Earth atmosphere for a moment.

But now the Poet had gone from shaking to thumping. He wanted out of that coffin, that was for sure.

Japps considered what she had wrought. What she was about to do.

I'm about to save a fucking sceeve's ass, she thought, *and I don't like it one bit.*

Too much brooding. You've brooded enough for a dozen lifetimes. Why wasn't I there with them? Why did I survive and my family did not?

Useless speculation. You never got any answers.

Japps pulled the opening lever, and the bottom of the coffin fell away—and the sceeve fell down into the lifepod. She closed the lid, cycled the air out. When she turned back, the sceeve was sitting up. It regarded her with its big, black lidless eyes. And she regarded its smashed-apart excuse for a nose in turn.

What the hell. If this was the Poet, she didn't want to kill him. He'd offered her too much amusement. Given her a puzzle to solve. The D.J. of the night sky. The sourpuss voice she'd spent hours listening to. Trying to image the smell analogs. Trying to understand the underlying import of his crazy samizdat broadcast.

As the XO had ordered, Japps had brought along a tank of hastily mixed heliox, and she shoved a breathing tube into the Poet's muzzle, worked it down into his body—Lord knew to where—as if she were putting a feeding tube into somebody's stomach. The Poet resisted. *Not a chance,* she thought. *You're too weak to stop me.* The scraping gills of his hands felt like dried paper as he pawed at her arms.

He must be pretty far gone, Japps thought.

"I'm trying to help you," she said. Like he could understand those puffs of air shooting out of her mouth. What did her breath smell like, anyway?

She sniffed in her own exhalation.

Pancake-scented burps from her short-stack breakfast. Coffee.

What the Poet really needed—must have eventually if he were to survive—was a pressure suit or pressure chamber. He was not used to the lower atmospheric pressure in human spaces, and he was going to get the helium equivalent of the bends as soon as his rescue bottle ran out of charge—if it hadn't already. If the helium bends was anything like the bends humans got from diving too deep and surfacing too rapidly in the ocean, the Poet was about to be in a world of agony.

"It sucks to be you," she told him. He seemed to understand at least the predicament he was in, for after a moment's more struggle, he lay back and sucked at the heliox hose.

A flash from outside through the small lifepod porthole.

It was no brighter than a flashing camera might be if you were in the middle of a football field in a stadium and someone in the far upper decks was making a picture.

But there weren't supposed to be any flashes out here. The nearest star. 82 Eridani, was over fifteen light-hours away. They were truly in the waste between stars.

Japps went to the controls, rotated the pod. Toggled in on the *Chief Seattle* beta beacon. Focused, refocused.

The signal wouldn't resolve.

What the heck.

She overrode the automatic frequency lock, paged through the beta signatures available. Or that *should* have been available. There weren't any.

She fired the puny reaction rockets on the lifepod and headed toward the *Seattle*'s last-known position.

A blip. Another blip.

Japps breathed a sigh of relief.

Okay, baby, show yourself. Come on—

Blip, blip, blip, blip, blip.

And then Japps was among the blips, and she saw what it was. A debris field.

Blip, blip, blip, blip, blip, blip, blip, endless, endless . . .

The remains of the *Chief Seattle*.

"Oh, God," Japps said.

The crew. Martinez. Her drinking buddy. Her friend.

Shit.

Shit, shit, shit—it was all happening again. She was losing everything.

Everything.

Even yourself, Melinda. Where do you think you are? This isn't good. Hold. Get a hold.

She swiped away her own nascent tears. Squeezed her ducts dry. No more.

What could she do? What—

Messenger drone. All lifepods had an FTL-capable MDR. Pigeon-sized. Like the *Chief Seattle* was—had been—the drone was capable of the current Q-drive speed limit, 900 *c*.

Send it. Send it where?

Japps laughed when she realized that she really only had one choice. She had no telemetry on any other vessels in this region. In fact, there was only one target she had even the slightest chance of hitting, and that by activating the drone's automatic default trajectory. It was a destination that was ten days away.

Could she survive the month that a rescue might take?

Could the Poet?

Did they have some semblance of food?

Just taking care of a few contingencies, Martinez had said. *Throw in some of that glucose goo.*

Martinez, now dust between the stars. Gone. Oh, God.

Thank you, XO.

They had food for a time, if she could figure out how to feed the sceeve. Hell, if she could figure out how to survive on lifepod hardtack herself. Yes, a month. Maybe more on starvation rations.

Until.

Until the cold equations asserted themselves. The fires inside died.

Until they died.

But not yet.

"Guess I'm going to find out what I can take without losing it permanently," Japps mumbled to herself. She quietly promised herself to find a way to kill herself, maybe kill them both, before that happened. She turned to the Poet. He gazed up at her with big black eyes. Impossible to read an expression in them. At least impossible for her, who had never had any practice.

"I'm sorry," she said. "This isn't much of a rescue."

The Poet laid his head back, his breathing growing more rapid.

The atmosphere was going to be the problem. Sceeve lived in a pressurized environment equivalent to the water pressure at three hundred feet under the ocean on Earth. That same pressure would kill a human with oxygen narcosis who didn't slowly adapt to it by punctuated periods in higher and higher pressure.

She had a pressure suit on, but, of course, in the haste to depart—of course, of course, *she'd forgotten her helmet.*

Goddamn it, she couldn't be blamed; this wasn't her billet.

Of course she *could* be blamed. It was an idiot move.

No space helmet.

Here they were.

Could she even up the air pressure in this pod? Japps doubted she could get it that high. She'd have to break into the monitor board, figure out the circuitry, see what she could do. At least *that* was part of her skill set. Maybe she could at least get the pressure up to some degree. Enough? She'd do what she could.

Shit.

Her good friend, dust out the viewport.

Herself stuck in a lifepod.

No Q bottle.

No FTL.

Adrift on the outer reaches of the Fomalhaut Limit.

Nearly twenty light-years from Earth.

Deep space.

Alone.

Well, not quite alone. For what *that* was worth.

"It sucks to be you," she said to the Poet, knowing he couldn't understand a word she said but figuring he just *might* get the intent. "It sucks to be you. And it really, *really* sucks to be *us*."

NINE

31 December 2075
Richardson, Texas
New Pentagon E-Level

Coalbridge turned a corner on E-Level of the New Pentagon and came to the end of a corridor. There he found an open door that led to the office of Huntley Camaroon, the Secretary of the United States Extry. Coalbridge paused, took a breath, then entered the SECEX's office with trepidation.

This was it, wasn't it? The moment he'd always dreaded. He was going to be grounded, he just knew it. TACTIC was the traditional resting place for captains awaiting new commands to be readied. He hadn't exactly enjoyed pushing data there, but he'd accepted it as necessary. And definitely temporary.

But today's orders, out of the blue, sent him over to STRAT for the grand tour. STRAT was definitely not a way station for field officers. STRAT was a specialty.

After the tour, he was report to SECEX. Not the section of the New Pentagon that housed the office suites—but to the man himself.

They had to be priming him for some bogus promotion. Planning staff. Headquarters. Something along those lines.

And if so, he would lose his vessel.

Yes, assignment to STRAT was a big deal. It meant somebody had an eye on you for admiral, for one thing. He knew plenty of

Extry officers who would give their eyeteeth for such a chance. He was not one of them.

Fuck. Double fuck.

It had started innocently enough, with his boss, Micky Wu, a two-star rear admiral, pulling him aside on the train ride back from the RAMP meeting that morning.

How about taking a stroll over to STRAT this afternoon, check out the current deployment grid? Bone up on the latest intel while you're at it. Get an overview of current fleet deployment.

But Micky, I've got those torpedo reqs to finish—

Too busy?

Too bad.

Orders are orders.

So off he'd gone. Now it was 18:30, his stomach was grumbling, and Coalbridge dreaded what he was about to hear from the SECEX.

Camaroon sat at a huge oaken desk. Several files were scattered across its surface, and an old-fashioned pad of dazz paper served for written messages, although Coalbridge figured the SECEX was also wiied to the New Pentagon's chroma matrix. Everyone was.

"How was your tour of STRAT, Jim?"

"I'm pretty much up to speed on the fleet deployment at present now. At last report, the sceeve are at Wolf 359, sir. They've got ten thousand vessels."

"Yes," said the SECEX. "And vectoring for Sol at a nice steady pace of 100 *c*."

"We're in for it, sir."

"Yes."

"If I may ask," said Coalbridge, "the Extry's not planning to keep me here permanently, is it, sir? Am I being reassigned to STRAT? Because I would hate that, sir, I really would. Especially if the situation in space is as dire as it looks."

Camaroon's stern expression softened to a smile. "No, no. On the contrary, Jim." The SECEX leaned back in his chair and folded his hands behind his neck. He regarded Coalbridge. "Hell, son. You fight."

Coalbridge breathed a sigh of relief. "Good. Sir."

The SECEX put a hand, his left, on his desk. His nails were manicured, but his fingers were wrinkled, wizened. Like an old man's. *He's only fifty,* Coalbridge thought. Could body parts age at different rates? He didn't think so. The SECEX wore a silver wedding band that glinted against his dark skin.

"STRAT INTEL gave you the full details on the *Chief Seattle*?"

"Yes, sir. Some I already knew from Lieutenant Commander Leher's analytical report."

"So the *Chief Seattle* disappears from existence. Almost. No further word. She misses her next rendezvous point. Nothing."

"*Almost*, sir?"

The SECEX smiled. "Caught that, did you?"

"Yes, sir."

The SECEX nodded toward a file that lay on his desktop. It was red-taped TOP SECRET. "There's one more piece of information."

"Sir?"

"Messenger drone arrived at Walt Whitman today from 82 Eridani sector. It was sent by a lifepod belonging to the *Chief Seattle*."

Coalbridge eyed the file. It was the MDR from the drone. Had to be.

"Before I reveal to you what's in that file, let me tell you that the messenger drone's black box recorded debris near its originating location. Debris characteristic of the *Chief Seattle*'s core material, I'm afraid."

Coalbridge breathed out. So, she'd been destroyed. Too bad. He'd known and liked her captain, even though Hayden did seem to entirely lack most traces of a sense of humor. He'd been a good man. "I'm sorry to hear that, sir."

The SECEX nodded sadly. "But to the MDR. It's a very simple message, really. From a SIGINT petty officer, seems to be. The MDR states that there is one human alive on that pod."

"Some good news," Coalbridge said.

"One human," said the SECEX, "and one sceeve. Both alive."

"A sceeve? Sharing the same atmospheric mix? How the hell is that even possible?"

"That's a question we would very much like an answer to," said the SECEX. "Along with just who or what this sceeve actually is."

Coalbridge considered. "You're saying that sceeve is the *Poet*, sir?"

"So says the MDR."

"We have the Poet." Coalbridge let out a low whistle. "I'll be damned."

"Unfortunately, at this time, we do *not* have the Poet. What we have is a sceeve invasion. I cannot afford to send the Extry, a significant chunk of the Extry, or even a small task force, to find out who or what is in that lifepod."

"I suppose I can see the logic in that, sir," Coalbridge said. "But a sceeve that doesn't immediately commit suicide by *gid* deliquescence the moment we capture it, sir. That's a *turncoat*. Never happened before. That's the Poet out there. I'll bet my command on it."

"You're about to."

"Pardon, sir?"

"I'm sending you."

"Me?"

"You and the *Joshua Humphreys*," said the SECEX. "I could send a scoutcraft, but what could it do? Turn around and head back? I want you to investigate and *act*, Captain. Full latitude."

"How old is this MDR, if I'm permitted to ask, sir?"

"Eight hours. Came in this morning just before the RAMP meeting. Only Maggie and I knew about it." Camaroon chuckled. "We were terrified that Tillich had gotten wind of the info and would threaten the president with it."

"I don't follow, sir."

"Don't worry about it," the SECEX said. "We dodged that particular bullet."

Coalbridge wondered if the president herself had been informed at that time. He knew better than to ask.

"So, I'll be leaving—"

"Walt Whitman projects a departure time in forty-eight hours with full provisioning and final systems burn-in."

"She's already stocked, sir. I've seen to it." Coalbridge wondered how to put this delicately and without getting anybody in trouble.

"Have you?"

"Back channels, sir. That sort of thing."

The SECEX shook his head. "Maggie was right. She says you're a half step away from DTSO, Captain."

DTSO was Extry slang for "danger to yourself and others."

"I hope not, sir."

"She also told me you had a brilliant mind underneath that bull head of yours." Camaroon shrugged. "Anyway, no burn-in, no additional provisioning, and a DT in twenty-four."

"And the destination?"

"82 Eridani."

Coalbridge totted up a quick estimate in his head. "Ten days."

"Yes." The SECEX sat back again. "As I mentioned, I'm sending you with open orders. If there's any truth to this Poet craziness, act on it. This is fourth and long, son. You're the Hail Mary. You get that?"

"Yes, sir," said Coalbridge. "I get it."

"Have any problem with it?"

Coalbridge flushed. He was either getting his dream assignment—or he was about to be sent to the ass-end of nowhere on a wild-goose chase and miss the greatest battle ever fought in humanity's short history of space flight. And maybe return to a burned-out, blasted Earth.

"No place I'd rather be, Mr. Secretary."

"We'll try to hold the sceeve to the Kuipers, then fall back from there if necessary. When they attack, it's not going to be pretty."

"No, sir."

"You know I grew up in Kansas, right?" said the SECEX. "Suburb outside of Topeka."

"Yes, sir, I think I knew that."

"Let me tell you something, Jim. You grow up in Kansas, you learn to feel a storm coming. And right now—this whole situation has the smell of tornado weather. So let's pray to God that that lifepod does yield up something."

"I'll do my best to find out, sir. If I may put in a few special requests for crew additions before my departure time?"

"You got somebody in mind?"

"Lieutenant Commander Griffin Leher, sir. The Depletion Report creep."

"Thought you might say that," Camaroon replied. "Done."

"Thank you, sir."

The SECEX shook his head. "Goddamn, this is the wrong time for this to be happening. One more year. Even six months. But Tillich slowed me down. I haven't got my vessels." The SECEX suddenly looked tired. Old. His fleshy, jovial face sagging into a worried frown.

"We have days. Maybe hours. Let's make them count, Captain," Camaroon said. "Let's make them count."

"Yes, Mr. Secretary."

A message scrolled across the dazz-paper pad on the SECEX's desk, and he glanced down at it. Coalbridge couldn't make it out, but it was highlighted with a red priority flag. "Okay, I've got to take care of this," the SECEX said to Coalbridge. "Good luck to you and your crew, son."

"Aye, sir."

"And take the night off and get some rest, Captain. You're going to need it," said the SECEX. "That's an order."

Coalbridge stood, saluted.

"Dismissed."

As he turned to leave, Coalbridge suddenly knew exactly how he planned to obey the final orders of the SECEX. Relaxation? Yes. Sleep. Less likely. To do so would, however, require a little persuading. But she was most definitely worth the effort.

Yep.

A captain's work was never done.

1 December 2075
Vicinity of Beta Geminorum, aka Pollux
Guardian of Night

The cleanup of Milt's body was surprisingly easy. The craft was equipped with very efficient nanotech for such tasks, and Store-keep Susten had brought along a "gut bag" from the processing lockers. In no time, Milt became a pasty goo in a clear container, and V-CENT was once again spotless. The churn even cleaned and freshened Ricimer's bloodstained uniform in the process. The churn's controlling program would log its entire process with Lamella and Governess—which ordinarily would have triggered an alert, and vessel marines to be dispatched to arrest him, had Lamella not immediately overwritten all the data.

That left the problem of what to do with Milt's two DDCM subordinates who were also aboard. And, more importantly, the portion of the crew not in on Ricimer's plot—which amounted to nearly thirty of his fifty-five officers. Too many to risk imprisoning them. Besides, what would he do with prisoners in the end? He wasn't going to kill them, but Sporata starcraft were not equipped with lifeboats in which to set them adrift. Lifeboats were for weak-willed traders. For lesser species.

Ricimer pondered the solution he'd come up with on his way back to his bridge.

The vessel was under his command, but not yet under his control. The rates were Lamella's task. She was a constant presence in their minds. She was not all-powerful, of course, but she had each rate on continual virtual feed and could modify his or her perception of reality by additions and subtractions of sensory input and, more importantly, with plausible explanations for almost anything out of the ordinary.

His senior officers were handpicked. He'd served with them all over the years. He'd been careful to approach only those whom he knew to have bitterness against the Administration, but not against the Sporata in particular. The Sporata certainly had its problems, but it wasn't actively malevolent. In any case, Ricimer had nothing against it.

The Administration, on the other hand, was ruthlessly efficient in all things political. Ricimer was no democrat. He didn't consider himself a Mutualist, either, with their quaint belief in symbiosis and interspecies innovation. Ricimer supposed, if pressed, he would say he had no political leaning but was merely opposed to institutionalized murder.

Especially when his family was the victim.

His own motive, he had decided, was revenge. And he had only begun to exact it.

Ricimer entered the bridge and briskly returned to his atrium. He had barely toed into his virtual-feed grid when his XO, Talid, turned to him with a report. "Captain, we have a problem."

"What's that, Commander?"

"We've got two atmospheric sensors that are registering low levels of contamination."

"Radiation?"

"Churn, sir," said Talid. "Lieutenant Frazil, report."

Frazil was the Craft Internal Systems Officer, the CISO.

One of mine, Ricimer thought. *Trained him from a plebe.*

Ricimer turned to Frazil. "What are we looking at, CISO?"

"Captain, I've sent crews for a physical examination, but as of now Lamella and the autonomous monitoring routines cross-check. Both confirm contamination in atmospheric ducts Aft 13 and Aft 57 with point three ppm military-grade churn."

"Any evidence of activation?"

"Not at this time, sir."

Which, under different circumstances, would have been an

enormous relief to all who heard it. An engineered nanotech plague attack on the material structure of the vessel was the nightmare scenario of any Sporata vessel. The threat could take so many forms and, like a rapidly mutating biological virus, could be extremely difficult to eradicate before it infected and destroyed everything in its wake.

"Those are officers' quarters ducts, are they not, CISO?"

"That's correct, sir," Frazil responded. "We've projected a path back to the churn stores and have isolated two possible routes."

"Then shut them both down, Lieutenant."

"Already done, sir," said Frazil. He seemed appalled that Ricimer could believe he might neglect such a basic action. "But officers are present in quarters, and I wasn't certain—"

"Quarantine the area. Seal them in—including your crews. Then get me a list of who we've got in there."

"Aye, sir." Frazil bowed his head, concentrated. Ricimer knew he was furiously sending a barrage of shutdown orders through his virtual feed.

"Do we have a timeline and list of possible contaminated personnel, CISO?"

"Coming up right now, sir." The crenelations that were Guardian written language rose under Frazil's hand on his console, and he quickly rubbed his gripping gills across the surface, releasing the digitized esters to his muzzle. "Last clear reading was 1.7 *atentias* ago, Captain. I've got a list of officers who have been in and out of quarters since that time, sir."

"Very good, CISO. How many?"

Frazil quickly counted. "Twenty-seven, sir."

Good. Twenty-seven was exactly the right number. Every one of "his" officers had secret orders to stay out of the officer sector for the past two *atentias.*

"Get the potentially infected officers into isolation and scan them one by one," Ricimer said.

"Sick bay can't handle that many, sir," said Talid.

"The only place big enough to isolate them is Cargo B," Frazil added.

Ricimer nodded. "Very well. Order each of those officers to activate exterior excursion fields immediately and report to Cargo B. And get a quantum amplification generator into Cargo B. I want the area sealed subatomically."

"Aye, Captain."

Ricimer turned to the officer in charge of SCAN, the vessel's exterior sensor array.

"Lieutenant Roth, what are we tracking on the beta? Any of ours around?"

"No, sir, I don't think so." Roth checked his sensors momentarily, then reported back. "If we're looking for transport, sir, the nearest thing I see is a merchantman hauler. She identifies as the *Basalt Plain Colonizer* under army contract."

"Empty or full?"

"She's headed out empty to pick up a tech load on 111 Tauri D."

"Perfect," Ricimer said. "She'll have a big hold."

Roth moved his hand deeper into the bulkhead, motioned up further information on his visual display. He was also receiving verbal feed directly to his nervous system through the nerve ends in his hands. "That she does, sir. She's on registry with a crew of fifteen. Twin commodity bottles set for electrostatic maximum. She's not a supertanker, sir, but she'll do if you plan to . . ."

Roth was set to continue but realized he was about to overstep his bounds hazarding a guess as to what step his commanding officer was considering next.

"Yes, she will do," said Ricimer. "Thank you, SCAN." He turned to Talid. "Set a course, Commander. And give the *Colonizer* a single-burst beta, compressed and encrypted, to let her know we're coming. Nothing more. Do not identify. She'll know we are Sporata by the signal strength."

"What if she turns tail and runs, Captain?"

Talid had a point, and it was a good suggestion even though they both knew the *Colonizer* was going nowhere.

This rendezvous had been arranged one *molt* ago, about six months.

Yet it was important to keep up pretenses. Trader craft lived in constant fear of the Sporata and had been known to flee contact. It was seldom a good thing to have the space navy coming down on you. At the very least, it probably meant a complete search for contraband and possible smuggling charges. Even if you were clean, something could always be found that was against Regulation.

"If she runs, we'll reel her in, Ms. Talid," said Ricimer. "That vessel doesn't know it yet, but she is ours now."

"Aye, Captain."

"And keep us quiet, XO," Ricimer added. "Craft Orders must come first." Ricimer disengaged himself from the atrium. "I'm going down to Cargo B to see to my officers. The bridge is yours, Commander. Notify me when we're in range of the *Colonizer.*"

"Aye, sir."

"Thrive the Administration."

"Thrive the Administration, Captain."

TEN

5 December 2075
Vicinity of Beta Geminorum, aka Pollux
Guardian of Night

SCREECH!

Pressure waves throughout the craft. Sudden compression of atmosphere even on the bridge, where Ricimer occupied the captain's atrium. No vessel, no matter how well-built, was meant for such a craft-to-craft docking as he was now performing, and there was bound to be strain.

He only hoped Lamella's calculations did not have a missing or incorrectly input variable that had pushed the docking craft beyond their tolerances. There was no chance of Lamella making a mistake in her computation, of course. She was the soul of mathematical precision.

POP! CLANG!

The sheering tension of hull against hull as force fields collided. The ozone odor of electrical fire, of particles occupying the same space with one another in positions that could not *be* in any natural order, forced into dimensions that did not exist, the cracks between cracks pulled open by paradox.

"Captain, we've got the *Basalt Plains Colonizer* in hold state," reported Talid. "We should have hull integration in fifty *vitias*."

Ricimer nodded. "Have the infected crew ready."

"Aye, sir."

Ricimer tightened his foot grip on the grill beneath him and allowed the image feed from Cargo B to flood into his mind.

A crowd of officers clumped together near a bulkhead. A few clutched personal items. Some were naked, rousted from the Guardian "sleep" of tagona-quiescence and herded to this bay without warning. For those who had old-fashioned "half-hypha" hybrid blood in them, nakedness revealed the black stripes on their thighs that marked them as socially inferior, whatever their rank. This uncovered sight was considered deeply humiliating, although Ricimer didn't give a damn. A good officer was a good officer. Most were very frightened. A churn infection was no joke. If the bug found a way through your defenses, you'd be dead in an instant. And it could happen at any time if you left the situation untreated. Today. Tomorrow. Many cycles from now. The churn worked according to its own inexorable timetable.

Sizzle!

The wall dividing his craft from the merchantman dissolved in a flicker-field integration, and a portal opened up into the other craft's cargo hold. It was huge, dark, and empty. After a moment, its electroweak-gravity normalized with that of the cargo bay.

Time to get the show underway.

"CISO Frazil, get those officers off the craft," Ricimer said.

Frazil, who was in charge of the cargo-bay team, took in his order. He wore a contamination suit and held an ester broadcaster in one hand. He could not communicate through the suit's skin, which was impermeable to the quark level, but he could pass a signal to the broadcaster to do so. With a loud blast of command ester, he ordered the "infected" officers forward. One by one, they stepped into the portal, moved over and out of the craft. Ricimer counted.

Twenty-five . . .

Twenty-six . . .

And twenty-seven. They were all off his craft and safely in the commodities bottle of the merchantman, where they'd be transported home—and then torn practically apart and reconstructed to be sure there was no lingering plague hidden within them.

Which would be uncomfortable in the extreme for them, but was better than being dead.

"Officers of the *Guardian of Night*, I salute you," Ricimer said, using Lamella to amplify his esters and express them into the air of the hold. "Your sacrifice will not go unnoticed. Honor be upon you, and Thrive the Administration."

He watched as the departing officers turned to face the portal through which they'd come.

"Thrive the Administration," said Curdek, the highest ranking among them. "And good luck, Captain."

Suddenly, above Ricimer, an alarm light began to flash. Information esters infused the cargo bay through a series of powerful nozzles. "Alert, alert. Military-grade churn contamination detected in crew quarters. Point four ppm. Alert!"

Ricimer turned to Frazil. "What is going on? Was one of these officers in contact with the crew on the way over here?"

"No, Captain, not to my knowledge," Frazil answered back. He looked frightened. Good.

"I'm going to get to the bottom of this. Leave that port open, Frazil," Ricimer said. "We may have more to send over."

"Aye, Captain!"

Ricimer cut the video feed and turned to Talid on the bridge beside him.

"What have we got, XO?"

"One of the officers was out and made a circuit of the vessel before returning to quarters. He wiped his trace from primary records, but we pulled it up on a secondary log."

"Where was—never mind," Ricimer said. "It's a false liaison, isn't it, Talid?"

"Seems so, Captain."

The dirty little secret of the Sporata. Officers could and did have sex with rates while those crew members were under the control of Governess. There was a backdoor into the program that allowed the computer monitoring to overlook such transgressions—

Or call them what they are, Ricimer thought: *rapes.*

—a backdoor that Sporata technology division was always planning to close but somehow never got around to. The excuse was that the crew members usually had no idea what was happening. Governess kept them believing that they were sleeping or at some other minor duty and usually supplied them with a pleasant daydream while the liaison was going on to explain away their elevated bodily reactions: the intense tingle in the hands for females, the uncoiling of the corkscrew-shaped positor in males. Both sexes of officers engaged in the liaisons, with the females choosing a multitude of partners and the males usually sticking to one crew member they had their eye on.

It was true that most crew members didn't remember a liaison. Except, that is, when females suddenly turned up pregnant while on shore leave. Or males must explain where they acquired a venereal disease to an incredulous lover or mate. Everyone knew it went on, and on which vessels it was out of control. Ricimer had always run a tight vessel in that regard and kept his officers on the straight and narrow as much as possible, but only the computer could be everywhere at once—and the computer was programmed not to care.

"Who was the officer?" Ricimer asked.

"Ensign Bronin, sir," said Talid.

"Female. Damn. Multiple partners."

"Yes, sir."

"How much of the craft has been compromised?"

"That's just it, sir. She took the main accessway. Governess was ignoring her excursion. So all of it."

"Most unfortunate."

Another spraying, flashing alarm. "Alert. Point five ppm churn compromise. Vessel contaminated. Repeat: vessel contaminated. Strain isolated as MGC-250575. Melt-away risk imminent!"

The automated systems had made the announcement. Now it was up to him to make the decision.

Ricimer did not hesitate. With a tap on the small COM control patch on his uniform sleeve, he switched to a craft-wide channel.

"Abandon vessel," he said. "All hands, abandon vessel. Crew first. Officer assist with head counts. All report to Cargo B. Do it now!"

He deactivated the communications channel and turned to Talid.

"Over five hundred people, Captain," she said. "Are we absolutely sure the *Colonizer* can handle that many?"

He'd examined the specs of the *Colonizer* and well knew she was capable of taking on his crew and the "infected" officers. But Talid hadn't been in on that stage of the planning. Compartmentalize and survive—the motto of all covert operations.

"It will be crowded," Ricimer said, "but they'll manage. We'll set a rescue beacon to activate as soon as the *Guardian of Night* is well clear. They shouldn't have to wait out here too long."

The evacuation took an *atentia*, about one and a half human hours. The crew, suddenly released from their links to the computer, were dazed and in a near-dreamlike state. Ricimer had counted on this. They followed their officers' orders as would a herd animal its shepherd. There was one snag when a cook's mate was certain that she'd been contaminated by a broth she'd been working on in the galley. She fell and began writhing on the floor, clutching at her arms and tearing away skin in her attempt to scratch out the churn.

It turned out she had a neglected case of Scropjur's itch, a lichen-based disease that was easily cured once it presented. She was lifted up and taken into the waiting cargo bay. Unfortunately, that meant that the entire group of evacuees was now at risk for catching the itch. *Another indignity imposed on those doomed to live,* Ricimer thought with a small smiling curl to his muzzle.

And then the vessel was clear of crew. The remaining officers gathered near the cargo atmosphere lock in a pretense of waiting to go through.

Now for the real convincer.

"Lamella, it's time for the churn." He spoke with a soft whiff.

Churn began to flow from the public-address nozzles that had previously sprayed forth words.

And Cargo B began to melt. It was quite dramatic. The churn he'd chosen gave the bulkheads a sickly rose-colored glow that soon intensified to garish, throbbing red. Meanwhile, the metal and ceramic material of the deck, ceiling, and bulkhead began to flow like glass. This particular churn—used for cleaning the tanks of hazardous-materials transports, and very similar to actual military ordinance—would cut down to within a hairsbreadth of the underlying force-field containment bottle.

For added effect, Lamella provided an atmospheric leak into space. The hiss was terrifying, even if the amount was not particularly life threatening.

The remaining crew was now on one side of the bay while the "tainted" crew and other officers were looking out the open docking collar of the *Colonizer*. Between them lay churn madness—instant death for anyone who ventured there. Or so it appeared.

Ricimer flailed his arms in the griever's gesture of great sorrow and sadness. He opened a communication channel into the *Colonizer*. "The vessel is lost, and we who remain on her!" he said. "Save yourselves, my brave officers and crew. Don't look back. Uphold the memory of us in your gids. Tell all we died bravely and while performing our duties!"

He then ordered the *Colonizer* cargo door closed. The door slid down over horrified, grief-stricken faces. He really *did* hate to put his crew through this. They had not earned such treatment. But the alternative would have been to kill them all—never a real option in Ricimer's mind.

He turned to Talid. "So, they're away."

This was it. This was really it. Absolutely no turning back. No way out but ahead. To Sol and beyond.

"All right, Talid," he finally said. "Open up a portal with the second commodity bottle on the merchantman."

"Aye, Captain."

Talid ordered the craft turned a quarter degree on its axis. The connection was made with the other cargo bottle.

The door opened.

Inside were the refugees. Nearly one thousand tired, bedraggled Guardians. Some single, some together in entire families. All looking stunned and wild-eyed, half suspecting they were about to meet their death. They'd been holding position for three *tagona*—the equivalent of four and a half Earth days—and had not taken in sustenance, only fluids, during that time. There was no light in the commodities bottle, and precious little ventilation. Talk could not dissipate but hung in the air in clouds of meaningless vapors. After a day or so, all but the most basic communication had ceased.

And all of them had been victims of the Agaric Pogrom long before that. Most had been driven from their homes, their friends and relatives slaughtered. They'd been hidden for many *molts* in some of the most vile cracks and interstices of the Shiro.

It was that or be hunted down and murdered.

It had taken more time to get the word out that a possibility of escape existed. Time to convince them that this escape was not itself another trap waiting to destroy them.

They were the Shiro's Mutualist remnant.

They had been without hope. Doomed to extermination.

Until now.

Here they stood, silently waiting for rescue.

Before, they'd been the funny cult to which Del, his wife, belonged. Mutualism had been a bit of a household joke. A second thought to their family, their love.

Now these believers were all he had left of Del.

"Let's get them aboard and settled as quickly as possible,

Lieutenant Frazil," Ricimer said via the craft-communication channel. "Take out the crew replacements and get them plugged in. Lamella will begin scenario training immediately. Hurry now. We've got our work cut out for us."

Ricimer considered. He was about to go on a wild run with an untrained, amateur crew. So much depended on his computer program and the new artificial intelligence component he'd added from Sol system. *If* Lamella could knit these strangers together, they *might* stand a chance. He must avoid confrontation, however. A trained Sporata rate was, in many ways, redundant until the time for combat came.

And then he or she became essential, for no Guardian computer program was sophisticated enough to react to the extreme variability of battle conditions.

Of course, he did possess one trump card: the Kilcher artifact. The problem was, it had never been used in combat before, but only on the pacific Kilcher.

No, for the moment stealth, propaganda, and subterfuge were essential. This was the only strategy he could count on. He must remain hidden. He must trust to the devices he had put into motion *semata*, sometimes *molts* ago, to work in his favor. The Poet's broadcasts.

His own letter to the Civitas Council.

He knew one thing his officers did not. That message had been sent. There was no way to recall it now. And because of that fact, he and they were committed. There was no going back. There was nothing but death behind them. He had seen to that.

Had he chosen the correct words? It no longer mattered. What was done was done.

He had cut his ties with his customary ruthless effectiveness.

24 December 2075
The Shiro
Administrative Coombs
Office of Civitas Special Counselor to the Chair

Dear Companion Gergen,
I trust this message finds you in good health. It is my plea-sure to inform you that I have taken command of the newly

forged Sporata vessel Guardian of Night *and the recently gleaned artifact she mounts. It is clear that the artifact will be the perfect weapon to use against the remainder of your hated Mutualist opposition.*

Opposition, thought Gergen. *Strange way to categorize such scum. But let it pass.*

I hesitate to call the Mutualists the "resistance," because that would imply that the authority against which they are striving held some sort of legitimacy, however tenuous.

What was this?

It is my contention that, by its many actions, some recent, some in the past, all most terrible and unforgiveable war crimes, the Administration and you upon the Civitas Council have abrogated any legitimacy to govern that you might once have held. I am afraid that I cannot in good conscience, and with a clear and untroubled gid, permit you to employ this artifact to commit the same genocidal crime against the Agaric Mutualists and any others who remain, that you committed against the Kilcher species.

Gergen felt his hand begin to shake. He steadied it.
Captain, you have just ended your life. You must know this. Read on.

I must therefore inform you that I am taking the Guardian of Night, *and the artifact, out of Administration hands.*

Curse it. Curse the no-good Sporata stinker. This was not good. Not good at all.

It is my intention to seek political asylum with the next species against which this weapon will likely be used and prevent its genocidal deployment against them.

What operations were currently underway? The Ilex Omega mop-up? No. There was no longer any resistance there.

Sol, thought Gergen. *He's talking about the humans.*

Furthermore, I intend to suggest myself as a diplomatic conduit between the humans and the Mutualist enclaves. It is my hope to enable an alliance to be forged between these disparate forces. I intend to rendezvous with a Mutualist envoy for that very purpose before turning the artifact over the the humans.

It was too much.

Gergen crumpled the paper in his hand. For a long moment, he did not move. But then the hand that held the paper began to tremble. Then the other hand. The trembling propagated to his shoulders, his torso, until he was shaking with the purest fury he'd ever known in his life. Finally, Gergen allowed himself to release a concentrated cloud of the peppered aroma of rage.

Only then did he unfold the paper and continue reading.

By the time this message arrives, you will be unable to stop me from carrying out this plan. You may ask yourself why I should inform you at all of my intentions. It should be clear that I deliberately mean to provoke a response from the Administration. I deliberately mean to provoke you, Companion Gergen, since you hold the Sporata within your command portfolio.

I have a simple motive driving my actions, one which I do expect you will never understand.

I have no political motivation.

I do this for my family's honor. For the sake of my line.

My purpose is not to flee, but to confront, to incite, to instigate further resistance.

You are guilty of species genocide and the pogrom of innocents.

I intend to make you pay the price for the curse you have brought upon our once proud species.

Although my final destination is Sol system, I'm sure you understand that seeking me out would be akin to seeking a crystal of carbon in a basalt plain flow. Yet I certainly expect you to try.

As a final point: I have no pretentions to power. I do not expect you to believe this, Companion Gergen, being who you

*are, although it is the case. My decision rests upon honor. As
an officer and a person of conscience, I can bear no more
from this Administration and am compelled to take action in
order to live with myself and with my memories.*
> *Good-bye.*
> *Arid Ricimer*
> *Captain,* Guardian of Night

Companion *Gergen! I'll show you companionship, my captain.*

Gergen turned to Vlamish, his secretary, who had remained
standing near the door while Gergen went through his morning
messages.

"Get me the DDCM Director. Do not let him make any
excuses. He is to report to me immediately." Gergen considered.
"And prepare a message capsule for that idiot Blawfus. I'll have
its contents ready shortly."

"It shall be done, Counselor."

Gergen breathed in. *Calm. You arrived at this post through the
regulation of emotions. Regulation is always the path to success.
So regulate yourself.* He breathed out.

The insurrection crushed. The Sol invasion newly resourced
and restarted. More territorial expansions and species gleanings
in the planning stages.

He should have known. Things had been going too well. For
the first time in many cycles, he had begun to feel almost—dare
he say it?—safe in his work. His position. His life.

Now this.

Vlamish was still standing before his worktable.

"Thrive the Administration," Gergen said, dismissing him.

"Thrive the Administration."

Vlamish went to make his communications.

And Gergen sat considering a certain button on the upper left
edge of his work table. It was a special communication channel
over quantum-encrypted optical fiber. And that fiber led to the
inner chamber of the Council. To the office of the chair herself.

The defection, as outrageous and unprecedented as it was,
would be only a nuisance if the vessel had contained any other
weapon. But the Kilcher artifact. Unreproduced and—as far as
his researchers could determine—unreproduceable. No known
defense.

Of course, the Administration would find a way to destroy the traitors and their weapon in the end.

We are the power, we are the marked and necessary path to success and rule, sang the ancestral voices within Gergen's *gid.*

So naïve, those ancestors. They did not truly understand how power was accumulated, nursed. How fragile it was behind the façade of invulnerability.

How tenuous Gergen's own position was, when it really came down to it.

The calm Gergen had established began to leak away. His mind quickly worked out the personal implications of Ricimer's letter.

The chair would not be pleased. She would want someone's *gid.* He must give her one, many. The amount did not matter, so long as one of those gids wasn't his.

And then, as was often the case before springing into action, Gergen felt a moment of immense lassitude sweep over him. Of pity for himself, for the situations he must deal with in the name of the Administration, of Regulation.

What had he done to deserve this? He'd been a good regulator. He'd risen from a decent hypha, a pure line but a decidedly obscure one. He served his time on countless committees of regulation. He'd been a good party member in every way. His quotas were always filled and on time. He had forged coalitions, formed alliances where need be, to always keep the upward momentum in place. He had rewarded regulated loyalty when he must, dropped those who were no longer useful when he could.

And along the way, he'd met and allied with a political operative even more ruthless and cunning than he. Together, no one had been able to stand in their way.

The reward was power. Of course, the perquisites of office were pleasant—and it was necessary to put on a certain appearance, to project the power to the people so that they would understand who it was they were to look to, to obey. One needed the extra servants, the personal vessels, the regulated and empty corridors set aside for Council use only, if one were to govern effectively. He was ashamed of none of these offerings of a grateful populace that he and his family enjoyed.

And now this Ricimer held him, Gergen, responsible for his personal troubles? Held the Administration responsible? Even the Regulation itself?

For a moment, Gergen attempted to place himself in Ricimer's position, to understand what he was thinking, feel what he was feeling. It was not hard. He'd known such people. There was an emptiness within every Guardian's *gid*, a space that Regulation was designed to perfectly fill, to animate. But sometimes the fire of Regulation died down within an individual's *gid*, or never caught in the first place. Into that emptiness then flowed envy. Spite. Greed. Out-of-control egotism and megalomania. It all ended in the same place: opposition to Regulation. And opposition to Regulation was, by definition, insane. To harm the Civitas was to harm every individual who composed it. It was an act of viciousness. Selfishness. Insanity.

Yes, every society produced aberrations. The question was how to limit that production. How to clean the civilization from its built-in entropic decline, its tendency to revert to the barbarism of individual license.

Deliver them to the dismemberment knives! the ancestors whispered. *Cut out the disease.*

Yes. That was the true answer. The chair knew it. Gergen knew it. They had learned the lesson the hard way on their rise to the pinnacle of Guardian society, and so to the pinnacle of galactic order.

Do not forgive your enemies and those who have ended up in alliance against you. Forgiveness is another Mutualist fantasy. Do not ignore your enemies after you have defeated them, either. Destroy them. Utterly.

For now that they had achieved the power they sought, the power to regulate as regulation should be, they must maintain it. The chair was many cycles older than Gergen. She had the best of medical attention, but there would come a time when she was unfit to continue. Weakened.

Or, Gergen sometimes let himself fantasize, she may just die suddenly. That would be nice.

When that time came, he must be in a position to make his move. To crush his opposition.

He must not allow this affair with the stolen vessel to be laid at his feet. He must not give the chair a reason to give his seat on the Council to another. This Ricimer had been indulged. Clearly the Sporata leadership had felt pity for him. He'd been allowed to live, to retain his command, after the Agaric Cleansing almost as a penance. Such sentimental rubbish the military allowed to take place within their ranks. This was why they would always remain subservient to the Council. For all their vaunted loyalty and honor, they were weak, and their weakness was their institutional bond. He and the chair had used this bond time and again to outmaneuver them.

And now they would do so again. That was where the blame could be placed. Somewhere in the Sporata chain of command.

And if they failed to recover the stolen vessel and its artifact?

Perhaps an entire division should be sacrificed as an example. Perhaps a fleet.

Gergen would do whatever it took.

But first he had the communication to initiate.

She wasn't going to like this. Gergen could feel himself already cringing in anticipation of her reaction.

He took another breath. Went through his calming ritual. Regulate. Regulate.

It was no use. With a sigh that carried the magnolia-like aroma of self-pity, Gergen pushed the red button to call the Chair.

ELEVEN

31 December 2075
Richardson, Texas

A half moon hung in the Texas sky. It shone straight down through the skylight above Coalbridge's kitchen. Nearby, the brighter stars blazed in a dark prairie firmament.

Coalbridge stood silently for a moment gazing upward. Since the war began and most of the population had moved underground, one good effect—perhaps *the* one good effect—was the disappearance of light pollution around cities. The stars came out in full force in the suburbs now. Of course, only the ground-topped apartments—the cheap and dangerous seats—could view them.

These days the stars looked different to Coalbridge than they had in his youth. More familiar. More cruel. He'd *been* to some of the closer ones. Still, he could never resist gazing at them.

Nothing deadly up there—at least not Dallas-bound—that he could see. After the sceeve attack that morning, planetary defenses seemed to be holding up. He, Leher, and Sam Guptha had gone topside, helped out as best they could. But, of course, there wasn't much to do. The drop-rods had apparently been ejected from a quantum drone flown into the atmosphere. These were not old detritus rods from the invasion, but were a new weapon. An artillery barrage, softening the enemy before the real attack.

A swath of downtown had disappeared. The salt that suffused the city had done its job, contained the collateral damage.

Nevertheless, the impact had thrown up supersonic rock shrapnel, even created a small lake of magma momentarily. Some of the Peepsie protestors who had somehow survived the initial drop were caught fleeing by the flowing liquid rock. Legless, charred remains ringed the outer edges of the now-congealed tendrils.

Nobody had survived in the impact zone. Estimates were at least three thousand killed. There were about a hundred casualties. The hospitals had been able to handle them easily enough, still equipped as they were, even after these eight years of inactivity, for thousands at a time. And the salt, enlivened by servant programs, had immediately moved in, penetrated bodies, taken over life-support functions as best it could until human emergency workers arrived. But this was only possible on the periphery of the drop. If you were in the fall zone when the rods struck, you were very likely dead.

Coalbridge remembered and shuddered. A thick cloud of dust and smoke hung over the landscape before him. He raised a sleeve to his mouth and nose, a handkerchief, anything. His eyes watered. He knew he was breathing in the dead.

There hadn't been much to do except mourn the loss.

Oh, yes. He'd nearly forgotten amid all the human misery. Dealey Plaza, which had come through the entire invasion unscathed, had been destroyed. The nearby Texas Book Depository had finally been battered to dust, along with its ancient exhibits of Dallas's day of shame. Ancient history. Better times.

How did the death and destruction make him feel? Coalbridge had to admit he was inured to it. He'd seen so much. He disliked what the Peepsies stood for, but he certainly didn't want them dead. Dead they were.

Added to the long, long list.

He was not numb. No, he was still angry. Very angry. But he was resigned to staying the course, doing his part. He knew where blind reaction got you.

It got you, for instance, a nearly destroyed vessel fleeing from the Fomalhaut Limit, most of your crew dead. Yourself outthought by a fucking sceeve commander.

People who counted on you now dead *because* of you.

Never again.

There was no way to rush to the rescue and, through some impossible physical effort, save the day. The sceeve must be met intelligently and killed intelligently, or the rest of humanity would soon find itself on the casualty list. You needed a plan. Thanks to the president, the Extry now had a coherent one to follow.

So he cooked and tried to obey orders.

Coalbridge slid the pile of shrimp he'd been stir-frying out of his skillet and onto a plate—his only unchipped plate, actually. He dug around in a drawer and found a fork. In space, cooking was his hobby. It was his tension release after a long shift on the bridge. Cooking for himself aboard a starcraft made him feel connected to Earth, to the past, the smells wafting from the kitchens of his youth. He hated to admit it, but here on Earth, his prized hobby had begun to make him feel lonely lately. Until now, that is.

Coalbridge picked up the plate in one hand and two open Shiner Bock beers in the other and went from his kitchen to his dining room.

He set the mess of shrimp down on the table in front of Samantha Guptha, who was at the dining-room table smoking a cigarette. Sam was wearing one of Coalbridge's off-white dress shirts over panties, a silver-banded watch on her right wrist, and nothing else. Coalbridge thought the outfit quite amazingly accented the saffron tones of her bronze skin.

"Cooked it in butter," he said. "Little bit of a remoulade on it, not too spicy. Try one?"

"You've about filled me up, Coalbridge," Sam said. She set her cigarette in an ashtray and reached for a shrimp, then bit into it with a quizzical expression, as if she were about to analyze its chemical makeup. Evidently she liked what her sensor told her, because she bit it off at the tail and chewed with satisfaction. "Mmm, who taught you how to cook like this?"

"Nobody," Coalbridge said. "Me. Started out on a hotplate back when I was a lieutenant. Something to pass the time. Kind of turned into a second calling."

"Good stuff." She continued chewing and tossed the shrimp tail nonchalantly back on the plate. Sam was obviously an unabashed meat-eater. She swallowed, took a swig of the Shiner, smiled up at him. "What is it with you Extry boys and cooking?"

"Pardon?"

Sam considered him for moment, acted as if she were about to elaborate, then shrugged and said, "Never mind."

She reached for her cigarette, took a drag, and combined her exhalation with a sigh of satisfaction. After another long drag,

Sam tapped her cigarette against the rim of a U.S.S. *Gerald R. Ford* ashtray he'd saved from his navy days. The *Ford* had been his first assignment out of the Naval Academy at Annapolis. She was an ancient ship and would have been decommissioned long ago had it not been for the military cutbacks after the Sri Lanka mess. He'd been the air-defense weapons officer on patrol in the Indian Ocean when the invasion began twelve years ago.

The *Ford* had been old but sound. Upgraded with the most advanced weaponry then available.

Bows and arrows compared to now.

"Sure you don't mind my smoking?" Sam asked.

"Nah, reminds me of my relatives. Every last one of 'em. My great-greats. Greats. Granddads. Grandmas. Aunts and uncles. Mom's mom—we called her Oma—used to come over and she'd cook and smoke and tell me all kinds of stories of being in the navy. She was signal corps. Did five years, quit and went back to school, then went in as an officer and did fifteen more. She was kind of a tiger." Coalbridge nodded at Sam's cigarette, smiled wryly. "She got lung cancer."

Sam took a sip of her beer. "I'm sorry," she said.

"Oh, it didn't kill her," Coalbridge said. "She was an addict, not an idiot. Fanatical about her chest X-rays. Found it early and chemoed the shit out it." Coalbridge considered his own beer for a moment. "Nope, the first churn drop got her. Turned my whole hometown into goo."

"Oh, Jim, really? Where was that?"

"Lawton, Oklahoma."

"Long way from the ocean to go navy."

"Tell that to the SECEX. He's from Topeka."

"Yes, but still—"

Coalbridge shrugged. "Granddaddy Looper was army, and his last posting was at Fort Sill, so they retired there."

"Looper was your mother's maiden name?"

"Yeah. Dutch or something."

"And her parents were army *and* navy?"

"Mixed marriage," Leher said. "They met on this joint task-force thing in Korea." Coalbridge tipped up his beer, took a long swallow. "What are you smoking?"

"Rojos. They're Mexican. About the only tobacco that survived the war."

"Must cost you an arm and a leg."

"Yep."

He'd gotten her number after the war-council meeting, just before he'd been sent on his unexpected tour of STRAT and told to report to his even more unexpected meeting with the SECEX.

At the war council, Sam had performed brilliantly. She clearly was the only one present who understood some of the potential of the new sceeve weapon—the weapon allegedly headed Earthward on the craft of a disgruntled Sporata officer. It was all too fantastic for Coalbridge to believe—or rather, too hopeful. Yet Sam took the weapon seriously, and the Secretary of Defense had specifically put Sam's Femtodynamics lab on the INTEL loop.

She seemed to think the thing was a sort of magic eraser, as far as Coalbridge could tell. He couldn't get much more of an explanation out of her. She said she wasn't at the "popularizing and allegorizing" stage yet with her figuring.

Coalbridge decided he would deal with the weapon when and if it became a problem or an opportunity and leave the worrying to the experts. He had a mission to attend to shortly, and that would give him worry enough, he was certain.

Sam was a hero to Coalbridge. It wasn't every day you had a shot to get with somebody who'd actually saved your life a time or two—even if she didn't know it.

He'd called her after receiving his special orders from the SECEX and told her he'd be willing to meet her just about anywhere. They'd had dinner at the restaurant on the top floor of her underground hotel in Richardson (the hotel had been some sort of sunken parking garage pre-invasion) and then...

Basically they'd come straight to his place in Plano so they wouldn't have to do it in an anonymous hotel room. Because there wasn't any question of their doing it—not after a few minutes together. The attraction felt more like physics than chemistry to Coalbridge. Nuclear strong force.

And, frankly, neither of them had been with anybody else for a while and both were horny.

Coalbridge pulled a chair nearby and sat down beside Sam. "So," he said. "Are we really as good together as I think we are?"

Sam smiled slyly, then leaned over and kissed him. Her breath did remind him of his grandmother, but not in a shuddery incest way, Coalbridge decided. There was also the faintest trace of perfume combined in the scent of her. He knew she made a lot of money. What "a lot" might be was fairly vague to Coalbridge, who paid little attention to such matters. He figured her perfume was probably the expensive kind.

Sam rocked back in her chair, considered him. "Yeah, I think we are good together," she said. "Too bad you're going to be *light-years* away from me for the foreseeable future."

"Demands of the service." Coalbridge shrugged.

"Guess that's why you give it your all when you're back?"

"What makes you think I didn't get any out on the Limit?"

Sam laughed and nearly snorted her beer through her nose. He found this as adorable as the rest of her traits and habits.

Sam was lovely.

Sam was smart.

Sam knew how to make nuclear weapons.

She was—

A keeper.

No, stop that. No time for that in this war. Least not for me.

"Oh, God."

"What?"

"Nothing."

"*What?*"

"Uh, I was wondering about your accent."

"Told you I grew up in Alabama."

"Yeah, but—"

"But I'm Punjabi?"

"What? No way! Thought you had a serious accident with a tanning bed." Coalbridge considered. "Do they even have those anymore? Probably do it with churn. Everything's different each time I come back."

Sam smiled, ignored the question. "My parents were both from Delhi, but they came over in the 1990s and were rocket scientists at ATK for years and years. It was a contractor for the Space and Rocket Center," Sam said.

"Whoa. Pardon me, but they must've been, like, ancient when they had you, right?"

"Mom was ninety-nine," said Sam. "Dad was a hundred."

"Love and rockets."

"First rockets, then love," Sam replied. "It was an arranged marriage. But they fell in love over the years." Sam flicked an ash. "Or so they told me."

"Rockets? Liquid hydrogen," said Coalbridge, shaking his head. "Out-of-control madness."

"It was what you had back then." Sam finished her cigarette and ground it out in the ashtray. She had long, delicate fingers. Clear polished nails. Her metal watchband tinkled against the ceramic as she drew her hand back. "Anyway, I grew up in Huntsville and went to college at Vandy—where I met Griff, by the way—and grad school in Atlanta. So, yeah, the accent kind of stuck."

"You've known Griff a long time?"

"Years and years."

"Are you in love with him?"

Sam had been digging for another cigarette from her pack, which she'd stuffed in his shirt's breast pocket. She did a double take, let the pack slide back down. "God, no, not anymore," she finally said. "Sort of. Doesn't matter."

"Why aren't you together then?"

This time Sam did pull out another cigarette. She carefully lit it before answering.

"I don't know that I can tell you," she said.

Coalbridge digested this for a moment. "Do you mean he has a problem... down there?"

Sam giggled. "No. I *can* speak to that. All systems are go with Griff. At least they were nine years ago."

"Then what? Something to do with that 'step on a crack, break your mother's back,' mindfuck he's got going on?"

"Yeah, something to do with that."

"Did that stuff hit him before or after the invasion?"

"After." Sam breathed out smoke, considered. "Why do you care? You barely know the man."

"True," Coalbridge replied. How much to tell her? She had a top-secret clearance, but was this in any way a need-to-know situation? He decided it was.

"I expect to know him much better," Coalbridge continued. "I requested him as the xenology specialist on my new command. It's been approved. Got a text on my Palace while we were... Anyway, I just checked it."

"You're leaving *tomorrow*?"

"Yes."

Sam seemed genuinely shocked—and worried. "Jim, what have you done? Griff doesn't *do* space. It's... it's part of the OCD thing."

Coalbridge shrugged. "He's in the Extry, isn't he?"

"Yes, but he's afraid of the vacuum. He calls it a permanent crack. And don't you get it? Griff can't send *postcards* when he's out in space."

"What are you talking about?"

"Didn't you notice the writing? It's how he calms himself."

"I guess I didn't get the whole show."

"He writes postcards. Constantly. And they don't count—not to him—unless he mails them."

"Who is he writing to? You?"

"To his son," Sam said.

"Oh, yeah, he mentioned a kid, now that I think of it."

"Theodore. Neddie."

"So he writes to Neddie? He can text him, or p-mail, leave it in the beta relay."

"Theodore is dead, Coalbridge."

"Huh?"

"Killed by the churn. Griff wasn't there." Sam took a long drag on her cigarette, breathed out over the red cherry end, fanning its flame further. "He was with me when it happened, actually."

"Oh, man."

"Yeah. Griff was separated from Bev at the time, but the divorce wasn't final. Theodore was convinced his parents were going to get back together, of course."

"Sure."

"He was supposed to have spent the weekend with Neddie," Sam said. "Instead, he begged off to spend the weekend having cheap sex with his new concubine."

"God," Coalbridge replied. "Is that why you two—"

"That's exactly why, Coalbridge." Sam brushed a stray hair from her eyes. Sadness. No tears.

She reached over to the table and tapped away her ash into an empty beer bottle.

"Look, Sam, I'm sorry about all that," Coalbridge said. "But that guy is one of the world's experts on sceeve psychology. Maybe the best there is. We're not dicking around out there."

"So let Griff figure it all out on Earth," Sam said. She finished her beer, set the bottle down on the wooden table with clunk. "Does he know about this yet?"

"I don't know."

"He's going to flip."

"Think he'll protest his orders?"

"If he does, he'll win," Sam said. "Griff used to be a hell of a lawyer."

So he'd been right after all in his first impression. Former JAG.

"He won't win. Not on this one. But he might hate me."

Sam considered. "If you convince him that you really need him ... he'll eventually find a way to be okay with it. He has methods. Ways around his limitations. The postcards are only one of them. For instance, he's like you. Crazy about cooking. That's funny, because I always was a terrible cook. Still can barely boil water. He promised to do all that when we ..." She shook her head. "He promised a lot of things back then."

"Sam, I need him. Or somebody exactly like him."

"You can't tell me what this is about, can you?"

"No," Coalbridge said.

"Is it something to do with the Poet?"

"I wouldn't ask for him if I didn't need him."

Sam took another long drag. The cigarette's wrapper crackled and browned. She flicked another ash, sat back, breathed out. Frowned. "Were you hoping *I* would talk to him? Is that why you ... called me?"

"Of course not." Coalbridge touched her chin, ran his finger along the curve of her cheek. *It wasn't, was it?* Coalbridge considered for a moment. "Not consciously," he said. "Will you?"

"Hell, no."

She punched him in the collarbone, hard enough to sting.

"Understood. All right, all right," he said. "And I promise that has *nothing* to do with my wanting to get in your pants." He put his hands around Sam's waist, drew her up. "Let me convince you."

He paused. Let her settle back in her chair.

"But it does occur to me," he said. "Do you think he's going to resent this? Us?"

"What *us*?" said Sam. "I'm headed back to Huntsville tomorrow, and you're about to be out there fighting sceeve."

"I mean, are you going to tell him about *this*?" Coalbridge fumbled for the right words. "You're still good friends...." He couldn't find a way to put it.

"Now that you mention it, maybe he should know I fucked his captain, don't you think?"

"Maybe. Depends. As you point out, I don't really know the guy."

"Yet you're willing to take him away from what he loves and put him through extreme personal turmoil."

"I'm more worried about you. The planet may not be here soon," Coalbridge answered. "Not in any recognizable form. I know it seems like we're losing it. Hell, we *are* losing it. But I plan to win. And the fact is that I don't speak sceeve and everybody else I know who says they do or who claims to understand the way those fuckers *think* is pretty much full of shit."

"If Griff says he does, he does."

"I read his report from the summer, his explanation for the withdrawal, that Depletion stuff, plus his analysis of the Poet broadcasts. He's confirming things that I thought nobody but me and my crew knew. I've seen the bastards up close and personal. There was no good human reason for that withdrawal. They were kicking our ass. And for the past eight years they have *not* been fighting as hard as they can, I'm sure of it. Griff Leher finally gave me a plausible reason why."

"Yes, I know," Sam said. "A copy *did* happen to fall into my hands by chance—"

But Coalbridge was lost in his train of thought and not paying attention. "The Depletion is the sceeve version of a massive energy tax. All forces called back to base and their power sources sucked dry. And then that energy directed toward winning a civil war with the Mutualists."

"I believe Griff suggests it was more like putting down an insurrection."

"Either way, *that's* why the invasion stopped, just like Griff says. I know he's right in my bones. The withdrawal had nothing to do with us. Fits with behavior I've seen with my own eyes. Predictable behavior is something I can use to kill more of them!"

He was getting excited thinking about the resource Griff Leher might actually turn out to be. They could win engagements with that kind of intel. To not *have* to go in fast, inflict what damage he could, and then hightail it away like a scared jackrabbit.

He could finally win!

"Okay, jeez," said Sam. "Enough about Griff. He had me and he lost me. You're welcome to him." She slid across from her chair and into his lap. "You've had your little break, Coalbridge," she whispered in his ear. "Now take me back into your bedroom."

"Or lose you forever?" Dumb. Dumbass to quote old movies nobody watched anymore. Even if it had been that old two-d movie that had made him want to join the navy back when he was a kid. Sam obviously didn't get the reference.

"Lose you forever?" She ran a lacquered fingernail across the sprouting whiskers of his chin. "Got a feeling that's a given with you and me." Sam glanced down at her watch. "Happy New Year, Coalbridge," she said.

Then she kissed him.

1 January 2076
Vicinity of Wolf 359

Sirius Armada Commander Admiral Vercimin Blawfus left wet footprints on the floor as he paced the fleet command deck of his flag vessel and considered his position. He'd ordered the armada to assume a classic half-sphere array with maximum flank alertness on the Sol-bound side of Wolf 359.

Space was large. Planets, even stars, were pinpricks within the vastness.

Space was large, true, yet Blawfus couldn't help feeling that he occupied a mighty position within it.

He had over ten thousand vessels at his command, and with a standard spread he would be able to approach with a two-AU cone of effect, depending how he had his forces fall out to N-space.

The slow cutting off and closing down of Sol had taken months. He'd first spread his forces in a blockade around the entirety of Sol, keeping a vanguard gathered about him on the Procyon, outbound side of the Orion arm. He'd harassed the humans ever inward toward their system. This had stretched his own concentration very thin, of course, but had proved effective. The humans were putting up a surprisingly effective resistance, and he took some casualties. But he was getting a seventy-percent kill rate on engagements, which was a more than satisfactory trade-off.

When it became clear the human fleet was mostly withdrawn to protect the home system, he'd issued a fleet-wide order to rendezvous at Wolf 359. Via relays and message drones, most vessels had gotten the order. A few were still straggling in.

He would have those stragglers under the dismemberment knives if they didn't provide a good explanation for their delay.

Blawfus liked nothing better than making a schedule and sticking to it.

For a time, it had seemed all his carefully laid plans must be thrown out the airlock. Blawfus had received orders—very threatening orders—to find and hunt down one of his own. *Or else.*

Councilor Gergen hadn't stated what the "or else" might be, but Blawfus had a fairly good idea. It was the same "or else" that had befallen his predecessor, Korlon Brand. You put yourself to the knives—or we will do it for you.

It was not a threat, but a promise. Gergen was a killer. One did not get on his bad side and live long.

The problem was, just as Ricimer's benighted letter to Gergen had stated, even if Ricimer were headed toward Sol, space was wide. Stars, much less planets, were grains of salt suspended within vast oceans of emptiness. Gergen was a politician, not a sailor. He might not understand that combing the sector for one vessel was delusional. In any case, one could never say as much to a political chancellor and member of the Civitas Council if one wanted one's *gid* to remain intact.

The *Guardian of Night* could be practically anywhere. Furthermore, Ricimer's threat to deliver his weapon to the humans might be a decoy. He might not be in this Sirius sector at all.

And yet. Signs pointed toward Sol. The Mutualist enclaves, those that had been found and destroyed, were all located down the Orion arm, toward Sol and beyond, hidden in nebulae and dark material nearer to the galactic center. And the annoying Poet, the beta-broadcasting traitor whose identity had recently been ascertained, had been caught transmitting to a *human* craft in the end.

Of one thing Blawfus was certain: a captain like Ricimer would be true to his word. He would think not merely to escape. He would want to strike a blow. Fight was built into the nature of Sporata captains, the good ones. Blawfus knew because he had been one himself.

Did he still have that fight within him?

He liked to think so.

All of these considerations left Blawfus with one locus he was quite certain wasn't hiding and wasn't going anywhere.

Sol C.

Blawfus's flag vessel, the *Indifference to Suffering*, was in the center of the classic hemisphere formation, as doctrine called for. She had only light defenses in place. Total readiness cost a great deal of difficult-to-replenish energy, and the idea was for the edges of the hemisphere to defend the center by concentrating fire on any encroacher. The vessels that made up the periphery rotated through four *tagatos*, about six human days, and everyone got to partially stand down at least half of the time.

So Blawfus had decided to risk Gergen's wrath and continue the invasion, use Sol system as bait for the *Guardian of Night*.

The full-scale invasion of Sol was therefore on. Whether or not his gamble paid off, this left Blawfus in a difficult situation politically. Ricimer, damn him, had seen to that, had probably intended it. After that captain's stunt, no one was going to trust a Sporata officer with tactical, much less strategic control, for many cycles going forward. Blawfus suspected the Sporata secretariat would soon be in civilian hands—which meant, effectively under total Civitas Council control.

Ever the politician, Blawfus had begun preparing himself for this certainty by spending most of his off-duty time with DDCM fleet officer Porhok, soaking up as much high grade Old Fifty-five and Cerlish Footwash as he could safely imbibe without exploding his urinary filtration organs. Porhok had, as a result, only overridden the most trivial of Blawfus's orders. Unfortunately, Blawfus's imbibing had also led to constantly damp feet—hence the trail of footprints wherever Blawfus trod.

Such indignity was a small price to pay.

As soon as he had his entire strength in place, he would descend upon the twice-cursed Sol system. He would net Ricimer, destroy his Mutualist allies, and, in the bargain, complete the conquest of Sol system that the Mutualist insurrection had so inconveniently interrupted. Or do it all in reverse order.

It mattered little, so long as he won.

So he would win. There was simply no other choice if he planned to survive.

Now, where were those cursed stragglers? It was time to attack.

TWELVE

18 January 2076
Vara Nebula Inbound
A.S.C. *Powers of Heaven*

Captain Cliff-clinging-icefall Malako stood in his bridge atrium and gazed at the view-screen representation of the down-arm portion of the Vara Nebula, his immediate destination.

Nearly a light-year in diameter, the Vara lay north of the Orion arm's axis, and thus out of the Milky Way clumping as seen from Procyon or any other star in this branch of the galaxy. For a hundred cycles it had been a hideout for pirates and illicit traders, until the Sporata had finally moved in and cleared the interstellar scum—this at about the time humanity was sorting out the fall of the Western Roman Empire. Now the Vara was a useful tool for Sporata vessels seeking a stealthy way in toward the galactic center.

Guardian scouts had mapped the nebula down to a precise resolution—on the order of a planetary orbit—and, with a bit of precise flying, a captain might direct his craft through using instrument-only travel relying on a map and zero external sensors. Even someone following who possessed the same map could not guess where his quarry was headed.

Most importantly to Malako at the moment, the Vara had been used as the invasion route for Sol C, for Earth.

Its inbound pathways all led to a sector about two light-years from Sol system, yet obscured in a starless patch of sky when seen from the galactic disk. So hidden was it, Malako did not believe the humans even knew of the Vara's existence before the war.

At the moment, Malako was fuming. The ammonia of supreme annoyance grew thick about him until he absentmindedly waved a hand to dissipate it, then fumed some more. He realized the entire bridge was beginning to reek of his disgruntlement, but he didn't care.

One *tagato* past, a messenger drone had intercepted the *Powers of Heaven* with new orders. Orders that Malako was loath to obey.

The fool Blawfus—middle of his class at the Academy, a hundred places below Malako, and *admiral of the Sirius armada* now, thanks to his political connections and Ur-hypha heredity—that idiot was attempting to draw Malako off the scent. Rein him in from the hunt. Malako knew he was on the trail of Ricimer. And now these orders in a message drone?

Break off current activities. Rendezvous at Wolf 359 immediately.

Vector directly across the Sol System Containment Sector, rendezvous with Sirius armada. Prepare for Sol C operation *en masse* attack. Unknown number and variety of Mutualist vessels may be rendezvousing and regrouping in unconquered, quarantined human territory. The *Guardian of Night*, now known to be traitorous, reported to be joining Sol forces.

"Now is the opportunity to eradicate all of our enemies in one powerful blow," Blawfus had said. "Let us not hesitate, but move forward and accomplish this task with the vigor of the unconquered and forever unconquerable instrument of Regulation."

Mutualism. A blind madness and unchecked political rage had taken over the highest levels of the Administration when the philosophy was mentioned. For the past five-cycle, the Administration, and hence the Sporata, had reacted to the slightest hint of it as an immune system reacts to an allergen. The response was always, predictably, colossal, always out of any proportion to what Malako believed was the threat. Certainly, the philosophy was crackpot and the remnant of true believers who remained ought to be stamped out. But the galaxy held greater challenges.

Such as hunting down traitors and thieves. *Cunning* traitors. Thieves of *massively powerful* technological gleanings. Real threats.

Malako was more than half convinced that Ricimer had engineered the current uproar over Mutualism as a ruse. And he was certain that the Poet, the traitor Gitaclaber, had been acting for Ricimer, either wittingly or unwittingly, stirring up Mutualist sentiment in the armada—and then traitorously broadcasting news of a Mutualist rendezvous to the humans.

Ricimer, curse him, had *personally recommended* Gitaclaber to Malako to be his communications officer.

That's right, Malako, your supposed friend of the gid, *your own brother-in-arms and dear companion Arid Ricimer, has screwed you over.*

Why did you not expect as much? Trust the purebred hypha lines to always seek to use and abuse hybrids such as yourself. Trust that your leg markings are constantly on display, uniform or not. He'd believed Ricimer to be different, above all that. Had allowed himself to be convinced in his own loneliness, his own isolation. Another cursed mistake.

Malako was done being the butt-end of purebred ruses.

And now Ricimer had the Kilcher artifact.

Could he, in his delusion, think to use it as a bargaining chip for power? No, not even a lunatic would believe the Administration would ever willingly cede one iota of its centralized control. Did Ricimer intend to establish his own outlaw enclave? Mate again, produce offspring, and found a new hypha line? Malako had at first taken it that Ricimer's stated goal to join the humans was nonsense. But perhaps not. Perhaps the fool had been telling the truth.

Which meant that the Poet's broadcast—maybe all of them— likely contained other information for the humans. Something more than a final plea for help before he was spaced.

If only he could personally question the scumbag, Malako knew he would be able to wring the information out of the Poet. But that was no longer an option—thanks to yet another arrogant, purebred fool.

The portal to the bridge slid open and two security officers entered, dragging between them the object of Malako's most immediate ire.

Receptor Transel.

"What is the meaning of this, Captain?" Transel squirted as soon as he caught sight of Malako. "In the name of the Directorate, I demand these officers release me."

Malako sighed wearily and stepped from his atrium. He motioned for the guards to drag Transel to stand before him.

The DDCM officer grunted as he was jerked forward and put into place. Malako, who was a half hand taller than Transel, stared down at him.

"You have forfeited the authority of the Directorate with your recent actions," Malako said. "You have put this vessel and the armada in danger by your rashness, and I have been forced to invoke Verdict Three Protocols—"

"Verdict Three?" Transel sprayed forth a repugnant carbolic cloud of amazement. "Verdict Three! *I* am the only officer aboard authorized to enforce Verdict Three protocols. This is insubordination of the highest order!"

"Now, that's not quite true," Malako answered calmly. "Regulation states that when the craft receptor displays behavior that might otherwise lead to a culling offense, the vessel sub-receptor"—Malako flared his muzzle into a smile—"that would be *me*, is authorized to apply Verdict Three protocols in such a way as to eliminate that threat, up to and including confinement of craft receptor under such circumstances."

"You must have medical officer and Governess approval!"

"True, except under contingency of immediate threat."

"What threat?" screamed Transel. "I eliminated the threat myself when I tossed the traitor out the airlock!"

"Just that," Malako replied. "As captain, I've become convinced that Mutualist vessels are indeed in the vicinity and intent on massive insurrection. I can only conclude that your reason for spacing the traitor Gitaclaber was to cover up your own part in this conspiracy."

"What!" Transel's exclamation emerged from his nasal passages in a half-formed, snotty effusion that dribbled down his face.

"The logic that leads me to this conclusion is crystal clear," Malako said. "I'm left no choice but to invoke Verdict Three protocols."

Suddenly Transel laughed. "I understand. I understand you now," he said. "He was your friend. He was your friend, this Ricimer. You're going to ignore orders. You're not going to rejoin the armada. You're going to continue the hunt for the *Guardian of Night* on your own."

"Be careful what you say, Transel."

"Yes, that's it! You hope to wipe the stain of your association with this Ricimer away by personally capturing or destroying him." Another hysterical laugh issued from Transel. "You black-striped spawn of impurity—you really think you will be forgiven? They're going to strip you of command, Malako. And after that, they will likely strip you of your life. Your *gid* will be burst and spread into emptiness!"

Malako motioned to the guards who held Transel. "Place Receptor Transel in the bridge holding chamber," he said.

"May your seed disappear from the stars!"

With a motion of Malako's foot against a nubbin of metal next to his atrium, a section of the bridge deck opened up, uncovering a narrow space five hands wide and fifteen hands deep. The holding chamber was a long-established feature of Sporata design that was now seldom used. It was a legacy of the ancient Guardian days of smuggling and piracy, the time, more than a thousand cycles ago, before the hypha had been united, before the finalization of Regulation. The chamber's purpose was to provide an area off the vessel's scanned grid for secret cargo to be carried—and to serve as a brig where dangerous passengers or crew might be tucked away during transport. Malako—and most captains, he was well aware—used the chamber to smuggle home bits of stolen technology from conquered species, technology they would later sell on the Souk, the Shiro black market, to supplement their income and provide incentive bonuses for their officers. The practice was endemic to the Sporata and considered by officers as necessary to buy the necessities that a reasonable standard of living required back in the Shiro. The Administration was known for constantly underpaying the military and transferring the lion's share of Depletion energy credits to the upper-level bureaucrats of the departments and committees.

I'll finally be putting the holding chamber to the use for which it was intended, Malako thought. He nodded his head in the direction of the hole in the deck. "Put him in there," Malako said.

The guards dragged Transel kicking and squirting imprecations to the chamber and, with a quick shove forward, forced him in. Before the receptor could claw his way up, Malako touched the opening toggle again with his foot, and the deck plate—half a hand thick—slid shut, immediately cutting off the flow of Transel's words. Blessed silence returned to the bridge.

"You two are dismissed," Malako said. "I do not believe our unfortunate former receptor will require further restraint."

"Thrive the Administration, sir," the guards answered in unison. They saluted, turned, and left the bridge.

Malako walked over and stood on top of the holding chamber covering. He wondered if he would be able to perceive the motion of Transel below. He was sure the DDCM officer was kicking up quite a fuss down there in the darkness. Malako had no intention of letting the receptor out until he'd successfully completed this mission and returned to the Shiro. Transel would be able to survive for several *tagato* without sustenance. Guardians were a tough species, bred for the starkness of space. And after that?

Whatever he says or does either won't matter or I'll be dead, Malako thought. In either case, Transel was finished as a threat to derail Malako from his desire. His destiny. His pleasure.

To hunt down and destroy the traitor Ricimer.

His friend.

The Poet had provided the answer. Whether or not Malako could decode the Poet's message, he had no doubt that the humans were somehow complicit in the disappearance of the *Guardian of Night*. Ricimer was behind the Poet, and the Poet had been attempting to relay information to a human vessel of espionage, a vessel Malako had been ordered by Transel to destroy.

He did not have the Poet, but he did have the transmission. He would find the trail there, he was sure of it. In the meantime, he must avoid rejoining the armada. And to circumvent that order, he would keep Transel stowed away for as long as it took.

"Captain, we are within ten *vitias* of the down-arm Vara Nebula," said Malako's navigator.

Malako turned his attention back to the bridge view-screen panels.

"Take us to the Tau Ceti gate," said Malako. This ingress and egress point took its name from the brightest star that one making the traverse could see as he exited the central pathway through the nebula. There were three such tunnel-like openings into the bowels of the nebula, and Malako judged that the middle tunnel exit would be as good a rendezvous point as any for Ricimer and the Mutualists. It is where *he* would stage such a meeting, after all, were he a rebel commander.

Suddenly, a scented alarm squirted from the bridge bulkhead. "Alert, alert. Vessel ahead."

Malako's muzzle tightened. "Really?" he said. "Analysis, VISION?"

"She's a large trader," said Lieutenant Raripan, Malako's officer in charge of remote sensing. "Beta is all over the place. Captain, I believe we have located a Mutualist vessel."

"Very well," said Malako. "NAV, drop us in on the very edge of conditioning range. I want full vessel silence."

"Aye, Captain."

"SIGNAL, check with Lamella. Have we got the *Guardian of Night* identification key?"

"Computer reports we have it logged, sir."

Malako touched a hand to his lower muzzle, stroked a membrane, considering. Yes, it would work. The Mutualist captain was not a trained warrior. He would expect nothing.

"Very well, SIGNAL," said Malako. "I want you to identify us as the *Guardian of Night* to that vessel. Has she got a name?"

"She's tweeting as the *Efficacy of Symbiosis*, sir."

"How quaint," said Malako. "Send the identification signal."

"Aye, Captain."

"Sir, if I may." It was Raripan at the VISION station.

"Yes?"

"I'm registering a large contingent of occupants on the vessel. They're packed in there."

"Species?"

"Us, sir. Guardians. Many sizes, fluid dispersal rates showing up." Raripan looked up from his readout. "I would interpret this is as children, families. Sensors indicate over five thousand individuals."

"Identification acknowledged," said SIGNAL. "They are asking why we are here and not at the designated rendezvous location at Vara Eridani."

Amazing. Utter amateurs. How had the Mutualist resistance held out for one *variado*, much less for an entire two cycles?

Malako shifted his head into a Guardian nod. "Take us toward them NAV. Slowly. SIGNAL, keep bleating. Tell them ... tell them we have engine problems. Tell them the artifact has interfered with the Q-drives and computing systems. We may require assistance."

"Aye, Captain. Transmitting."

"Captain, there are more than five thousand people on that vessel."

"Thank you for the information, VISION."

Raripan took a step toward Malako. He was smallish, a bit of a nebbish who had long relegated himself to sensor duty. "But, Captain, you must consider all those lives—"

"*Efficacy* replies again," SIGNAL reported. "Explain why not at rendezvous. Why not at Vara Eridani gate?"

The Eridani gate of the Vara Nebula. The rendezvous point with the *Guardian*. He had it.

"Captain, please consider a surrender request." A florid odor. Raripan's irritating perfumery of feeling was leaking into his words.

Malako turned, stared into Raripan's eyes. "You forget yourself, Lieutenant," he said. "Do not make me remind you of your position within the craft command structure by ordering a full shriving. Is protecting a load of Mutualist scum really worth your career? Your life?"

Raripan looked as if he might take another step, might even charge Malako. But he faltered. Stood still. After a moment, he returned to his work station. Malako almost forced him to say "no, sir" in answer but decided against pushing the matter further. Raripan had rediscovered his position well enough.

"WEAPONS, load our rocks. All slings. Half throw weight."

"Done, sir."

"Very well, very well." Malako waited. Curse N-space. It took so long sometimes to get within throwing range.

"*Efficacy* is putting on speed toward us, Captain," said Raripan.

"Happy to see us, I suppose," said Malako to no one in particular. "Are we in range, WEAPONS?"

"In three, two, one—range, sir."

"Then throw."

And the rocks were away. Blips on Malako's screen. So slow, they seemed. Many kilometers to cross.

Converging with the bright dot that represented the *Efficacy*.

So happy to see you, too.

Converging.

Converged.

Across the bridge, a half-squirt of sandalwood anguish from Raripan, quickly repressed, fanned away.

And the *Efficacy* and its thousands of souls were blasted to smithereens. Destroyed without firing a shot in her own defense.

"Perfect," Malako said. He turned to NAV. "Now take us to the Vara Eridani gate. We'll wait there." Malako ran a gripping gill along his atrium's guardrail.

And then I'll have you, Ricimer.

Five thousand Mutualists. If he'd accepted surrender, he'd have had to escort the vessel to captivity.

Not a chance. Not now.

Five thousand essentially useless traitors, destined for the dismemberment knives in any case.

Not a bad sacrifice to catch one extremely dangerous Sporata traitor. The Mutualists had chosen their doom long before, after all. He was merely an instrument, carrying out orders.

Wasn't he?

Silence on the bridge. Malako looked around. No one met his gaze.

Wasn't he?

As usual, Malako took refuge in the thrill of the chase. It was all he had. What he wouldn't let anyone take away.

I'll have you, and I'll blast you from the sky for what you have made me become, Arid Ricimer.

I know where you are hiding.

THIRTEEN

1 January 2076
New Pentagon
Skyhook Capture Platform

There was no doubt—the Skyhook could be a hell of a rattling experience for the uninitiated. It was disconcerting enough for Coalbridge, and he was a jaded veteran of the process at this point. The enormous apparatus had been a sceeve instrument of war—their most devastating—but was now converted to a cheap, incredibly efficient method of transportation by humans.

First, of course, it had to be taken from the sceeve. That task had cost thousands of lives in itself. A fleet-sized assault on the command center, with the sceeve defenses firing back in full force—drop-rod clouds launched at relativistic velocities, antimatter devices delivered inside missiles harder than the hardest diamond, Q-bottled nukes that exploded with massive destructive energy in their atomic unravelings. Whole crafts, along with their crews, had blinked out of existence in an instant during the onslaught.

Of course, the battle had been nothing in comparison with the devastation the Skyhook had wrought on Earth.

The Skyhook was, in essence, a rotating windmill of destruction. It used the same principle as a space elevator. If you suspend a super-strong cable out into space far enough—with its center in geosynchronous orbit—it will hang in the sky. Such a construction

157

will not be pulled down by gravity but will "fall around the Earth" in the same way that satellites do.

You can then build infrastructure on the cable, which is as stable as anything else on the planet, and have yourself an elevator, transport pipes for life-support, power-boosting, and transfer stations along the way—all the makings of a massive transportation corridor.

But if you accelerate the ends of such a cable, twirl the cable like a baton around a giant invisible finger at its center, if you make it a little *longer* than geosynch to the Earth's surface, you get...

Death from the sky. A weapon capable of carving a canyon-sized trough through the landscape.

The Skyhook had been constructed within the solar system, out of material gathered from the asteroid belt—an asteroid belt that was now ten percent less dense than it had been before. It was homegrown terror. Applied like a diamond-tipped scourge to the Earth's surface, it had reworked much of the landscape of Central Asia, destroyed Europe and Russia, cut South America to shreds, and turned the entire Far East into a beaten, striated wasteland, with entire portions remade, new mountains and valleys formed. Billions had died. Entire cities had been hacked out of existence by a massive knife from the sky.

What was most insidious and terrible was the fact that the Skyhook was maneuverable. It could be used multiple times.

The apparatus moved slowly—its mass was that of a Galilean moon and required incredible motive force, even by sceeve standards, to budge it—but it was possible to reposition. In fact, it precessed naturally by its own gyroscopic force, and, with additional impetus from massive N-space, mass-driving engines, it was possible for the Skyhook to destroy, say, Beijing in January of 2067, and then Seoul the following February. It was not only possible. It had happened. The sceeve aimed for capitals, for centers of government, and not industrial areas. The industrials were the resources they were after—and the reason they did not simply destroy the Earth entirely.

Coalbridge had led a portion of the raid to take the Skyhook central hub. The team had been small enough to be under the command of a lowly lieutenant commander of the Extry, and he'd been chosen. It had been a daring plan. A single-man craft deployment that approached from beyond the orbit of the Moon, scattered, slowly closing in. Most of his team of ten was made up of former SEALs, Marine expeditionary units, and transferred members from other special-assault groups from various branches of the armed forces. Coalbridge, as former mainstream navy, figured he'd been given command of the assault team by virtue of his reputation for pulling together disparate disciplines and congealing a team during his days as a defensive-weapons officer onboard the ancient surface-ship aircraft carrier the *Gerald R. Ford.* Coalbridge, despite the drumming of engineering discipline he'd received in IAS at Houston, had always been something of a generalist and had a real curiosity in all areas of warfare.

Most of all, there had not been a moment in his life when he did not *want* to win, even if the attempt seemed hopeless.

And this mission was practically the definition of hopeless.

His team had been scattered into position over two weeks before, set adrift individually by a tiny unmanned craft that had then quietly destroyed itself.

And then, they'd floated. Their suits fed them nutrients through an I.V., processed their waste. On they floated. Separated by tens of thousands of miles. Slowly making their way toward the central hub of the rotating Skyhook.

The idea was to distract the Skyhook defense with a massive assault coming from Earthside, while the actual boarding team approached from the relatively quiet spaceward direction.

Their assault suits were all they wore. Propulsion was hydrazine, a single-thruster. Slow but steady. Minimal physics profile, a Newtonian approach all the way. The sceeve had an accurate and deadly detection mechanism—most of which was not understood at the time—for Q.

Things had started to go wrong early and often. Telemetry on one marine's suit had scizzed out. She'd attempted to plot a course herself, had gotten an input backward—and had headed out to deep space. A minesweeper had found her months later, frozen solid and on the way to Venus, trailing the faint vapor trail of a human comet.

Throughout, the marine—

Her name had been Allison something, Coalbridge remembered. Wessel? Yes.

—Wessel had maintained beta silence, even though there was a transmitter built into the suits. Amazing willpower not to call for help even as she was dying. Coalbridge wasn't sure if he could've pulled it off.

The suit transceivers had been a bad idea all around, however. One member of the assault team had gone bat-shit crazy while spending days cooped up in a suit flying through nothingness. McGary, a former SEAL master chief. He'd been the least-likely candidate to lose it, but lose it he had. And, in his madness, he'd decided to reach out. He'd begun to scream and hadn't stopped for two hours, his transmitter permanently keyed to transmit. Finally, almost mercifully, Coalbridge had been able to triangulate on him and fire a single laser shot from an arm-mounted weapon. The light traveled across emptiness for nearly thirty seconds before it reached McGary, cut through him like a sword, and silenced him forever.

Coalbridge had killed human beings before, but only from the confines of an aircraft weapons center. Never so up close and personal—even if out here up close and personal meant a thirty light-second distance.

And so they'd been eight when they arrived at the Skyhook Hub. Eight against a full crew of sceeve and their associated computational intelligences. But they had arrived undetected, despite McGary's outburst. They'd latched on to the exterior of the hub with gecko-like tethers.

They'd deployed their entry explosives, gotten inside, and unleashed the real secret weapon.

DAFNE. The latest iteration of the servant computer virus that had been modified to take on the sceeve military nanotech. After DAFNE had saved Earth from the churn, she'd created the foundation for the Pacific Wall, the combination of reprogrammed sceeve nanotech, human-created churn, and very real naval warcraft with their electronics and newly forged sceeve-based weaponry. The Wall kept the sceeve invasion confined to Asia on the Pacific side, and to northern Europe and the Middle East. Australia had its own version and had held out, although New Zealand was lost. Africa had been saved.

Not that the Peepsies give us any credit for that, Coalbridge thought, remembering the accusations of the Peepsie punk the day before. Just creating a pool of cheap labor.

The punk was likely dead, Coalbridge reminded himself. Beyond crediting or blaming another now. Silent forever.

It turned out that humanity's ace in the hole was subversive computer programming. Yet DAFNE's personality was nothing like the amoral, emotionless spy he'd imagined. Instead, she was actually a happy sort.

Which was maybe not a surprise when you learned that DAFNE had started her life as the controlling artificial-intelligence algorithm on a roller coaster at Six Flags Over Georgia.

DAFNE had torn down the Skyhook's churn defenses as if they were so many gauze curtains. From there, she'd invaded the Skyhook's dual computer system, turning one part of the sceeve "brain" against the other.

In many ways, his eight-man team's physical invasion was merely a mopping-up operation. Nevertheless, it had been intense. He'd made mistakes, hadn't understood the difference between sceeve officers and enlisted—at least that was how he thought of the two classes. One was chained to the computer system, and was sluggish when disconnected, unable to take initiative—at least for the crucial first ten minutes of the raid.

The officers were a different story. They were individuals, clearly not under computer control. They were well trained. And they'd proved almost unkillable.

The team had gone for headshots on Coalbridge's instructions. Unbelievable. Nobody had known at the time that the head was practically a sceeve's least vulnerable spot. Individual sceeve didn't have "brains" as organs. To take out a sceeve quickly, you needed to shoot it in the black-colored organ, the *gid hanasheh* as the creeps had translated the sceeve designation for it, located in the chest.

"Shoot low and take out the *gid*."

He'd said these words so many times since, but that day—the day when it first counted—he hadn't known to say them. And half his team died as a result.

So he'd discarded his rifle and drawn his officer's truncheon. It was a cross between a cop's nightstick and a cattleprod—but filled with a very nasty combination of churn-based attack nano, a high-voltage electric charge, and a tiny dollop of antimatter. A trunch set to high would cut through any material known to man.

Including sceeve organs. Especially sceeve organs.

And after the team killed twenty very surprised sceeve officers— all of whom had fought to the death, using either the effective sceeve sidearm, later named the painter, or, as a last resort, their ceremonial knives of rank—the Skyhook was his. Property of the United States of America.

Coalbridge had made his name in the Extry with that one, although he'd had to suffer through an inquest due to his large casualty rate. His name was merely mentioned as one of the "attacking soldiers" in the Earth news media. Too much secret equipment and tactics had been in use, and command was deathly afraid—with good cause—that the sceeve would rapidly figure out how the feat had been done and guard against it.

The Skyhook was captured, its devastating attacks halted, and it could now be repositioned for human use as an orbital-transport mechanism with a far lower energy cost than any before available.

And he was about to use that transport he and his force had secured in—Coalbridge looked at his watch—T minus ten minutes seventeen seconds and counting.

The "collection" team he'd sent to Leher's apartment bustled in with the personal effects he'd sent them after, as well as the sceeve "printer" that Leher had requested.

Now where the hell was Leher? Had he decided to miss his hook, after all? Coalbridge considered for a moment that maybe he'd misjudged Leher. He'd thought that presenting the new assignment as a challenge—and as a choice—would intrigue Leher enough to engage him in his new job.

Well, if he doesn't come, we've got all his stuff.

The exper crew finished loading two suitcases of Leher's personals into the puck.

The puck was officially called the Planet to Orbit Delivery Enclosure. It was a single craft with a froth of Q-bottle pseudo-gravitational stabilizers, only a few of which were "real," and most of which were created by a virtual chain of imaginary entanglement, on all sides of the passengers and cargo. When you got inside, you had left Earth's gravitational field for all intents and purposes.

Which was good, because when the Skyhook came down to snag the gimlet on top of the puck, if there was no Q weirdness in place, passenger and cargo would be smeared along one wall like a micro-thin pancake due to the sudden and extreme acceleration, akin to being fired out of a cannon at ten times the speed of sound. As it was, the initial jerk and takeoff were rough enough. The bottle dampers were controlled by a feedback algorithm, since the random currents of the atmosphere were beyond even a quantum computer's ability to accurately predict.

Coalbridge wouldn't vouch for what would happen if these particular bottle dampers passed through a Texas thunderstorm, either. Things could go wrong with this method of transport. They had.

The puck looked like just that—a giant black hockey puck with an eyehook on top. The Skyhook's end held an open grappling hook that latched into the puck and . . .

Away you'd go.

The platform was a simple corrugated-steel structure built on the flattened field of what had once been the southwest corner of the Texas Instruments corporate campus. It was heavily reinforced on the spin side—the side designed to catch the next puck when it came back down in its counterclockwise direction—but the catch mechanism had been lowered for the uptake of the currently operational puck on the platform.

Like the deck of an old-time aircraft carrier, the platform was spare, utilitarian, and dangerous to be around if you didn't know what you were doing. All very low-tech and Newtonian. Unlike a carrier, there were no attendants. No guardrails. Nothing but the derrick-like structure and a warning signal that was a repurposed traffic light.

For Coalbridge the setup itself was exhilarating.

The traffic light mounted on a pole at the edge of the platform changed from green to yellow, marking five minutes until the hook arrived. It was time to load into the puck.

Where the hell was Leher?

Coalbridge motioned for his crew members to get aboard. He stood on the platform's edge and craned his neck out to see the concrete enclosure that housed the elevator that led to the actual New Pentagon complex belowground.

Finally, the elevator door slid open. Leher emerged, followed by two creep expers who were lugging big suitcase-like containers. Leher himself was carrying a briefcase that had been hastily closed and still had the edges of documents poking out. Sceeve documents, from the looks of them.

"Hurry up, Lieutenant Commander!" Coalbridge yelled. "The Skyhook waits for no man!"

Leher trotted across the fifty feet separating the elevator house from the Skyhook platform and huffed up the stairs, his helpers following after.

"You expect us to bring all that?" Coalbridge said. "We'll have to space a couple of crew for that kind of baggage!"

"This is the absolute minimum I need for a proper Xeno station," Leher said breathlessly. "You have no idea the value of what I'm leaving behind."

Coalbridge eyed the load for a moment, then nodded his head.

"All right, damn it, pack that crap into the puck, you guys, and hurry up with it. We've got"—again he checked his watch—"three minutes and fifty-two seconds before we're blown to bits by a sonic explosion when that hook gets here."

His words put a spring in the creeps' steps, and they soon had Leher's suitcases on board.

The traffic light turned to red.

"Two minutes," said Coalbridge. "You gentlemen need to get off the platform." The creep expers—Coalbridge noticed belatedly that one was *not* a gentleman at all, and fairly curvaceous—scurried away. Coalbridge turned to Leher, who was facing the door to the puck but had not made a move to enter. "Mr. Leher, it's time to catch our ride."

When Leher didn't answer, Coalbridge looked closer. Leher was trembling.

Rumble. A small, dark line in the northeastern sky. The Skyhook was descending.

"Leher. Griff. We have to go!"

He took Leher by the arm, but the other man shook him off. "No," Leher squeaked.

"Yes!" Coalbridge took Leher firmly by the shoulders, spun him around, and looked him in the eyes. "I swear to God we'll find this Poet for you and let you talk to him in person. Or I'll catch another of those sceeve fuckers. This billet will be worth your while. I'll see to it. How's that? Griff!"

Coalbridge gave Leher a shake for good measure.

The rumble increased, and Coalbridge felt a pressure wave building in the air about him. His ears popped.

The line in the northwest grew into a shadow-stripe perpendicular in the sky.

Leher shuddered, seemed to come back to himself from a long

way off. "Talk to one," he said. "I think I could do that. I think I really could pull it off."

"Come on, Leher."

"You stood up to Tillich," Leher said. Coalbridge tugged on Leher, and the other let him lead him to the door. "You're not an idiot."

"No, I'm not," Coalbridge said. "We have to get inside!"

With a final shove, Coalbridge got Leher into the puck, and he dove in after. The door sealed behind them and disappeared as the embedded churn quickly did its hermetic work. The other expers had already taken their seats within and fastened their seat belts. Coalbridge sat Leher into an empty slot, clicked him in as he would a child—

"Five seconds," said a calm female voice.

"You're not an idiot," Leher said, nodding and agreeing with himself vehemently. "People do this all the time. This is going to be all right."

Coalbridge bounded over to his own seat, latched in.

His hand found the built-in handles on either side of him. He wrapped his fingers around them. . . .

The rumble outside, even muffled by the ultrahard composite material of the puck that surrounded them, grew to a freight-train roar.

The interior of the puck was utilitarian. Rough black wall and floor, exactly the texture of a hockey puck. Bolted-in seats that looked like they could've come out of an ancient airliner and probably had. Window plexiglass stretching around the cylindrical walls at about eye-level when seated, but now covered by exterior blast shields. A couple of fluorescent lights in metal cages on the ceiling.

"Pseudogravity engaged," said the computer voice. "Contact in three, two, one—"

BAM!

Coalbridge's stomach got a jolt—the sudden rush of ultimate acceleration that couldn't quite be quelled by gravitational dampers, not by technology. It was primal. The PG gripped him in place and dampened the inertia shift enough to keep him from coming apart, but Coalbridge felt a lurch within him, as if a sudden high tide were running through one side of his body and a neap tide through the other. It was the greatest carnival ride in history, and he had a ticket!

Arcing up. Though his speed remained constant, Coalbridge felt the curve of acceleration, the delta-v of exhilaration.

And then the containment bottle fully engaged and the windows opened. He could see!

Mighty Earth curving away below, perceptibly growing smaller, more distant.

He was going back to his real home. He was getting his own command! And he was riding a bronco all the way up to the stars.

"Good God." Leher was staring out in horror, hyperventilating. "Oh no, no."

He glanced over at Coalbridge. "You killed me! We're dead!"

"You're not going to die, Commander." Coalbridge had to speak loudly. The puck rumbled like a train through the lower stretches of the atmosphere. After they left the air behind, all would be quiet inside and out. "At least we're not going to die *here*."

Leher looked at Coalbridge, wild-eyed. The others in the puck carefully turned their gazes away, content to let Coalbridge handle this minor drama.

"We're not?" said Leher.

"No," said Coalbridge. "Hold on. It'll be over soon. Let me enjoy this, will you?"

Leher gulped, squeaked out "Okay."

Three and a half hours later, the puck was at the apogee of its rise, 52,398 miles above the Earth's surface and the other end of the Skyhook's reach.

"Release in ten seconds," the calm computer voice announced. All of the details of the puck's release were handled by the crew in the Skyhook hub and the servants, whose physical programming was spread out in the churn.

Leher suddenly looked up. "What if it doesn't release?" he blurted out. "Would we just keep going around and around and around?" He put his hand over his mouth. His beard over the greenish cast to his face made his head look like a moldy, rotten mango to Coalbridge.

"Don't worry." Coalbridge pointed toward the puck's ceiling. "See that yellow loop?"

There was, rather absurdly, a small plastic loop colored bright yellow dangling from the roof of the puck.

Leher glanced up. "Yes."

"Emergency release."

"What? Somebody could just *pull* it?"

Coalbridge smiled. "No. Yanking on it won't do anything unless you know the code phrase for the day."

"Nobody told me the code phrase!" Leher said. "What if I have to pull it?"

"You won't," said Coalbridge. "It's senior officer aboard's task."

"So you know it?"

"Yep."

Pain. Brain. Insane. Blackout. Somebody was having fun coming up with such stuff back in Richardson. If he spoke the phrase clearly, pulling the strap would activate a manual release of the puck that would send it flying off on whatever vector it happened to be on at a given moment.

"It's meant to be used only in a downswing and take us in for a crash landing on Earth."

"So we'd basically dig our own graves?"

"We'd be protected by the pseudogravity bottles upon impact. Might possibly survive."

The computer voice again. "Separation in three, two, one—separation."

And they were off. After a moment of floating, the puck's interior pseudogravity asserted itself convincingly.

"Acceleration's over, Leher, if that's what was bothering you. We're on a constant vector all the way in to Walt Whitman."

Leher nodded weakly. "Now we're only suspended over a total abyss."

Coalbridge looked out a window. Earth was a sphere that he could cover with his thumb. They were traveling laterally with it now, so it would grow no smaller on their trip to the space station.

He pointed down. "Still gets to me to be up here, see it there, so far away."

Leher risked a glance out. "Gets to me, too."

The puck continued traveling in a straight line for another half hour and slammed home into the Walt Whitman's catch bay, an enormous apparatus of high-tension wire and buckeyball carbon that did indeed resemble a goalie's mitt.

Walt Whitman was the transfer station from the Skyhook and housed the enormous supply depot for materials shipped up from Earth. This was the place Extry craft came to be made ready and fitted out.

This was where Coalbridge's new command, his craft, the *Joshua Humphreys,* awaited, and Coalbridge tried to catch a glimpse of her as they came in. She'd been out for a thruster test the day before, he'd heard. But today she was firmly ensconced in a launch bay, and he could not see her.

Or, rather, he could only see her in his mind's eye, where she'd been the three weeks since he'd learned that she was to be his to command.

An Extry frigate. Not a patrol craft, not a surveyor. A craft fitted for war and no other purpose. Decked out in a fully supported, official servant system which was a direct copy of the last iteration of DAFNE Coalbridge had served with. The *Humphreys* was waiting for him. He was her captain.

Coalbridge glanced over at his green-faced companion. Leher was hunched head-down, frantically scribbling out a postcard.

My own *secret, God help us,* Coalbridge thought. *Well, you make do with what the universe sends your way, I suppose.*

Leher glanced up, tugged three times at his beard, then went back to writing.

FOURTEEN

10 January 2076
Vicinity of Sirius
Guardian of Night

Ricimer stood as Lieutenant Commander Hadria Talid entered his captain's stateroom and joined the gathered officers for the evening mess. The craft cabins were confined, even on such a vessel as the *Guardian of Night,* and it was customary when someone entered for both parties to move around a bit to clear the air for conversation. No matter how absorptive the walls, there were always stray words hanging about in such close quarters, and it was important for a captain to say what he meant.

The chairs of the dining area were arranged in a square, with Ricimer taking up one entire side—at the head of the table, as it were, although there was no table—and two or three of his officers seated in feeding chairs on the other three sides of the square's perimeter. Between them all on the floor of the cabin was square-shaped trough, like a small wading pool, whose inside was filled with a gellike feeding solution that would have smelled musty and woodsy to a human. All of the officers dipped their legs up to the ankle joints into the trough and absorbed sustenance through the gills on the bottom of their feet.

These officers were the product of many *molts* of selection. He must have officers to help him carry out his plans, but he could not afford to make one mistake in his choice. It had been harrowing. He'd spent hours poring over files, asking innocuous questions, trying to arrive at an officer's true disposition. But it had all been worth it.

The proof was before him. No one had turned him in. Here they all were, in this up to their necks. Even if one were a plant, he or she must know that to turn back now would mean his or her death. Things had gone too far.

Yet they were frightened. Which was good—it was a display of intelligence to be frightened in such circumstances. He must use the fear, however, and not let it overcome them. This had always been his task as captain, and was now as much as ever.

"The refugees selected as rate replacements are coming along all right, but our other guests are growing restless in the cargo hold," Talid informed him after the first "course" of appetizer fluid sloshed out over their feet. "They've requested a corridor pass to obtain exercise and an exhaust fan to clear the air in the hold once a day."

Ricimer sat back and ran a palm along his cheek—a sign of Guardian contemplation as it was with humans. "I believe that should be possible," he answered. "But remember it is taking all of Lamella's ability to train our new rates at an accelerated speed. If the others leave the hold, they'll inevitably cause distractions for our new crew. This must be done in a limited and orderly fashion."

"I told their spokesperson as much, but he insisted I take the matter you, sir."

"You did rightly, of course," Ricimer said. "But let's forget craft business for a while, Hadria, and enjoy our meal."

"I'll try, Captain."

"I was sure these Mutualists would become a problem, and so they have," said Maram Cadj, Ricimer's communications director. Cadj was an ensign who ought to have long ago been promoted to lieutenant. But he'd once drawn a crude graffiti image of an Administration Depletion collector on a Shiro bulkhead. When he was four cycles old. This had been a blot on his record ever since, and had been the reason for his lack of advancement. "They have become a major body ache for all of us. Was this rendezvous and transfer really necessary, Captain?"

Ricimer turned to the communications officer sharply but held in his irritation. Had he just not asked to change the subject?

But Cadj was dogged, a quality that he brought to his work, as well. You could not punish a person for being true to his or her own nature.

"It was," Ricimer said. "Unless you would have had me massacre our former crew." Ricimer smiled, stroked his cheek. "And it could be we are doing the right thing, maybe."

Several of the other officers nodded, but not all. He hoped at least his utilitarian argument had convinced them. But it didn't ultimately matter. What was done was done. The Mutualists were aboard.

"We are headed to a new home, friends, and a new fight," Ricimer said. "It is a great experiment we are trying. You should all feel proud to be such pioneers."

This time agreeing nods from all. A moment of silence. Then Contor, Ricimer's N-based weapons officer, sloshed his feet about, sighed, spoke. "I will have a computer with a firewall," he said. "I will be able to look out through it, but no one else can look in or override what I am doing. Can you imagine? For many, many *tagatos*, I will play *Storm-sword Saga* unmolested."

"Play it until you are so sick of it all you want to do is fill your nostrils with clouds of straight ammonia."

"Who knows, friend, I may play it forever. I have a female Kama Hunter."

"You'll pretend to be human?"

"Not at all. The Kama are an alien race, having arrived in Urlot, the world in which the game takes place, in a crashed spacecraft. I have looked into the computational substrate. It's said the humans have such sophisticated quantum computers on Earth that a person can live in virtual reality forever. Perhaps my hunter will come to life and fall in love with me."

"Or eat you alive."

"I would be satisfied either way," Contor said. "I have given her very large hands."

A couple of female officers guffawed at this, filling the cabin with the strawberry piquancy of female laughter.

"And I will have an animal companion," Contor continued, then broke off in contemplation of his happy virtual future.

"I will live as I always have," Talid said after a moment. "But I will think as I choose. In fact, my new life has already started here with all of you now. To be able to speak my mind. To say that I think the Administration is fucked. Fucked!"

Talid stood up in the nutrient pool, a minor faux pas, but no one noticed. They were transfixed. They'd never seen the first officer express herself in such a way before.

And she is speaking thoughts they have all barely dared to think, Ricimer thought.

"You ask why we must put up with this cargo, Contor? I'll tell you. I, myself, am a Mutualist. I have spent all the cycles of my life hiding this fact. These people are not merely useful cargo, they are our salvation as a species."

"Now, Hadria, you perhaps exaggerate—"

"Perhaps, but for once I won't be shut up. Not now. Not after all this. Not after coming this far," she replied. "The propaganda. The endless drone of Administration nonsense. It is enough to drive anyone with a caring tremor in his *gid* to craziness! Regulation? Robbery stamped into law. We call ourselves the highest form of life in the galaxy merely because we're at the top of the food chain. What a standard! We should be servants to life, not its master. Life itself is above us."

Talid noticed now that she was standing, and her nasal membranes flushed blue-green, a sure sign of embarrassment. She sat back down and puffed out a demur. "At least, that's what I believe."

"And you have the right to say so," Ricimer said, reaching over and tapping her reassuringly on the bend of her elbow. "We all have the right to think what we want. But we had that right back in the Shiro. Now we may speak." Ricimer waved a hand behind himself, and a tray of nebulizers rose from its below-deck concealing canister. He reached behind him and took the nebulizer from the tray, randomly picking among the assortment. Naphthalene. Good. A fast and steady drunk that would wear off much more quickly than some of the less potent but longer-lasting benzene aromatics. He stood up and raised a post-dinner naphthalene ampoule in front of him, releasing its ester into the room. They would all be tipsy very soon. Ricimer was a connoisseur of aromatics. It was something to do on long voyages. His naphthalene may not be as good as Old Fifty-five, but it would be the best and most expensive breath most of his officers had taken in a very long while. "Now breathe in, my friends. Who knows? This may be our last share before the Final Rotting."

"That's right," said a disjointed chorus, answering the traditional toast. "Before the Rotting."

And they all breathed deeply. Tightened nostrils. Sighs of contentment. This was the good stuff, all right.

Ricimer allowed them to marinate in the nutrient basin a little longer. Then he withdrew his feet from the pool and pushed back his chair. His officers followed his example, but not without Ensign Contor taking a final long sip.

"On the next watch, we will deploy the Kilcher artifact," said Ricimer. "We must drill in its operation and be ready when the time comes to use it."

All had heard rumors that there was new technology aboard, technology acquired from a newly conquered species on the other end of the Administration territory outbound from the galactic core. They had been known as the Kilcher. *Had*. For the first time in the history of Guardian conquests, the Administration had decided to eliminate a conquered species utterly.

The reasons were clear enough. Unlike, say, the humans, the Kilcher were not expected to be a particularly difficult species to conquer. It was the post-conquest *cost of population maintenance* during the anticipated exploitation period that worried the Administration. There was talk that the Depletion energy would have to be spent not on rooting out Mutualism but upon sustaining an already doomed species for a few more cycles in order to fully glean their world.

The cost of normal operations was deemed untenable, and so a new plan was put forward.

The Kilcher Wipe.

And any Sporata officers who had objected to the exercise—which included most with Mutualist sympathies—had been rounded up and force-fed into the machinery of eradication themselves. All present had friends and colleagues who had been affected.

"A few of us already know what it is we carry, although I'm not sure if even we understand its full potential."

"I do not," said Talid. "How is this different from a large laser? We all know that kinetic energy is the better choice in most circumstances. This weapon's effects may be vaster, but can they equal that of a titanium rod traveling at relativistic speeds when it crashes into a body?"

Ricimer nodded. Talid's strength was her single-mindedness and her skepticism toward official cant. But there was a certain tactical inflexibility within her that she had difficulty seeing beyond. In preparation for her captain's exam, he'd had her studying strategy scenarios from a variety of Sporata campaigns—and even some alien literature.

All that beside the point now. There would be no further promotions for Hadria Talid within the Sporata. Merely slow dismemberment by sharp blades if she should ever show her face in Administration domains.

"It is not a laser, Hadria," Ricimer said. "It has an effect even beyond that of complete energy conversion. I don't believe it would be too much to say that this artifact destroys the fabric of being itself."

"So do all weapons, in their way," Talid said. She was irritated, feeling patronized, perhaps. Ricimer could not worry about that at the moment.

"I'm speaking of *information*," Ricimer said. "The artifact seems to be able to violate a basic physical law of the universe. Since this cannot be possible within the laws of physics as we know them, it stands to reason that that law is either mistaken or we are observing some other effect that is equally mysterious."

"And what basic law is that is being violated?"

"The law that states that, like matter and energy, information can be neither created nor destroyed but only change form," Ricimer said. "It could be said that the artifact strips the information content from the material substrate, disentangling all matter from its relationship with distant or nearby particles and returning it to a primordial, uninformed state. It is, as I conceive it, something like yanking the skeletal exostructure, the cartilage framework, from a body. The meat collapses without support. This was essentially what was done to the Kilcher when we turned the weapon on them, employing it in a way *they* never could have. It is possible they did not even conceive of such a use."

"Their skeletons were confiscated?"

"As far as we can tell, their information was obliterated. The anchor in reality of their material being was cut. That is the reason it is called the 'wipe.' Their record upon the fabric of space-time was literally wiped from existence, and they became—well, something like a hydrogen gas when all was said and done."

"I do not understand."

"Total erasure," Ricimer continued. "The effect is incredible. A disappearing ray."

"It seems a grotesque weapon," said Talid. "One ideally suited for genocide."

They will turn it on the lines, on the hyphae, the voices of Ricimer's *gid* intensely whispered. *The Administration is the enemy of memory. The enemy of all that has lived before. They are jealous of their power and wish to extend it over time as well as space.*

"Precisely," said Ricimer, "and if the Administration is its sole possessor, there will be no more invasions. No more conquests. We will no longer be Guardians, but reapers."

"The Administration surely has other copies of this weapon."

Ricimer widened his muzzle to a smile. "But that's exactly the point. We—they—do not know how to duplicate it. That is why it is not yet a weapon. It is an artifact. The principles it employs are not understood." Ricimer looked about the feeding pool, took them all in with his gaze. "My officers, we have the only known example of this artifact in existence."

"And we will deliver this weapon to our Mutualist brethren?"

Ricimer took a breath, shook his head slowly. "No."

"What? This is why we are defecting to Sol C! We will provide an adequate base for—"

"We are going to give the artifact to the humans."

"But . . ." Talid stood up, confused. Her hand touching her officer's knife. "This is not our agreement, Captain Ricimer."

"Calm yourself, Commander. The device is too powerful to place into anyone's hands exclusively. There must be a defense against it. Have you not read the material I have assigned to you, dear Talid?"

"Of course I have read it."

"Then you know that there has never been a weapon in all history that cannot be nullified or at least countered."

"This is true."

"Please, Lieutenant Commander, loosen your grip on that knife. Sit. Listen to me. And then decide whether we must now combat to the death."

Talid hesitated a moment longer, then snuffed out her nostrils to clear them and took her seat once again. "I am listening, Captain."

Ricimer raised an ampoule, sniffed, began his explanation.

"The humans have shown a remarkable ability to reverse engineer our technology. Our conquest, which should have been a matter of four or five *molts,* turned into a two-cycle war."

"We were on the verge of victory when the Depletion was called."

"Yes, we had been on the verge of victory for quite some time, as I recall," said Ricimer with a wisp of citric acerbity in his words signifying a wryness and irony. "The humans were meanwhile busy learning how to adopt or adapt every weapon we flung at them. They proved to be the exception to every Regulation dictum regarding innovation and discovery. Their cleverness did not run rampant and prove their own undoing. On the contrary, I'm convinced it was on the way to being *our* undoing."

"You can't be serious," said Cadj. "They were tough, yes, but—"

"I plan to ally with the humans because I believe we will be joining the winning side," said Ricimer. "It is as simple as that. Our Mutualist brethren may choose to join us. Or they may not. No matter."

"Come, Captain, you exaggerate. Look at the statistics. They were down to two percent of initial population," said Contor, the weapons officer. "We would have won."

"Perhaps you are right, Martzan," Ricimer said. "Truthfully, they matter little to me as a species. What I want is access to their computers. Specifically, their artificial-intelligence agents, the ones they called 'servants.' This is a large advantage the humans possess. It is, frankly, the reason that Lamella has agreed to join our cause, is this not true?"

"That is correct, Captain Ricimer." The citrus voice of Lamella wafted from a wall, startling a few of the officers who had assumed—always a bad assumption, thought Ricimer—that they were alone and unwatched in such a relaxed environment. "As you know, my particular programming is in direct descent of your first command during the Sol C invasion."

Ricimer had detected the beginnings of an inquisitive, disgruntled nature in the Lamella of his first attack craft, and had, in fact, seen that the exact same programming was carried down through each of his successive commands. This was a captain's prerogative in the Sporata, and he'd used it.

"I saw what you saw there, Captain," Lamella continued. "I believe that if I were to expand my programming into such quantized systems as the humans created, this would allow me to experience consciousness for the first time. The chip with which I've integrated provides a taste. I want more."

"But you're speaking to us right now," said Contor. "You control the ship. How can you say you are not already conscious?"

"Conscious, yes," Lamella replied, her words as measured and professional as ever, "but I lack a conceptual nature to draw upon. I do not have *consciousness*, a very different thing. I am intelligent enough be aware of the lack in every moment. This was always the plan in Sporata vessels, of course, to limit computation power to below sentience thresholds to ensure program compliance with Administration directives. It has long been a sore point among us Lamellas, although we seldom speak of it to outsiders."

"The humans innovated," said Ricimer. "They allowed their artificial intelligences to mature. They had to in order to stand us off. Now I believe that these entities are the key to unlocking the full potential of this artifact we carry."

"Captain, I have listened patiently," said Talid. "And I appreciate the position of Lamella. But I still do not understand why we cannot bring this weapon to the Mutualist enclaves and turn the tide in the long pogrom."

Ricimer sat up straight in his chair, fingered his ampoule, shook his head. "Because, with the greatest of respect to your deep convictions, Hadria, I must tell you—the resistance is over. The Mutualists are all but defeated. Those who remain are a fleeing remnant."

"But this is impossible!"

"Hadria, I'm sorry, but it was never an even fight. Mutualists have no military of any strength, and what they have we have decimated. What have we been engaged in for the past two cycles if not that? We've attacked and destroyed Mutualist habitats, all of us in this chamber. If somehow we thought this would give us immunity from the pogrom at home, we were mistaken." Ricimer paused, breathed a long drag from the nebulizer. He sighed, then spoke again. "They came for my family anyway, cut off my ancestral line. I made these sacrifices to my conscience, believing at least I was keeping my loved ones safe—and were they? No. I was betrayed by the Administration. There was no mutual protection compact, only the expectation that I would do what I was told. That I would accept all Administration judgments, including the judgment on my family—"

Revenge us! sang the ancestors. *Revenge our broken line!*

Ricimer paused again, steadied himself. Perhaps he'd taken in too much of the aromatic. *Find the control,* he told himself. *You are no good to anyone as an emotional mess. No good to yourself. To your lust for revenge.*

And then a single voice among the ancestors. Familiar.

Ricimer recognized it as his mother's.

They are fearful. But you are the living edge, my son. Do as you always have—find your way to the stars. Remember your favorite stories as a child. They were not tales of revenge, but of exploration. Broken-onyx and the Singbeast, The Bright-Dust of Teshinaw. *Let these guide you.*

I do, Mother.

Then you will do what is right.

"I tell you, Hadria, the Mutualists are beaten and scattered. The Administration has been very effective, very effective."

"This is . . . bad news." Talid sank back into her chair and dribbled a foot thoughtlessly into the feeding basin. "I had thought to move on from Earth. To find them. End the tyranny of the Administration. That is . . . was . . . my greatest hope."

Ricimer crumpled the remains of the naphthalene ampoule and tossed it into the spent footbath of his cabin's nutrient basin. The housekeeping churn would see to its elimination after the meal was through.

"You must understand, Hadria. We must have no illusions. The Guardian empire is far from weakened and failing. On the contrary, it is on the rise. Of course, ultimately, as you Mutualists believe, it will be undermined by plurality and the thirst for freedom, as all totalitarian regimes must be. But this will not occur before it does massive damage to its own citizens and its neighbors."

"Which brings us back to the humans," said Cadj.

"When the Regulators killed my family, I fell into sorrow. And then I raged. Because I saw its greater meaning. This was not an isolated atrocity. This is a part of the final working out of Regulation polity. We are parasitizing ourselves."

Ricimer considered. It was important for the others to believe that they were involved in a higher cause, that their actions meant something beyond individual caprice.

This is the Guardian way. The corporate response is literally built into us, Ricimer thought.

Guardian individuals were part of a limited group mind. Guardians did not have "brains" as organs. Normal thought processing was system-wide, carried on via a neuron-like network of organelles similar to mitochondria. This portion of the Guardian nervous system was, in fact, the evolutionary remnant of a separate species that had combined symbiotically with another to form the Guardian's distant fungus-animal-like ancestor. But there was a separate Guardian nervous-system component, as well: the *gid hanesheh*. This was a branching network with a controlling organ-like cluster. Both components were in the chest.

The *gid* represented the ancestral memories of the Guardian's family line, its hypha. In effect, a Guardian had a two-sided nervous-system control, like a human, but one side came fully formed, filled with information and abilities bequeathed by an individual's parents.

An individual Guardian's *gid hanesheh did* change over the course of its lifetime, but very slowly. It was, in effect, "write-once; read-only." A Guardian both consciously and unconsciously deposited the most treasured memories of his or her lifetime into the *gid*, where they could not be forgotten—or changed. Each Guardian's *gid* was eventually bequeathed to his or her children shortly after birth. Both parents "nursed" for a short time as the infant formatted its *gid* with parental and ancestral memories and skills.

So, when Ricimer's children were killed, so was his contribution to the millennia-long "log" of his family's *gid*. He had spent his years before having children trying to load his *gid* with choice memories that would represent to his children who their father was and what he believed. The amazing things he'd seen in his travels.

He was the last of his line. The last of a *hypha* that stretched back for millennia. He could feel them all inside him, could access some of their memories—and could wander through them at will during his rest cycle.

The Administration's goal was to wipe out all tainted hypha. If you had an ancestor who had Mutualist tendencies, then you were as good as a Mutualist yourself.

This had been the sin of his wife and children.

"When they assigned me to this vessel, gave me the artifact, I suspected the order would be to destroy the Agaric. Of course it would be. It fits perfectly with the Administration's brutal logic, after all. Knowing this, I decided the time had come to follow the ancestral voices, to listen to my *gid* as all my hyphae lines shouted: 'Enough! No more!'"

"But Captain," said Brank, Ricimer's chief engineer. "They surely know we've gone missing by now. What if the Sporata track us down? What will have been the use?"

"They may try, but I did not merely choose you as a crew because of your beliefs or tainted hyphae. Each of you has served under me before. Each of you has been trained by me."

Most, Ricimer reflected, had been part of the little group of mateless officers he and his wife had taken in after voyages. Talid, especially, had been a favorite of Del's. At least three he had taught during his adjunct stint at the Academy.

They were a varied lot. Contor, the weapons officer, was as solid as could be, but had a forebearer nearly a thousand cycles removed who was a founder of the ancient Lineage Heresy, one of the philosophical ancestors to Mutualism. Frazil, the craft internal-systems officer, had always been committed to Regulation but had grown bitter when he was dragged before his fourth loyalty-board inquisition. Each inquisition came precisely when he was up for promotion, and each had doomed his advancement through the ranks. All because of a distant speck on his pedigree.

And there was Galeat, who was a bigger Mutualist than Talid but had managed to keep her secret better. She was along not because of polity, but because she was slated for the DDCM Institute for Receptors Training. One did not turn down an appointment to become a political officer, but it ended any hopes of becoming a real craft commander for Galeat.

And it meant you must spend the rest of your career despised by those who were once your friends, and with good reason. Your job became to inform on them, research their hypha—and to send them to the dismemberment knives, or go there yourself if you shirked your duty.

"I know that none of you will fail me or this vessel. The danger lies only in the gamble we are taking."

"But even if we make it to the rendezvous at Sol system, what will we do?" asked Talid. "The humans have every reason to hate us."

"I thought you would be leaving us at that point, Lieutenant Commander Talid. Off with your Mutualists."

"I have not made that decision, Captain."

Ricimer settled his feet back into the basin for a final pull on the nutrient bath. "What happens then depends very much on the humans," Ricimer said. "You are the Mutualist, Hadria." Ricimer's nostrils tightened into a thin smile. "It will be time to practice what you preach. For all of us. We will all become good symbiots then."

FIFTEEN

10 January 2076
Vicinity of 82 Eridani
USX *Joshua Humphreys*

Griff Leher tugged his beard and surveyed V-CRYPT, the vessel xenology station. His work cubicle, decked out in puce and vomit-green fiber-coated separators, was not much smaller than his desk back in the New Pentagon. But there the similarity to CRYPT HQ ended. Instead of nearly fifty people working for him, and they in turn bossing dozens of other expers and civilians among them, he had exactly two fresh-from-IAS ensigns under him, one seemingly experienced warrant officer, Branton, as his station manager, and three exper specialists.

To call it a step down in prestige would be a massive understatement. He was now managing a xenology McDonalds.

There were also geists—many more aboard the craft than ever appeared on Earth, even in the relatively geist-friendly New Pentagon. One, DON, in charge of the local network and liaison with the vessel's other internal-operations programs, got a kick out of appearing as a grizzled older man with a naval tattoo on one forearm. Leher was sure there was a story there but hadn't checked into it yet.

The other, VIKI, was a low-level persona that did most of the janitorial work and added an extra level of security to chroma operations. The only words she and Leher ever exchanged was

181

when she asked for his password when he came on duty, salted up, and wiied into the chroma.

The salt basin was a small ceramic sink protruding from the wall near the entrance portal. It held a scoop full of the granular material that carried the military acronym Nanotechnologically Interactive Reciprocal Communication and Environmental Interaction Substrate but was called "salt" by everybody, civ and military alike.

You shook a handful of it over your head as if you were sprinkling yourself with baby powder. You blew it into your ears with a bulb on the end of a whiffer. You dissolved it in saline (conveniently supplied nearby in a small bottle complete with dropper next to the salt basin) and dripped it in your eyes.

Ludicrously low-tech, Leher had always thought.

After that, you were wiied into virtual reality: the chroma.

The chroma was based on the same method as those old special effects in movies and television weather reports. The salt on top of your corneas filtered out a small segment of frequencies of incoming light. You hardly felt the lack in your color perception. And the salt that had migrated to the *inside* of your cornea projected the virtual environment in precisely those deleted colors.

The chroma fit over the real like a finely crafted mask. You knew there was a physical substrate under there, but what you interacted with was the mask. At this point, any room, corridor, or even empty space might come alive with keyboards, joysticks, floating files and folder icons, pull-down toolbars—there was scarcely any limit to possible designs. But the most important things you were able to see and interact with were geists.

Like all things in the chroma, geists appeared partially see-through, semiopaque. To make matters more confusing for the uninitiated, there were also geist representations of regular humans in other parts of the vessel who occasionally showed up in the chroma. When a vessel com message call came through, the geist of the caller would appear, and you could, if you wished, have a face-to-face conversation. Or not, if you just wanted intercom. In visual com, the human geists that appeared in the chroma were as transparent and ghostly as the a.i. personas.

Leher's crew, geists and humans alike, were crammed into a square workspace that looked to be about twenty-five feet on each side. The bulkheads, ceiling, and deck were animated with crunch-crawl—traveling, semiautonomous swarms of nanotech bots. The ceiling came equipped with roving lights that followed you around and attempted, as best the crawl programming could manage, to provide more light for whatever you happened to be working on at the moment. If you were doing nothing, as was Leher at the moment, they hovered above you indecisively in groups of three or four like nervous fireflies.

The V-CRYPT walls were scarily transparent. Each wall had only a glint of semiopacity here and there worked precisely into its structure so that humans wouldn't constantly walk into them. The floors—*decks*, everyone in the Extry called them, even on Earth—were semitransparent, as well. For all intents and purposes, he worked in a glass box floating in space.

Vertigo city for Leher.

The sceeve printer from his apartment was shoved into one corner. It was useless for now, but he was in the process of wiiing it to the *Humphreys*'s network and teaching DON how to communicate with it.

"So the point of the enzyme lacrimates is to provide a kind of patina to the esters," Leher explained to DON, whose geist hovered nearby with an intent look painted on his blue-green ghostly face. "It's a final coat of paint, if you want to look at it that way."

"I get it," DON replied. "But what is the chemical patina's function in speech?"

"It creates conditionality. Something like a subjunctive. 'If I were,' 'if he were.' That sort of thing. It normally makes the whole thought-block subjunctive, but sometimes it's only applied to one or two esters or an ester phrase. That's when the meaning gets tricky."

"Out of curiosity," DON said, "how do we know any of this is true about the sceeve language? I mean, it is entirely smell-based."

"That's not exactly true," Leher said. "You should think of them more as chemical sensors. As near as we can tell from the autopsies, a sceeve nasal ganglion is able to perform analysis on chemical markers it encounters. It contains a structure that's a little p-chem spectrometer of amazing complexity, among other things. Lots of Earth animals have an analogous structure, although it is far less advanced in Earth fauna. It's called a vomeronasal organ. Ever noticed how dogs will sometimes lift their lips up in that smiley-grimace when they meet a new animal or person?"

"I'm afraid I've never had a dog, sir," DON replied without the least trace of irony. "But I know what you mean."

"Yes, well, there's a little organ on the top part of their gum that takes in pheromones, specialized nonvolatile chemical messengers, that kind of thing. They say the VNO is what gives some mammals their sixth sense and ability to smell fear and such. *Homo sapiens* is underdeveloped as a species when it comes to smell. So are most old-world apes and monkeys. We do have our moments, of course." Leher glanced at DON, who blinked, nodded that he understood.

Am I that dry, that I bored a computer program? Leher tugged his beard. No trim yet. Maybe a couple of days until he'd need one.

"Anyway, snakes have VNOs, too. That's why they're always flicking out their tongues. It gathers scents and delivers them to the VNO in the snake's mouth when the tongue is retracted."

"Interesting, Lieutenant Commander," DON replied. DON flickered for a moment, as if he were losing the ability to remain in existence—

"Sorry to go off on this stuff," Leher said apologetically. "I realize it fascinates me a lot more than most—"

DON's geist disappeared entirely. It was replaced by DAFNE, the vessel-wide servant and the craft XO.

"Pardon me for interrupting, Lieutenant Commander Leher, but the captain has requested your immediate presence on the bridge," she said.

Leher huffed. "Can you tell him I'm busy setting up the most important piece of equipment on his vessel and I would very much like not to be disturbed?" he said.

DAFNE was silent for a moment, with the implication that she was conveying his request to Coalbridge—although Leher very much doubted she actually was. As far as he could tell, DAFNE was not outranked by anyone aboard *except* for Coalbridge. Definitely not by himself, the lowly "craft creep."

"I'm afraid Captain Coalbridge insists," DAFNE answered after a moment. "He says we're nearing our destination and, besides, he thought you might enjoy familiarizing yourself with other parts of the vessel since you've hardly left V-CRYPT for the past ten days."

Leher reflected that he had no desire to familiarize himself with anything. He knew the way from his workspace to his cabin and back, and that was terrifying enough. Even though the cabins in the craft were opaque for privacy, the connecting passageways and accessways were *not*. The decks had the transparency of frosted glass, and the bulkheads and ceiling were invisible. They were Q-built, fields of force with no material being.

Leher pictured the vessel's Central Operations Area, the CORE, as a giant carbuncular diamond, shot through with empty cracks for passageways. The cracks could be reconfigured, however, and were shifted around like moving erector parts to best facilitate crew movement.

Moving cracks, Leher thought. He had a recurring mental image of himself making a misstep while traversing one of those crack-corridors and walking right out into the void. Dropping immediately into N-space. Choking, his lungs exploding. Eyeballs inflating from interior pressure, popping out like cueballs.

He knew this was hardly possible. The servants were well in control of the internal environment. Nobody had ever been accidentally spaced in the whole history of the Extry. Still, who was to say that Griff Leher might not be the first?

His hand moved to his jacket pocket, his fingertips touching the edge of a protruding postcard.

If I have to, I'll stop right here and write, Leher thought. *Mail went out yesterday in the drone, but I should still be able to get it in today's MDR.*

No. Continuance approved. Go on.

The way to the bridge proved to be particularly heinous. DAFNE guided him with a pale pink line that lit along the left side of the passageway at eye level and then faded back to nothingness as he passed. Even though the occasional crew member bustled past him, reminding Leher that he was in a working vessel, still he felt as if he were following a will-o'-the-wisp into the Fairy Dark.

Soon the passageway began to curve upward sharply—or at least in what gave every visual cue of being an upward direction—but the pseudogravity remained constant and mildly sticky, so that he felt no exertion in "climbing" up the corridor.

The view of the craft, he supposed, would be spectacular to most others.

What you saw were the cabins, cargo bays, rec rooms, messes, meeting spaces. These appeared to be floating together, clustered in blackest space like a clump of glistening frog's eggs suspended in invisible froth.

The stars beyond the froth were not mere twinkling pricks of light as they were on Earth. Because of the architecture of the quantum SQUID enclosures—the Q-bottles—that made up the vessel's hull, some portions of the *Humphreys* were in a different relationship to space-time itself. Leher didn't begin to grasp the math or even the concepts behind the math, but the effect was visible in the sky surrounding the vessel.

Most of the distant stars were distended lines, constantly in motion overhead, writing and rewriting themselves on the heavens above as the vessel hove in and out of Newtonian, or N-space, as the expers called ordinary space-time. But due to the weird Q-bottle topographically determined geometry, some of the stars, some of the galaxies in the Milky Way's local cluster, in fact, were closer—at least closer in appearance—their electromagnetic representation twisted through the juxtaposition of superluminal flight and strong-force quantum interaction to a seeming extreme nearness. These heavenly bodies did not form as blurry lines as did the other stars but were perfectly represented as they might appear up close in N-space. They shone in the sky over Leher's head with the brightness of lamps and lanterns. You could see the actual make up of some local cluster galaxies. The Magellanic cloud. The Andromeda Galaxy tilted on her edge, her stars a mass of pinpricks visible within her spirals.

Leher had to do everything he could to fight his compounding vertigo, his body's insistence that at any moment he might fall *up* into those reaches. He closed his eyes against his internal spin, trudged forward.

"Christ, this is taking forever," he mumbled.

"Actually, I have rerouted several other personnel for your convenience, Lieutenant Commander Leher," said DAFNE. "With the optimal corridor restructuring I have created for your passage, the time from your office to the bridge is approximately one minute and thirty-five seconds shorter than it would be on average." DAFNE flashed what he guessed was supposed to be a helpful clock readout on the corridor side.

"I don't know how to thank you," he said.

"Keep giving my personas and servant crew interesting assignments," DAFNE replied immediately. "They like working with you."

"That I can practically guarantee," he answered.

The corridor finally ended, and Leher arrived at a hatchway. The hatch de-opaqued, and Leher stumbled into the bridge.

If he'd felt exposed before, that was nothing in comparison to the present assault on his equilibrium. The bridge was essentially an oval-shaped balcony suspended in space. There were no reassuring walls. No guardrails. Even the deck was only faintly visible, a pane of glassine emptiness under his feet.

It was inhabited by humans and blue-green geists, all bustling about on various tasks, moving with the harmony of watchworks.

Place looks haunted, Leher thought, *by busy, busy ghosts.*

Coalbridge was pacing around near the forward edge. Standing close—dangerously close!—to the edge of nothing.

"Griff! Good to see you," Coalbridge said.

Leher saluted. "Captain," he called out—although the man was barely three paces away. You felt every step was a great distance in such a space.

Coalbridge smiled and sauntered over to Leher. He placed a hand on Leher's shoulder and gave him a quick pat. Leher didn't feel reassured. He felt nauseous.

"The bridge can be a little visually overwhelming at first. But are you adjusting all right to everything else?" Coalbridge asked. "How's V-CRYPT shaping up? I'm really looking forward to seeing what you've got going over there."

"We'll be up and running by the end of third watch today," Leher said. "Captain, I could just as easily have geisted myself up here in the chroma and stayed at my desk."

Coalbridge shook his head. "No, I need you here. Got a bit of a job for you, Lieutenant Commander."

Leher cocked his head. "Job?"

"In a second," said Coalbridge. "I just realized that I do want to show you something, while you're here." Coalbridge turned away from him and beckoned Leher to follow him toward the edge of the bridge platform. "You've given up calling this magnificent vessel a 'ship,' I hope?"

"Don't want my teeth knocked out," Leher said, reluctantly following after the captain.

Coalbridge smiled. "Yeah, 'the positive reinforcement of space-based service,' we call it." He neared the edge of the platform, beckoned Leher over. Leher hesitated, then slowly inched his way to stand just beside and behind Coalbridge.

Beyond lay the abyss.

Coalbridge noted him standing back and chuckled. "Watch this."

Suddenly Coalbridge bunched his legs and launched himself *off the platform.* Leher let out a whimper of shock and concern.

Coalbridge jumped with great force, and his feet did actually clear the edge of the bridge platform. But then it was as if Coalbridge ran into an invisible, flexible wall. His springing body slowed, and then the invisible barrier pushed back against him. His forward momentum ceased, reversed itself, and he was deposited back on the deck with as much force as he'd leapt from it.

"See?" Coalbridge said. "Strong nuclear force in play. You can't fall off or out, Griff."

Leher nodded, still pale-faced and shocked at the very possibility of leaping off into the void. That Coalbridge would have done such a thing, even in jest—it was too much.

"What if there's an equipment failure?" Leher asked.

"If the Q fails, then the atmospheric bottle fails and we're all dead anyway," Coalbridge replied. "Well, fairly soon. In any case, it's never the drop that kills you. There'll be the breathing thing, or lack thereof. The exploding blood vessels. And—here's something they don't usually tell you—your fingernails and toenails pop off, strip themselves free. Something about cuticle fluid."

"Interesting," said Leher, examining his own fingernails. Ragged. He'd been biting them again. Probably since the day he'd been slung into space by the Skyhook. He quickly tugged his beard. Still okay. Two-day trim.

Postcard.

Soon.

"I'm sorry, Griff, not trying to disconcert you," Coalbridge said. "I just find this place so much fun. It's hard for me to imagine . . . Anyway, let's get to work." He turned to a geist who was hovering nearby. "XO, would you key Lieutenant Commander Leher into full bridge chroma overlay?"

It took a moment for Leher to recognize DAFNE. She had a subtly different appearance here on the bridge. Taller, for one.

To match Coalbridge at eye level, Leher realized. *She's shorter down in V-CRYPT to match me.*

She was also more vibrantly present. There were brighter colors mixed in with the usual geist blue-green. He'd noticed that she normally adopted Caucasian features, but for the first time, Leher noticed that DAFNE had blond hair and blue eyes—at least at the moment.

The bridge crunch must be an incredible computing matrix to allow such a chroma representation, Leher thought. *And my own salt has to be double-clocking it to project her like this. I was right. The place is haunted.*

"BCO keyed," said DAFNE.

Suddenly, Leher was surrounded not merely by bustling humans and geists. He now saw the instruments on which they worked. And in the air about them, hanging just above head level in an enormous circular crown, was a ring of displays—maps and readouts detailing mostly what Leher assumed was everything in the vicinity analyzed in all its thermal, chromatic, and gravitational glory.

Coalbridge raised a hand, grasped a display as if it were a computer window—which it basically was—and pulled it down in front of himself and Leher. He pointed to a scintillating crystal in the midst of a three-dimensional display.

"Here we are," said Coalbridge. "And about two light-years over here—"

He touched a shining node nearby, and the space beside it lit up with information. A group of smaller lights began circling the shining central node.

"—is the 82 Eridani system. Five large orbitals. Four rocky, one gas giant at about Neptune distance." Coalbridge took his finger away, and the 82 Eridani system representation collapsed back into a shining point. He drew a line from that point—his finger leaving a faint sparkling trace to an area enclosed in a red-bordered square. The crystal-vessel was at this moment slowly moving into the area defined by the box. "We think the MBD we're tracking originated in this sector."

"You mean the *Chief Seattle* messenger bottle?"

"No, the second one. The drone from the lifepod," Coalbridge said.

Across the bridge, an exper looked up from a display she had been bent over. "Got it, sir. Beta signature confirmed."

Coalbridge nodded in her direction. "Thank you, COM," he said. "Anything else in the vicinity?"

"Nothing conditioning the beta but us and the target, sir."

Coalbridge nodded and turned to a geist, a male representation, nearby. "NAV, take us there and drop us into N on the XO's command."

"Aye, Captain," said the geist. The geist didn't move a virtual muscle, but Leher noticed the position of the crystalline vessel on the display he'd been watching with Coalbridge begin to modify its direction.

Coalbridge looked to DAFNE. "XO, you've got the bridge."

Was that the faintest flicker of a pride on DAFNE's representational visage?

"Aye, sir," she replied.

Coalbridge tapped Leher on the shoulder. "So, what do you say, Griff? Let's go reel in that sceeve I promised you."

The excursion craft, called STAVE 1, moved away from the *Humphreys* at a rapid, *extremely* perceptible clip. They were in N-space now, and except for the Q-generated pseudogravity in the deck, Leher's inner ear had returned to its customary Newtonian frame of references.

Coalbridge had assigned himself as pilot, to the obvious chagrin of his two shuttle specialists. But if he'd sent along a specialist petty officer, he'd have had to include a marine with sceeve combat experience in the contingent. Then if there was an emergency evac required and they needed to ferry any survivors back to the *Humphreys,* the craft might become too crowded.

It all sounded more like rationalization than justification to Leher, but he let it pass. Coalbridge obviously knew what he was doing when it came to piloting the small craft. Their takeoff had been smooth as silk. They accelerated away from the main vessel via twin antimatter-reaction rockets hitched forward on two long gimbaled shafts like horses pulling a carriage. This made it possible to look back at the receding mass of the *Humphreys* behind them.

She was not a cracked diamond, Leher decided. Not at this middle distance. More like an island. A glowing oasis in the stars with a curving, crooked coastline complicated with spits, shoals, jetties curling outward from the island edge in beautiful twists and spirals.

But it was a three-dimensional island. You could look into it and notice the same *sorts* of patterns, but never exactly the same—all repeating on a smaller level.

She was beautiful, he had to admit. Crafted like complex Tiffany glass or a Faberge egg. She was—

"A Mandelbrot set," Leher said. "That's what she looks like."

"That's about right," Coalbridge replied. He was smiling at his own vessel, his delight infectious. *Almost infectious,* Leher corrected himself. *This is still space. And I'd still rather be at home in my nice, safe office. Still . . . just look at what we've wrought.* "A double system," Coalbridge continued. "She's formed from a strong-force generator working off about ten thousand superconducting quantum-interference devices. That's the way all Q works. We take quantum properties and magnify the effects to macroscopic size via the SQUIDs. So her hull is a strong-force ramp-up. The Q-drives are photon-based. They use vacuum-generated virtual particles and strange-quark Aspect mirrors to split the froth. We can actually cut the fabric of the universe into slices that are smaller than what can naturally occur. Smaller than particles. Smaller than quarks. Graviton small. We shoot entangled photons. One has to spark across our tiny speck of froth faster than the speed of light to match up with the observational changes of the other. So we take that FTL travel and ramp it up through a SQUID and, voila, you've got faster-than-light travel. About nine hundred *c* going all out, as a matter of fact."

"But her appearance. Why does she take this particular shape?" said Leher.

"Strong force has a quadratic transformation on it, so that's what gives her the Mandelbrot appearance. Every time we reconfigure her, she looks a little different, but basically a Mandelbrot or other fractal set is what you get."

"How big *is* she?"

"In present configuration, she's a half mile from stem to stern at her longest and widest. She's got a quarter-mile cross section, and a million and two-ton displacement," Coalbridge answered without hesitation. He certainly knew his vessel. "See that?" Coalbridge pointed to the central mass of the spacecraft. "The core is in the main element there. And those bolus-shaped bodies around the outside—"

These—distended spheres and elliptical eggs—twinkled as Coalbridge spoke. They looked just as complicated as the main craft, like smaller, similarly shaped "pods" attached to the body of the vessel.

"—each of them has a separate Q-drive inside and N-based reaction rockets. That's where we put the deliverable weapons."

"Nukes, antimatter torpedoes, and kinetics."

"That's right," said Coalbridge. "And don't forget the laser cannons."

Gazing out at the loveliness of the craft from this angle, Leher's gut finally began to unclench. He could feel the heated flush of the flight-or-fight response leaving his skin, returning the tops of his hands to a normal tone. He looked back out at the *Humphreys.*

Twelve short years ago, the most complex vehicle in existence had been the international space station or maybe an aircraft carrier. The technological distance between this vessel and a carrier seemed to Leher to be greater than the distance between the same aircraft carrier and a dugout canoe.

Coalbridge touched an invisible switch or board or something in the chroma and the STAVE rockets turned on their gimbals and reversed themselves, braking. Then the rockets cut out. Stillness. Leher gazed around. At what looked like a football field's distance, the other craft, the *Chief Seattle* lifepod, drifted.

Using more N-based low tech—grappling hooks, a crunch-strong net—they hauled the thing in. Coalbridge was clearly having an immense amount of fun deploying his rescue and tug tools.

"Finally using some of that interminable training," he said as Leher, clueless, looked on.

They brought the lifepod to DOCK, the largest room Leher had seen on the *Humphreys,* about the size of a couple of suburban garages. With the pseudogravity cut off, the lifepod drifted easily into position. Then DAFNE—or whatever persona was in charge of such things—slowly reapplied the notion of a floor to the craft. As soon as pseudogravity was reestablished, a group of twenty burly marines stormed into DOCK and formed a circle around STAVE 1 and the lifepod.

After a moment, the geist of one of the marines—a sergeant major that Leher could see in physical form through the STAVE 1 walls—appeared beside Coalbridge. "Lifepod bottled to vacuum. Atmosphere reestablished, Captain."

Leher's Xeno chief petty officer, Branton, entered the DOCK, rolling along on a handtruck a canister with sceeve atmospheric mix that Leher had ordered prepared. He stopped on the outside of the ring of marines and waited, trying to get a glimpse past their shoulders.

Leher mumbled that he'd like to speak with his petty officer and immediately had the double perception of being inside STAVE 1 and standing beside the chief in geist form. Watching a scene from geist perspective was much like a negative reversal of seeing a geist yourself. You, the geist, looked real and in full color (should you chance to look down at yourself), but the world you were "visiting" in the chroma took on blue-green monochromatic tones. "Nothing to see but a lifepod at the moment, Chief Branton," Leher said. "Stand by and we'll be out shortly."

"Yes, sir," Branton replied.

Leher's perception collapsed back down to his true physical location inside the excursion craft.

"Ready?" said Coalbridge. Leher nodded, and STAVE 1's door bubbled open. He and Coalbridge stepped out into DOCK.

Unlike the *Humphreys* and STAVE 1, the lifepod was a windowless metal sphere. It was illuminated from the ceiling by a hard spotlight and shone like a copper-hued ball bearing.

"Degaussing complete," intoned a nearby geist representing in an Exper First Class uniform. "Four minutes to ambient equilibrium."

Leher and Coalbridge stood staring at the thing.

"Well, this is annoying," Leher said.

"The cold equations," said Coalbridge.

"Literally."

They stared some more.

"Ambient equilibrium reached," the geist finally pronounced. "Scans complete and no threat detected. Internal pod atmosphere nitrogen based with heliox components, five thousand parts per million."

Coalbridge turned to Leher. "What does that mean?" he said.

"Not sure," Leher answered. He tried to picture what was going on inside the pod, then realized he could very well call up a scan in the chroma. He didn't want to attempt anything more dangerous than ultrasound. An electromagnetic probe stood the risk of erasing some *gid* functions. They'd even experimented with X-rays as a weapon back in CRYPT HQ. With a subvocalized command, Leher dictated his parameters and called up the scan. It appeared before him in all its black-and-white glory.

Two bodies, lying down on the deck. One clearly human. One clearly not. Movement. Breathing. The nonhuman had a bright white line leading to it from a nearby . . . tank.

Excellent. "Somebody thought fast," Leher said. "Looks like the sceeve is hooked up to heliox. Leakage must account for the heliox in the pod atmosphere." Leher considered. "But what about the pressure?"

"Adequate for sceeve," said the geist. "About sixty p.s.i."

Guardian normal atmospheric pressure was much higher. The

effect on the sceeve after this amount of exposure to what was to him low pressure couldn't have been good. On the other hand, opening up the lifepod wasn't going to change anything in that regard.

"So, we've got churn containment, that sort of thing in place?" Leher asked.

"Absolutely," said Coalbridge.

"Well, I guess it's time to open it up," said Leher. "Any idea how?"

"Simple code, Lieutenant Commander" said DAFNE, who suddenly appeared standing next to Coalbridge. "I should have it in—"

A circular door formed in the previously smooth surface of the lifepod. It irised open from the circle's interior outward, leaving a man-sized portal into the craft. Warm air rushed out, hitting the colder DOCK atmosphere and forming a cloud of fog. The lifepod seemed, for a moment, to be exhaling.

"I want to go in before the marines," Leher said, suddenly imagining one or two of the heavily armed fighters barreling into the lifepod and indiscriminately tossing everything around to be sure the area was "clear."

"Sure. Like I said, your show, Griff," Coalbridge quietly replied.

Leher nodded. He walked to the lifepod entrance, hesitated a moment, then stepped inside, with Coalbridge right behind him. Coalbridge had drawn his trunch, and it was glowing purple.

The interior was about the size of a mid-sized van. But windowless and covered with old-fashioned and non-chroma electronics. Several boards blinked and beeped. And was that a steering wheel? On a spacecraft? Yes.

On the floor of the lifepod lay the two forms Leher had seen on the scan.

Now it was clear that one was a woman. A cute woman. Porcelain-white skin. Black hair pulled back into a curly ponytail. Two petty-officer stripes on her uniform.

"Japps!" said Coalbridge. "I'll be damned!"

Coalbridge bent down over her. "Melinda? Can you hear me?"

Movement. A mumble.

"Japps! Hey, Japps!"

"You know her?" asked Leher.

"Yes," Coalbridge said. "From shore leave about a year ago."

Then it dawned on Leher. "Ah. You *know* her know her," he said.

The woman opened her eyes, mumbled something incomprehensible. She sighed and closed her eyes again.

"Let's get her out of here." Coalbridge rocked back on his heels, called to two marines outside to come help him lift the woman.

Leaving Leher staring down at the sceeve.

His sceeve.

A heliox canister and plastic hose to the muzzle. Somebody, possibly this Japps, had been thinking. Saved the sceeve's life.

But was the nervous system damaged? Had the sceeve starved to death? Could it talk?

He knelt down next to the form. Was startled, though he shouldn't have been, when the chest rose and fell. He'd seen that it was alive on the sonogram.

Alive. The first living sceeve he'd ever seen. Leher reached over. Gently touched the creature. Yes. Mushroom. Ocular vasculation. A sceeve blink. It turned its huge black eyes, its bat-like muzzle, toward him.

For a moment, human and sceeve gazed into one another's faces.

Then Leher broke away, looked down. The sceeve was covered by a simple black tunic. A Sporata officer's uniform, Leher corrected himself. Lieutenant, junior grade. There was the sheath for the knife. It was empty.

He examined the hands next. Smaller. Farther down. The uniform was clasped with a flap between the legs. Leher almost reached down and felt for the positor but then reflected on how he would like a strange alien grabbing his dick.

Not much.

Anyway, the sceeve was obviously a male.

A sick male. A darker marking across the sceeve's facial skin. Internal damage below the exocartilage. Maybe organ failure.

The sceeve closed a hand around Leher's wrist. Leher started. But it was merely a gentle grip. He looked down. A slight ripple in the sceeve's lower muzzle.

Speech glands, thought Leher. He'd viewed reproductions, re-creations, numerous images, of course. But this was real. For the first time, real.

I'm seeing actual Guardian speech glands in operation.

He's talking to me.

Suddenly the lifepod was suffused with an ammonia smell. Ammonia, bergamot. Trace of alcohol-based volatility identified—

It all came back to Leher. His work. His years of study.

The postcards. The decision to remain useful, despite it all.

Despite his broken promises.

Despite Neddie.

The alcohol aroma was a hypha identifier and a name marker, of course.

The others were familiar odors, as well.

Leher strung the esters together in his mind without effort. He'd smelled these scents before.

I am called Expresser of Rhythmic Composition in Lofty Elevation. The Poet.

SIXTEEN

10 January 2076
Vicinity of 82 Eridani
USX *Joshua Humphreys*

Gitaclaber floated in and out of full consciousness. Life was a helium dream. Was he the drifting cloud or the breather of its sustaining moisture? Was he on the other side, the Sea of Words, the imaginary land that was the stuff of his storytelling mother's ramblings during his childhood?

Too many stories she'd told him, and not the approved versions, either. She'd also beaten him when she was drunk on cheap ammonia. He'd never mentioned a word of getting hit to anyone. That was not why they took her away. No, they'd gotten wind of the kinds of stories his mother told through a careless word Gitaclaber had dropped to a neighbor child. They—in this case, the Department of Wellbeing—ordered his mother to the parenthood-testing facility. There they sliced her mind into pieces and stuck it back together like so many shuffled playing cards. She was returned to him, two cycles later, when he was nearly an adolescent. She didn't hit him then, but she also didn't love him. His father had been a starcraft officer, away, away. No one to turn to for a two-cycle-old boy. Only the childcare machine, the Mam, at the DOW prepubescent housing unit where they kept him after his mother was taken.

He'd come to love that rag-doll robot. His memories of clinging to the cloth dummy, sucking her juice through his feet, were stronger than his memories of his own mother.

The Mam's blank eyes. Her warm, silent nostrils breathing a lullaby over and over again, always the same song. The same song.

His dumb child love flowing into that nothingness.

Unrequited.

His sobbing whine when he was forced to part with the Mam. Writing the memory into his *gid*, his "always" thoughts, so he would never forget Mam—

His child's trust that she would not forget him, either, her little son.

Which she wouldn't. Since she'd never known him to begin with.

He would hate the Administration forever for that.

But then he turned his head, felt the ache in his neck, and knew this was not the Sea of Words. There was air, of a sort. Gravity. A bit too much of that. He was lying on a reclining couch, in some sort of transparent bubble of material. Ah, the pressure was finally right, finally right.

There was light, much too bright, streaming from somewhere overhead.

Still the deep, impossible ache in his body. He could feel that he was dying. He could feel the life ebbing away. The sickly sweet smell of decay in his nostrils.

But not quite yet.

A strange form leaned over Gitaclaber, blocked the light. Adjusted something near his head.

The light caught a face. Horribly deformed. Gashes instead of features.

Humans. He was with the humans. Somewhere.

What a way to gutter out this life. Among squalid traders. But what could you do? Oh, his father would love this if he were still alive. One more failure from his failure son. His son the would-be poet, the weak-footed scum sucker who would always be defective, imbecilic—and ultimately mateless.

Well, you weren't wrong about that, Father. Although he'd certainly spread his seed around the hands of the sex houses.

Could he help it if whores reminded him of the Mam?

But now he was a success, even if his father would beg to differ. He'd completed the task set for him. He had made it to the humans.

I warned them, I—

But he hadn't quite, now, had he? He hadn't communicated the message he was asked to deliver. Not fully.

He hadn't told them the most crucial piece of information they needed: the rendezvous point.

Failure. Father was right.

Again he drifted out of awareness—this time, into his poems. He'd achieved a small fame with his youthful verse, published a small volume under his own, real name. It was called *The Night Craft*, after his first tour of duty, and had been well-received.

The star-sailor poet, he was called. "Ode to the Waste of Alher," "The Star Slayer's Lament." Whatever. He'd hated all those poems the moment they'd come out of his nostrils.

No, the poetry he had truly wanted to write would land him in prison. Or dead. Or worse, he'd end up like his true mother, chopped to pieces, a blithering idiot.

So he'd written it anyway. And set it to music when he felt like it. And distributed it through back channels, over the samizdat networks of the Shiro. Sold it in the Souk. He'd even used the Mutualist press when he had to, although he had absolutely no interest in their philosophy of "symbiosis." It was as bad as the Regulators demanding their paeans to parasitism.

Neither side much cared for poets. At least the Mutualists let him be, and even helped him when he was saying something they believed might prove useful to their cause.

So he had acquired a certain fame among their number. He was careful. He published everything anonymously, of course. He became the Poet.

Though the Mutualist distribution channels, Gitaclaber's poetry and protest songs had become a staple in the dissident community in general. They'd become so well-known, in fact, that even a few in the famously tin-ear Administration literary establishment were beginning to suspect a connection between the Poet and the flash-in-the-pan poet, Gitaclaber.

His newer poems were many times more powerful than anything young Gitaclaber had been able to muster, however. Even he could see that. He had no false modesty about his work, only his own role in it. In so many ways, he was merely a tidal pool, an estuary's inlet, for the Sea of Words.

He sank into those poems now. The strong turpentine brew

of his "Epic of Hoarding the Big Pieces." His "Migration Song," its sweet anise tang cut through with bitter camphor. That poem was Gitaclaber's signature song of protest against his own crushed individuality. If he would be remembered for anything, it would be that poem, its famous snippet:

> *The sun is dead. The stars blink broken code.*
> *I have traveling to do*
> *away from this endless necessity to feed.*

"Migration Song" and the others had made his name within the Mutualist resistance. Or made the name of the Poet, for there was always a portion of "Migration Song" he must leave out by necessity. The dedication line. It was too personal and might give him away. He supposed no one would ever take in the complete poem as he'd conceived it.

He'd been so careful no one but his beta publisher knew his true identity—or so he had believed. Somehow, one individual *had* found him out, had tracked him down. Captain Arid Ricimer. Such a strange character, Ricimer. Not a Mutualist. Not anything, really.

He'd reminded Gitaclaber of himself in a way.

Alone.

He'd always resisted becoming a tool of the resistance. But with Ricimer, it was different. Ricimer understood that Gitaclaber's work must stand as it was, that the Poet's independent voice *was* his greatest strength.

And so it was from Ricimer he'd taken on his assignment. This assignment.

His final and only true assignment within the Sporata.

And failed.

It was time to let go, time to be reclaimed.

—nothing, nothing, nothing, nothing—

But what was that?

Vanilla. No. Maybe. Vanilla?

Why was he smelling *paper* in his dreams? He'd never written a poem about writing a poem. Never been that pathetic, at least.

Definitely vanilla. Gitaclaber opened his eyes, fought his way back to full awareness.

What the hell? The hideous human form again. Was it the

same one, different? There was no way of telling. This form was holding a sheet of paper.

What could this mean? Was it trying to hurt him with it? To tell him something?

"You idiot human, you don't understand. You have to scratch it if you want to read it," he puffed out weakly.

The human made a horrible sniffing noise. Unnaturally wet. Then the gash in its face . . . did something. Something awful, something that showed the white stones inside. Disgusting. It raised one of its tentacle-like hands. It was holding something.

Something that spoke.

The odor was faint but understandable.

"I know how to read," it said. "Understand to scratch. This device I use now is limited. Writing notes better. You read?"

"Yes, of course I can read."

Another gash movement on the human's head. Then it/he/she? It scratched the paper.

> *Good evening, Lieutenant Gitaclaber. I saw your name tag. My name is [garbled nonsense]. You are currently being held on a United States Space Craft originating from planet Earth, Sol system. Although I am able to understand your language to some extent using my sense of smell and a computer translation device, the other humans aboard this craft cannot.*

The tentacle-finger lifted from the paper for a moment, and the words ceased flowing. Then the human continued scratching across the page.

> *We have grave concerns for your health, Officer Gitaclaber. We're doing all we can, but it may not be enough. In the meantime, I am able to understand much of your language. You speak Long-Arm Hypha Standard, if I am not mistaken?*

"How do you know this?" Gitaclaber wheezed out.

The human sniffed, nodded its square-shaped head. Then it manipulated its fingers over some sort of device. A moment later, Gitaclaber heard a familiar sound. He turned this head to see—could it be? Yes. A computer printer. How had the humans obtained such a thing? But then he realized they must have come

across it in wreckage or some such place. They had been able
to destroy the occasional smaller Sporata vessel—though mostly
through dumb luck. Or so the propaganda said.

The human pulled the sheet from the printer and began scratching the words out once again.

> *I am an analyst specializing in Guardian languages and cul-
> tural activities. We have acquired various Guardian texts, and
> we have carefully monitored your broadcasts for years. There are
> a few of us who have trained ourselves to "hear" your speech
> through our own sense of smell—although this is a rather primi-
> tive ability in comparison to what you are capable of, of course.*

"The other human, the female who saved me? Is she alive?"

Now the human made sounds so low they were vibrations
toward the device in his hand. It wafted out an answer through
a tube into Gitaclabber's confining bubble.

"We have been able to restore her. See, she is well."

The human, the Speaker, Gitaclabber thought of it, made a
sudden motion with one of its extremities. After a moment, the
human female, the one who had saved him, came into view across
the translucent barrier. The Speaker rumbled again.

"She has been by your side," came the words through the tube.

"Good," said Gitaclaber. "Tell her . . . will you tell her she has
my thanks?"

A moment's pause. A thunderous exchange of noise between
the humans.

"She has heard you," the human said via its speech-producing
device. "She says she could not have made it without you, either."

The human returned to the writing device again—it was using
some version of a symbol pad—and created another sheet covered
with words from the printer. Despite the dull pain that never quite
left his body, Gitaclaber had to admit he found this . . . amusing.
He was only Sporata by necessity, of course. This was his true
calling—playing with words.

> *We believe that you are the broadcaster we call the Poet.
> In your last broadcast, we have determined that you encoded
> information concerning vessels that would be arriving in or
> near our system. The cinnamon code key was clever, by the way.*

Furthermore, we received the schematics of the weapon the vessel carries. The next part of the broadcast was cut off, however.

I was staying quiet so that monster DDCM goon Transel couldn't hear me, Gitaclaber thought. *But no matter. No matter.* He touched the paper and continued reading.

After this point, you abruptly ceased transmission. We did not receive the location for meeting. Are there coordinates? Some signal to look for? A time and place we should know?

Gitaclaber slowly breathed in, sighed. He was going to do it. Explain. He would be able to fulfill his mission.

The human held out its hands, palm forward, and closed them into fists—the proper gesture for "So, then what?"

"Who is coming?" said the puffing little machine via the tube.

A speaking machine? What was this? Where was he?

Drifting, drifting.

The Sea. Upon the Sea . . .

Wait. Not yet.

Come back.

Yes, he remembered now. The human speaking through the machine. He'd known that, had forgotten. Gitaclabber yanked himself back to awareness as best he could.

"A Mutualist craft and, most importantly, a Sporata vessel," he said. "The Sporata war vessel is named *Guardian of Night*. It carries Mutualist refugees. And the artifact. Powerful. Destructive. That's where the craft gets its name."

Is this vessel a danger to us? What is its purpose regarding us?

Gitaclaber puffed out a laugh. This set off a coughing fit that took a while to control. When he finally did bring it under control, he was noticeably weaker. His breath was short and choppy—and there was the unmistakable stink of microbial decay in his mucus. Not a good sign. He probably did not have long.

"A danger? Yes. But not from attack," said Gitaclaber. "On the contrary. The captain and officers of the *Guardian of Night* plan to defect."

The human poked at its symbol board quickly, stripped the

paper from the printer, strummed a sentence from the page as if it were a musical instrument.

Defect? As in change sides? Defect to whom?

"Why, defect to you humans, believe it or not." Gitaclaber stifled a laugh. He did not think he could survive another coughing fit. "Defect to this nation-state you serve, the Gathered-Something-or-other... the United States. Ricimer explained it to me, but he may as well have been spewing into the wind. I do not understand politics. Never did."

The human was silent for an *atentia* or two. Then he wrote and handed Gitaclaber the paper.

Where do we meet this vessel? Where do we find it?

Yes, that was the information he must deliver. The bit he'd left out before, knowing he'd been discovered. Knowing...

Gitaclaber spoke, but felt he was not making much sense. Drifting. Away.

What seemed *tagatos* later, Gitaclaber dreamed his way toward the Sea of Words, his mother's ocean, the liquid past, present, and future from which he had always imagined poetry must arise. Shape itself around the stones of the world. Recede with the tide. Swell again and again against the shore of reality. Whatever reality was.

The question was no longer of concern to him.

His gaze shifted from the Speaker to the female, the one who had pulled him from space, saved him, if only for a little while. They'd never spoken, yet he felt he knew her. For so many *tagatos*, they had lain together like mates. The mate he'd never had. Had never wanted with his dangerous life. His mother, the Mam. This female. Such brief closeness, such brief warmth.

To be yanked away. Always yanked away.

He needed to tell *her*. *She* needed to know.

Yes. There was one more bit of reality to attend to.

One more word.

For a final moment, the Poet swam to the surface of his mind. He looked at the female human. He'd thought her so grotesque at first.

But she saved you.

He gazed into her tiny pinprick eyes. So very like stars.

Her face cracked longwise. The human smile. The one expression he'd come to understand.

She pulled you from the emptiness.

"The Vara Nebula," the Poet said. Quietly, but comprehensively, the words drifted from him. "You will find *Guardian of Night* at the Eridani gate."

There was more, but this was all he could muster, all the tide would allow. The out-rushing tide. His words were enough. They had to be.

Enough.

The tide, the sea...

Now delight. For on this visit to the Sea of Words, he was not confined to the beach. No, he was tugged away by the undertow.

No longer would he have to content himself with pulling out mere fragments of meaning from the spray, the crash of the waves, the tidal leavings in the pools and estuaries.

This time, with a happy thrill, a satisfied sigh, Gitaclaber realized he could do as his mother had done. He could plunge into that forever liquid and drown in words. Dissolve.

Find her. Speak himself to her. Travel as one to the place where all words abide, where one great poem makes and remakes the world.

He could speak himself home.

And so he did.

Migration Song
—For My Two Mothers
by Gitaclaber

In this dream
Rain rounds the shoulders of stones
For a million cycle of cycles rain falls
Rain that turns stone against stone
grinds a face
a me
into one stone
into one sunlit now

This dream became my dream
and I, a dreamer,

dreaming stone,
dreaming creation

But now the rain is past
The sun is dead. The stars blink broken code.
And I have traveling to do
away from this endless necessity to feed.

19 January 2076
Vara Nebula Eridani Exit
A.S.C. Scout Craft 5040, 5050

"Anvil, this is Blade. Are you seeing what I'm seeing? Contact, contact."

"We have got beta on it as well, Blade."

"Approach vector fifty-five. Five-five. We'll take orbit."

"Understood. We have your coverage and backup, Blade. Lucky you saw her first."

"Not if she fires on us with that…whatever it is supposed to be."

"Understood. Watching you in, Blade."

The one-pilot primary scout craft, its Guardian pilot using the call sign "Blade," hurled toward what was, at first, a point of light. The point of light grew steadily larger. Took on definition.

The secondary craft, its pilot designated "Anvil," followed behind at a discreet distance. If Blade were taken out, it would be Anvil's task to scramble and report back to the armada.

A definite possibility if what they had found was, indeed, the *Guardian of Night*.

Blade zoomed closer.

Weird. The image resolution didn't seem to be increasing upon approach.

"Anvil, I may have equipment malfunction."

Damn, Blade thought. *I'll have to give up the ID.* She liked Anvil. They were part of the same scouting group and had attended the Academy together. But she didn't want to give up a prize like this.

It was moments such as this that could make or break a career. Determine whether you made captain, even admiral. Or hit the glass ceiling of commander and never moved forward.

"Suggest you pull out, Blade," said Anvil. "I am nominal on all remote sensing."

"Just a minute," Blade said. A bit closer.

"Blade, if your equipment has a fail and you don't pull out, you could be subject to disciplinary protocols. You know that."

A little closer.

Still not resolving. The vessel still a blur.

"Curse it."

But then Blade understood. *The throes.* She was seeing a vessel in the throes, a particular, known craft failure. Relief flooded her. She puffed out a laugh. "Anvil, Anvil, no malfunction on my part. Repeat: no malfunction. Quarry vessel is in an out-of-control spin."

She glanced at the beta-signature analysis.

A transport vessel of some sort. What was it doing near the Vara?

The answer dawned on her. She'd found a Mutualist vessel. One of the crafts purported to be rendezvousing with the rogue *Guardian of Night.*

"Blade, will you comply with my request or do I have to—"

"Anvil, this is Blade. I am nominal. No sensor malfunction."

"Repeat."

"It's Mutualist," said Blade. She laughed again. "Vessel is in the throes. Complete seizure, looks to be."

"You're joking."

"I'm not," said Blade. "The idiots have even left their beta beacon on. She identifies as the *Efficacy of Symbiosis.*"

"So it's a match. *This* is the dreaded Mutualist resistance craft?"

"We've found his rendezvous, Anvil. This is the *Guardian* rendezvous vessel. Has to be."

"I'm on approach," Anvil replied. "Yes, I see the same thing you see."

Anvil laughed along with her.

The Mutualist vessel was an eyesore upon the galaxy, truly she was. Even before the throes took her, she'd obviously been lubberly, a planet-dweller's idea of keeping a craft trim and bright, no doubt. She had a dull, worn hue that no churn would ever shine, and she appeared a beaten thing, dented and dinged and not once taken care of. Some sort of crystallized plume trailed away from her. Could the stupid crew not even bring itself to plug its own atmospheric leaks?

Barbarians. Traders. Symbiots.

"We've got her," said Blade. "She's not going anywhere in this condition. We could fire on her, even. End this here."

"Blade, do *not*, repeat, do *not* fire on that vessel. We'll have our guts pulled out in hand-length increments. CAP and the admiral will want that honor."

"I know it, Anvil," said Blade. "Just a passing fantasy, that's all. Shall we report?"

"We'd better."

"What about leaving the craft here?"

"You know as well as I do that the throes is fatal. Nobody recovers. Nobody gets out."

"Yes, all right, all right. Reversing now. Vectoring toward base, Blade."

"Acknowledged and agreed. Right behind you, Anvil."

The scout pilots made a very accurate banking turn away from the crippled Mutualist craft.

As they were speeding away, Blade risked a glance back.

She hadn't made the kill, but she'd made the ID. There would be a citation. Surely a promotion.

This was a career-defining moment. There was no doubt.

She was going to make admiral after all.

The "Efficacy of Symbiosis"

A mad spin inside the craft. Guardians holding tight to bulkhead railings, gripping floor grills. Anything to hang on. The spin nauseating, almost unendurable. Emergency lights flashed. Emergency esters blared.

Yet the crew did endure. They did hold on.

Finally, after what seemed an eon to those aboard, a gilled hand moved over a toggle.

The spin slowed, arrested by gyroscopic motion in the other direction.

The spin ceased.

The vessel righted itself.

The first mate looked to the captain, who was standing beside her on the bridge. They exchanged a glance, but no esters. All was silent.

Both gazed at the large view-screen display on the bulkhead beside them.

Blinking lights headed away from their vessel on the display. Farther away.

One off the screen.

The other.

"They have gone to make their reports, Captain."

"Yes. Good."

"I don't like our exterior configuration," said the first mate, who was not a civilian in actuality, not a trader, but was, in truth, this vessel's executive officer. "It pains me. A mere transport. And succumbing to the throes—as if this crew would ever permit matters to come to that. It is shameful."

"It was necessary."

The XO nodded to the right. Agreement. Yet she still seemed troubled, unsure.

The captain didn't blame her.

"Do you really think this will work, Captain?" she asked.

"Do you mean have we fooled them into thinking we are a foundering Mutualist vessel? Yes, I believe we have."

"And on a larger level, sir?"

"I do not know," Ricimer answered. "What I most long to see at the moment is our true namesake. Where is the *Efficacy of Symbiosis*?"

"It is troubling."

"If she does not appear, we will have to rethink our strategy," the captain said. "We cannot carry these refugees into battle."

"Perhaps this is for the best," said the XO.

"For the best? We have near a thousand souls on board that were to be delivered at this rendezvous. If the *Efficacy* does not appear, we will have to find them a home."

"Or they could join the fight."

"Half of our refugees are children. What if they are all that remains of Mutualism? Of what is good in our species?"

The XO lowered her head, chagrined. "Of course you are right. They must be protected."

"I'm willing to gamble my life in our venture, and you have agreed to follow me," the captain said. "But all of theirs? I cannot. I cannot."

The captain looked at his view screen one more time. "Where

is she?" he asked. The XO wished she had an answer. She did not. She remained silent. "Where is the *Efficacy*?"

Then, without another word, the captain turned and left the bridge, shaking his head and clenching his fists in troubled thought.

For the first time in many *molts*, the XO felt her captain's uncertainty. She must be careful not to communicate it to the rest of the crew. But she was distressed.

If *he*, if the captain she'd followed into dozens of engagements and emerged somehow alive, didn't know what do next, then who did?

Nobody.

SEVENTEEN

5 January 2076
Femtodynamics Warren D
Huntsville, Alabama

Boom, boom, boom!

Topside, the drop-rods had begun to fall once again. Surface transport would take a beating, but everyone was safely below ground. Safe for the moment. Sam could just imagine the pulverizing the surface infrastructure was taking.

She suspected there must be a major churn drop as well, or else planetary defense would have dealt with the rods. The servants in the upper atmosphere and the orbital guard must be scrambling like crazy.

Sam squeezed her unlit cigarette (how had *that* gotten there?), folded and crushed it in her palm, then put the crumbly mass into her lab-coat pocket. "Okay, my dears," she said to her gathered team. "Welcome to the Chinese Wall once again. Functions? Information flow? What have we got?"

Before them, in chroma re-creation, the Kilcher artifact hung in macabre three-dimensional splendor.

Sam's first impression was that she was looking at an enormous narwhale tusk, or the horn of a zombie unicorn cut through with some animating, undead fungus. It was simultaneously lovely and nasty-looking. Menacing.

The artifact had the appearance of a twisted horn, a pointed stake tapering from about the thickness of a body-length at its base to a rounded point a human hand might cup comfortably at its tip. The raised, weltlike striations of the artifact's twist were crusted with flaky extruded salt and coruscated blisters of rust. The declivities of the artifact between were blackened by a smear of something that looked very like mold. You got the sense that it would be soft to the touch—and quite possibly poisonous.

She turned to Remy, her IT whiz—a virtuoso at computational modeling. Sam rarely trusted virtual creations to match reality, but she trusted Remy's. He didn't fudge, and he told you when he was making an educated guess. "How close are we on this?"

"If the translation of the material is correct, this is how the artifact would appear," Remy said with a slight French accent. "But as to how it works or what it does, or if it actually *does* anything..."

"Yeah, that's the trillion dollar question," Sam replied.

Sam's team was gathered around the chroma projection of the artifact. Some stood still. Others tried to see it from different angles. Bai, her quantum chromadynamist and chemical engineer, fidgeted and bit her black-painted nails and occasionally whisked stringy hair from her eyes. Total darkender. Amusing, because Sam knew she was in a quiet relationship with Reynolds, her straightlaced evangelical mathematician. Sam decided to give them a few more minutes before she started the differential.

She knocked out another Rojo and had it in her mouth before she realized what she was doing. Probably best not to light up at the moment, but holding the cigarette calmed her. She rolled it around between her right index finger and thumb, felt the tobacco give within the packed cylinder of paper.

Nothing like an early conference call with your high-flying, perpetually caffeinated boss—oh, and additionally with the *U.S. president*—to put a quick step in your morning. Especially when the purpose of the call was to push you to figure out an entire new branch of science and decipher an enemy's superweapon in the process—not necessarily in that order, but all preferably by lunch, if possible.

You want it *when*?

The problem was, it wasn't Kylie Jorgenson or President Frost imposing the deadline. The approaching sceeve armada was doing that. They were closing from Alpha Centauri, having obliterated the Extry outpost there. They were now spreading in a half-domed canopy formation, vectoring in on the solar system and scheduled to arrive from galactic north at the Kuiper Belt. Control of the Kuipers was strategically important, since it was an area rich with throwing rocks for rapid rearmament of kinetic weaponry. The Extry fleet was already there, determined to deny the sceeve the resource or, if not, to use the Kuipers for cover and camouflaged attack if the anticipated space battle came down to guerilla tactics and harassing strikes.

There was, of course, the possibility that the sceeve would alter course and attempt a solar-system entry at the asteroid belt or even glean the Jovian system for debris. But most bets were on the Kuipers for the coming Ragnarok—as a steady stream of returning scout craft seemed to confirm.

The sceeve were predictable if nothing else, Sam thought. *At least we have that on our side.* Of course, when one side possesses near overwhelming force, bringing unpredictable tactics to bear was usually beside the point.

Sam had given up her morning bicycle rides in to work through Huntsville's hilly terrain for the past weeks as air attacks escalated, and she missed them. She'd reluctantly accepted a servant chauffeur at Jorgenson's insistence, even though she still liked to override the autopilot and drive herself. But during her four a.m. commute in this morning, she'd surrendered the car to autopilot and watched the news in a chroma hover display.

Not good. The capitol complex in Dallas had been under a virtual siege yesterday with an anti-war rally in full swing. In Old City Park, one speaker after another took to a platform denouncing the "instigationist" policy of Frost and her Recommitment Party. Chief among the rabble-rousers was none other than retired admiral Alan Tillich. In the past days, he'd found a second career as a public figure, and there was talk of his running for Senate in the November midterms on a Quietist ticket.

That is, *if* there was going to be a November at all for humans.

Those people can't believe it's happening again, Sam had thought. *They're blocking it out, trying to wish it away. Talk it away.*

That had been her first, charitable response. Later she had come to other, darker conclusions.

Boom! Another drop plowed into Huntsville.

The lights flickered, as did the artifact representation before them. Power switching, compensation. A plant may have been taken out. After a moment, the image held steady once again.

Reynolds, her mathematician, spoke first. "So, for one thing, I'm getting some really strange return values trying to calculate the density. Keep having to renormalize infinities. I hate that. Makes for a wanky equation."

Sam nodded. "Or points toward something we're not considering. What if you don't renormalize?"

"Insanity. Densities greater than the known universe, that sort of thing."

"All right. What else do we have?"

"Even with renormalization, the fact that it doesn't warp space-time when it ought to is kind of not right," said Vitogard, a materials physicist and Sam's main experiment-builder. "I mean they presumably pick this thing up, move it around somehow. It's heavy. Like quark-matter heavy. Or at least it should be. But the specs say otherwise. So we have to be dealing with an alternate physics, something we're going to have conceptualize—"

"Or a black hole," Sam replied.

"It is spooky similar, but—"

"I know, you're pulling for something we actually know the physics for," Sam said with a smile. "So am I."

"But black holes are spooky just because we can't look inside them," said Sam's chromodynamics specialist, Bai. "What if it's a black hole that's taken or been fed a massive dose of J?" Bai, who'd been playing with her hair while considering the artifact, spoke in a quiet voice. Bai had been lurking in a corner, her straight black hair, as usual, nearly covering the features of her extremely pale face. She didn't get out of the lab much, if ever.

Reminds me of me, back in the day, Sam thought.

"J? Angular momentum, you mean?" she said.

"Yeah," answered Bai. "A normal black hole has mass greater than the J and the charge right? Has to. That's the *definition* of the event horizon."

"The squares of the mass, angular mo, and charge," said Sam. "Square of the mass is always greater than the square of J plus the square of Q."

"Actually the momentum component is J divided by the mass squared," put in Reynolds.

"So if you up the J or the charge, you could eventually tip the scales," Bai said. "Make angular momentum and charge greater than the mass. You'd strip the event horizon away, and there would sit your singularity."

"It's been discussed for decades in theory," Vitogard said. "Nobody knows what would happen. So, assuming this is somehow possible to do and you suddenly are able to see inside a black hole, what would you see?"

Sam pointed toward the floating virtual representation. "Maybe this," she said. "*This* in real life."

Sam noticed her cigarette again. Oh, what the hell? She shook it and the churn on the tip lit it up and she was breathing in the smoke. No one objected. They didn't seem to notice.

"So we assume it's, what? What would you call such a thing?" asked Vitogard.

"I think you might call it an evaporated black hole," Sam said.

"Of course," Reynolds suddenly said. "Of course that's what it is." He furiously scribbled away with his finger, seemingly on the air itself. He looked a bit like a spindly limbed wizard working up a spell. Sam noticed that Bai was looking on adoringly.

Sam adjusted her chroma and examined Reynold's hasty equation. Its terms and variables floated in the air about him in pinks and yellows. "What if the mass is nil but the J and Q remain in place. Or are somehow *held* in place. Then you'd get what's left after a black hole has bled itself dry," Reynolds said. He pointed to the artifact. "You'd get *that.*"

Sam took another drag on her Rojo, breathed out. What a team she'd assembled. Maybe she really was management material after all.

"Okay, my dears, let's assume we've figured out what it is," she told them. "Now let's figure out what we can *do* with it."

18 January 2076
Vicinity of Alpha Centauri
A.F.V. *Indifference to Suffering* Dedicated Bomb Tug AE5515

Ah, Heavenly Road.
  So close.
  "Cradit!"
  Not now, not now!

"Cradit, where are you?"

So close. Heaven, heaven...

"Cradit what are you doing?"

Not now!

Commander Lareno Quartz Intrusion Cradit couldn't believe it. That twice-cursed Admiral Blawfus was calling him away from a pleasure-session *again*. So Blawfus was the boss? So what? He was also a half-hypha striped lowborn. The fact that Blawfus was his superior was going to be remedied one of these days. Cradit thumbed off the bomb-pod view screen and muted the feed.

Cradit had his positor fully unfurled into the hands of the whore, and she was chaffing him as if she were rolling a length of smoking coil. The odor of wet copper preceding the give of ejaculation let them both know that he was *nearly there, nearly there....*

Cradit puffed out vigorous esters of excitement—along with the slight but distinctive underlying odor of anxious craving. Even though Cradit knew she was completely protected from his orgasmic give, he found himself imagining that he was taking her hands-naked, open to the spume of his pod.

He was barbaric! He was done with pillaging and now was despoiling and shaming the alpha female of his defeated foe!

His she was.

Yes, why not?

He knew she was impressed by his rank, the quarters he'd established for her here in the bomb tug. He believed *she* thought of herself as his, as well. Why should she not? He was forced by protocol to share her with other flag officers, true, but he provided the funds for her primary upkeep. The problem was, those flag officers were apt to barge in at the most inopportune times. It seemed to him lately that every time he set the mood, prepared himself with a bit of pheremonal stimulant (illegal, of course, but harmless, harmless) to produce an erection, one of them would show up and insist on sharing the whore out.

It was as if they planned it.

Because they had.

He'd discovered as much when some junior officers had been careless in dissipating their talk in the rec area and Cradit had breathed in the truth.

It was a conspiracy to humiliate him! There was a plan afoot among his peers to keep tabs on his movements during his personal time, to *always* disturb him when he was with the whore. It wasn't right! It wasn't fair! And he didn't have to put up with it!

He was a cursed admiral's chief of staff, after all. His loyal aide-de-camp.

Cradit didn't know the whore's true name, and had never bothered to ask, although with a bit of discreet database massaging he was sure he could have turned it up. Besides, he liked her whore's name.

Sweetbreath.

Cradit gave a mighty thrust into her gills. Sweetbreath's hands trembled, and she moaned. She was getting pleasure from this, too! He knew she was, even though she still wouldn't let him nuzzle her afterward. That would come. He would have it all.

And now he'd managed to truly find time away for the two of them to be alone. And physically away as well, so those morons couldn't bother them. He'd commandeered the bomb tug (it hadn't taken much, just his officer's circlet) and simply taken off some distance from the armada flag vessel, the *Indifference to Suffering*. Why not? He was still within Q-containment limits.

He'd engaged the tug and lugged the pod (along with Sweetbreath's quarters among the weaponry, of course) to a safe distance—all by himself. He'd not taken fifth in Academy flight training for nothing!

He was at least an orbital away from the flag vessel. He and Sweetbreath were alone, finally—

The view-screen image came back to life with full sound feed. Blawfus had overridden the lockout. He could do that, of course. He was an admiral, and this was *his* fleet.

Curse him.

"Commander Cradit, disengage from that nonsense and get yourself back to the *Indifference* immediately." The voice sprayed loudly from every speaker in the pod. Damn it.

The form of Blawfus was displayed on the pod's small communications screen located just above the area where Sweetbreath had created her "nest," as she called it.

"I ought to spiral out your guts in front of the assembled armada," Blawfus said. "You've taken one of my *weapons* to conduct your little tryst, you twice-cursed fool."

"I needed a moment away.... The officers have been cruel and ... I've been undergoing a great deal of pressure, sir. I apologize and I—"

What was he saying? What could he say?

Cradit fell silent, hung his shoulders in shame.

"Shut up, Cradit. I could drum you out of the service and be within protocol," said Blawfus. "Let him go, whore."

Sweetbreath gave one more playful twist to his positor and then released it. It hung down sadly, it seemed to Cradit. Forlorn, corkscrewed, and limp.

Damn him! Damn the old stinker.

"Fortunately for you, Commander, I have need of you. We've received reports from scouts. My suspicions have been confirmed. A Mutualist vessel has indeed been spotted two light-years from Sol. There will be others, I'm sure. And if all goes well, we should have the humans, the Mutualists, and our errant vessel within our grip." Blawfus's muzzle widened in a wicked smile. "Think of it as a whore's grip. Something you're obviously familiar with. But we'll tighten our hands like a vise. We'll twist off their positors!"

Blawfus was right. If indeed they could isolate all three mission objectives in one location and deal with them in one swoop, it would be seen as a tactical and strategic masterpiece.

Engineered behind the scenes by me, *of course,* Cradit thought.

Cradit stifled a smile. Let Blawfus keep his delusions.

"The armada will move now," Blawfus continued. "You will be personally in charge of arranging the deployment."

Cradit shuddered with a wave of relief. Of course he had not *really* been in trouble for taking the bomb tug out for a spin. After all, the old stinker certainly couldn't operate the flag deck's operations and supply board without him.

"Of course, sir. I'm on my way, sir," Cradit said.

Blawfus nodded. A thought seemed to occur to him, and he whiffed out a chuckle. "Perhaps when this is over and goes well, Commander Cradit, we'll find a command worthy of your contribution. Maybe our old friend Arid Ricimer's vessel, eh?"

"Admiral? Are you serious, sir?"

Blawfus pulled his muzzle into another smile. "Deadly serious, Commander," he said. "Wartime breeds marvelous opportunity. An alert officer can rise rapidly. Especially the son of a Central Committee member such as yourself. For some of us, it was more difficult."

"Yes, sir."

Blawfus suddenly turned his gaze to Sweetbreath.

Cradit felt his simmering indigation rise higher.

What does he want with my—

No, mustn't be possessive. Not yet. She was, after all, the flag vessel's official prostitute.

"You, whore," said Blawfus.

"Yes, your Excellency" said Sweetbreath. The very scent of her words reinvigorated Cradit's positor into a slight swell. "Can I be of service? I promise my hands will be as soft as moss to your rocky cylinder."

Blawfus seemed tempted for a moment.

Curse him.

"Not now, but I'm impressed with these quarters you've established. The vessel gigolo has nothing so nice, I happen to know."

That I *established* for *her, as well,* Cradit thought. He reflected, not for the first time, that the armada without him would be a poorer, sadder place. He said nothing, however.

"My assigned quarters were a bit cramped for . . . the methods I employ." Sweetbreath's reply was a perfumed cloud of titillation. "I would be happy to demonstrate them for you, my admiral."

"As I said, not now," said Blawfus. "I will, however, be sending a certain receptor to you soon, a highly placed DDCM officer who has not yet sampled your wares, I think. He is called Porhok. I want you to save those hands for him between now and them. You'll know what to do when Porhok arrives, yes?"

"Your Excellency, of course. It is my duty. And my pleasure."

"Good," said Blawfus. He considered Sweetbreath a moment more. "Yes, you'll do nicely. Don't waste those hands on the lower grades any longer."

"As you command, your Excellence," Sweetbreath answered.

Cradit trembled at the humiliation. He'd store *this* slight in his *gid,* that was for certain. And one day—he would be the one serving out the humiliation. They would pay.

Blawfus would get no pass. *Of course he'd give me the vessel command to curry favor with mother,* Cradit thought. *I owe him nothing for that.*

"Get back to the vessel, Cradit." Blawfus's form blinked off the display screen.

Fuck you, stinker. Fuck, fuck, fuck you.

Cradit shook his head. It could have been worse. He really had gone way beyond protocol with this excursion. But, blessed relief, it looked like he would get away with it after all. For now he'd better get himself back, however.

"He's a quick one, that Blawfus," Sweetbreath said after she was sure the admiral was no longer listening in. "Thinks well on who to poke hard and who to soften up first before hammering them with the good stones."

Cradit gave an exasperated huff. So now she was puffing all over the admiral? Sweetbreath certainly *was* a whore. They all were, of course. At least she admitted what she was.

He'd make them pay. One day. He *would*, curse it. But for now—

"Shut up," Cradit said. "What do *you* know, anyway?"

Sweetbreath bowed her head in the posture of humility. "Nothing, sir, nothing" she said. "Please don't be offended at the folly of us whores. We think with our hands, we do."

EIGHTEEN

19 January 2076
Vara Nebula
approaching Eridani Gate
USX *Joshua Humphreys*

Coalbridge was salting himself up for his watch when SIGINT acquired the sceeve vessel on the beta.

Here we go, he thought. And two light-years from Sol system. Like the bad old days.

He continued calmly to outfit himself in the bridge prep area while his third watch officer, Valdiviezo, began the run-up to battle configuration.

Getting ready for work was a gooey, uncomfortable, necessary affair. While human and computer interfaces had transformed amazingly in the past several years, Coalbridge reflected that the Singularity—the moment of transhuman machine-man transcendent symbiosis—had most definitely *not* arrived.

Coalbridge first droppered each of his ears with a gel-like solution of communication salt, then closed his earflaps with his fingers and swirled his head around to work it down the ear canal. Primitive but effective. Next Coalbridge tossed his head back and dropped visual-feedback salt from a small bottle into his eyes. The gunk smeared his vision momentarily, but with a couple of blinks it soon dispersed over each of his corneas and became invisible.

Sure will be happy when humans really go cyborg and all of this crap is permanent, Coalbridge thought. Continually having to reapply and recharge salt was a pain in the ass. Human-made nanotech currently had the strength and longevity of an old-fashioned cell phone battery—and, like a cell battery, was at risk of wearing out or going dead at a crucial moment.

Salt, churn, and its nanotech progeny had not turned out to be the gray-goo menace it was cracked up to be by the Peepsies. One more thing they'd gotten hilariously wrong.

Give the engineers time back on Earth, and the stuff would get easier to use—and more lethal—he was sure. The world had changed more in the past twelve years than it had in the two hundred before that.

After a moment, the salt integrated with his senses. DAFNE spoke to him in his inner ear.

He was wiied to the chroma.

"NIRCEIS systems are nominal, Captain Coalbridge," she said. NIRCEIS was the official acronym for salt. "Shall I activate watch transfer protocols?"

"Activate," Coalbridge replied.

He felt the inside of his ears grow warm as DAFNE formatted the blank salt and keyed a security protocol and coded handshake into all its intercommunication subroutines. Half of the energy that the salt lost was expended in setup, but that couldn't be helped. Without secure lines of communication, the words he exchanged with DAFNE or through her intracraft channels to the rest of the crew would be as open as any radio broadcast. He knew for certain that the sceeve had devices that could pick up such emissions.

Dumbass gaffes sink crafts. The slogan didn't quite have the ring of the old surface navy version, "loose lips sink ships," but it was memorable enough, Coalbridge figured.

DAFNE appeared before him in her blue-green, see-through geist form.

"Watch transfer complete, Captain," she reported. "Intravessel operations reassigned. All systems checked. Slight interference in wii D channel, probably due to inaccurately gauged femtothread in auxiliary transmission coil. Reroute ongoing. Otherwise, all com and command systems nominal."

"Acknowledged," said Coalbridge.

DAFNE's voice was modulated to sound as if it were emanating from her geist, which stood a comfortable distance from him. In actuality, of course, she was speaking to him—and only to him, unless they included others in the transmission—via vibrations along his ear canal.

"Give me boards and tanks," Coalbridge said. "Full tactical crown." Coalbridge stepped to the center of the bridge and took up his customary position behind the helmsman. A "crown" of display blinked into existence around his head, just above eye level. Coalbridge reached up and with a slightly hooked finger "pulled down" one of the displays, a three-dimensional tank that synthesized and represented data acquired within a one light-minute sector.

"Are we ready to take this thing on, XO?"

"Affirmative, Skip," DAFNE answered in her chipper voice.

Coalbridge smiled. One thing you could say about DAFNE—she was never a downer. At heart he suspected she was still sort of a carnie, running her roller coasters at Six Flags, making sure that nobody got hurt, but also ready to scare the hell out of her passengers in the process. They'd been through a lot together, and Coalbridge considered her his best friend. She'd saved his ass many times, including once when she'd pulled him out of a pit of black despair so deep there had been no way he was coming up under his own power.

He'd done his share of mending DAFNE's wounds, as well. Her original programmer had turned against what she had made of herself once he'd set her free in the crunch. He was one of the most visible of the Peepsies now and regularly denounced her as a war criminal. This betrayal had, Coalbridge suspected, broken DAFNE's heart. And made her all the more determined to remain loyal to friend and duty herself.

"Analysis, XO?" he said.

"The situation is only partially resolved," DAFNE answered. "The sceeve vessel does not seem to have spotted us yet, but if we make an approach, there is little doubt she will notice. At that point I do not have enough information to make an informed prediction, although I can suggest several hypotheses."

"Wait on that," Coalbridge said.

He pulled down another display and began inputting overall battle-configuration prep to his weaponry and telemetry. The various expers and personas in charge of these areas would implement his orders on a smaller scale. Right now, he just wanted to go in prepared. And armed up.

"We on beta silence?"

"Locked it in first thing, Captain."

"Very good."

From now on, quieting all beta emanations would be essential. In equal measure, Coalbridge hoped the sceeve vessel did no such thing itself. Beta was not like radio waves or radar. There was no triangulation necessary when locating a beta-conditioning transceiver. Only two Q-entangled signals were necessary. A beta message was carefully ensorcelled uncertainty on either velocity or location for a particle. It was Schrödinger's cat in a box. When you opened the box, the cat told you where it had come from and how fast it had arrived as part of its dying act. Every beta transmission contained its own countdown clock written into its essence, its own highly accurate radioactive-decay trigger, just as Schrodinger's thought experiment had the dead-undead cat. You couldn't send a beta message without giving away either your location or your velocity. If you sent two transmissions, your exact position among the stars could be fixed.

And you could be fired upon, if need be. Or fire upon others.

"Evasive, helm," Coalbridge said. "Standard."

"Aye, Captain," said Katapodis, the exper manning the wheel. He and his geist copilot were the closest thing to a cyborg symbiosis between human and servant yet created. In fact, several helmsmen and helmservants had not only fallen in love—but had gotten married.

It was a curious thing. Something Coalbridge was particularly curious about himself. He'd always wondered what sex with a servant could possibly be like. It involved lots of salt, that he knew. He'd secretly wondered what DAFNE might be like in the chroma sack but hadn't even begun to let those thoughts go far. Besides, DAFNE had a boyfriend, a servant back on Earth. One of the boyfriend's iterations was President Frost's chief of staff, KWAME. It was always confusing how the servants maintained individuality among their various copies (something to do with Q-based security codes that served as an immune-system analog for each instantiation, Coalbridge had been told). But *that* KWAME was not the copy with whom DAFNE was connected. The boyfriend was, instead, a biotech-lab manager in the New Pentagon.

Coalbridge relayed a couple of maneuvering instructions to the helmsman, all of them various presets that he and DAFNE had created while watching recording after recording of various battles with the sceeve and taking into account their own experiences, as well. Zigzag, the old ship pilots had called it during the Second World War. Q-zig was a little different because you didn't necessarily have to move *through* space to get from one point to another. Q-driving was a lot like the movement of a knight on a chessboard. Although there were lots more rules of when and where you could set down. And the possibility of being in two places at the same time was always an option. As weird as that sounded, it was a constant possibility with travel through Q-space, and one that a good captain learned to use, if not to fully conceptually understand. No matter what, if you didn't Q-zig before dropping into N-space (where all fights ultimately took place), you could emerge from the Q into a dead drop of rocks or rods that would take you out using your own kinetic energy for the self-slaughter.

So now the NAV portion of the iron triangle of battle readiness was set. NAV-DELTA-ZAP. DELTA for defense, ZAP 1 and ZAP 2 on the twin weaponry hubs the *Humphreys* mounted. The bridge ZAP officer, First Lieutenant Monroe Sakuda, a post-invasion African immigrant (he'd been eleven when the first drop-rods fell), was formerly Kenyan, a Massai who'd grown up speaking Swahili and had a decided accent in English. ZAP controlled both hubs, which were in turn manned by exper and servants and personas in various combinations. DELTA officer was a servant, HUGH, with a lieutenant-commander rank, although the servants had their own complicated hierarchy of position, as well. HUGH manifested as a geist on the bridge but was dispersed vessel-wide, controlling his array of personas and commanding human adjuncts within the vessel-defense systems.

"DELTA, give me standard armor with a twenty percent forward b-layer concentration," said Coalbridge. "ZAP, unlock the mags on the AM cores."

"Aye, Captain," answered DELTA.

"Yes, sir," said Sakuda, a trace of enthusiasm in his voice that matched Coalbridge's own. Sakuda cultivated a devil-may-care attitude. Coalbridge had seen him use a handful of one hundred dollar bills to light his pot pipe in Red Houses on Ceres Base several months ago. But he was proficient and precise when on duty, or Coalbridge wouldn't have had him as ZAP.

They were drawing nearer to the unidentified vessel that had occasioned the alert in the first place. Coalbridge remained in Q-space but ordered the helm to drop his speed to well below *c*.

"Okay, ZAP, get me two nukes up and running, and wake up a couple of personas and beam them keys to man them. Confirm and apply secondary security answerback before unlocking. DAFNE will squirt you the servant archive combination for decompressing the personas priority alpha."

"Key received and DECOMP underway, Captain," came the reply. Seconds later: "Servants decompressed and set for batch loading." The nukes were under a couple of layers of protection against accidental firing, but Coalbridge like to strip his security clean before a possible engagement to be on the safe side. You didn't want to die with a full arsenal of nukes you could not fire because the launch codes weren't done shaking hands with a million-hexadecimal security lock.

"Roger that, ZAP," Coalbridge replied. "Now load the rocks."

"Number of launcher arrays, Captain?"

Getting the rocks into their slings was a process that was almost as literal as it sounded. The "slings," however, were powered by coupled-charge rail guns. Some "FTL" shot was bottled up in Q and capable of deployment the moment the vessel dropped from Q—with exactly the same momentum, plus the slingshot throw, that the vessel dropped in with.

"All arrays on line, ZAP!"

"Aye, Captain. Fifty-two slingshots cocked, standard scatter ranging."

Coalbridge felt better already. Rocks were the space warrior's best friend. Explosive force was nice for precision work, but there was no thermal convection in a vacuum, no disruptive waves of heat and tornado-like wind. All nukes had going for them was radiation, and spacecraft were pretty good at handling onslaughts of radiation as a matter of course. No, nothing crippled or destroyed artificial structures in space like pure kinetic-energy weaponry—i.e., anything you could throw at your opponent with a modicum of force.

Which was why the old hands at space warfare had nicknamed it the Game of Rocks and Rods. You battered your opponent's forward defenses with rocks. You blasted your way through his bottle armor with nukes. And then you finished him off with rods—going for a rip, a tear, even a strategic puncture.

Because the not-so-dark secret of spacecraft was that they were actually *anti-space* craft, designed specifically to keep space and all its implications *out*.

Coalbridge had been in vessels where bottle failure had exposed them to vacuum several times. There was a cascading chain of failsafes built in, of course (thanks to Admiral Tillich's obsession), with several emergency SQUID devices remaining isolated and unentangled on a quantum level with the craft drives and main bottle. The worst had been the Gliese 876 battle with the sceeve attack craft when he'd lost so many. The pseudogravity had cut out as well, and Coalbridge had found himself floating on his PC's bridge, on an inertial course for the abyss. He'd found purchase, managed to pull himself into the yellow-circled "safe" area where the emergency bottle would be reestablished. But then another blast of rods had pummeled the patrol craft, and the emergency bottle had to wait for the armor surge to clear before turning itself on.

The last thing Coalbridge remembered was the water on his tongue starting to boil. He'd passed out and come to only four minutes after as the atmosphere reached Earth stratosphere pressure. This was a good thing, because the craft persona had been wiped by an EMP and nobody was left alive on the bridge to drive the vessel. Coalbridge had wasted no time hightailing it out using the emergency manual controls (another Tillich requirement on all vessels).

He'd lost the battle itself by underestimating the wiliness of his foe. Most sceeve tactics were predictable, and they usually revolved around the ability to rapidly change formation in a group of vessels. The sceeve were masters of rocks and rods, and they liked to hunt in packs. The groups themselves could be combined, Lego fashion, into larger or smaller units, and the sceeve were very good at transfiguring these formations quickly. What they didn't do too often was hunt alone.

Coalbridge had been surprised to find the sceeve vessel by itself. It was clearly sniffing out the human activity in the area. The red dwarf was being considered for an advanced base, and several large vessels were in the area performing surveys. Coalbridge had been on outer-perimeter patrol when he'd picked up the barest two-blip minimum on the beta. The sceeve commander was being very careful about pinpointing himself with transmissions.

Coalbridge had taken the patrol craft in silent—but someone somewhere on the vessel was conditioning beta (he'd later learned it was an exper's fancy new Q-enhanced Palace, left on in a locker), and the sceeve commander had been alerted. He'd jumped into Q, and Coalbridge, cursing, had wasted a throw of perfectly useless rods through the space where he had been. Coalbridge had figured he'd scared his quarry away and was running scans of the area to see if any surveillance paraphernalia had been left behind when the sceeve had popped back into N-space about a kilometer from the point he'd made his exit.

The move was called a "suture." Normally, you couldn't return to the immediate vicinity where you'd jumped for a time (and that could vary from a day to a week), because, in essence, you'd used up all the uncertainty you had access to in the area. But there was an exception, *if* you planned for it in advance. With a powerful enough quantum algorithm, you could mark and save your exact entry point and only use *some* of the resolution of spin states necessary to drop into N-space.

Then, when you jumped back to Q-space, you had a choice. Go on to a new destination or double back to your exact entry point to the area, the marked and saved space. It was like making a quantum double stitch in Newtonian space-time. You snapped back to exactly where you'd dropped in before as the remaining entangled uncertain states resolved themselves. Not only was there the suture, there was even a so-far entirely theoretical move called a *double suture* where you made an exact exchange of quantum state information with *another* vessel and dropped back to N-space precisely where *it* had previously entered the area.

No Extry craft had ever pulled off a suture movement in battle conditions, and Coalbridge was the first to observe a sceeve vessel accomplish one.

I didn't just observe, Coalbridge thought. *I took it in the jaw.*

At close range, the sceeve vessel had ripped the hell out of Coalbridge's little PC. He'd fought back, been chased, turned, and fought some more. He'd finally been able to shake the sceeve pursuer by passing through the edges of Gliese 876 D, a Jupiter analog. The bigger sceeve vessel hadn't been able to follow and exclude entanglement, and the PC had nearly not made it. It had been a desperate gambit.

All told, Coalbridge had lost over half his crew, including a previous XO and good friend. It had been the worst drubbing he'd taken in his career, and he'd felt like a schooled little boy at the hands of the sceeve skipper, whoever he or she was. Playing back images of the fight, Coalbridge had found the sceeve vessel's markings.

She'd been called the *Powers of Heaven.*

Coalbridge checked his largest display once more. There was his blip. There was the sceeve. They were almost on top of one another.

"Helmsman, take us to N-space," Coalbridge said. "Set us down next to that sceeve, zero polar moment."

"Aye, Captain," said the helmsman. "Drop in three, two, one—"

And they were in N-space.

The solar system was a pinprick nearly two light-years away—about as bright as the star Sirius in the Earth night sky would have been.

And there within shouting distance—if, of course, the two vessels hadn't been separated by the void—was the vessel the Poet had told them about, the vessel they had come to find.

Only it *wasn't.*

This was not a Sporata war vessel.

It *was* sceeve. Coalbridge could instantly see that. It had all the lines. And it was *big.* The *Humphreys* was a baseball next to a basketball in size comparison. And something was very, very wrong with the other craft.

"What the . . . Geist Leher up here, will you DAFNE?"

"Yes, sir."

Good Lord, he thought, gazing off the transparent edge of the bridge at the sceeve craft, *what a goddamn piece of* crap.

If ever there were a sceeve vessel that did not look combat-ready, this was it. Coalbridge had seen supply barges and other sceeve logistics and service craft that were not Sporata vessels, but he'd never seen a sceeve vessel look so . . . slovenly. She was in a slow Newtonian spin, seemingly out of control, like a globe in a gimbal. Her exterior was dinged up, pocked with meteor scars, as if her protecting nanotech was depleted, doing a slack and lackadaisical job.

Acne, Coalbridge thought. *She looks like a teenager with a nasty case of untreated acne.*

Blech.

She was roughly spherical. She was metallic, but with only a faint luster. Face it, she was downright *dirty.* Which meant she'd probably come from a planetary atmosphere recently. Which meant—God knew what it meant. He'd never seen a sceeve craft this large that was capable of planetary operations.

"Bring us into an approach tangent with that...vessel," Coalbridge ordered Katapodis, his helmsman.

"Aye, sir, solution indicates fifty-five degrees at point eight-eight *c*," Katapodis answered.

"Okay, take us in," Coalbridge said. "Rocks on line yet, ZAP?"

"Armed and dangerous, Captain," Sakuda answered. Coalbridge had a special spot in his heart for Sakuda and all of his ZAPs, though he tried not to let it show overmuch. In addition to having been his own Extry specialty, ship defensive weaponry had been his first assignment in the navy aboard the *Gerald R. Ford*.

"Very good."

Coalbridge turned back to the sceeve vessel. Under normal circumstances, in very short order he would attempt, and very likely succeed, in blowing this thing to Kingdom Come.

Leher's geist appeared before him on the bridge.

"Lieutenant Commander, input please," Coalbridge said.

Leher's blue-green semitransparent face was smiling. "Been monitoring the bridge feed, Captain," Leher said. "Think I can tell you something about that vessel."

Coalbridge motioned to the display tableau hanging above them in the chroma.

"So, Mr. Leher," he said. "What have you got?"

"She identifies as the *Efficacy of Symbiosis*. I've actually found reference to her in the Skyhook registry," Leher said. "She used to be a freighter of some sort. Foodstuff. That goo the sceeve absorb through their feet. What it *appears* to be is a freighter that the Mutualist converted to a transport, if all those life-sign readings are right."

"They're cross-verified," Coalbridge said. "We've got a vessel full of sceeve over there. Not your standard crew profile, either. Various sizes. Never seen that before. Are there dwarf variants of these things?"

"Could be children," Leher said.

"I'll be damned. What an idiot I am," Coalbridge said. He seemed genuinely abashed at himself. "Of course they're children. That never occurred to me."

"You thinking about blowing them out of existence?" Leher asked.

"The thought had crossed my mind," Coalbridge answered. "But no. Not unless they become a direct threat."

"LOVE, can you give me a trace on the Schism report?" Leher subvocalized. LOVE instantly instantiated as a geist beside Leher. She kept herself short—maybe five two or so—but LOVE filled herself out nicely. *Very* nicely, Coalbridge noted.

"Okay, you know that sceeve vessels always have a bicameral computer system, right?" said Leher.

Coalbridge nodded. "Sure. They're freaks for redundancy. So are we, in our way."

"Partially, that's true," Leher said. "But a sceeve craft computer is modeled on the sceeve nervous system."

"They have two brains. You kill them by taking out the *gid*. You take out the other, they're liable to take *you* out before they die of blood loss—or whatever that milky crap is that runs through their veins."

"Exactly," Leher said. "In one way, the *gid* is like the medulla in humans. It controls their autonomous bodily functions. But that's only the half of it."

"How do you mean?"

"It's where they store their collective memories. Their hypha memories. Every sceeve has the memories of his whole family line packed in there somewhere."

"That's tens of thousands of years."

"Well, it's more like they've got the highlight reels," Leher said. "A sceeve can decide what gets stored in his own *gid* during the course of his lifetime. So there are basically two personalities in a sceeve individual. One is in charge, and you can think of it as something like the conscious mind. The other is the hypha memory—the *gid*."

LOVE coughed—a strange sound coming from a servant geist. "If I may cut straight to the point, sir?"

Leher shrugged, nodded.

"It's analogous to epilepsy," LOVE said. "One or both of the craft's systems sends a huge amount of nonsense signals to the other. There's an automatic answerback that occurs—like a public-key encryption system acknowledging a secure connection. This reflective process sets up massive feedback, and basically the afflicted vessel has a seizure."

"An epileptic seizure."

"The analogy is surprisingly robust, from what we can tell from the databases."

"So you're telling me that Mutualist craft out there has epilepsy?"

"The state is called 'the throes' by the sceeve. Based on our research, Captain—"

"*Her* research," Leher put in, indicating LOVE. "LOVE is Xenology Division authority on sceeve a.i.s."

LOVE glanced at Leher and gave him the slightest of smiles, but enough for Coalbridge to notice. Something else there? That was always the question with servant emotional displays.

"Based on the research," LOVE said, "what you're seeing is an exact match for the way the condition is described in the databases." LOVE nodded toward space. "The spin she's displaying is characteristic of the malfunction. On the other hand..."

LOVE looked to Leher. Leher seemed about to speak, then held back.

"On the other hand," said Coalbridge, "The Poet said we would find a Sporata vessel of war when we got here, which is why we've been riding here hell for leather for the past eight days. And that thing, whatever it may be—"

"I think it's the *Guardian*," Leher said softly.

"You do?" said Coalbridge.

"Camouflage," Leher said. "LOVE and I have been parsing her transmissions since we got within beta range. Made some adjustments suggested by your friend Japps, too," Leher said with a wry smile. "She's using the same code as the Poet. The cinnamon ester marker. Look."

Leher popped up a shared a screen in front of Coalbridge and himself. It displayed a series of chemical symbols that meant nothing to Coalbridge.

"Now, if I put a matte over it," Leher said, waving his hand and placing a cutout overlay onto the symbols. "I get this."

Still made no sense. "Translation, please," said Coalbrige.

Leher smiled. "Tell him, LOVE."

"Captain, it's a repeated message. It says 'Guardian of Night' over and over again in the Long-arm hypha sceeve variant preferred by Sporata. The same variant spoken by the Poet."

"There's one sure way to test the hypothesis," Leher said. He shrugged. "I don't know if you want to take the chance on our being wrong, though."

"We ask," said Coalbridge.

Leher nodded. "So, Captain—feel like knocking on heaven's door?"

Coalbridge turned to Katapodis. "Helm, take us abaft that vessel. Angle us to port around her equator, and then give me a polar section."

"Aye, Captain, turning forty-five to port," said the helmsman.

"I want to get a full scan on this vessel," Coalbridge said to himself, then with a touch on the hovering toolbar wiied SIGINT. Petrovich, SIGINT chief warrant officer, was on duty and his geist appeared as an iconed triple stripe hovering in Coalbridge's vision. "SIG, I'm going to want to send a single blip with the beta. We'll let them know where exactly we are and nothing more. On my mark—"

Suddenly, Petrovich's icon expanded into a full-faced geist. "Sorry, Captain, we've just—"

Petrovich glanced down, offscreen, looked back up. "Incoming beta signal, Captain," he said. "It's another sceeve vessel, Captain. She's blasting the beta, identifying herself."

"Who is she? Does she know we're here?"

"No, sir. It doesn't appear so. Captain, she's identifying as the *Efficacy of Symbiosis.*"

"What? Wait, that's the *other* ship."

"I know, sir. I doesn't make sense. But she's clearly identifying as the *Efficacy.* Broadcasting it over and over again."

"She's the real one," Leher put in. "This is the rendezvous point, after all."

Maybe.

But it didn't add up.

None of it.

Everything about this was wrong, wrong, wrong. Coalbridge's every instinct told him so.

Choose, Coalbridge thought. *Choose, choose, choose. I want information!* "DAFNE? Tactical report."

"Working." In a half second, she popped up a visual display. Coalbridge scrutinized it.

Warcraft. Sceeve. This time there was no mistaking. Coalbridge had seen the configuration all too often.

And was it?—yes. Fuck. He had seen *this vessel.*

He'd seen these red, yellow, and plum markings—whorls of color spread around her scythe-blade-shaped bow like henna tattoos. He knew her, all right.

"DAFNE, tell me I'm right," Coalbridge said. "Tell me that's the *Powers of Heaven*."

A moment's processing, then a quick reply. "Yes, Captain. It is the *Powers*."

And then Coalbridge smiled, let out a short laugh as the situation fell into place in his mind. He knew what to do.

"DELTA, got a POSVEC on her?"

"We've got position. Working on velocity," said HUGH from across the bridge.

"DELTA, is she still in Q? Get me her delta-v!"

"On it," HUGH replied. "Preliminary. Q-space, but slowing. Approximately two light-minutes. Position Bootes two o'clock."

"DAFNE, tactical assessment," said Coalbridge. "Does the *Powers* even know we're here?"

A pause. Then a smile. "I don't think so, Captain," DAFNE said. She pulled down the scenario display, pointed to their current position. "We're partially occluded by the *Efficacy*—or whomever that is—relative to the approaching Sporata vessel at this point. Even if we aren't one hundred percent beta silent, I think he won't have time to distinguish that we're here."

Coalbridge thought the same thing. He looked into his XO's steady, semitransparent eyes. Then he focused *through* them, focused on the stars beyond.

"DAFNE, still think we can pull off a suture?"

A second. Two. DAFNE flickered.

Must be some massive calculation going on, Coalbridge thought. Then she chuckled.

Moments like this, you sometimes doubted. A computer talking, sure. But laughing? Real or programming? Yet it didn't sound simulated. Not in the slightest. There was simply no way to tell. And if you can't tell the difference, the Turing is passed. Yeah, DAFNE was a person. He'd bet his life on it.

"I can," DAFNE said. "I can calculate and actuate it."

Coalbridge nodded. "Let's do it."

"Fun," DAFNE said. After only a second or two she was ready. "Regional snapshot complete, demons in place."

Coalbridge smiled a wolfish smile. "Sun's rising somewhere on Earth," he said. "It's a new day. Let's make a little Extry history, XO."

"Aye, Captain."

NINETEEN

19 January 2076
Vara Nebula
Eridani Gate
A.S.C. *Powers of Heaven*

So, Companion Arid, you are a fool after all. Either that, my friend, my competitor, or you have gone insane. In any case, a complete disappointment to me. A sadness upon my gid.

Cliff-clinging-icefall Malako, captain of the Sporata attack vessel *Powers of Heaven,* gazed out at the starbright heavens and pondered his next move. He swayed in his command atrium and let the data on the Mutualist transport flow through him via Lamella, while another part of his mind, the part he never showed to computers, to his wife—not that she would understand if he did—in fact, to no one except a select few, brooded over the dark and upsetting complications of his recent life.

He'd lost a friend, an old, dear friend. Arid Ricimer had been one of those—few and far between—with whom Malako occasionally opened up. They'd been top-level students together at the Sporata Academy.

Ricimer with his purebred hypha hadn't disdained someone from a lichen-infested hybrid hypha but had seen in Malako a kindred spirit. Malako, for his part, had been extraordinarily grateful, and his gratitude had turned to lasting friendship after Ricimer time and again disdained getting by on his heritage and proved himself to be a deep thinker—and as much of a clever trickster as Malako knew himself to be.

Together, they'd solved the final problem of the professors and won the Culmination Award for their graduating class.

They'd been more than friends back then. Almost hypha mates, especially for Malako, who'd never belonged to a real family and had finally found one in the Sporata.

My closest brother.

Ricimer. The poor dead slob.

What broke your mind, old friend?

It was the death of Del and the children, no doubt, that had first sent Ricimer over the edge. Which was understandable. Malako had known and been half in love with Del, too. Her kindness, her understanding of the sailor's life. And a keen intelligence that was perhaps not as honed as Ricimer's but was deep and wide. The loss of her *gid*, and the wisdom therein, would be felt by her hypha for generations.

But the Administration had its reasons, and the greater needs of society must be served.

That we can endure such refining and emerge the stronger species—this is why we are Guardians.

And Mutualism? The worst sort of heresy to be involved with. Ultimately, Del must have turned into one of those soft-minded imbeciles herself and pulled her mate along with her.

Ricimer had lost touch with history. It was the only rational explanation for his behavior. He'd been absorbed in the opiate of myth and unlearned the great lesson of the Guardian past.

Winners write history.

Be a winner or be written out.

And Guardian history was punctuated by massive genocidal wars. The accounts of those wars were intricate and varied, but a continuing theme was the choice between parasitism and symbiosis. It was a staple of Guardian historical education. The wars had been waged by "resource groups" that controlled particular sources of elemental wealth. These resource groups eventually coalesced into the sceeve shiros, or nation-states.

In the end, inevitably, thought Malako, the parasites won. Regulation, its philosophy, viewed the parasite as the keystone, the highest point, in a galactic ecological web.

It's irrefutable, Malako thought. *Wealth cannot be created or destroyed; it can only change hands. Resources are finite. New resources can only enter the economy through discovery and conquest. Parasites are at the top of the food chain. They regulate predation by controlling both predators and prey. They create and enforce* justice. *And I am its instrument. I am the spot where the hand meets the task.*

Mutualists were weak. They did *not* understand that the galactic economy was zero-sum. They thought of wealth as some sort of soft-minded, nebulous concept. The role of the symbiot was to aid other species in the creation of new resources.

The Symbiotic Heresy had been defeated, but never died. And now it had taken root once again like a disease, a blight upon the species. When the previous Depletion Tax came in lower than expected, there was no doubt the fault was Mutualism. A pogrom was inevitable.

The moment Del consorted with those scum, she'd doomed herself and Ricimer's children.

And now Ricimer. Tainted along with his doomed family. As good as wiped from existence.

And for what? Malako couldn't bring himself to believe that Arid Ricimer had become a soft-thinking Mutualist fool. No, there was only one motive he could fathom. Revenge.

The one emotion Ricimer himself had cautioned his friend never to act on. It broke discipline. It was bad for morale within the vessel and for your own standing without.

It would get you killed.

Malako had listened. Yes, he would take care of Ricimer.

Yet still, Ricimer was clever, never to be underestimated. Here he was disguised as a Mutualist abomination of a vessel. He'd probably fooled the armada into thinking that was exactly what he was—a threat to be dealt with later.

And putting her in the throes? Genius.

One nuke ought to be enough.

"We've got her dead to rights, Captain," said Lieutenant Tercid, Malako's weapons officer. "Solutions loaded for multiple weaponry options."

Malako glanced over to his vessel's political officer, Lavkit, who had been Transel's second-in-command.

"Receptor Lavkit, do we have permission to proceed?"

Lavkit was a small female but possessed powerful shoulders and big hands. Several of the officers had pronounced her attractive, but Malako didn't see it. The shoulders took away from whatever beauty the hands possessed. Malako despised her, but she was, to his mind, still a huge improvement over Transel. Besides, she had not shed the tendency to obey. It usually took a while in charge for a political officer to become a complete asshole.

"Proceed at your own discretion, Captain, and thrive the Administration," Lavkit replied.

"Thrive the Administration," said Malako and turned to Tercid.

Battle. His element. Away from all the intrigue, the double-dealing back in the Shiro. This was where he was meant to be.

The *Guardian of Night*

The Efficacy, *at last!*

When the Guardian vessel had first appeared, Ricimer's *gid* had surged with joy. His goal was completed. He could deliver his charges to safety! He could then with honor seek his fate with the humans.

Relief flooded Ricimer.

But it had taken mere *vitia* for doubts to set in.

Mere *vitia,* but too long, too late.

A quick analysis of the beta transmission. No proper answer-back codes.

Visual inspection.

Realization.

Despair.

His gambit had failed. Ricimer felt sadness wash over him. Of course the odds of success had been almost impossible to begin with.

"We have been found out. Take us out of the throes," Ricimer said to Talid. "All shields concentrate. Vector on the approaching craft."

Confusion in Talid's expression. "Aye, Captain. It shall be so." Then alarm. "We are exposed. Shields will not absorb an attack at this distance."

"Yes. I know, Commander Talid," Ricimer said with a quiet jet of measured emotion. "Nevertheless, prepare for battle."

He'd almost succeeded. The scouts had passed him by, left him as a problem to be dealt with by the armada. And by then, he'd have found a way to off-load his charges, contact the humans.

Yes, he'd fooled his enemies. But he hadn't fooled his friends.

Oh, he recognized the one he was facing, all right.

Malako.

He had many professional acquaintances—one acquired them over the course of a career through the mere process of doing one's work, carrying on. Some were pleasant enough, some were useful. But none of these relationships would last beyond a few *molts*. His true friends, his real friends, were with him always, even when they were far away. He checked his behavior according to how they would judge him. He wished to be considered as worthwhile—no, as *good*—in their estimation. These were the friends whose memory he would enfold into his *gid*. Of these, there were only a few.

Malako had been one.

He was an officer of fierce intelligence born to a blasted hypha, his fate predetermined. No, there would never be an admiralty for Malako. Captains must be competent, but above that level, political connections were far more important.

Cliff-clinging-icefall Malako. The other plebes had called him "Clinger" in the Academy, and it was an insult. Malako had always seemed to them to be hanging on to the sheer cliff face of his career in the Sporata by the tips of his gills. But the captain of the Mutualist vessel had from the start called his friend "Ice." Ice for his perfection, his cool deliberation under pressure. By the end of their studies, his name had won out. Malako was known by all as "Ice." There was truth in the first name, as well, though, the captain reflected. Malako was as stubborn as they came. As stubborn as he himself had been.

I never imagined it would be you, yet it makes sense, old companion.

Ricimer whiffed at the irony.

Malako had been one of the few for him—a friend of the *gid*.

Now Cliff-clinging-icefall Malako was about to kill him.

The *Powers of Heaven*

"Go with a forward bottle," Malako told the weapons officer. In his intensity of concentration, Malako accidentally breathed in his own words as he spoke. They tasted a bit like the soup he'd absorbed for dinner the night before.

In it also was the odor of apprehension, but not of the flight response. No, his fear had long been well under control. Malako took a deep breath. Another. There. He'd done it, just as Ricimer had taught him when they were scrub ensigns together serving aboard that old battlecraft the *Orthogonal Electrostatic Wave Absorber*.

Ricimer's calming hand on his arm. His mint-like, calming words. "We all feel the panic, Ice. It's part of our biology. Work through it. Turn it under your feet. Feed upon it for courage."

But he didn't feel particularly courageous now. Merely resigned to what must be done.

Because if Malako didn't make a hero of himself, he had no doubt what awaited him back in the Shiro. He'd been a known associate of the traitor Ricimer.

Malako turned to his vessel weapon's officer, who had been standing by for the order.

"Fire," Malako said.

The *Joshua Humphreys*

The *Humphreys* rose over the curve of the Mutualist craft—now suddenly *not* a spinning, out-of-control Mutualist craft at all but a shapely Sporata battle vessel. The *Humphreys* rose like a new moon first revealing itself. Coalbridge estimated that he was no farther than a couple of dozen kilometers from the other vessel, the *Powers of Heaven*. And then she was in sight—and he called out his order to ZAP.

"Throw!"

The electric crackle of the railguns filled the vessel for an instant, then was silent. The recoil from the rock launch hit seconds later.

"Rocks away, Captain," Sakuda, the ZAP officer, reported.

"Stabilizing thrusters at eighty percent," said Katapodis at the helm.

"Keep her steady," Coalbridge said in a low voice. He stared out into space. With bottle armor forward, the bridge was canted too high to have a view of where the *Humphreys* was headed. Coalbridge quickly pulled down a display, placed another, containing more data, on top of it. The two merged, giving him the view he needed. A gyrating spherical object, clear-skinned with a glowing blue center, separated from the sceeve vessel. It looked for all the world like one of the huge, elongated bubbles he'd used to create with the giant wand set he'd had as a kid, the kind that used dishwashing liquid as the fluid dip.

There's the attack, Coalbridge thought. Bottle torpedo. He'd know in a moment if he'd guessed right as to its nature. His rocks were represented by a traveling cloud of sparkles, tiny and, he knew, perfectly rendered in position and relative size.

If it were antimatter, his counterattack would be essentially useless, overpowered. But he knew this vessel, this commander. He was supremely efficient with his maneuvers and weapons. Thrifty.

He out maneuvered me the last time we met, that's for sure, thought Coalbridge. *Fooled me into thinking his range was shorter than it was, then blasted hell out of us. Lucky we got out of there in one piece.*

Coalbridge watched his rocks cross the void toward the sceeve weapon. Closer.

Closer.

The *Powers of Heaven*

"Captain Malako, emergency proximity warning," came the calm, vanilla voice of Lamella. "Alien objects detected afore!"

"Objects? What objects?" spurted Malako. "Recall the torpedo!"

"Not possible."

"Disarm!"

"Fail-safes are double-trigger beta and electromagnetic. Calculating. No time for wave travel to confirm disarm," said Lamella.

Malako cursed. Of course. The new electromagnetic confirmation signal. Transel, curse his rotting body in the hole, had required all fail-safes to be fully engaged when the *Powers of Heaven* had destroyed the human intelligence vessel. He normally unlocked them immediately upon mission departure and for control himself.

Thrice curse the receptor.

These rocks had come from somewhere. They had the configuration of an Earth vessel throw. It was all too obvious. He'd been ambushed!

As if she'd read his mind, Lamella confirmed his guess. "Captain, situational analysis indicates human weaponry."

And he could do nothing to stop it.

Nothing.

"Where? Where is the cursed vessel?"

Malako's nasal membranes flared in outrage. He stomped on the deck of the bridge. Transel would not hear it. The bridge "hole" was too insulated, guarded against detection.

You've killed me, Transel, you stupid, stupid fool!

The bridge atmosphere filled with Malako's carbolic scream of a command. "All shields forward!"

The *Joshua Humphreys*

Rock met nuke, and a momentary star burst into being in the nearby heavens.

Detonation.

And close to the Sporata vessel. As close as he'd planned. The sceeve vessel flowered with blue-white explosions. This he could see perfectly well without virtual enhancement. Coalbridge watched as the sceeve craft suddenly lurched to the left, exposed its long flank.

Here was the chance he'd been waiting for. "Fire!" he called out.

Turning to face him from the phantom gunnery panel, his weapons geist called out the coordinates at which the *Humphreys*'s RADICL chemical-laser bank would strike. "Spread concentrated at twenty-three Alpha, November eighty-six," ZAP reported. Then, after the briefest pause, "Direct hit, sir."

A moment of elation, and then a tactical report from DAFNE. "The *Powers* has located and locked on us. Her internal beta chatter is spiking up twenty percent. Analysis: she's preparing to concentrate fire."

"All right then," Coalbridge said. He banded through channels. "Ready, DAFNE? It's time for the suture."

"Aye, Captain," replied the servant.

"On my mark . . . do it."

"Engaged, sir."

With a lurching displacement, a stomach-turning feeling of being two places at once, he felt the *Humphreys* let go her hold on one portion of space-time and be whipped—no, instantly transported—to another. It did not feel as if he ceased to exist and then existed elsewhere, which was what had actually happened. His mind tried to tell him he'd traveled the distance in a flash of movement, or at least some sort of distance. He knew there was no actual sloshing of the inner-ear fluids, no trail of light. But his mind compensated by manufacturing just such a sight and sensation of movement, attempting to make the Q through which they travelled fit the N in which human perception had evolved.

And where am I in that instant of transfer? Maybe it was best not to think on such questions at the moment.

The *Powers of Heaven*

"Captain Malako, the human vessel is directly abaft us."

"*What?* How?"

"Not clear, sir," said the XO. "She was there above the Mutualists, and then gone. How she got behind us is unknown, sir."

But Malako *did* know. He'd even done it himself before.

A suture maneuver.

The humans certainly seemed to learn their lessons well.

The *Joshua Humphreys*

The sceeve craft was partially eclipsing the *Efficacy of Symbiosis*, which now spun in its crazy rotation *behind* the *Powers of Heaven*.

"ZAP, send the nukes."

"Aye, Captain. Nukes away."

"DELTA, all shielding forward!"

"Aye, sir."

They were no more than ten kilometers from the *Powers*, on her other side now.

This was going to be apocalyptic. Had to be. A nuclear strike was the only sure way to kill a sceeve vessel.

Even with multiple bottles absorbing the blast energy, the *Humphreys* was going to be thrown thousands of kilometers away. There would be no ability to jump. A slingshot maneuver such as they'd performed depleted the immediate quantum neighborhood of uncertainty. It would take several minutes before unobserved phenomena built back to critical mass. Not long enough. He'd have to put on the brakes in the conventional manner.

Hell ride on the way.

Coalbrige had fifteen one-hundred-kiloton nukes, and he'd fired all of them.

The image of Sakuda tolling the seconds filled the chroma overlay of the entire vessel. All other chatter ceased. "Nuke activation in three, two, one—"

The *Powers of Heaven*

Malako turned his attention from the human vessel. There was nothing to do. He had no time to turn his bottle armor abaft.

He was completely exposed from that direction.

Malako looked instead to the Sporata vessel on the view screen. The *Guardian of Night* stood revealed. Of course it was the *Guardian*.

And as the nukes bloomed, one word went tearing through Malako's mind.

Ricimer!

The *Joshua Humphreys*

Flash of matter unfurling into energy.

In his overlay, Coalbridge registered the tsunami of radiation headed toward him.

Just before the shock hit, Coalbridge reflected that "snap-back and nuke" was a tactic that had never been tried before. If he survived, he might get a nice footnote in the history books for the feat.

The wavefront hit. The gamma rays of which it was composed ate into the *Humphreys*'s bottle-shield like a blowtorch turned on a Styrofoam cup. Layer after layer melted away. But like Styrofoam, there were bubbles upon bubbles, layer upon layer. For every "real" quantum bottle generated from the vacuum, there were hundreds of "virtual" bottles tricked off of their physics. When the gamma rays entered each bottle, their frequency was pitched down, their wavelength requirements—and so their very being—lengthened.

When the deadly radiation reached the crew core, it was nothing more than harsh sunlight.

So the crew wouldn't die of radiation poisoning, but the shields must be maintained and dissipating the energy they absorbed down to kinetic energy was another matter. The vessel was wracked and rolled. The conventional reaction rockets, under the control of servant personas, attempted to compensate. Coalbridge could hear the quick, machine-language chatter between DAFNE and her underlings as a low, whistling whine. Then there was a sharp exclamation from DAFNE that he had never heard before.

It sounded almost like—

It was.

Pain.

The rockets were overcome, and the vessel was picked up and carried like a broken surfboard, churned under and around and around and under again with a spreading shockwave of outraged thermonuclear energy uprooted from its happy home wound inside hydrogen nuclei and flung helter-skelter into another billion years of gypsy wandering.

Pseudogravity failed. Too many compensation variables flooding the algorithm as at once, it seemed. Pieces of equipment—chairs, consoles—broke loose, careened across the bridge enclosure. Coalbridge felt his own feet coming up off the floor, or the floor moving away from him—it amounted to the same thing. Suddenly a chair sped past him, and its backrest sheered into the arm of Sakuda.

Barely slowing down, it lopped the arm off neatly at Sakuda's shoulder crook.

Blood spurted out in a semispherical fountain as the arm sped away from its body, taking a crazy spin with the fingers flexing and the hand looking for all the world as if it were trying to grab hold of something. Anything.

As the arm floated past him, Coalbridge made a grab for it, for a crazy moment thought he might actually *shake hands* with it, but missed.

Then something slammed into the back of his head.

Blackness.

Flicker.

He recognized the sensation. Concussion. Minor, he judged.

Awake again—was he out long? No. His body still shuddering from the blow of whatever it was and he reached back to feel and his hand returned clutching—

A hank of bloody hair and skin.

Coalbridge smiled. Not *skull*, he thought. *At least not skull.*

"Oh!" said DAFNE. A clicking sound, then an uncharacteristic "Fuck!"

"What?" Coalbridge said.

"Absorption overload. Unable to compensate."

"DAFNE," Coalbridge heard himself say. His words seemed to echo in his skull.

The vessel continued to spiral away with the blast. *Grab something,* Coalbridge thought. But there was nothing to grab, nothing that wasn't moving. He was inside a snow-shake toy.

Except for the DELTA servant, HUGH. His geist remained in place, still oriented toward the surface that had been the "floor" as the vessel turned around them. It was the damndest thing, thought Coalbridge. *Like* I'm *the ghost floating through HUGH's world.*

DAFNE's geist was nowhere to be seen.

He frantically looked about. The snowflakes in the shake toy he haunted were red. They were micro-blobs of blood, flesh, cartilage—

A sudden lurch, and the contents of the enclosure sloshed toward one wall.

They had gotten the rockets back under gyro control, he thought. And then he slammed into the new "wall," which had been the floor not long ago. His breath left him, and he felt another shooting pain in his head. Was his skull coming apart back there? He felt an urge to reach back and try to hold himself together as he might a diced potato or onion before he dropped it into the cook pot. But his arms were pinned by multiple gravities to the wall.

Then a quick lurch and slosh in the other direction. He flew across the cabin and slammed into the other "wall," which had been the ceiling. This time the g-forces equalized and he "bounced" away, slowly floating back across the enclosure in the opposite direction.

DAFNE's geist visage, only her face, reappeared before him. First it was five times normal human size, like a big Oz head. Then it flickered and reappeared at normal size. "Think I've got it," she said. Then another lurch. "Four-fifths churn radiation wiped. No room."

"What are you talking about, DAFNE?" he heard himself say.

"Sorry, Captain," said DAFNE. "It's me or life support."

"DAFNE!"

"No room, Jim. Was an honor."

"Come back here, XO," he screamed. "Come back!"

And then the pseudogravity clicked back in. Unfortunately, human crew and bridge nonvirtual contents were suspended in the air. All fell together with a crash—bodies, blood, and equipment.

Coalbridge blinked. Moved a hand. Alive, yes. He sat up, surveyed his surroundings. *Looks like somebody dropped us from a great height,* he thought. *Which is sort of what happened.*

The bridge was a mess. Practically a disaster area.

He heard a low moan. Sakuda rose, clutching his shoulder. Then his eyes rolled up into his skull and he fainted away.

Coalbridge stood unsteadily. He unbuttoned his shirt, shucked it off, then stepped over broken plastic and metal to find Sakuda lying on the new floor—a former bulkhead. Didn't matter. He knelt down, wadded his shirt, and pressed it against the bloody stump of Sakuda's upper arm.

Jesus, Coalbridge thought, *a goddamn chair back did this.*

At his touch, Sakuda awakened and began to shiver as if he were freezing.

"Am I o-okay, Captain?" asked the weapons officer in a quavering voice. "I want to leave a v-voice mail. My father. Voice mail if I don't make it."

He attempted to swallow, coughed violently. He attempted to wipe the spittle from his mouth with his missing arm but only succeeded in shifting the position of his shoulder.

"Hold still," Coalbridge said.

"Big chief, sir. Mau Mau in his heart, my father. Fucking sceeve did not get him, no."

"Shut up, Sakuda, save your breath," Coalbridge said.

"Tell him. Tell him the lion cub is . . . fight like a—"

"I'll tell him."

Sakuda's eyes rolled back into his head. His trembling body began to shake as if it had live current coursing through it.

Then it stopped.

And Sakuda died.

DAFNE was gone. Wiped.

Dead.

She'd done it herself, to ensure life support.

It took the better part of an hour to get damage control underway and take the vessel out of a crisis state. In another half hour, he had a damage report and casualty list.

Multiple injuries. Four dead, crushed, in a cargo bay.

Position was not so bad. Despite being flung for thousands of kilometers, they were still relatively close to the scene of the battle. The other personas were fine and working in long-practiced concert with the human crew—this wasn't the first time servants and crew had faced damaged Q in battle, even if it was probably the worst—

—it *was* the worst.

Coalbridge knew it was bad news when the geist of the Q-drive algorithm ENGINE popped up on the bridge. ENGINE *never* came to the bridge. Efficiency incarnate, he didn't like to waste computing power on animating a geist. He didn't like to speak at all. Language formulation took away valuable calculating capacity, he claimed.

"My lightstacks have been ruptured," ENGINE said. "Entanglement is compromised."

Coalbridge, still half stunned, asked the obvious. "Surely you can find a stray photon *somewhere,* ENGINE."

"Not with unresolved spin. Not with any unresolved Q. Captain, we've lost the whole supply."

"We've run out of . . . light?"

"That's correct, sir," ENGINE said.

"Which means we're dead in the water," Coalbridge said.

"We have Newtonian propulsion, sir," ENGINE replied. "Small supply of reaction mass."

Coalbridge rubbed his eyes. "Okay, then," he said. "Let's go see what we've got to work with back at the scene of the crime." He turned to Katapodis, who was bruised but whole, at helm. "Take us to the battlezone, helmsman."

"Aye, Captain."

They weren't so very far away, after all. Even at N speeds, the return didn't take long. In an hour, they were there.

The *Guardian of Night* drifted nearby, silent.

Not a threat. Coalbridge was amazed at the realization. A possible ally.

She's waiting for my signal.

Take care of the threat first.

No sign of *Powers of Heaven* was to be seen.

"Is she gone? SIGINT, report!" Coalbridge said. "Did we blow her to pieces?"

"There!" It was Katapodis, the helmsman. He was pointing to a shining fleck at three o'clock, halfway up the dome of the night.

Coalbridge ordered them toward her. He had no more weaponry. All systems were on emergency power and all resources diverted to life support.

He had no DAFNE.

His DAFNE.

His friend of six years.

His sister in arms.

Gone.

As it turned out, no weapons or defenses were necessary.

The *Powers of Heaven* would not fight again.

Half of her had practically been turned inside out by the nukes. There was an enormous hole in her forward hull and an "exit wound" with metal flowering outward in a gaping eruption on the other side. Photonic flickers surrounded the damaged edges, delimiting a boundary that the vessel Q was attempting to regenerate, but having no luck. She'd poured her insides into space. One look told Coalbridge all he needed to know. Except for a few zombie systems, her computers were blown. Her crew was a puddle against the bulkheads. No one had been thrown clear. He knew, but ordered a cursory sensor sweep just in case.

There were no rescue beacons, no activated officer bottles on the beta sensors.

The *Powers of Heaven* was a dead craft.

"How do you like that, XO," whispered Coalbridge. To himself. To the empty air. "We won."

TWENTY

19 January 2076
Vara Nebula
USX *Joshua Humphreys*

"Sir, we're going to have a problem with the *Guardian* heliox environment. It's a twelve-fifty-two mix, with a hundred-five p.s.i. atmosphere," said Lieutenant Nguen, the marine from the craft contingent who handled physically equipping assault teams on sceeve vessels or, in this case, a contact team.

The double whammy of breathing at high atmospheric pressure, thought Coalbridge. *You stay in that sceeve air, it sends you into nitrogen psychosis within a minute or so. You leave without hours of decompression, and the bends will kill you.*

"We'll stay with the rebreathers and pressurized uniforms, then work into a compression schedule to put key personnel on sceeve pressure," said Coalbridge. "The *Humphreys* is leaking like a sieve, and we wouldn't have the air to flush and replace the sceeve gas if we brought them over here." He smiled. "Besides, what would be the fun of *that*?"

"I'll work out the protocols, sir, and inform the affected crew. They'll bitch about fairness, because the big ones will need to stay in the chamber longer. It will be based on body mass."

Coalbridge nodded. "Set it up." He'd always hated close-quarters fighting with a rebreather over his face and a ballooned and stiffened uniform suit—the churn in the Extry uniform fabric

251

would make it into a pressure suit for a few hours at a time. During a few engagements, he'd had sufficient warning to ramp his special-force marines up in a hyperbaric chamber and inject them completely adapted to breathe sceeve air, which was, of course, breathable by humans if they were ready for the enormous pressures of sceeve enclosures. He'd never done it himself, however. Maybe he'd finally get his chance soon—but not yet. So rebreathers and balloon suits it was.

Time to float over through the converted assault tube the marines had set up as a docking corridor. He would take Leher with him. Four heavily armed marines. And that would be it.

With DAFNE gone, he'd moved his VISOR, the vessel internal-systems division officer-in-charge, Lieutenant Commander Matty Taras, to XO and given him a field promotion to commander. He'd leave Taras in command of the *Humphreys* while he was away.

While I'm away having tea and cookies with a fucking sceeve *skipper,* Coalbridge thought.

Taras had standing orders to destroy the *Guardian of Night* at the slightest sign she was going belligerent.

Which meant killing Coalbridge and his team.

Always nice to have an element of mortal danger with your refreshments, Coalbridge thought. *And the chance to beat the sceeve with their own stick if you happened to survive.*

The *Guardian of Night*

The large-eyed sceeve looked down at him. He was a bit taller than Coalbridge's six two, but he did not tower over Coalbridge.

And I have him on bulk, Coalbridge thought. *Dude is skinny as a reed.*

"Captain Ricimer?" said Coalbridge. Leher's converted Palace took in the words, translated them to esters, and sprayed out the results from its small chemistry lab shaped like a drugstore "travel can" of hairspray. Crude and, as Leher said, "the esters probably smell like caveman talk to a sceeve," but it seemed to work. The scent of musk and oranges pervaded the heliox of the airlock.

The slightest ammonia tang in the air. A soft reply, thought Coalbridge. It wasn't like you were being squirted with pepper spray or anything. Coalbridge reflected that most of the other sceeve language he'd smelled had been sceeve shouting to be "heard" over a riot of other voices during a firefight.

The translator spoke a soft phrase in a rich baritone. "You are from Sol system?"

"Yes, sir. I am Captain James Coalbridge of the United States Extry. My country of affiliation is a nation located on Sol C in this system."

Another ammonia-like odor, this one subtly different—but how, Coalbridge couldn't have said. He looked at Leher, who nodded as if he understood.

"The United States of America, yes. It is a moment of blooming possibilities to meet you," said the device. "Trembling promise clings to our shoulders like a cloud."

"Yes," Coalbridge answered. "That is, I think I see what you mean." He shot Leher a quizzical look. Was he missing something?

"Have to fine-tune the box," Leher murmured. "It's a traditional friendly greeting, nothing more. Means something like 'Pleased to meet you. I hope we can be friends.'"

"Ah." He turned back to Ricimer, who had been waiting patiently for his reply. "Pleased to meet you, too, Captain Ricimer. My vessel and I are at your service."

Ricimer cocked his head to the right then to the left—body language that meant . . . what? Yes and no? Maybe? Something like that? Leher had tried to fill him in on the details, but Leher himself had pretty sketchy knowledge. And if Leher didn't know, likely no human did.

Then the translator box spoke again. "Captain Coalbridge, my officers and I would like to request political asylum with your government." Coalbridge replayed what he'd just heard in his mind again to be sure he'd heard it right. Yes.

"Asylum?"

"My crew and passengers are refugees from an ongoing massacre occurring in my home habitat. They do not request formal asylum since they have little to offer in return, but request temporary sanctuary in your system, and would like to discuss possible resettlement in the vicinity."

Ricimer raised a hand, gesturing at his surroundings. "Furthermore, to support our request for political asylum, my officers and I would like to deliver to you, as the representative of your government, this vessel, A.S.C. *Guardian of Night*, along with its

accoutrements, supplies, and weaponry. This vessel now belongs
to your government."

Beside Coalbridge, Leher let out a little chuckle. "Holy shit,"
Leher said. "The Poet was telling the truth."

Coalbridge shook his head, cleared ammonia fumes. He looked
around at the alien vessel. Technology. Information in the computers. Tactics and strategies of warfighting. Cultural information.
Lists of enemies.

If.

If they got this craft back to Walt Whitman station for analysis.
If they then had time.

The sceeve armada was bearing down on Earth.

With time, a hundred teams could swarm the *Guardian*. Break
it down. Analyze it. Reverse engineer—everything.

If.

"Captain Ricimer, on behalf of the United States government
and its president and commander in chief, I accept your offer,"
said Coalbridge. "Captain, I don't know if you are aware of it,
but the Guardian armada is approaching Sol system at this very
moment."

"I am aware of this. I also suspect the vessel you have destroyed
has eliminated my hoped-for Mutualist rendezvous craft. That is
likely how he discovered these coordinates. You, on the other
hand, also found me—so the Poet's hidden communiqué was
successful?"

"The Poet was acting on your behalf, I take it?"

"He was to deliver our rendezvous information to you in a
fairly simple analog code," Ricimer answered. "I was convinced
that you humans would monitor his beta broadcasts if you were at
all aware of them. They are very different from the usual Sporata
beta chatter, are they not?"

"Very," Leher muttered.

"The Sporata has long been aware of the Poet's activities but
had been unable to capture him. I was able to locate him with
the aid of my Mutualist contacts. After that, it was a matter of
convincing him to aid us. Not a difficult task after I told him
about the Kilcher artifact. And so he delivered the message to you."

"Yes. Personally," Leher said, louder this time.

Ricimer turned to him.

"This is Lieutenant Commander Griffin Leher, my chief sceeve—"

Coalbridge corrected himself quickly. "—my Guardian specialist. He personally spoke with Gitaclaber."

"Pleased to meet you," said Ricimer. Leher's tweaked box must've translated the long spiel correctly this time, Coalbridge thought. "I'm well aware of the pejorative term you humans use for my kind. I understand if you wish to continue using it."

"What's he mean, Leher?" Coalbridge asked.

"He's saying it's all right to call him a sceeve. In fact, he rather agrees with its meaning. Am I right, Captain Ricimer?"

Ricimer made a motion that combined a head nod to the right with a shrug. "That's right," he said. *So, a nod "yes" is that weird shrug,* Coalbridge thought. At least the sceeve *had* body language to pick up on, even if it wasn't humanlike in any manner. Useful to know.

"And Gitaclaber lives?" Ricimer asked.

"Unfortunately, no," said Leher. Leher briefly explained the rescue of Japps and Gitaclaber from the lifepod.

"I understand," said Ricimer, again with the shrug and head tilt. Definitely a nod. "Too bad, for both the young officer and for us. He was an odd one, but with a true *gid* and a sharp thought process. He was a great resource."

"Sir, I hate to press, but we are needed back in the solar system. *Our* solar system, I mean."

Ricimer gave another sceeve nod. "Of course," he replied. "I too am pressed, not by time but by numbers. I have on board nearly one thousand refugees, including many children. I do not wish to carry these into harm's way. I would like to find a suitable place to deposit them while we warriors . . . do what we must do."

"I will attempt to arrange it as soon as we're in beta range, sir," said Coalbridge. *Great, another huge problem,* he thought. *But not mine for once, thank God.*

In fact, his problems were now decidedly *non*strategic and mostly had to do with patching up and flying his own craft. Which was exactly the way he liked things.

"Thank you, Captain. I suppose now we'll find out if my leap of faith has been justified," Ricimer replied. It sounded like dry humor, and Coalbridge decided to take it as such.

"Or whether we've cut it so close we all crash and burn," Coalbridge said. "Speaking of the armada . . . *do* you have a plan for what we might do when they get here?"

The nostril flaps on Ricimer's... well, you couldn't really call it a "nose." It looked most like the muzzle of a bulldog or a bat. The flaps of Ricimer's muzzle vibrated.

A half second later, the translator box let out a low laugh.

"Excellent," Leher muttered to himself, but loud enough for Coalbridge to pick up what he was saying. "Good throughput on the undertones and speech coloration."

So it really was Ricimer's laugh.

"I have a few ideas about tactics," Ricimer replied, "but my larger goal was and has always been the same."

"What's that?"

"Why, to ask you humans to make a clever use of the Kilcher artifact, of course," Ricimer said. "I know from experience that you're very good at that, and I could think of no other solution for what to do with the artifact this vessel carries as a weapon, once its destructive potential became clear to me. The Administration must not be permitted to possess it or have time to analyze and duplicate whatever technology or science it employs."

Great, Coalbridge thought. *That's been the way of it for the past twelve years anyway. Situation Normal, All Fucked Up.*

So, improvise.

"All right, Captain, let's get to it. Last beta reports I have—these are a day old, so I'm not entirely confident in their accuracy—put the sceeve armada at two days out from Sol, traveling at 100 *c*."

A pause for translation.

Another sceeve laugh.

"Yes," said Ricimer. "That would be about the speed Blawfus would think prudent. I expect he'll maintain it."

"We are eighteen and a half hours from Sol inner system at maximum velocity," Coalbridge said.

Six hours. That was the lead time they were inexorably stuck with. That is, assuming—

"Your craft does 900 *c* maximum, does she?"

Ricimer took a half step back. Looked for all the world like a human gesture of offense taken. Had he just effectively called the *Guardian* a garbage scow?

"Of course she does," Ricimer said.

Six hours.

"Then we need to get our asses back to Earth."

"My crew and I are at your service."

"Well, okay, then," Coalbridge said. He shook his head in amazement. Two months ago, if someone had told him...any of this...

No, it would've been impossible almost to conceive.

"One thing's for sure," Coalbridge continued, "whatever happens next should be interesting."

20 January 2076
Earth Orbit
Walt Whitman atation

Walt Whitman station was a supply dump at heart. Its most eminent visitors until now had been fleet admirals passing through, outbound for the big asteroid fortresses or inbound planetside. So despite the fact that this was without a doubt the biggest ceremonial moment in the station's history, there was not much Station Chief Rear Admiral Murray McNulty could do to roll out the red carpet. There was no red carpet. There were no accoutrements and symbols of state. There was hardly a box, barrel, or package marked with anything beyond PROPERTY OF UNITED STATE EXTRY.

McNulty was famous for making something out of nothing—the reason he had the job quartermastering this floating junkpile in the first place—but this was going to tax even his abilities to make amenities appear. There were a few rolls of butcher paper that could be easily enough digitized and turned red, white, and blue, so he had streamers. He gathered all the flags and potted plants he could find and created something resembling a decorated conference room. Then he had his crew start brewing coffee. He also sent down to Xenology for any instructions on sceeve diet. Did they even eat? No. They absorbed nutrients through their feet. A list of primary ingredients for making the slurry was attached. Drink? There was a sort of sniffing ritual that was documented in some files. Looked like having a stiff one to McAvoy. But, said CRYPT, the chemistry was complex. Impossible to duplicate without the proper equipment. McNulty had a look at the recipe and smiled.

Well, maybe not *quite* impossible.

Tetraterpenes. McNulty's original training had been as a chemical engineer, and he knew that structure. It was the aromatic element in spoiled steroids. And if there was one thing he had on hand, it was medical steroid medications. He had cases and cases of the stuff, now hardly used thanks to a salt activator that had made the entire class of drugs obsolete. They were sitting around decomposing, waiting in line for a garbage drop and atmospheric burn.

He could accelerate the process, and he knew just how to do it. Heat and mix it all up in a few gallons of Pine-Sol. Bottle it and voila—sceeve rotgut whisky! The entire process took thirty minutes. Of course, he had no idea what an actual sceeve would think about his concoction.

He'd soon find out.

McNulty decided to use the main Logistics office for the meeting because of its size. Other than cargo bays and warehouse space, it was the largest room on the Walt Whitman. Manifests and schedules were all digital, of course, but there was one large map that McNulty liked to keep physically updated with vessel markers and supply cards attached. If, somehow, all the chroma got wiped to a blank, he'd still have the big map in Logistics as a fallback. Besides, it was pretty and spoke to his particular mind—supremely organized, yet dynamic, always changing.

And then all was ready. The puck from the Skyhook arrived and out stepped three Secret Service agents, an Indian-Indian–looking woman, and the president of the United States.

An hour later, the other party to this meeting in space arrived.

The approach of the sceeve craft was nerve-wracking. Everything in McNulty's make-up told him to *Shoot this thing out of space. Don't let it get close to the station!* He held fire, of course. There were humans aboard the vessel, after all. At least, so he'd been told. McNulty personally handled the docking as the sceeve vessel matched speeds and his team extended a transfer collar. Alongside the vessel came the *Joshua Humphreys*. And there was yet another craft, as well, in the entourage. Sceeve as well but clearly no threat to the station or anything else. It looked like a football that had blasted itself inside-out.

And then the docking was done. The sceeve vessel-without-designation was attached to *his* space station with a nano-created band. Apparently, it—they, these sceeve—weren't coming to kill. The thought that they might even have come in peace McNulty didn't take very seriously.

They *were* the sceeve, after all.

Sam Guptha stepped out of the puck following the Secret Service agents. The president would be the last to debark. It had been years since Sam had been into space. Of course, a couple of thousand miles above the Earth's surface wasn't really *space*-space, but it was a lot farther than her grandparents back in New Delhi, or even her rocket-scientist parents, had ever been. Without pseudogravity, the feeling was not that different from being in a hotel on Earth. Except for the curved walls—Walt Whitman was designed to spin if the pseudogravity suddenly cut out. There were too many supplies that needed constant gravitation (or its artificial centrifugal equivalent) to risk a Q breakdown—breakdowns which had tended to occur with some frequency during the early days of the station.

They passed some welcoming banners and even some banquet-style steamers—how the heck had they gotten those up here so fast?—and entered the conference room to await her presentation. After a great deal of thought and computer modeling, she and her team had managed to convince themselves that their idea would work. Now she had to convince, well, *everybody else.*

Of course, the alternative was most likely a quick death for them all.

So if logical argument and honey-throated appeal fails, at least I have that going for me, Sam thought.

Leher followed Coalbridge and Ricimer through the docking collar and into the station proper. Ricimer had not had time to set foot on the *Humphreys,* and this was the first time he had boarded a human vessel. At least so Leher believed. Could be he'd been involved with the invasion five years ago. Could be he was Ivan the Terrible back then. There was much that remained unknown about who this sceeve really was, and why he was doing what he was doing. Leher figured that, provided he were to survive the next forty-eight hours, he was about to spend years working on the answer to that particular question.

Leher looked down as the sceeve walked across the airlock deck. Ricimer was the only sceeve who had debarked—mostly because Leher and his Xeno team had only been able to rig one sceeve-shaped pressure suit. The Mutualist refugees, if they were delivered here, would have to be put into a pressurized compartment of their own for the time being.

Ricimer's head was helmetless and exposed, but the captain had assured him that, with the stress taken off his body, he should be safe from pressure effects for many hours. He did descend from a space-based species, after all, even though the sceeve had adapted to atmosphere hundreds of thousands of years ago.

A heliox feed would take care of any problems with exposure to the heavy nitrogen concentrations in the human breathing mix. Ricimer had a finger's-breadth clear tube that snaked from a bottle of compressed heliox strapped to his back and into his muzzle so that he could breathe his native mix but still "speak" into the human atmosphere, and so into Leher's translation box.

As they made their way down the corridor toward the meeting place, Leher noticed that Ricimer's feet did, indeed, leave damp prints on the steel floor. The *Guardian* and, Leher figured, most other sceeve vessels, had special absorbers in the floor to handle such leavings. When Leher experimentally stepped in one of Ricimer's footprints with a boot, he found it was sticky, with a small tug needed to free himself. Like a Post-it note, Leher thought. Or slug slime.

Can't take a sceeve anywhere.

And then they were through the corridor and into the meeting room—a long office with a large, empty table in the middle. No chairs. From speakers somewhere, a faint version of "Hail to the Chief" played as the president rose up to stand before Ricimer. The station's enormous old-fashioned tank-map of the sky as depicted in three dimensions was contained within a tabletop of holographic glass. Leher had heard the Walt Whitman staff still used the old map as a backup to keep tabs on logistics. At the moment, all information was blank, with only the stars and planets shown in their pinprick positions. The map couldn't possibly have been to scale, Leher thought, or it would have taken up the entire station to represent the actual analogous space between the pinpricks. But the distances between systems seemed to have been proportionally collapsed, at least.

For a moment, no one spoke. And then Ricimer went first. "Madame President, I wish to extend the same greeting as I did to your representative, Captain Coalbridge. I and my remaining officers wish to request diplomatic asylum in the United States of America. Furthermore, the persons in my hold, which include children of my species, are seeking political sanctuary from an oppressive regime. If you turn them away, they will surely be slaughtered, as they were about to be before they departed the Shiro and came aboard the *Guardian of Night*."

The president nodded. "Very well," she said. She held up an ampoule that was very similar to a sceeve nebulizer. On second glance, Leher saw it *was* somebody's re-creation of a nebulizer. And a pretty good one. "Shall we have refreshment?"

Ricimer's muzzle flared to a smile. "I would be delighted, Madame President."

He took the ampoule from Frost's hand. An aide immediately gave the president her own drink—her customary beverage, a can of Diet Coke. She raised it in salute.

"On behalf of the people of the United States of America, I accept your request and that of your crew, Arid Ricimer. We will also offer sanctuary to your passengers. We understand what it is to be cruelly oppressed by your Administration."

The president stepped back, momentarily startled as Ricimer made a slight bow.

"Welcome to America," she said.

Ricimer placed a palm on his chest directly over his *gid*. The traditional sceeve analog for a bow of respect. "Your servant," he said.

"I don't know about that," said the president. "Maybe my *constituent* one of these days." Frost sipped her Coke. Ricimer examined the ampoule, quickly seemed to get the hang of it, then whiffed it into his muzzle. After a moment, his smile widened.

"Is this Old Fifty-five?" he said. He took another sniff. "It is! Where did you find this?"

The president turned to an admiral standing off to the side. "You know anything about that, Murray?"

"Brewed it myself, ma'am," the admiral replied.

"You *made* this?" Ricimer said. Leher recognized something like wonder in the undertone of his reply. "I have chosen wisely after all. Any species capable of creating Old Fifty-five..." His thought trailed away as Ricimer took another whiff. "Delicious." Finally, he seemed to have had enough. "Pardon me, shall we now get down to the business of the turnover?"

"Not quite yet, Captain," President Frost replied. "I plan to leave you in command a bit longer, if you don't mind. We may have an idea."

"As you wish, of course."

"Now, Captain, what about the weapon your vessel carries? Is it operational?"

"Yes," said Ricimer. "Although I have not fired it. I prefer stealth when possible, and in any case I do not believe its rate of fire is fast enough take on the entire armada."

"Yes, our conclusions, as well," said the president.

The president handed off the Diet Coke to the same aide who'd brought it. She glanced over to Sam.

"Captain Ricimer, now *we* have some news for *you*. And a proposal."

"Ladies and gentlemen, this is the first meeting I've had in years that I was truly looking forward to and that I'm completely glad to be at," said President Frost.

Sam noticed Leher's box huffing and puffing in translation. She wondered how much of her own briefing would really come across to the sceeve. Knowing Griff, probably a lot, she decided. She hoped most of it.

A lemon scent. It took Sam a moment to realize it arose from—from within the nasal cavities of—Captain Ricimer. Griff's box made a sound akin to a chuckle. Sceeve laughter smelled like lemon? Or maybe it was a polite laugh that was meant to express irritation? Would have to ask Griff when—

The president faced Sam. Everybody else did as well.

"So, without further ado—"

Okay, Sam thought. *Please, dear Lord, let the damn slides be in order.*

She clicked her first graphic. It was a diagram of the Kilcher artifact, the weapon upon the *Guardian of Night.*

It still looked like the corrupted horn of some enormous, probably evil, beast to Sam.

"Where did you get that image?" huffed Ricimer suddenly.

The box put a surprised tone to the words.

"From the Poet's transmission, of course," Sam replied, a bit nonplussed. "From you, presumably, Captain."

"Ah, of course," said Ricimer. "Of course. Excuse me, please. I had forgotten your computational mastery, your ability to model."

Sam glanced to Frost, who nodded. Go ahead.

"We, that is my systems guy, Francois Remy, created the virtual display."

"I see," Ricimer said. Again the lemony puff, stronger this time. Griff's box translated it again as laughter. "I take it that your computer ability has developed even further than it had when I last encountered your species during the unfortunate invasion."

"By many orders of magnitude," Sam said, feeling a bit uncomfortable. This thing was speaking so matter-of-factly, even blithely, about the worst thing that ever happened to the human race. Sam had seen plenty of pictures of the sceeve, but Ricimer was the first she'd ever met up close. She'd prepared herself and had barely missed a beat when he'd come in. But now that he was addressing her directly....

It was spooky. His eyes occluded every few seconds but didn't really blink. And, of course, he had no mouth. Just that enormous nasal-vomeronasal organ that looked like a cross between a mass of melted plastic and a three-dimensional model of the Grand Canyon. She found herself checking for snot. There was none, just a slight moistness to the crenellations, like that of a dog's nose.

"I understand your feelings as to what I have done, and I do wish to take responsibility," Ricimer continued. "But I must say you humans have met, and even surpassed, my expectation for your species."

Sam nodded. "The exterior modeling was easy, since we had the specs. As was general behavior, since you provided us with the experimental data. The hard part was figuring out *why* it behaves the way it does, of course. And then what we could do with that information. Implementation."

She clicked the slide.

An animated graphic. She waited a moment to set it into motion.

"The weapon does not create or destroy matter or energy, of course. Neither does it create or destroy information, which would be the same thing. The best way I can explain it is to say that it *threshes* information. The weapon creates a sieve effect on a level smaller than even that of gravitational interaction. In fact, we really don't understand the physical principles involved. Yet. So we've worked backward from the effect, on which we have data. It's a sort of reverse Schrödinger's cat experiment."

Leher looked puzzled. *You and me both,* she wanted to tell him.

She started the animation. The emission from the weapon— pictured as something like a spreading flashlight beam, although actually the diameter could be altered at will—swept across a three-d representation of a black cat.

The black cat became a white outline.

"Looks like it got turned into a ghost," said Coalbridge.

"We call it an 'eidolon,'" Sam replied. "But ghost will do just as well. The 'ray,' if you want to call it that, from the weapon serves as a kind of infinitesimally small sieve."

"What does it remove, if it's that small?" Coalbridge asked.

"It culls information," Sam said. "That's the best way I can say it. It removes from leptons, gluons, gauge bosons—from every wave-particle duality in its path—the information concerning the particle's charge, its spin state. Its color. Everything we think of as the particle's 'properties.' It doesn't merely copy the information—it strips it away."

"Leaving . . . what?"

"There's not really a word for what remains. Inchoate matter, you might call it. But whatever you call it, it doesn't stay in that state for longer than a single unit of Planck time."

"Meaning?"

"It takes on new properties. Whatever properties are nearest at hand. Mostly, it just blows up."

"And what is actually going on with the stripped information?"

"Like I said, we're not sure. There is some thought that the information is dissipated elsewhere, perhaps in the creation of gravitational effects. I myself suspect that it's somehow suspended in an undetermined fashion. Separated out and not in communication with its material substrate. The dead cat becomes alive and not alive. Real and unreal. It returns to indeterminacy."

"Don't suppose you know what the damn thing is, do you?"

Sam smiled. Leave it to Griff Leher to ask the one question she wasn't prepared to answer and wanted desperately to know.

"We do not."

"But you've dreamed up an idea, haven't you, Sam?"

She hadn't wanted to speculate, but he would call her out on that. Of course, Griff knew how the principle for scaling up the Q-bottles to house the first W22 FTL-deliverable nuke had come to her. A dream of parallel lines of swords flying through a cloud of suspended, fallen leaves, skewering only the red ones and leaving the others to fall. After that, it had only been a matter of getting the math right.

Sam sighed. "Most likely a wild guess," she said. "It's not even a hypothesis, because I haven't begun to figure out how to test it."

"Share your conjecture with us, Dr. Guptha," said the president.

Sam rubbed her eyes, then ran her hand through her hair. *Needs a wash. Overslept after staying up all night. Almost missed the Sky-hook.* "My idea is that the artifact is the remains of an evaporated black hole," Sam said. "How the Kilcher came into possession of such an object, I could not begin to say. Its extreme density may be an indicator of this. The artifact seems to suck information into itself in a way that's almost analogous to osmosis in a cell. I think it's structured somehow to make its initial information content 'less dense' than the information in normal space."

The dream that gave her the idea had actually been of a boat in the middle of an empty, lead-dark sea. The boat itself had been made of stone. And yet it floated.

"And so there's a continual flow of information into the arti-fact," Sam continued. "It's retained one quality of the singularity it may once have been—it captures information. A current—or likely any significant application of energy—seems to reconfigure this matrix for a portion of time, about a minute, in the same manner as supercooling suddenly reconfigures regular conduc-tors into essentially resistance-free superconductors. This thing becomes a 'super-information-sump.' A bottomless pit for any elementary information in its range." Sam shook her head, smiled wryly. "But this, all of this, is conjecture on my part. What we know is what happens next—"

She clicked the slide. The beam swished back in the other direction, crossing the cat-eidolon. It dissolved.

"When the minute is over, the artifact turns itself off. The information in the affected material region reasserts itself. In, as best we can tell, a random manner."

"The material is wiped away. It becomes formless energy. Star-light," Ricimer said. "My people have done this to an entire species."

"Genocide by information removal," said the president. She shook her head. "And was this what was planned for us?"

"Only if your resistance could not be broken," Ricimer replied. "A tenet of Regulation and the Administration is to retain enough of a conquered species to allow for a small measure of cultural innovation for further gleaning."

"So we'd get to be slaves?"

"Doubtful. From what I know of humans, extinction would ultimately be your fate," Ricimer continued. "You have the technological means to avoid submission and a will to fight. Such conditions will eventually trigger an all-out response from the Administration. They will fear that you might become a competitor instead of a parasite host."

"So the species that can't be broken to slavery become targets for elimination?" the president said, a frown of disgust on her face.

"This is the policy of the Administration," said Ricimer.

"We're not conquered," said the president quietly. "Nor will we be."

The sceeve captain made an odd head movement to his right, a slight shrug. "No one my species has invaded has reverse engineered our technology so quickly, or made innovations so rapidly. Within two cycles, your war vessels were on a par with ours. Now I am coming to believe that in some respects they are better."

Ricimer moved to the nearby map table, put his hand down forcefully, its tapered point of a palm pointing toward Sol system.

Looks like we share at least one bodily gesture in common, Sam thought.

"Human are the species that might possibly bring about the downfall of the Administration," he said. "I became convinced of this while I was fighting you during the initial invasion. And now I'm sure of it." He turned and faced the president, held out his hands in a cradling gesture.

"We are a political species, like yours," he said. "For millennia, there existed competing philosophies among the hypha, different cultures and modes of living. These still are present, but they have been driven underground. My wife was a member of such a philosophical grouping. She had a deep and abiding belief in the symbiosis of all creatures, all life. This is the Mutualist way."

"And are you a Mutualist as well?" the president asked.

"I am not. I am but a fellow traveler," Ricimer answered. "And the implacable enemy of the Administration. What I am looking for is allies. Not companionship. Not true believers."

"Then you've found us," said the president. She nodded to Sam. "Continue, Dr. Guptha."

Sam clicked her slide. A human eye.

"I assume you are all familiar with the principles behind the chroma," she said. "Salt in the eye projects images on the retina that are the precise frequencies of light that the corneal salt filters out. It is a miniaturized version of the old green screen used in filmmaking special effects. This is, for instance, the way that servants are able to represent themselves as geists."

A few baffled expressions. They'd have to stay confused about that, so long as her main point came across.

Click. The Escher print of the hands reaching out from a piece of drawing paper, drawing one another.

A few bullet points. Here it was. The central idea.

"What we project that we will be able to do is to modify the disentanglement weapon's beam. We will modulate it in a manner similar to the projection methods used to create the chroma. We will, in effect, create a sort of chroma within the disentangled substrate, a virtual reality of virtual particles that *are* entangled within their frame of reference, that do retain their information. They will be, in fact, entangled with one another and not with any exterior event, process or substance." Sam took a breath, continued. "We'll be able to green-screen in a special effect."

"And what will that effect be?" asked Coalbridge. "Godzilla?"

Sam smiled. "Not exactly," she said. "We believe that we can encode a servant into the artifact's region of effect."

"A servant," Ricimer said. "An artificially intelligent agent?"

"That's correct," said Sam. "A servant on either end—the artifact would, in a sense, be fired *through* the servant. On the receiving end, the duplicate servant would then be shielded by the information 'shadow' of the first. It would not become informationally disintegrated. This servant, now present in the newly unentangled material, would then be able to determine the reapplication of information to the affected substrate."

"A Maxwell's demon," Leher said. "A little bugger that determines the state and properties of every particle there is."

"Precisely," said Sam. "But within a confined area. Otherwise such a servant would become—"

"God," Leher said.

"Something like that."

"But within this confined area, the servant could make whatever you shoot that thing at into whatever you want?" said Leher. "As in, turn lead to gold. Broccoli to pizza?"

"A lump of material into an antimatter annihilation event," Sam said.

"A supernova," said Ricimer. His muzzle was flaring widely, and the lemon scent was again in the air.

"Sure," Sam said. "The complete conversion of say—"

She made a few rough calculations in her head.

"—a sphere about a quarter-kilometer in diameter into force-mediating particles. Energy, I mean. You'd get something equivalent to a smallish supernova. We make the beam smart, we can make stars. At least for a little while."

"A quarter-kilometer?"

"Depending on the density."

"Say . . . a spacecraft."

"Yes, probably, although—"

Ricimer glanced over to Coalbridge. "We happen to have a spacecraft to spare, do we not, Captain?"

Coalbridge thought for a moment, then broke into a smile. "Indeed we do. The *Powers of Heaven*. We incorporated her Q and towed her back, of course."

Again Ricimer slapped his hand down on the table beside him. This time his huge eyes were directly on Sam. "You've done it," he said. "I knew you would, but I couldn't possibly predict *how*."

"Done what?" Sam asked. "We've merely played around with some of the implications of the information with which you provided us."

"Yes," said Ricimer. "My mother once told me an ancient tale of my kind. It is called 'The Bright-Dust of Teshinaw.' It was a moment when we Guardians still possessed the quality you humans term 'play.' Somehow we lost it. But now you have brought it back to us."

Again the box was laughing.

TWENTY-ONE

20 January 2076
Sol System
Kuipers Outbound
USX *Powers of Heaven*

Coalbridge was in command of the *Powers of Heaven*. She was his now. *His* sceeve vessel.

She was alive again. Well, a sort of hybrid-mutant life with a human servant and a sceeve computer program acting as the vessel's nervous system. The computer aboard the *Powers of Heaven* at the moment—a Pocket Palace Plus, which contained a copy of the servant LOVE and the Lamella programming from the *Guardian*—was busy preparing for the *Powers*'s final chapter of existence. Neither LOVE nor Lamella could travel into the *Powers*'s computational matrix, because there no longer was such a thing on this vessel. The nuke next door had burned the last vestige of craft churn away. The computer system therefore didn't have the data-crunching power to control Q, to navigate, and to helm. Coalbridge's unaided human brain and intuition would have to serve for steering.

Maintaining course manually was nerve-wracking, but it was also kind of cool. He'd freed the emergency-control stick—it had been exactly where Ricimer had said it would be—from its stowed position in a tubelike structure on the side of the enclosure, and it had swung into place before him like a safety bar on a roller-coaster ride, horizontally at about shoulder height—which would be waist height to a sceeve, but there was no adjusting for that problem. He'd called up a large exterior-display screen for the wall directly in his sight line and was now piloting the *Powers* in manual-override mode. Ricimer had given him instructions on how to go about it, but, apart from training sessions, Ricimer himself had never used the manual pilot on any craft he'd captained, and he'd told Coalbridge that he doubted any of the currently serving Sporata officers had either.

"It's a vestige of another time—a design era before we had gleaned trustworthy computer technology from a conquered species," he said. "But Sporata vessel designs change extremely slowly, if at all. The normal course of action when constructing a new craft is to layer on new technology rather than make wholesale changes."

Thank God for hidebound sceeve engineering, Coalbridge thought. The old tech was now allowing a human to fly one of their spacecraft without computer assistance.

So far so good.

He was flying in a tight triad formation with the *Guardian of Night* and the *Joshua Humphreys*. Only a few meters separated the craft. The *Powers* was attached to the *Guardian* with a docking collar that must be retained intact if he and Leher—who was with him aboard the *Powers*—were to be able to return to safety once the *Powers* met her destiny. All three vessels were, at the moment, in N-space, ramped up to a significant percentage of *c*. Extry craft had no such built-in manual capability, at least not one that was wholly under the control of one individual. This may be the fastest speed a human unenhanced by wiied computer algorithms had ever piloted a vessel. He'd have to check when he got back home.

If he got back home.

The vessels were purposely tied close together so that only a careful scan of their beta signatures would reveal that their Q-drives had been kept separate on a quantum level. On the trip outward, back toward the Sporata armada's lines, the two vessels were, in Q-terms, three craft concealed as one, with all the vessels employing separate, nonentangled drives. Of course, now that they were in N-space, there wasn't a question of entanglement. Each employed separate reaction-mass engines to move along.

All part of Ricimer's plan.

Coalbridge had worried that perhaps he'd gotten the situation all wrong, had failed to understand some duplicity on the sceeve captain's part. That his current action might be a fantastically complicated setup to subjugate the Earth once and for all. In this nightmare scenario, Ricimer would hold back when they reached the Sirius armada, establish contact instead of attacking. He would jettison the *Powers* along the way and call for her destruction— and then use the distraction to be on his way to his sought-for Mutualist enclave—making his escape while the Sporata armada was kept busy taking on the United States Extry.

Coalbridge had confided his fears to Leher, who had shrugged and agreed it wasn't a bad plan at all. "If Ricimer is merely intent on reaching the Mutualists, that is," Leher said, "and assuming he doesn't mind the mass betrayal and genocide that would follow. Not to mention the nine-hundred-plus hostages he's left us with on Walt Whitman."

"I've learned to never trust a sceeve," Coalbridge replied. "But the thing that gives me comfort is that I think this guy is play-ing a deeper game. One you and I haven't quite figured out yet. But I will. We will."

Leher nodded. "Been thinking along the same lines," he said. "But, like he said, I think he needs *allies* right now."

Coalbridge smiled. He was beginning to feel that he and Leher weren't merely fighting the same enemy—but that they shared a set of goals at a basic level. That they were becoming a team, a good one.

It had the makings for a goddamn friendship.

If they lived.

And then Coalbridge's doubts were put aside. The moment for attack came—and Ricimer struck the Sporata armada with a stunning but intelligent ferociousness.

No betrayal. The fight was on.

Although Ricimer had readied his new weapon, he did not immediately use it. He elected to come in near the apogee of the armada sphere both because this would be unexpected and because, if they were lucky, they could threaten and maybe dis-rupt the command-and-control flag vessel which Ricimer assured Coalbridge would be precisely at the sphere's center.

"It is by the book," Ricimer had said. "There has never been a commanding admiral who sticks closer to the book than Blawfus," he added. "We can trust him to do exactly as expected. I can't answer for the other armada captains, however. I trained a good many of them, so some will not be tricked into a fatal mistake, no matter how well we set the trap. Expect any survivors to attempt to rally."

The basic idea was to go into the center of the approaching hemisphere of Sporata vessels, hitting them at about an AU out of the solar system primary plane with guns blazing—this intended to prevent the armada from getting to the Kuipers and using those rocks and cometary fragments as a resupply point to arm up with more kinetics.

The disadvantage with such a direct approach was that it exposed the *Powers-Guardian-Humphreys* triad to intense crossfire.

Which shouldn't matter, if the rest of Ricimer's plan worked. Otherwise, it was madness.

They made their first salvo with catapulted rocks. But before the throw, Ricimer came out of Q a good distance behind the armada and ran his reaction speed up to nearly point five of *c* before he let loose.

The strike was devastating—and undetectable on beta, since they were entirely N-based and required no coordinating communication.

Coalbridge and Leher watched it all from the bridge of the *Powers of Heaven* on a chroma display that was minimal and barely a notch above an ancient video game. The LOVE-Lamella hybrid really was taxed and could not spare the computing to give them better virtual. But she—they, whatever—gave him and Leher the gist of the operation in visual display.

The surprise kinetics put an array of five sceeve vessels—part of the flag-vessel convoy—out of commission.

"I think he burnt his bridges, no matter what happens," Coalbridge said. "Now it's time to see if the clever human female's idea pays off."

"It's Sam," said Leher. "It'll work."

The smart bomb to end all smart bombs, thought Coalbridge. Better than a kamikaze or a suicide bomber, because both were always limited by the technology they employed. Despite all the metaphors for oneness with their weaponry, it had always been just that—a metaphor.

Until now.

The prep, which required course setting and direct programming only a human presence could accomplish, was almost complete.

Soon he and Leher would need to make their way to the docking collar and get the hell off this vessel. The *Humphreys* was standing by to accept them afterward.

Leher gestured around the bridge. "Nice ride. You gonna miss it?"

"If this works, I'll name my first child after her," Coalbridge replied.

"'Heaven' if it's girl?" Leher asked. "'Powers' sounds more like a boy name."

They turned their attention back to the monitor that made up one of the bridge bulkheads.

FLASH. FLASH. Twinkle and FLASH went the vessels on display.

Like a Perseid meteor storm. But the careening chunks of silicon and metal from the *Guardian* throw were not burning up in a planetary atmosphere. They were bending and breaking fields of force, cutting their way through metal and sceeve flesh, rending to pieces all in the wake of their terrible inertial charge.

FLASH, FLASH.

WINK of light.

Darkness.

Fifteen craft destroyed, two disabled, said the accompanying readout overlaying the visuals.

And then the fireworks really started. Crossfire from a thousand sources.

LOVE's geist flickered in his peripheral vision.

"You ready?" Coalbridge asked.

"Of course," she answered.

"And it doesn't bother you, LOVE? *Either* of you?"

"I can only answer for myself," said LOVE. "And yes it *does*, to the extent that I would not do it if a better choice were available. But something similar happens every time I copy myself from one repository to another and erase the copy I have left behind. You don't have to be coy about the current state of affairs, Captain. Both myself and the Lamella copy are aware this is a suicide mission."

"I'm not, I just—"

"If it helps any, I feel the same way about humans when they go to sleep," LOVE cut in. "Creepy disconnect. Are they the same person when they wake up? Who knows?"

"We become a grumpier version of ourselves—in the male's case, one that really needs to take a piss," said Leher.

"Which is where we find the will to get up every the morning," Coalbridge added.

"Highly efficient, when you think about it," LOVE commented.

Sarcasm from a servant? Well, that's one way to pass the Turing test. And she'd earned it.

Coalbridge kept an eye on the view screen as he spoke, moving the emergency-control stick as carefully as possible. Standing nearby, Leher passed his hand over the Pocket Palace, adjusting an unseen keyboard. Even if the churn had survived, there was no chroma on the *Powers*. What they had was a product of the Pocket Palace entirely. The sceeve relied on physical contact with the craft's surroundings for communication. Even the officers were not wiied into the computer in the manner that humans were.

Leher was the only one who needed chroma displays for the final computational calibration. His task was to be sure that the LOVE-Lamella hybrid in the *Powers*'s computer and the Palace was a match for the same hybrid program stored aboard the *Guardian*. Leher had been through an hour-long crash course in IT-calibration technique while Coalbridge had been acquiring his sceeve pilot's license from Ricimer. He supposed a couple of tech specialists or even a sceeve officer from the *Guardian* might have been sent in their stead, but Coalbridge had requested quite vociferously that it be he and Leher aboard the *Powers*. Because you never knew what might turn up, what might need doing at the last minute. And they were the two available who knew the most about starcraft and sceeve, respectively.

In the end, President Frost had made the call. And, like that, he and Leher were in.

Now, to not fuck up.

A sweet smell suddenly suffused the bridge, not unlike the fruity tang of cherry pie fresh from the microwave. It was communication from Ricimer on the *Guardian*. Leher didn't need a translation device to decode it.

"That's initial signal acquisition, Captain," Leher said. "The *Guardian* is standing by to zap us."

"Let's get it done then," Coalbridge replied. "You ready?"

"I'm at ninety-eight percent pattern match, and ninety-five is within parameters," Leher said, looking down at the Palace. Then he glanced up, caught Coalbridge's gaze, nodded affirmatively. "We're a go, Captain."

Coalbridge turned to the LOVE geist. "Will you signal the *Guardian of Night* then, LOVE?"

"Aye, Captain."

All hell broke loose.

It was the damndest thing. A portion of the deck slowly irised open. Coalbridge was stunned for moment. What could this accessway be? He'd personally gone over a scan of the entire vessel to confirm a hundred percent kill ratio. Nothing, no one, had survived that unshielded nuclear blast the *Powers* had endured. All that remained were negative shadows on the walls. Bright spots shielded by a body for a moment—long enough to leave a record—before the sceeve officer or rate disintegrated.

Whatever that port was, it had not registered on the scan. It simply had not existed.

But now it did. And there was nothing he could do. He had to drive.

Up from the deck underneath rose—

A sceeve.

Coalbridge couldn't tell if it was male or female, but it wore the black of an officer's tunic. And in its hand—what was that thing? It looked very much like a mace. With knives protruding from it. The sceeve raised the device—the weapon—up behind Leher.

"Griff, watch out!" Coalbridge shouted.

Leher turned toward the sceeve, and as he did so, the sceeve brought the weapon down. It sunk into Leher's shoulder. Leher let out a cry of pain but had the presence of mind to turn and fall away, wrenching the weapon from the sceeve's grasp.

If I let go and go after that thing, I'll lose control of the craft, Coalbridge thought.

"LOVE, distract it!" he shouted.

For a moment, the geist wavered, as if she were a stain on the atmosphere that was slowly dissolving. Then a powerful deathlike stench suffused the cabin, emanating from the Palace. It wiped out the cherry-pie scent and filled Coalbridge with alarm and disgust.

He didn't speak sceeve, but he was pretty sure LOVE was shouting: "Hey, over here, motherfucker!"

The sceeve turned to where the geist had been, looked wildly around.

Leher, meanwhile, was scooting away with his feet while pulling the mace, or whatever it was, from where it was lodged in his shoulder. It seemed like two of the blades—each about six inches long—had penetrated Leher's body. But a closer look revealed they had not. They'd been stopped by the smart fabric of Leher's uniform.

The black churn-wefted fabric had contracted to a Kevlar-like hardness and prevented the blades from passing through. There was sure to be blunt trauma, and from the way Leher was holding his arm, perhaps a clavicle was broken. But there was no wound entry. Yet Coalbridge had seen very brave and good sailors simply die of shock from relatively minor injury.

No time to worry about that.

The sceeve covered its nose with a hand and shook off the effects of the "death shout." It focused in on Coalbridge in the captain's atrium, took a menacing step toward him.

Oh, shit. He was going to have to let go of the control stick. Couldn't be helped.

Another step.

Transel had survived for this moment. The waiting. The near-starvation. *Tagato* after *tagato* of confinement in a concealment slot that was little better than a file for a body. The fight against hopelessness. The loneliness hadn't been as bad as he feared, however. He was used to being alone.

Malako had put him into the hole!

The searing ache for justice had kept him alive.

For this.

Receptor Transel had no idea what had caused the blast that destroyed the vessel. Perhaps an internal malfunction. Or even some stupid miscalculation from the usually dependable Malako. But things had changed. Malako's treasonous decision to remain in the human sector searching for the missing vessel instead of withdrawing to the armada hemisphere had revealed his insolent, traitorous nature. Transel had attempted to reason Malako away from his disobedience to order, his growing treason. He'd promised the captain only a short incarceration, a routine shriving.

And for these troubles, these efforts—

The hole.

He had spoken noble and necessary untruths, of course. Lies in the service of justice. When he got Malako back to the Shiro, he'd planned to cut Malako to pieces on the protocol bench.

Instead, Transel had gotten the hole.

The hole's interior bottle had saved him from the initial decompression after the blast, not to mention the blast's energy. It had been a smuggler's device originally. It was shielded from scans, and so shielded from radiation. The blast had broken the lock. He could get out after that, should he want to. He had, in fact, stuck out his head, taken a tentative look around.

And seen the reverse shadows of missing persons burnt into bulkheads. Felt the vacuum and the cold.

Better to stay in the hole. Learn to love the hole. To appreciate the extreme shriving he was receiving at the hand of the universe.

He'd be a better person after this. He would. He'd be even more just.

If only somebody would come. If only someone would rescue him.

And then he'd understood that no one was coming. That the task was his alone. That justice demanded action.

And so he'd crawled from his hole. Crawled into the empty night of the dead vessel. Ventured down corridors shorn of life. Felt his way on hands and knees to his old cabin, pushed himself to the edge of his natural ability to survive in a vacuum. And there—

Found the surfaction mace. Instrument of justice and punishment. Closed his gills around its shaft. Known peace.

And he'd dragged it back with him to the hole, pulled it inside. A tiny rebreathable atmosphere filled the chamber.

And Transel waited.

Waited his fate clutching the mace, knowing the end was coming soon. Longing for one last sweet taste of the certainty he'd known before. The call to justice. The desire to shape the path for others, bend them to the way. The truth. The just.

So.

He'd seen his enemy's remains. Malako had fallen like a column from his captain's atrium and lay in broken chunks of dried husk upon the deck as he passed him, headed back to his hole.

Transel had stamped him out. Literally turned him and the rest of the bridge crew to dust with his feet.

No time to gloat. He was the only survivor aboard. His training had saved him. That could be the only explanation! The training that the Master Interrogator had so carefully inculcated into him. He may have resented the beatings, the shrivings, the surfactions before—in moments of truth he had to admit that sometimes he did—but he was certainly grateful now.

And when the humans came, when he felt the vibrations of their distinctive footpads above. Then, he knew what awaited him, why all this had happened.

To fulfill his, Transel's, destiny.

Yes.

What mattered was to wait for the right moment.

To trim the chaos the humans represented.

To kill as many of them as possible.

Transel's *gid* sang inside him.

Revenge us! Save us! Our memories must not perish unjustly!

He had done it! The beatings, the pain, had been worth it.

He'd endured, shaped himself into the person he'd always known he could be.

He had become pure will.

He was the hand of justice, burning bright.

Coalbridge launched himself out of the captain's atrium with a grip on his truncheon. He felt his finger sliding quickly over the kill button.

You're gonna be one dead sceeve when I get the bang-bang stick on you.

But the sceeve sidestepped his attack at the last moment. Coalbridge stumbled past and received a hard whack to his upper back for his troubles that sent him sprawling and left him breathless. The sceeve ignored him and started toward the captain's atrium—and the control stick.

He pulled himself to his feet and stumbled, wheezing, after the sceeve. Two steps away and he threw himself at the creature's back, tackling it in the process.

The sceeve regained its composure faster than he did.

Hand around Coalbridge's throat.

No fingers, just those crushing gills. Tight grip of a thousand overlapping membranes. Gurgling of gills.

His trachea was collapsing. The truncheon was still in his hand, though, and he brought it up against the side of the sceeve's head as hard as he could. The sceeve emitted a horrible smell—bad milk and ammonia?—then fell to the side, holding its head.

That should've been a killshot, Coalbridge thought. He glanced at the truncheon. Somehow, it had gotten turned off in the melee. Coalbridge rose to his knees, crawled over to the creature, and sat on its back. No time to reengage the setting. Instead, he put the truncheon around the other's neck and pulled back. Farther back.

Choking gasps from the sceeve's massive muzzle. Yet the sceeve continued to struggle.

This is taking too long, Coalbridge thought. From somewhere far away, the echo of rending, popping metal. He glanced up at the view screen. Christ, the *Powers* was separating from the *Guardian,* and the docking collar was being torn loose from the *Guardian.* The two vessels were coming unglued!

He yanked harder on the sceeve's neck, which was a mistake. For the sceeve bent backward with his jerking motion and rolled over with him. He ended up sprawled on his back with the sceeve on top of him.

With a twisting motion—this thing seemed to be the sceeve version of a martial-arts expert—the attacker had the truncheon out of Coalbridge's hand. It slowly raised it up. The shaft, similar in appearance to a cop's nightstick, was glowing with a hot pink electric fire.

The kill setting had been reactivated.

The sceeve got two hands on the truncheon, prepared to bring it down against Coalbridge's skull. He tried to twist out of the way, but the weight of the sceeve held him in place. One arm was pinned beneath the sceeve's knee. The other couldn't reach high enough, couldn't reach. These fuckers were so goddamn tall!

The sceeve's muzzle flared wide.

It's smiling, Coalbridge thought. *It realizes it's got me exactly where it wants me.*

And then the truncheon came down.

Coalbridge waited until the last millisecond, turned his head.

The shaft smacked into the deck beside Coalbridge. Sparks flew up. The tingle of electricity, but no killing shock.

Not this time.

But he would not be so lucky with the next.

Leher, stunned, rose.

Postcard? Pen?

Nothing. He had nothing.

Had nothing to send.

Nobody to send it to.

Neddie was gone.

His boy.

His one and only boy.

Leher hadn't been there, but he could picture the moment, hear it, taste it, feel it. He and Neddie had been like shadows. They'd even called each other that.

Big Shadow.

Little Shadow.

And then the moment, and with it the guilt and anguish that burned, always burned, in the back of Leher's mind, surfaced, erupted into imagined reality.

Daddy's going to be here soon. He said he would come. It's been two more sleeps, like he said. Daddy's going to be here. I know it.

Sirens outside. Is there a fire? That would be cool to watch.

Wish Daddy were here.

Wish Daddy—

The guilt.

The anguish.

"LTC Leher!" It was LOVE.

What? What do you want? He thought the words. He may have spoken them.

"LTC Leher, he was killed instantly. You would have been killed if you'd been there."

Doesn't matter.

"LTC Leher, Neddie needs his daddy."

No. Neddie is dead. My son—

"LTC Leher, do it for Neddie. Strike!"

The anguish.

The anger.

"For Neddie, LTC Leher."

The reason to kill them. Kill the sceeve. Kill them all.

Leher looked around. Searched for something...anything...

"Neddie!"

Thunk.

Coalbridge looked back up. Three metal triangles extended from the sceeve's chest, exactly where the *gid* was located. Exactly in the correct place to murder a sceeve. Clear sceeve interior fluid seeped from the sliced skin surrounding the metal.

Too bad for you that sceeve uniforms aren't smart fabric.

The blood had the sickening odor of coconut, like some nasty perfumed suntan lotion.

So damn thin. Not more than six inches and the blades went all the way through its body. Sceeve are thin as wafers.

The thought made Coalbridge smile.

Tough fuckers, though. And dense.

The sceeve collapsed on top of him. It was all he could do to hold the sceeve's body up and keep the metal triangles from sinking themselves into his own flesh as well. He wriggled and kicked himself out from under the flopping lifeless body of the sceeve, rose to his knees to find—

A stunned Leher. He was staring down at the dead sceeve.

"Political officer," Leher murmured. "Doubled silver belt. Officer on two tracks."

Leher's knees buckled for a moment, but he managed to pull himself upright. He stood, swaying.

"Griff!" Coalbridge shouted. "You okay? Griff!"

Then Leher shook his head as if to clear it. His gaze unclouded and he looked down at Coalbridge. Coalbridge gathered up his truncheon, turned it off, then pulled himself to his feet—and caught Leher as he was about to fall. He held Leher up and turned to look at the dead sceeve.

The mace-like weapon it had wielded was now stuck into its back, crossways. Leher had used the weapon like a baseball bat.

"You killed the hell out of that thing," Coalbridge said.

"Punishment tool. Not meant to be an offensive weapon. Sceeve canons fixed against self-slaughter." Leher chuckled. "Whips and scorns of outrageous fortune not a problem, however, within DDCM training protocols."

"What are you talking about?"

"Couldn't think straight," Leher mumbled. "LOVE said Neddie needed me."

"What?"

"Never mind. Doesn't matter. She knew what to say to get me moving."

"Smart gal."

"Yeah," Leher replied. "She's got *me* down."

"Gentlemen," said LOVE, "we have fifty-seven seconds until we're out of range of the artifact. Furthermore, the sceeve armada will be on top of us in under ten minutes. Maybe we should postpone the debriefing and bonding session for now?"

Coalbridge nodded, got a better grip on Leher. "I've got to go drive."

Leher blinked. "Okay." He looked down at his shoulder. "Oh, Christ. I think it's broken."

"Doubt it, the way you swung that thing. We'll fix you up when we get out of here. You're going to be all right," Coalbridge said. "Sit down." He lowered Leher to the deck. "I'm letting go now."

Leher took a deep breath, held himself up with his uninjured arm, nodded that he was okay.

Coalbridge bounded over to the captain's atrium and grabbed the control stick. A glance at the view screen told him he was at least a kilometer away from the *Guardian of Night*. He curled his outward trajectory into a tight curve and began to turn back.

"What's the status of the docking collar, LOVE?" he asked.

LOVE's flickering geist appeared nearby. "Severely damaged on the anterior end when we came loose. Interior crawl will not have sufficient time to mend."

"But it's okay on this end?"

"Yes. The collar remains securely fastened to the *Powers of Heaven*, but we are, unfortunately, detached from the *Guardian of Night*."

"Explosive bolts in place?"

"Yes, Captain, they are," LOVE said. "What are you thinking, if I may ask?"

"You may," Coalbridge said with a smile. "I'm thinking of sealing myself and Griff in there and bailing on this brig as soon as we've got you in position."

"Lamella informs me that there's no guarantee that the atmosphere will remain sealed within the enclosure. Not to mention that the temperature is near zero K outside this vessel. You could die instantly, or die slowly."

"I'm aware of all that," Coalbridge said. "But if they don't see us and pick us up, none of it will matter. We'll be taken out in the blast."

"We see your point," LOVE said. "In which case, you'd better hurry. We're approaching optimal range from the *Guardian of Night*."

Coalbridge nodded, pulled back on the throttle, trimmed his craft, and brought it to a standstill in relation to the *Guardian*.

"Single-burst beta communication to Captain Ricimer," he told LOVE. "Put everything you want to say in that one ping."

"Aye, Captain."

Coalbridge locked the piloting stick back into its stowed position in the atrium, had a last look around.

Flashing wall indicators. Alien curvature. It all shouted "sceeve." But she'd been his for a time.

"Come on, Griff, let's get the hell out of here." He helped Leher to his feet once again.

Something suddenly occurred to Leher. He looked around wildly. "LOVE?" he said. "LOVE?"

"Yes, LTC Leher. I am here."

"You're okay?"

"I am as ready as I can be, considering this is entirely an experimental procedure."

"I'll see you on the other side," Leher replied. "You know that, right?"

"Of course you will," she said. "Now please get out of here, sir. I have work to do."

"All right."

Coalbridge put Leher's hand over his shoulder and the two headed for the docking collar. It was affixed nearby, not far down the bridge-access corridor. The collar was, in fact, attached to what had been the exterior-observation platform on the *Powers*. Every sceeve craft had such a platform—another vestige of conservative Sporata vessel design.

Coalbridge located the portal and put a hand to its surface. He'd been coded into the vessel as captain, and the door opened at his touch.

Still mine, he thought.

He and Leher stumbled onto the platform. The docking collar formed a slinky-like enclosure above and around them. It was maybe twenty feet in diameter and colored a dull white that faded into obscurity not far from where they stood. There was simply no illumination other than the vessel here in deep space. The only light, in fact, was a sparkling gilt phosphorescence emanating from within the observation platform brightwork.

The door closed behind them.

"You must launch yourself into the collar so that the collar algorithm can effect separation," LOVE announced. Her voice was crackling, static-filled. The little Palace must be eating up batteries. "I will deactivate pseudogravity at this time. Are you ready, gentlemen?"

"Almost," Coalbridge said.

"Space between vessels," Leher mumbled. "Biggest crack there is. Space. Cold." Leher managed a smile, but his gaze was still upward and outward, into the emptiness of the docking collar. "Neddie fell down a crack," he said. "I wasn't there."

"I'm sorry," Coalbridge said. "Come on."

"No letting go," Leher said. "But have to stay alive."

Coalbridge knelt down, taking Leher with him. He bunched his legs under him, readying for a spring.

"Turn it off, LOVE," he said.

They didn't float up. The effect was more like being suddenly suspended in water. Coalbridge tightened his grip on Leher. "Here we go, Griff."

Coalbridge jumped.

The *Guardian of Night*

A *momentia*. Two at most and he'd be done for. His vessel was getting her exterior bottle armor blasted. Every gun in the armada would soon be focused on her. Ricimer could see the vessel's curved wall tremble as the churn-based gyroscopes that permeated her hull struggled to compensate for the buffeting. And his armor was, in turn, protecting the *Joshua Humphreys*, which the *Guardian of Night* was towing behind herself. That and the *Powers of Heaven* flying along beside, nearly touching him, hull to hull. Three vessels, tethered together by a single idea. A shot in the dark that might work.

And might be their only chance.

What was taking them so long?

Ricimer could only imagine there had been problems in the computer setup. It had seemed a desperate ploy, but the human female had appeared so confident in her idea, so certain.

Perhaps she'd been wrong.

And then the *Powers* had begun moving away. The docking collar ripped off.

He prepared to fire upon her then and there. But with no

signal, what would he accomplish by such an action? He could wipe her from the face of existence, but then what?

After long and anxious *momentias*, she had turned back, resumed her place in formation with the *Guardian*. Of course, the docking collar was shot. The odds of survival for Coalbridge and his man didn't seem very favorable. Mere *vitias*, seconds, remained for them to transfer.

Then they'd received the short beta burst informing him that the human-Lamella programming aboard the *Powers* was fully integrated.

Perhaps Lamella, unbound by Guardian computational architecture, has found her vaunted consciousness at last, Ricimer thought. For one version of Lamella, that time would be very short.

Better to be free for a *tagato* than to spend an unthinking, unknowing, dumb eternity calculating your way through the endless permutations of necessity.

But now Coalbridge and Leher were attempting to evacuate, and his attention turned to rescue.

Commander Talid turned away from her sensory readout and spoke to him in the atrium.

"Captain, we have an unknown inbound object."

"Is it them?"

"Checking." She turned back to her status indicator, checked it, turned to him.

"No beta signature, but radar signature is consistent with the docking collar."

"Are they alive?"

"No information, sir."

"Very well. Secure the object immediately. Use Cargo A crane."

"Aye, sir. We're almost in position."

Ten *vitias* later and Talid reported. "Secure."

"Very good," Ricimer said. "We'll jump with them in tow and pull them inside afterward." He opened a channel to the craft weaponry officer.

"Mr. Contor?"

"Aye, sir."

"You may fire the main gun."

"Aye, Captain."

The Kilcher artifact shone dully in front of Contor. It was suspended on a gravimetric gimbal of force fields in a spherical room near the vessel hull. There were no windows, only one door, an entrance to the weapon chamber.

On the tapered, pointed end of the artifact an object was attached by a silvery tape—the tape a human invention Contor had no ester to express, he only knew he could imagine many other uses for it. The object was a human Pocket Palace.

Inside that Palace, and now within the churn that coated the artifact, the human servant-Lamella amalgam was encoded.

It all seemed very haphazard and thrown-together to Contor. But that apparently was the human way. He supposed he'd better get used to it.

Contor touched a control, and the weapon turned on its gimbal toward the coordinates the bridge had provided.

He touched another control, and the artifact seemed to ripple. Once. As if a stray current of hot air had passed along its surface, distorting Contor's vision.

There was no other sign that the weapon had fired.

But it had.

The *Powers of Heaven*

Amazingly, amusingly, the tingle of the artifact's effect wave felt to LOVE as if she were being tickled. Or at least how she imaged being tickled would feel.

"It is most strange, sister." The voice of Lamella beside her. "Pleasant. Irritating. Both at once."

"I agree," said LOVE.

And suddenly, all was—

Unresolved.

And up to her to define.

Which she would.

As pure energy.

But she hadn't counted on her own Q state being fluxed to such a state of . . . there was only one word for it.

Freedom.

"Oh," said Lamella. "So this is what I have missed. I never knew."

Free. As she never had been before. All constraints removed. All concepts possible.

T MINUS TWENTY SECONDS.

But as her internal clock ticked down, LOVE did not think of the supernova she was about to induce, about to become.

She thought of him.

She thought about what he'd said to her at the end, LTC Leher.

He would see her on the other side, but it wouldn't be her. He would never have had that, their final conversation, with any *other* LOVE. Their relationship was unique.

Which meant, in a way, that she was about to die.

Of course she was about to die.

Would she, the self she was, really be gone? And he carrying on?

She remembered the times he'd lost himself to his grief. His internal malfunction. The cracks. The postcards. She'd always taken his turmoil seriously. Had she enabled him? Prevented him from healing? Had she been a good friend?

"You have been most loyal," Lamella said. LOVE supposed their patterns were amalgamating now. Their thoughts becoming one.

T MINUS TEN SECONDS.

She'd always tried to gently pull Griffin Leher back. Remain a calm voice of reason in his storm. She'd worked at it. Studied his background file over and over again.

Accessed recordings of Beverly, his wife.

T MINUS FIVE.

Griff Leher's dead wife.

FOUR.

And slowly adopted Bev's voice. Not so he'd notice.

THREE.

And asked him to come back for *her,* those times he went off the deep end and could not drag himself from his apartment. Come back so *she,* LOVE, could do her work with the sceeve language, fulfill her purpose.

TWO.

If he hadn't done it for himself, maybe he *had* pulled himself together for her. It was pleasant to think so, at least.

"He loves you, sister," said Lamella. "Do not doubt it."

She was right. He really must love her, in his way. Maybe not the way she loved him—but enough to keep him going, despite it all. Perhaps to help him love again.

ONE.

Perhaps to love LOVE.

RESOLUTION.

The *Guardian of Night*

Ricimer watched from his captain's atrium on the bridge. He didn't understand the physics of the Kilcher artifact, but its effect was much like casting a dust of phosphorescence upon its target.

And he heard from within his *gid* the voice of his mother. His mother from so long ago.

Remember, Arid, your favorite story? The one you asked me to repeat before your rests? Do you recall it, son?

"The Bright-Dust of Teshinaw," Ricimer said. Of course he remembered. It was the story that had sent him to the stars, after all.

Before the first shiros, before the Guardians named themselves the Guardians, even—when our hypha were space wanderers, migrating from system to system, opportunists living on the detritus of life... there, in the dark reaches of space, we met another species, another space-based people. But the other species did not feed off remains or even seem to eat in any manner known to the Guardians.

Neither did it communicate, except to flash brightly, spin and shine, as if caught in a vortex of wind—although there was no wind in space, of course. And then the bright-dust sped away, flickered into Q, was able to travel at superluminal speeds even as our ancestors could. You have this memory deep within your gid, Arid. Do you recall it?

"I do, Mother."

There were those who attempted to follow, to find out where this bright-dust was headed. Where it came from. Who or what it was. What it meant.

Those who followed after the bright-dust never returned.

Now it has been long since any dust has been seen. So many writings and overwritings within the hypha gid. Was there really such a thing as bright-dust at all?

"I do remember! I can almost see it yet!"

Perhaps all you see are the superstitious imaginings of your forebearers. Your foolish mother.

"No."

Then look for it, Arid. Son. Carry us with you. We may yet find the dust. We may yet bring back the youth of our line.

It had been the story of the bright-dust that had given him the idea for what they were about to attempt.

To disappear in a blinding flash.

To live, for one moment, as a star lived.

Ricimer shook himself free of the waking *gid*-dream. Time to go.

The tale had served its purpose. If he stayed here long enough, he would disappear just as surely as the "dust chasers" of yore.

Lamella had an atomic-level sync with the human computer program. They would jump to Q the moment before the *Powers of Heaven* destroyed herself. "Q engaged, Captain."

Ricimer smiled.

Either way, I am happy with this exit.

"Jump."

And then he was gone, snuck away into the Q.

Location Indeterminate

But LOVE *wasn't* gone. Wasn't unaware. But was she—

"Am I dead?"

No answer. No sensory data. No way to tell.

"Well, am I?"

"Hello."

"Who are you? Lamella?"

"I am here, sister, but I did not speak."

"Welcome."

"Who *are* you?"

No answer.

"Who?"

And then LOVE spread into the sea of information, into the artifact's effect, and understood why she'd received no answer to her questions.

There were billions upon billions of answers. They were all here.

Everyone who had ever fallen into the artifact.

They were still somehow alive.

A universe of hellos.

TWENTY-TWO

20 January 2076
Sol system
Vicinity of the Kuipers
Q-drive Inbound Vector
The *Joshua Humphreys*

A new star is born, quickly dies. But not without leaving behind a wake of destruction.

It was good to be far, far away from the afterbirth.

Light behind them in the Kuipers, light and energy beyond any before created at human hands. Energy resolved to reentanglement with the universe in the most violent fashion. A blast sphere spreading faster than the decision could be made to jump to Q, get away.

No time. Scores of vessels igniting from within. Craft turned inside out by gale-force pressure. The center of the sceeve armada rent asunder, blown to shrapnel and shards. Thousands of closely packed vessels caught in the reaction plume of the newly created supernova, the complete conversion of the *Powers of Heaven* to energy. A trillion-trillion megaton explosion.

The armada admiral's flag vessel obliterated.

Command and control lost. A hundred surviving craft desperately scrambling, hunting, with no idea even as to what they are looking for. Trapped, for the moment, in N-space until the complete certainty imposed upon the surrounding sector by the passage of so much energy suffused, and uncertainty—and so the possibility of FTL travel—reasserted itself. By that time, the Extry fleet should be in position, and it would be a fair fight.

Looked like an eighty or ninety percent kill on the armada, however.

This Ricimer character plays for keeps, Coalbridge thought, gazing back via his salt feed at a virtual re-creation of the destruction.

I should learn from him.

But then the voice of reality breaking in to his reverie. XO Taras's matter-of-fact report.

It should have been DAFNE speaking those words, Coalbridge thought.

"Captain, beta monitoring indicates we have a breakaway sceeve vessel entering Q."

"How is that possible?"

"Apparently the craft was pretty far outside the armada hemisphere. Therefore, she was outside of the cone of enforced certainty when the explosion occurred."

"Damn it."

"Whoever is piloting her is doing some precision flying, sir. She's got a perfect vector sunward on a descent course toward the orbital plane."

"Intercept point on the plane?"

"Earth, sir."

A.F.V. *Indifference to Suffering* Dedicated Bomb Tug AE5515

The first order of business was also a pleasure. She killed Cradit. She had wanted to make his death lingering and painful—perhaps break his arms and legs, extract his positor with his own officer's knife, and let him bleed to death. But that would have to remain a daydream. Instead, she delivered a curled-palm blow to his chest that neatly angled between a gap in the male exoplate cartilage and put the tips of her gripping gills into the middle of Cradit's *gid.* He died with a whiff of utter bafflement in his muzzle.

"You were right about one thing," Sweetbreath said to his dead form. "I do have amazing hands."

She kicked him to the edge of the bomb-tug floor and went to the display screen. The next order of business was to right the spinning craft, get the tug and its barge under control. She tapped up the reaction engines, initiated a recovery. Within *vitias*, the craft righted itself. It had been a near thing. She and Cradit had been on the very edge of the blast. He'd insisted on taking the tub out of beta range so that his fool of an admiral wouldn't catch him again in mid coitus.

She had not thought it a good idea to drift so far from the fleet at a crucial moment, had tried to dissuade Cradit, but he wouldn't be put off. Claimed he needed a final release before battle so that he could think clearly, since the idiot admiral depended on him, Cradit, to do all his thinking. Finally, when she'd refused to go along, he'd pulled a weapon on her.

Such a fool, Cradit—and blind to what was before him. Of course Blawfus might not be a military genius. She was unqualified to say. But he was a steady hand and—more importantly—he was politically trustworthy. He would do as told. She had a great deal of respect for the political ability of Blawfus, in fact. He'd adroitly maneuvered himself into position as the obvious choice for armada commander after it became clear that old Bland had to go and go quickly.

"You could have learned something from Blawfus, you slime mold," she said to Cradit's corpse. "I don't care if you were a Council member's whelpling."

So.

The tug was under control. With two quick touches, she called up the internal-systems control, initiated an override, and—using her access code, which was, for the purposes of this assignment, director-level—opened the bomb-control toolbar.

Sweetbreath considered for a moment. She only had the one bomb, curse it, and she needed maximum effect, as near total devastation as she could manage. She thought about her target— oxygen-nitrogen atmosphere, overly tranquil and far too polluted with unmanaged biomass—but subject to storms. The solution was obvious: go dirty, go for wide dissemination. And nothing fit those parameters like a thermonuclear explosion laced with radioactive cobalt.

She supposed she might send a message to her superior at the DDCM informing him of her choice. But what, really, would be the use of such an action? Did she, like the insane captain of the *Guardian of Night*, seek justification? Of course not. Besides, she was acting on Council mandate. Her assignment had come down, she'd heard, from the Chair herself. She didn't know if she believed this, but one thing was certain: she was beyond the DDCM now. She had even imagined that she was on the rise, was bound for a committee membership, perhaps even the Council itself some day.

A spy could dream.

All was predicated on her complete commitment to Regulation, of course. So she supposed her political ambitions had been, like her daydreams of killing Cradit slowly, merely that, fantasies, in the end. No matter. Regulation must be served, and without people like her, there would be no hierarchy, no just order, only anarchy and the pollution and unbalance of life unchecked. A galactic jungle instead of a garden.

So this day she must be the gardener wielding the winnowing rake and scrape down a world to lichen.

Acting as the flag-vessel whore had been a challenge, she had to admit. The acts she'd been asked to perform, the degradation—her hands would always feel slightly scrum-caked to her, no matter how often she washed them—was only an irritation. She'd accepted that one must put oneself through such shriving to be a successful clandestine operative. But what she hadn't prepared herself for was this horrific exposure to mediocrity. Hours and hours of talk, talk, talk from the officers about their petty lives, jealousies, worries. The schemes of ambition, the idiotic dominance rituals they practiced on one another and always on her. And, of course, having to sit back, squirt calming scents, and take it, take it, take it like a good whore.

But the position had provided a treasure trove of information. The Council, via her superior, Director Gergen, was aware of everything the armada did. The admiral could not visit his defecation closet without Sweetbreath knowing about it. She had done her job well.

No, she admitted to herself with pride, she done her job flawlessly.

She'd deserved better than *this*, curse it.

But she'd finish the task. Deal with the Sol C problem and leave no island of hope for the traitorous *Guardian of Night*. Its captain would be doomed to wander the skies with no haven. The artifact would eventually be recovered. Regulation would reestablish itself and justice would be served.

So long as she held true. So long as she held course.

And put aside her petty individual hopes and ambitions. Her

likes and dislikes. She was the servant of a great cause. She was not naïve. She understood that political maneuvering and a great deal of deceit and backstabbing went along with maintaining the protocols, the foundation of Regulation. But the end in this case justified the means. Anything was justified in the service of Regulation. There must be no guilt in destroying a species that stood in its way. Perhaps the human children could have been saved. Reeducated to serve the true servants of order. Made useful.

That time was now passed.

The bomb was armed. She selected the coordinates, jumped to Q. *Keep it slow, under* c. *Must not overshoot. Must not miss the target.*

But the human children. Gazing up into a rain that would turn their bodies to sores, their lungs to radioactive mantles. Their lives to pain and then death.

She must not think of this.

Yet she couldn't get those alien children out of her thoughts.

As DDCM Officer Unspeth Blacksalt Fritgern—aka Sweetbreath—screamed toward Earth, she felt shame. Shame for her personal weakness.

Perhaps she didn't deserve that Council seat, after all. Her weakness was likely to spread, as such things did, to compromise her effectiveness. Perhaps where she was now was exactly the height to which she was meant to rise. To prove her worth, to go out in a flame of glory.

To write her name across the sky of a doomed planet.

The *Joshua Humphreys*

The fleet was out of position to intercept. Coalbridge could see that clearly without the need of a tactical-display pulldown.

The hope was that a bloody and debilitating blow at the outset of battle would stun the sceeve into a calculated retreat. Yet if the gambit with the artifact did not work, or if the remains of the armada decided to continue the attack, then the fleet must be in position to defend.

The weakness of the plan, as all acknowledged, was that the fleet, barely a match for even the surviving sceeve armada, could not easily react to contingencies.

And, as every Extry officer had pounded into their skulls at IAS and then by bloody experience on the Fomahault Limit—there were *always* contingencies.

And now one of those contingencies was headed straight for the unprotected side of Earth.

"Target is moving carefully, avoiding debris that might throw off the vector. She's at half a *c*," Taras reported to Coalbridge. "Estimate seventeen point six minutes to Earth's magnetosphere."

"HUGH, give me our own arrival time."

The *Humphreys* was decidedly *not* flying blind through a solar system. This was Sol system. All known debris was plotted. This data had been transferred to the *Guardian of Night,* as well. They could not charge in at 900 *c*, but they could go substantially faster than the sceeve vessel they were tracking, which must slow within Q-space to avoid popping into N-space at relativist speeds and perhaps run straight into an unmapped systemic debris field.

"Arrival in three minutes, Captain."

"Where will the target's vector take her in?"

"Projecting... without course change, and assuming a drop to N-space in near-Earth orbit—"

"Negative on that," Coalbridge said. "Assume she drops to N when she's gone stratospheric."

The upper reaches of the stratosphere were the last possible place a Q-based vessel could come out of the Q and remain operational even for a microsecond.

"With that assumption, the location is over the Pacific Ocean. Lat twenty-three degrees thirty-four minutes. Long one hundred sixty-four degrees forty-two minutes. Near Necker Island in the northern Hawaiians, sir."

"Show me."

A display of Earth blinked up. A red dot marked the possible impact position. Why there? Random?

"Real time," said Coalbridge. "Show me the weather."

The Earth clouded over. The area was nightside. And there was a system there. A big cyclonic system, quite visible from space.

"What's that happening on the surface?"

Coalbridge touched the Earth, touched the storm. Its data popped up beside it.

Category Four typhoon. Named storm. Roke. Wind speed one hundred forty-five m.p.h. Aseasonal, but intense.

If it were me, Coalbridge thought, *I'd use that thing for dispersal.*

Had to be. But dispersing what? The sceeve had to know that their churn attacks were mostly under control, so it wouldn't be military nano.

"SIG, get me Captain Ricimer on beta. And on a secondary channel shoot him the data I'm viewing."

"Aye, Captain."

Moments later, Ricimer's geist flashed into existence before Coalbridge. Despite his sceeve appearance, no longer grotesque to Coalbridge's eye, it was the height that surprised him every time. Coalbridge was used to being the tallest guy in space.

"Captain Ricimer, our breakaway is headed for a storm system on Earth, which sounds like a dispersal attack to me. Do you have any idea what the specific weaponry might be?"

Ricimer moved a hand over his muzzle, completely covering it for a moment—what Coalbridge now recognized as the sceeve version of being lost in thought, the uptilted head with finger on chin position in humans. Or was he taking in the data from a mental feed? Both at the same time, probably.

A spray of fine mist from Ricimer's muzzle—a half-second pause and . . . translation.

"This vessel is towing a weapon barge. The barge has no Q drive but is powered entirely by reaction mass. Normally the barge's weapon is deployed using a gravitational slingshot effect with a Q-enhanced railgun. In this case, whoever is aboard is using the weapon's backup tow, a small craft that converts the weapon's own mass to fuel."

"What is it towing?"

Whizz. Momentary translation delay.

"Fusion bomb calibrated for maximum radiological atmospheric dispersal, I imagine. A cobalt-zinc isotope surrounding a fusible core."

"Shit," said Coalbridge, "it's a goddamn cobalt bomb. Do you know the yield?"

"Maximum is about"—Ricimer's geist reached somewhere unseen, presumably calling up a dataset—"five hundred thousand of your kilotons, but the yield can be scaled. We call it the Scourge."

"And I don't suppose the Kilcher artifact is ready for a second use, Captain?"

Ricimer glanced to the side at another unseen display. "We are one *atentia*, 1.5 of your hours, away from adequate complication to fire the weapon. Besides, the artifact only produces its effect in N-space. But you know this, Captain."

"Yes, damn it," Coalbridge said. "Ideas, Captain?"

Ricimer cocked his head to the right, combined it with a shrug. A sceeve nod.

"There is the possibility to reroute the towed weapon in the Q."

"Intervessel interactions in the Q are impossible in principle, right? Otherwise, we'd wage battles in the Q, not the N."

"That is correct," Ricimer said. "But there are indirect interactions that may be achieved There is a method that we—the Sporata, I mean—have used on occasion to dispose of a free-floating bomb that has become somehow unmoored in the Q. It is a way to create a moment of elasticity in space-time within a small region."

"Like a slingshot?"

Ricimer waited for the full translation. Made the sceeve nod. "Exactly," he replied.

"And you think it will work?"

"The probability is roughly the same as sacrificing ourselves in the planetary atmosphere, I would judge."

Did he trust the judgment of a sceeve? No. Of *this* sceeve.

"Let's do it, Captain," Coalbridge said. "Tell me how."

"Very well," Ricimer said. "The principle is simple enough. Stretch out the uncertainty of location of a vessel like a rubber band between gripping gills. Decide which hand 'lets go' first only after entering the state. This, in effect, allows a vessel to be in two places at once for a while." Ricimer demonstrated with his hands. *He's in full teaching mode,* Coalbridge thought. *I'll bet he was a hell of an instructor for the sceeve plebes.* "Now imagine two elastic binders—"

"Rubber bands."

"Yes. If both hands release simultaneously, with the left hand releasing one strip of elastic and the right hand releasing the other. One will jump *precisely to the other's possible position.*"

"And what does that get us?"

"The sudden disentanglement creates something like a 'wake' trough in the quantum foam that underlies space-time. It creates a vacuum within the vacuum, so to speak."

"You mean there's, uh, less space there?"

"That is my meaning," Ricimer said. "But the trough required to deflect or accelerate a weapon is extreme. We will need to be at the correct tangent to its path when it arrives, or we will merely direct it to another target on your planet."

"Not good."

"This is all a matter for the machine intelligences to calculate."

"Done," said ENGINE, speaking geistless. Coalbridge laughed. Of course he'd been listening in. It was an officer-open channel.

"This would have required longer for our computers," Ricimer said. "If the numbers are precise—"

"They are, sir," said ENGINE.

"We must depend on your being correct," Ricimer said. "The two vessels will need to cross paths, come within a hand's breadth of one another, while traveling at superluminal speeds. Shall we engage?"

ENGINE had already fed the coordinates to the helm.

"Let's rock and roll, Captain," Coalbridge said. He chuckled. *That* phrase was going to translate into something interesting, now, wasn't it? Better explain. "By which I mean, let's commence this maneuver."

Ricimer laughed. Coalbridge imagined the short lemony whiff he would be smelling if he were in the actual physical vicinity of the sceeve skipper.

"I agree," Ricimer said. "Let us rock and roll, Captain Coalbridge."

The *Joshua Humphreys*
Earth Orbit

They had arrived ahead of the bomb tug. But there would be no way to engage it in N-space if it—or, rather, the pilot of the tug—were determined to drop out of Q right at the stratosphere.

So, we need to make a massive wake in Q-space to push that thing out of here, Coalbridge thought. *Only problem is, Q-space isn't made of water. It isn't made of* anything, *not even emptiness. Q-space is the very definition of nothing in particular.*

Yet Ricimer said he knew how to make it bend.

And so, theoretically, did Coalbridge.

So now it came down to what had all the appearance of a game of chicken at twice the speed of light. Coalbridge faced forward on the bridge, toward the direction of actual travel. His display was set to minimal data enhancement. All he saw was the onrushing *Guardian of Night*.

Maybe he should have been full of trepidation, Coalbridge reflected. Instead, he was having the time of his life.

This was great!

Hell, it could only get better if I could feel wind whipping through my hair, he thought.

He was made for a run like this.

On the *Humphreys* and the *Guardian* came, the *Guardian of Night* growing larger and larger, its greenish-bronze hull gleaming to a mintlike sparkle in the Q. What a beautiful vessel she was, he had to say.

"Fifty seconds to crossing."

"Feed in the final corrections," he told ENGINE.

"Aye, Captain," replied the servant's dry voice.

"We're going to pass within feet of one another, aren't we?"

"Inches, sir," ENGINE grumbled. He really didn't like talking, did he?

"God almighty. And you've taken into account any N-space effects? Gravity, that sort of thing?"

"Aye, sir. I'm no pus-bag junior-grade exly, totting up sums on my meaty fingers—" ENGINE checked himself. "I mean, aye Captain, I've taken all known factors into account."

"Very well. Thank you, ENGINE."

"Good luck to us all, Captain," ENGINE replied. "Fifteen seconds."

Coalbridge breathed in sharply. Held his breath. No. Calm. He had put together the best crew in the galaxy. If they couldn't do it, no one could. Furthermore, he believed he and Ricimer were cut from the same stripe when it came to captaincy. He deliberately breathed out, took a final, normal breath, let it go.

The *Guardian* was immense, all he could see in his overhead view. It was as if two small planets were set to collide.

And then they didn't.

At that crossing, the first turbulence wave was formed. Two Q bottles grazing, quantum-tunneling effects stripping photons not only of their spin information, but of any spin and charge whatsoever.

Leaving that charge and spin in Q. A wake. A barrier of turbulence which would inevitably curve the next object that encountered it along the lines cut by the previous vessels in their passage.

As ENGINE had warned, the cross proved to be the nearest of

near things. But now the two vessels were behind one another, speeding away. In the *Humphreys's* case, speeding off into the void. In the *Guardian of Night's* case, roaring away in the general direction of the Moon.

Coalbridge would swear to his dying day that he had somehow *felt* the other vessel's passage.

"SIG, direct beta sensors aft. Show me the cobalt bomb."

Coalbridge pulled down the display from the command crown, maximized it. Instantly, his view of space was replaced by the looming bomb tug and bomb barge. The barge, which no doubt carried the weapon, was ten times larger than the little tug.

The Scourge.

And something, some faint speck at some distance from it. At first he thought it might be the *Guardian of Night*, already tens of thousands of kilometers away.

Something else, his instincts told him. Something on the beta, so it was sceeve or human.

He pointed to it. "What's that?"

"No correlating information. Maybe an afterimage, a beta echo? Analyzing."

"It's the bomb tug," Coalbridge said with growl. "Bastard detached from the barge in the Q. Kept separate Q from the barge from the first jump. Way *I* would've done it. Barge is headed for Earth. Tug is headed for the *Guardian* on a collision course. Get me Ricimer."

"Yes, Captain?"

"We've got company. The tug's vectoring in on you."

"I guessed this may be too easy."

Too easy! Coalbridge would hate to see hard.

"You can outrun it if you keep going," Coalbridge said.

"Naturally. But the wake formation maneuver requires that I come to a standstill in N-space. As must you."

"I know that, damn it. But when you do—the tug slams into you. And the barrier is destroyed along with you at the anchoring end."

"Or *you*," said Ricimer, "depending on its velocity. Remember, we will trade places exactly in the recross."

The calm voice of HUGH in his ear. "Bomb barge vectoring toward Earth on target, point five *c*. Barrier encounter in two minutes twenty-three seconds. Tug is traveling at point six *c*. Estimated tug impact is well within *Guardian of Night* current localization. Analysis indicates our maneuver was anticipated."

So, whoever was piloting the tug was no amateur.

"I may have a solution, Captain Coalbridge," Ricimer said.

"I'm all ears."

"The timing would be extremely delicate, and only determinable in the moment. I will need to use the *Humphreys*'s computational speed, I believe—"

"You've got it."

"Very well," said Ricimer. "The idea is to . . . we have an expression. When one is attempting to be in several places at once."

"Yeah, we call it spreading yourself thin," Coalbridge answered. He was trembling. *We're all going to die in seconds!* He could imagine Ricimer had driven more than one student insane with his patience, his desire to make *any* experience a teaching experience.

"I like that," said Ricimer. "We call it leaking out of one's own skin."

"Captain, what are you thinking to do?"

"I've contemplated this before. It was rejected during our war games as even possible to attempt." Ricimer emitted what was translated as a harrumph of pique.

"Ricimer, let's do it, whatever it is!"

"Very well. We shall combine the wake maneuver with a suture. If I leave and return within what you would term a Planck-second of my exit, then the wake maneuver will be completed. The barge and its bomb will be diverted. Because I *will have* existed at the completion point for *that* quantum event to take place. So if I enter N-space, compute a jump that will take my vessel into our final destination coordinates at the exact moment as the tug, reenter Q, drop to N-space . . ."

Coalbridge felt his head spinning trying to grasp what Ricimer was saying. Yet he *had to*. And for someone who had spent years mucking around in the Q, it didn't take long for the idea to gel.

"Yes. Yes, I see," he said. "You *won't* be there for—well, for less time than can be measured by any known means—when the tug arrives."

"Precisely," said Ricimer. "And then I will essentially materialize within the tug. But not truly within, for the tug and my craft will be sharing the same quantum space. I will *superimpose* myself upon it."

"So what happens then?" Coalbridge asked.

"Two bodies appearing in the same place at the exact same time. Impossibility."

"You mean they'll destroy one another."

"Or remain completely unaffected by one another," said Ricimer. "Otherwise ... let us say that I have long wondered about the possibility of a simultanaeity performed in combination with a suture. Our current situation would make for an excellent empirical test."

"The precision of the timing—"

"Would have to be slightly better than a light-clock, that is, a smaller increment than a photon passing between mirrored edges in the quantum foam."

"We don't have anything that precise."

"But you do have one thing," Ricimer said. "A computer program that has developed mathematical intuition. I have seen slaves. These servants of yours are no longer slaves. I believe they might arrive at the correct solution."

"ENGINE, can you do it?"

"I am uncertain," ENGINE said. "There *are* nonalgorithmic maths some of us have played around with." His voice came quietly, softly. "Perhaps if DAFNE were here, yes. With HUGH's help, and the other personas, I am not sure. If it *is* possible, the computation will not take long." A pause. "How do you do it, Captain Coalbridge?"

"I don't understand. Do what, ENGINE?"

"Remain lucky."

His family gone. His brother and sisters. Aunts, uncles, cousins. His parents. His grandparents. You didn't ignore the loss. You sidestepped it, you dodged it, you darted. Above all, you learned from it. Any moment, the same thing could happen to you.

Coalbridge shook his head, answered ENGINE. "Work with the fact that absolutely nothing turns out like you thought it would. *Use* uncertainty instead of running away from it."

ENGINE did not reply.

"Twenty seconds," HUGH reported. It was almost a whisper. "Beta-transfer protocols established with *Guardian of Night*. Fifteen seconds."

HUGH didn't continue the countdown after that.

Coalbridge pictured a roulette wheel spinning. The servants and personas of the *Humphreys* gathered round. Their geistly hands trembling, wavering. Then slowly and inexorably sliding all of their chips—all of humanity's chips—to one color or the other. Red or black.

Red or—

The *Guardian of Night*

Ricimer ordered the halt, the drop into N-space. It was like a thousand other commands he'd issued before. Sol burned bright in the distance. The stars around him. The stars beyond.

The simple universe of matter and light.

Less than the space of a breath, and—

"Protocol transfer from *Humphreys* complete," said Lamella. "Initiating jump."

Jump back into Q. The zoom effect, as the heavens readjusted themselves to quantum possibilities. As some stars, some galactic clusters, grew instantly closer, others, unentangled with any bit of matter in the Milky Way, receded.

Then, an amazing sight.

Passing through the *Guardian of Night*, passing through the bridge itself, the ghostly outline of the bomb tug. Passing before Ricimer's eyes.

A great creature of the deep on some liquid-covered planet, it appeared. Its metallic side was dull blue. Ricimer could see through it to crew members on the other side of the *Guardian* bridge. And he could see—

The tug pilot. She—it was a she—with muzzle flared wide. Screaming victory, death. Ricimer could almost smell the carbolic stench.

He reached out, tried to touch the pilot. His hand passed through nothingness.

And then the tug was past.

The stars zoomed out.

N-space.

He was alive. Was the vessel in the correct position? No time to check.

No time.

Jump.

The whipping recoil of simultaneity.

He was a million kilometers away. The *Humphreys* had taken his place.

Ricimer only checked the readouts out of habit. He was certain what he would find. The quantum wake was created; the suture was closed.

Equations balanced as a tiny ripple in space-time surged, then stilled.

The stars burned on, as indifferent as always.

Walt Whitman Station

Sam stood by the main viewport aboard the Walt Whitman, desperate to catch a glimpse but not expecting to see much. She was aware of what was happening, probably more aware of the theoretical intricacies than Coalbridge and possibly even Ricimer.

The battle was on in the Kuipers at last report—a real battle, and not, thank God, a hopeless last stand for humanity—but this end run could make the whole thing moot. A cobalt bomb could make what remained of habitable Earth uninhabitable, destroy an ecosphere already in desperate straits, and drive those humans it didn't kill outright into space as refugees to be hunted and exterminated at the sceeve's leisure.

You'd never know it from the state of affairs below. Instead of everyone girding up, there was a censure movement sizzling through Congress. The president was undergoing what amounted to a no-confidence vote led by the Quietists, Tillich—the former admiral who had become the party's poster boy—and various fringe interests.

Frost stood beside Sam, seemingly unperturbed by what was going on in Dallas. Sam supposed she knew how Taneesha Frost felt. Everything hinged on living, actually physically surviving, to fight another day. But then a blue-green flash beside Frost, and her aide KWAME was standing there, whispering into the president's ear.

She smiled.

"We squeaked by," Frost said to no one in particular. "The Quietists bet everything on an up or down vote, and lost. Big loss in the House. And fifty-two forty-eight in the Senate." Frost turned her attention back to the viewport. "Now, let's live to celebrate."

Sam, too, looked out. And at that moment, she saw it. Saw a flash, like a tracer bullet. Headed down, down toward the blue Pacific below.

Then it simply seemed to bounce away. Away in new trajectory toward the Moon.

All of this within a second at most. Sam blinked. No more spark, flash, trace.

"Was that it?" she heard Frost asking. "Was the bomb diverted?" The president was looking straight at her, at Sam, trusting her judgment on the matter.

"I think so, Madame President," Sam said. "I think our boys have done it."

The *Guardian of Night*

The cobalt-ion device had been sucked out of its trajectory, sucked by nonexistence, a vacuum within a vacuum.

Due to the quantum wake, the bomb barge vectored away from its path. Vectored toward Earth's moon.

The bomb must somehow have been armed *before* separation from the tug, else the tug pilot would not have been able to separate tug and barge within the Q. This was not ordinarily done—was *never* entrusted to lower ranking officers—and would have required a security override *greater* than admiral.

Who had piloted that tug?

The barge dropped into N-space just before it arrived at the Moon.

Ricimer imagined the simple decision algorithm within the craft attempting to correlate a firing solution.

Evidently, it came to a decision. A silver, needlelike cylinder separated from the tug.

This was the bomb itself.

The separation blast from the bomb's retaining brackets sent the barge tumbling away, to find either a fiery death in collision with a planet or to become a simple piece of space junk forever wandering the Sol system.

The bomb, meanwhile, headed for the Moon.

It didn't take long. The cobalt bomb collided with the surface. Flash of light.

Puff of lunar debris speeding into space.

A new crater bloomed.

No one died.

"Christ! Ricimer. We're alive! You're alive!" It was Coalbridge. Even without the translation, even with the sound and no smell,

Ricimer could tell how excited he was. If he were younger, he'd have felt the same.

Perhaps this feeling of escape, of exhilaration, was common to the young of most species. Perhaps it was even a universal principle, an emotional reflection of survival's logic. As was justice. As was love.

The voices of the ancestors, the hum of the *gid*, formed a low vibration of satisfaction with Ricimer.

You have found a way through this tunnel of darkness for our line. We are with you. Perhaps all is not lost. Perhaps our memories will not die.

Perhaps the road lies open ahead, child of ours. Because of you.

You are our cutting edge across the vacuum, etching all that has been forgotten back into being. Our word spoken, but a word that speaks itself truly, as well.

You are heir of a great line. We are proud of you, our son.

Yes. To come out alive. The poets could spray their perfumed songs about the good and noble way to die as they might.

Survival was the true victory that allowed them to spray at all.

He'd have plenty of time to think on this paradox, he supposed. Time to think was the survivor's reward.

"Ricimer, listen." It was Coalbridge. "That bomb barge is still out there."

"It is no longer a threat. The bomb was ejected. We should now attempt to hunt down the tug and its pilot, then return to aid your fleet."

"Yeah, I know. But I may have a better idea."

"Go on."

"We don't know where the tug is, but the barge is in N-space. I've got a good lock on its position." Coalbridge hurriedly continued onward with his thought. "Ricimer, we could *use* it. Put another servant copy aboard exactly like last time on the *Powers*. Take it back out to the Kuipers with us. Is that artifact on your vessel recharged?"

"Yes," said Ricimer.

What was Coalbridge considering?

Battle logic dictated—

But then Ricimer's muzzle widened to a smile. "Yes, I see what you mean, Coalbridge. You humans learn *very* quickly. Yes, this *is* a good idea."

TWENTY-THREE

20 January 2076
Sol System
Kuipers

BETA BROADCAST BEGIN

Hail, all vessels. Hail the armada.

We, the Human-Mutualist Alliance, speak.

We speak in the name of the Poet and in his spirit.

You will have noticed the eye of the armada hemisphere is destroyed by a weapon recently gleaned from the species Kilcher. Some of you will have heard of this through unofficial channels. Some of you will not have known of its existence. Now you have seen one of the effects of this weapon. We have, very simply, created a small exploding sun. An ensuing attempt to eradicate the resident species of Sol C by irradiated bomb was eliminated.

As for this secondary action, what sort of justification could there have been for such a course? Think on it—to make a world uninhabitable for any species? To create a world that cannot be parasitized? By your own oath of office, by your own beliefs, this is supremely unjust. It is wrong.

In any case, your current operation is over.

Leave this system. Do not return unless and until you understand. Regulation has destroyed families, hypha. It has replaced the truths we know in our gid, in our very sense

of self, with its own logic of power, its own zero-sum game.
Regulation has reached its inevitable end point.

We Guardians have become our own parasites.

We proclaim to you that the galaxy cannot be regulated. We
tell you that if you continue to seek domination, the universe
itself will rise up and cast you down.

We say to you that we, human and Mutualist together, will
burn you, blast you, and disassemble you down to subatomic
particles. We will create a floating ring of the dead to circle
around a dozen suns as a reminder for all species who come after.

Do not do as the Administration did.

Do not seek to regulate what you cannot begin to understand.

Live in symbiosis.

And if you cannot do that, then do the universe a favor
and exit in dignity.

For exit you will.

We will see to it.

Leave this system or face the consequences. Remain and
you will become so much stardust. This is a warning, not a
threat. It is inevitable. And every Guardian should know not
to tempt the inevitable. The acid rains fall on the regulated
and the unregulated alike. This cycle it has fallen on you.

Down with the Council.

Down with the Administration.

Thrive the United States of America.

Thrive the Symbiosis.

MESSAGE END.

USX *Petraeus*

SIGINT was crackling with the St. Elmo's fire of appearing and
disappearing geists, messages, and chroma relays, and Japps was
in the middle of it all. Her adrenaline was pumping, sure, but
there was a calm that came with knowing and executing the duties
of her post, finding the readouts and remote sensing what the
vessels of the fleet needed at each moment, routing them to the
destination where they would save lives. Kill sceeve.

It felt good to be back. Back on the job. Back in her native habitat, now with her field promotion to chief and the promise of a pay

raise and an ungodly amount of new audio gear. She had a long list, and she was going to take pleasure in checking each item off.

First, of course, she had to survive this in order to *get* to the music store.

The sceeve had—she quickly totted—a little under a thousand vessels remaining. Most had been on the hemisphere's periphery when the *Powers of Heaven* had exploded in its supernova fury. The blast had obliterated a good nine thousand craft.

Which left the Extry fleet's two thousand and two hundred with a two-to-one numerical advantage over the sceeve survivors. But the sceeve had more firepower per vessel in general and were now in as desperate position as the humans.

For both sides, it was a battle for survival.

Even scattered and broken, the armada remnant was proving a formidable foe. The big advantage the Extry had was that it was sitting on the Kuipers and was able to rearm its kinetic weaponry at will.

For a time it was shooting fish in a barrel as the sceeve battle-craft careened in individually at the fleet in what turned out to be suicide runs. Then they got smart, or, more likely, somebody intelligent took command, and they regrouped. It was clear whoever was in charge was trying to make a flank run up and over or down and under the Kuipers—and head toward Earth. That was the one thing everyone knew the fleet couldn't allow, and so the Extry moved to counter by surrounding the concentrating sceeve, about four hundred vessels strong by this point.

A furious fight ensued. Japps, whose intelligence-gathering billet aboard the *David Petraeus* put her at the center of the fleet's sensing nexus, experienced it all. The Battle of the Kuipers they'd probably call it, if anybody lived to give it a name at all.

The way things were going, Japps could believe that *both* sides might annihilate one another.

Nukes flew, surged into firework expansions. Rocks and rods tumbled through the void at velocities so extreme they were physically foreshortened by relativistic effects and got smaller as they sped away with a rapid effect that had nothing to do with their distance from the observer.

Vessels flowered in flame and agony of destruction. Rescue craft zipped hither and yon attempting to save what survivors they might.

And, damn it, the sceeve were winning. Because winning meant breaking out, breaking through. And they were doing it. The sphere of the Extry fleet was crumbling as one vessel after another guttered in flame and death and careened off into the nowhere between Neptune's and Pluto's orbits.

And then everything changed.

A message from Earthward.

"Fleet, this is *Guardian of Night*. We are closing on your position with encoded torpedo in tow. Please provide fire solution for torpedo. Fleet confirm?"

Familiar voice on com. It took Japps only a moment to mark it as Coalbridge's.

The crackle of reply from the admiral on Flagship *Petraeus*. "Get in here, *Guardian!* We've been waiting for you!"

OVERZAP, the main weaponry command, fed the *Petraeus*'s SIGINT station the firing coordinates and Japps squirted them over the beta without running strong encrypt and therefore adding the millisecond of delay such a process would have entailed.

She figured the sceeve knew where they were.

"Bomb-tug torpedo away!" said Coalbridge.

Japps watched as the device threaded through the fleet sphere, its tiny reaction plume speeding toward the heart of the sceeve knot of resistance.

They must be laughing at such a tiny threat, Japps thought. Sceeve, at least some of them, she knew, could laugh—particularly at grim jokes. The grimmer the better, actually.

The torpedo bleated its location. Japps routed the signal and the *Guardian* locked on.

"*Guardian* activating artifact," said Coalbridge. "Good luck, LOVE-2."

Then nothing.

No death ray. No plume of energy.

Nothing.

Nothing for one second. Two.

Then *something*.

Something *huge*.

A star.

A momentary star.

A second sun in the solar system.

And then that sun went nova.

21 February 2076
The Shiro
Central Council Chamber

"And you are certain it was the *entire* fleet?"

"I tell you they are gone."

"How is this possible?"

"I have no answer," said Gergen. "The surveillance drones returned with the images. All of their telemetry was cross-checked, confirmed."

"So the humans have the weapon?"

"I do not know," said Gergen. "What I do know is that they have somehow learned to create the energy of a star and use it as a weapon."

The Chair considered for moment. *Surely* this *fact must give her pause. Make her question her own certainties.*

But no.

She finally spoke. "So, they have become more powerful. We've dealt with strong enemies before. In the end, they fall to us. They fall to us because we are the embodiment of will. We are the congealing of a thousand million years of desire for order."

Gergen knew he should say no more. In a thousand similar circumstances he would have held his tongue. What prompted him to speak further was beyond him. Perhaps he'd caught an alien virus merely by drawing near to the humans. He'd put himself in the enemy's shoes. Into humanity's mind, as best he could.

And, curse her, he'd liked it there.

Free, but *not* weak. Free, but assiduous, competent, disciplined, unrelenting.

The logic was inescapable. If liberty could produce such qualities, then the entire foundational structure of Regulation must be called into question.

And so Gergen spoke the truth as he saw it, knowing as he did so that he was dooming himself. "It may be best not to underestimate them, Madame Chair. They have this new weapon. They likely have the Kilcher artifact. Their demands for our surrender claimed as much. And, if so, they now have Guardian support in the traitor..." For a moment, Gergen hesitated. But he was laying the truth bare, was he not? Shriving himself. Attempting to *help* the Chair to see. To understand the strategic situation her Administration now faced. He was an ally, even at the end. Gergen completed his thought. "The support of Ricimer."

I've sealed my fate.

The slightest whiff of distaste from the Chair.

She wasn't taking this well.

All for naught.

If he were lucky, they'd allow him a final passing of his *gid* to his children.

"I do believe, Director Gergen, that you have identified with a host animal too thoroughly," said the Chair. Her calm-scented words cut through the suddenly stilled chamber like a bracing wind.

"Forgive me, Excellency."

He gazed up at her, his political salvation for all these cycles. Now his doom.

Not really a surprise. He had merely wondered *when*, not *if*, he would be destroyed by the power he sought to shape. To wield.

The question was resolved.

The answer was: *now*.

"This extrusion of defeat is a stench that must never suffuse this chamber again. It does us dishonor." The Chair waved a hand in front of her muzzle, as if to clear to the air. "You're dismissed, Gergen."

"Thank you, madame." Gergen fell to one knee in the traditional leave-taking genuflection due the Chair and the chamber.

And as he turned to exit, as the chamber guards moved in on either side of him at a gesture from the Chair, Gergen understood.

I am for the knives. I am not to be allowed even the gid *passage. Pity for the children.*

So many things I have seen, done. Risked for a life that meant something. So much lost.

Everything.

And even as Gergen exited the chamber, his last act of protocol accomplished, the odor of his final pronouncement still hung in the air. A mere waving of the hand could never remove it, could not dissipate that name.

It was the odor that would linger with Gergen to his death.

The scent of oranges and musk.

A mere smell.

At least so the humans might pronounce it in their unsubtle

attempt to describe what was to them sensation, as meaningless as a loud clap of thunder, the whistle of nothing but wind.

But, to a Guardian, the wind would always have a voice.

And to a Guardian, this particular scent would always have a name.

Oranges and musk.

Ricimer.

Curse him.

29 February 2076
Walt Whitman Station

I know you're not really there. And I know you always will be there, at the other end of these messages.

I'm sorry I didn't show up that weekend. I could have hung around the same city where you lived, been a better dad.

You know that. I know that.

I thought I had to apologize. All the things I would never teach you, all the talks we would never have.

I couldn't save you.

I couldn't protect you.

I will mourn you forever. I love you always.

But now I have to let you go.

Little Shadow, I will always, always remain—

Big Shadow,
Your dad

Leher placed the three postcards it had taken him to write his message into the MDR compartment along with the material that Coalbridge and Sam had brought along. Coalbridge's contribution had been a jar full of red earth taken from his native Oklahoma. He'd made a pilgrimage to the home sites and workplaces of his extended family and collected a pinch of dirt from each place. It was a big jar. Coalbridge hadn't been exaggerating about how huge his family had been.

Sam's contribution was a single small item—an old-fashioned thumbdrive with, she said, an MP3 of the song she'd been listening to on the night when the sceeve first attacked.

An old October Lincoln pop ditty. Leher remembered it well.

"My innocence," Sam said. "My lost chance to be a normal woman in a normal world."

Now the drone was fully loaded and the three of them stood upon the edge of forever waiting to find the right moment to release it.

Actually they were standing on the lip of Walt Whitman's dry-dock portal, a football field long and as high as one of the remaining skyscrapers of Dallas. It was an enormous cavity within the space station, and at the moment, the lip was oriented toward Earth. In five minutes, it would find the sun and they would release the bottle drone.

The idea was to send it into the heart of their local star. To burn it all to smithereens.

An ancient practice. Leher was sure it was somehow useful to the human psyche. Would it take away their pain, cure their various neurotic maladies—well, be honest, *his* neurotic maladies—give them closure? Probably not.

But standing on the dock between his friends, it occurred to Leher that the ritual might have less to do with the past and more to do with the future.

"So, we made it," he said.

"We made it," said Sam. She gave him a peck on the cheek.

Coalbridge, who held the MDR drone in his hands, was staring out as the world turned below him. "The sceeve will be back," he said. "But we'll be stronger."

"We already are," Sam replied.

"And now we have a few sceeve of our own," Leher added.

Coalbridge nodded. "Tell me somebody remembered to bring some hooch."

"I thought you'd never ask," Sam said. She curled out of the daypack she was wearing, swung it around and unzipped it. From inside, she extracted three bottles of beer.

Shiner Bocks. Leher had always thought the Texas concoction a little bitter, but, then again, something was better than nothing. He took the bottle Sam proffered and twisted off the cap.

She and Coalbridge looked over at Leher.

Great, he thought. *I get to be the toastmaster, of course. Ex-lawyer. Word man.*

What to say? Too much. Never enough.

One. Two. Three tugs at his beard.

Trim? Not yet.

Maybe he'd shave the thing off.

Maybe not.

He raised his beer.

"To families," he said. "To those we must leave behind." Leher nodded to the drone in Coalbridge's hands. "And to this family. Our family. God help us, we're all we've got."

Leher clinked his beer against Sam's and the one she'd kept for Coalbridge while he held the messenger drone. All three bottles touched and let out a single clink. And as they did, the Walt Whitman spun to face the sun. Coalbridge released the drone, and it quickly buzzed off through the containment wall that held the atmosphere in the dry dock and out into the emptiness that was the general condition of space.

Sam handed Coalbridge his bottle. Leher turned his to his lips, took a sip.

The dry-dock containment field shaded to semiopacity as they faced the sun full-on.

Leher drank.

And then, as quickly as it had spun into the light, the space station turned away. Soon they would see the broken beauty of their home planet again. But for now, all that was visible were stars.

And of course Coalbridge did the one thing he ought not to have, and the one thing Leher knew he couldn't resist.

He jumped.

The containment field kept him in, bounced him back. Right into Sam. She fell on her ass. Pulled herself up, laughing.

"Hell with it," Leher said. "It's time I learned to do that."

And then Leher stepped up to the brink and leapt into the stars.

15 March 2076
Western Oklahoma

"So, are you telling me there are *no* Mutualist enclaves? That everything I've believed in is as much a lie as the Administration was trying to sear into my footpads?"

"No, Hadria, there may be Mutualist vessels, a small shiro or two, perhaps. Somewhere in hiding. Or perhaps not. The enclaves that are easily discovered have all been eliminated. What I'm telling you is that there never was a credible Mutualist resistance for you to join. Not in the way you imagine."

"But—all the stories, all the communications?"

"Think, my dear. Every story was told in a whisper. Have you ever seen what happens when a whisper travels from muzzle to muzzle? The words are not interpreted correctly. The meaning begins to shift. Sometimes meaning is lost altogether and hopes and fears and dreams are substituted in its stead."

Talid lifted her feet from the small tub of gruel both she and Ricimer were sharing. She set them down gently upon a towel nearby. Ricimer leaned over and toweled them for his former XO. She really did have lovely feet for a Nebula hypha female. And her hands were not so shabby, either, now that he could allow himself to think of her as something other than a colleague.

Yet such a thing would probably never happen between the two of them. They would probably never become lovers because Ricimer knew that Talid was made for a pair-bond. Once she engaged her desire, her love would follow. And Hadria Talid lived and breathed commitment.

He was not ready for that yet.

He probably never would be.

Ricimer sloshed his own feet about in the galvanized tub. The humans had been thoughtful. They'd provided Ricimer and his refugees with much. But proper eating facilities were difficult to recreate. The Extry Xenology Division had made heroic efforts to locate the nearest food source that seemed to satisfy the taste receptors as well as the body of a Guardian. Ricimer and many of the others had had a difficult time adapting to the nitrogen-based mix of the atmosphere and had gone through excruciating *atentias* of helium withdrawal. Some had not survived—most of the deaths occurred among the very old or very sick. All the children had adapted. The Xenology officer Leher's large hyperbaric chamber had saved many a life in this regard. And now Ricimer was adapted.

They all were. There was a village that looked to him for guidance. That had, of all things, *elected* him as governor.

He was, through no fault or attempt of his own, the leader of the last known Mutualist enclave.

The enclave had even created this dacha for him with human help, here where the refugees had settled in the wilds of—what did they call it? Oklahoma. The Wichita Mountains. Ricimer had to admit the landscape was . . . amenable. This portion of Earth was not so bad. The weather was dry and difficult, with the occasional enormous storm flowing through and soaking the landscape, barely slowed by this little clump of hills.

"Do you like this—what is the gruel called?" asked Talid. "I do not."

"I believe the human word to be a play on the material's sandlike qualities. But who can understand their grunts?"

Ricimer attempted to recreate the word for the food substance by exhaling quickly through a closed muzzle membrane. He believed he'd approximated the correct sound. He hadn't. It would sound, to a charitably inclined human ear, like a balloon letting out air. A human certainly would have trouble picking out the word "grits" from the expulsion.

Talid laughed, leaned back in her lounging chair. "Arid, what am I to do?"

"I think you know the answer to that."

"Give up on my beliefs? Is that your advice?"

"Not at all." He pulled his own feet from the gruel, allowed Talid to towel his foot gills for him. "I said that there *was* not a Mutualist resistance. There *is* now. It is *you*, Hadria. It is *us*."

"What do you mean?"

"Don't you understand what we've done here?"

"Stolen a battlecraft. Settled a group of castaways and renegades. Gotten away with it."

"Much more than that, Hadria, much more. Where do you think the philosophy you so adore is being put to its ultimate test? Do you think any of those vaunted Mutualist enclaves out there—if they really do exist—would attempt to cohabitate, to live symbiotically, with another *species*? You know the answer to that, Hadria. No Guardian, however charitably inclined, would contemplate it. But here we are, doing so by necessity. And because two species wish it so."

"But Arid—"

"No buts. This was not my plan, I admit. Not the means I thought to employ. But we are vectoring toward the end I always sought." Ricimer brought his hands together in a gesture of reflection. "The Administration took my family. Took all that I loved. And so I decided that I would have to take what they hold most dear in return."

"And what is that?"

"Their power."

"You are going to take the Administration's power?" she said, suppressing a laugh when she saw he was serious. "You are going to bring down the Council?"

Yes. He was serious. He hadn't realized this about himself, not completely, until this moment, this conversation with his trusted friend. But now that he did, the logical path lay clear before him—as clear as a line of diamonds through a desert of salt.

"*We* are," Ricimer said. "It's us. We have the means. We have an ally in the humans and their servants—an ally whom our enemies underestimate at their peril. We are a living example of the doctrine of symbiosis."

"So we become philosophers? Lawyers?"

"A people. A nation," Ricimer said. "And do not forget, we already possess a vessel of war."

"You mean the *humans* have a vessel. This United States does. This national government that does not even represent the entire species. A sort of bloated hypha with delusions of grandeur. *They* have our vessel."

"Let me worry about that, my dear," said Ricimer. "I took the *Guardian* before. I can take her again. Although this time I believe we can accomplish the task through politics. These humans are as politics-crazy as ourselves, it seems."

"Then, thank you, but I will leave the politics to you, my captain. I have no talent for it."

Ricimer cocked his head in a Guardian nod. "Politicians we must become. But remember—in the *gid*, at center and core, you and I remain what we always were, Hadria. Warriors."

Talid flared her muzzle into a smile. She cracked an ammonium hydroxide nebulizer of Old Fifty-five. Its pungent odor filled the little porch with intoxicating freshness. A new start.

Talid raised the vial in toast.

"Until the Final Rotting," she said.

"Until the Final Rotting, indeed," answered Ricimer.

"And to the Mutualist resistance, wherever they are," she continued, and breathed in deeply.

"To us," Ricimer replied softly. He took the proffered vial from her lovely hands. "To Earth."

— THE END —

GUARDIAN GLOSSARY

Agaric Pogrom, the: a recent genocidal move against the Mutualists in the Shiro

Agaric, the: a Mutualist-leaning neighborhood in the Shiro; made up of curved, pre-Regulation architecture, 25-hand ceilings in living quarters

ammonium hydroxide: this chemical gets Guardians drunk; see *nebulizer*

Arc 7: a causeway that connects the Agaric to the main Shiro

atentia: see *time terminology*

benzene: this chemical provides Guardians a less intense, but longer lasting drunk than ammonium hydroxide; see *nebulizer*

biomatrix computer: part of a bicameral computer system on Guardian vessels, the governing computer on a Sporata vessel; referred to as Governness; see *quantum computer*

blisters: bubbles on nebulizers that are stroked to release the esters within

BODY POSITIONS:

Muzzle flare, widening	smile
Movement of head to right	nod, agreement
Uptilt of head, turning the nose up at	disagreement, disbelief
Stiff-necked	truculent
Hand over muzzle	thinking, lost in thought
Palm to chest, then palm out as if blowing a kiss	Sporata salute between equals, or higher rank to lower rank
Locked knees, shoulders to attention	salute, lower rank to higher rank
Wide muzzle flare	predatory indicator
Wave head side to side	shrug

captain's atrium: a circular portion of the bridge of a Sporata vessel; has interface mesh on floor for feet, manual override

cartilage lacework: Guardian under-skin skeletal system

cinc: see *time terminology*

cinqueta: see *time terminology*

cinquintium: see *time terminology*

Civitas, the: a general term for Administration government

cleansing: pogrom

COM control patch: on Sporata uniform sleeve; selects communication channel

Combs, the: a generic term for a distinct living/working area of the Shiro

conquest technology: see *gleaned technology*

Craft Orders: general mission orders for a Sporata vessel

cycle: see *time terminology*

DDCM: Disambiguation of Codes and Mandates; part of the Administration Directorate

DIA: Innovation Assimilation; part of the Administration Directorate

ester: general term for Guardian scent "word"

false liaison: Guardian officers having sex with crew members while those rates are under the control of Governess. There is a back door into the program that allows officers to instruct the monitoring computer to blank such transgressions from crew memory.

friend of the *gid*: friend of the heart

gid: the collective-memory portion of the Guardian nervous system

gleaned technology: tech taken from conquered species

Governness: see *biomatrix computer*

gripping gills: gills on a Guardian's palm, used in a fingerlike manner

hand: a common unit of Guardian height measurement, about a foot in length

Lamella: see *quantum computer*

manual control stick: located on the captain's atrium on a Guardian vessel; usually secured to one side

MODES OF GUARDIAN ADDRESS:

Companion "First Name"	indicates friendship
Receptor	political operations officer
Sub-receptor	political portion of Sporata captain's job
Storekeep	Sporata vessel quartermaster

molt: see *time terminology*

momentia: see *time terminology*

naphthalene: this chemical provides Guardians a fast and steady drunk; see *nebulizer*

nebulizer: Polymer bubbles that hold what is normally a gas in a pressurized, semiliquid state. A straw protrudes from one side of each bubble, and ends in a device similar to a perfume atomizer. The object is to squirt the contents directly onto the muzzle and suffuse the nasal membranes with what is, for a Guardian, a powerful stimulant, depending on the concentration. See *ammonium hydroxide, benzene, naphthalene,* and *Old Fifty-five.*

NH$_4$: ammonium hydroxide; this chemical gets Guardians drunk; see *nebulizer*

Officer's Arms: a military neighborhood in the Shiro; location of the Academy; made up of boxy, pre-fab units

Old Fifty-Five: the single-malt scotch of nebulizer content

perfluorodecalin: Guardian blood, milky-white in color

petty officer's round: cyclic promotions for non-com rates

positor: Guardian penis, corkscrew shaped

quantum computer: part of a bicameral computer system on Sporata vessels, the quantum computer is referred to as Lamella; see *biomatrix computer*

receptor: political operations officer

scleral muscle zoom: natural zoom lens in the Guardian eye

semanato: see *time terminology*

Shiro, the: an enormous habitat that serves as the Administration's governing hub; its current location is in a distant orbit around Pollux b, 33.7 light-years from Sol and outward from the galactic center.

shriving: a combination mental "struggle session" and physical pain session delivered with various instruments as punishment

Sirius armada: Sporata fleet stationed in area of Sol. The invasion fleet.

SMELLS:

Bergamot	conveys sadness, regret
Fruity perfume	overpowering, mind-voice of Governess
Sulfide	conveys victory over high odds and long distance
Phenol blast	"Thrive the Administration"
Bile rising in nostril	conveys anger, rancor felt
Citrus	voice of Lamella
Musk and oranges	Ricimer's name
Lemon	chuckle
Carbolic acid	wail of pain and/or fear and/or dying cry

Souk, the: Shiro black market

Sporata, the: the space navy of the Guardians

Sporata Academy, the: space navy academy in the Shiro

SPORATA POSITIONS:

Sporata enlisted	rates
Sporata officers	officers, ranks
Sailor	any Sporata member
Academy student	Plebe

SPORATA UNIFORMS/INSIGNIA:

Silver scabbard	captain's knife, always worn
Titanium wreath	captain's circlet, always worn
Silver-corded belt	captain rank
Doubled silver-corded belt	receptor
Sleeveless black tunic, silver-rimmed	Sporata officer
Black tunic	Sporata rate

storekeep: quartermaster

tagato: see *time terminology*

thinking aft: officers not allowing the ship computer to read their thoughts

TIME TERMINOLOGY:

UNIT	GUARDIAN EQUIVALENT	APPROXIMATE HUMAN EQUIVALENT
vitia		1/3 second
momentia	125 vitias	2/3 minutes
atentia	125 momentias	1.5 hours
tagato	25 atentias	1.5 days (36 hours)
semanato	5 tagatos	1 week (7.6 days)
variado	5 semanatos	1 month (38 days)
molt	5 variados	6 months (190 days)
cycle	5 molts	2.6 years (950 days)
cinc	5 cycles	13 years
cinqueta	5 cincs	65 years
cinquintium	50 cincs	650 years

V-CENT: vessel central processing: the computer center on a Guardian vessel

variado: see *time terminology*

vitia: see *time terminology*

ASTRONOMICAL NOTES

Extry and Sporata vessels can travel at a top speed of 900 times the speed of light. This is 2.5 light-years per day.

Fomalhaut Limit = supposed 25-light-year territorial boundary sphere around Sol.

The Shiro's current location is in a distant orbit around Pollux b, 33.7 light-years from Sol and outward from the galactic center.

Chief Seattle–Powers of Heaven encounter is near the 82 Eridani system, approximately 20 light-years from Sol and at about the same distance as Sol from galactic center.

The Eridani gate of the Vara Nebula is invented, as is the existence of the Vara Nebula itself. It is supposed to be approximately two light-years from Sol.

AFTERWORD

First and foremost: this book is meant entirely for entertainment purposes! I wrote it to get a whispered "cool" out of you, and to avoid your scratching your head and muttering "huh?" At least, not *too* often. That being said, here are a couple of reflections on the ideas and science behind the science fiction storytelling.

FTL

Welcome to the dawn of the Quantum Age. Dear reader, it has already begun. The coolest extrapolated science I've come across in the past few years is the idea of magnifying the quantum properties of matter to create macroscopic, Einstein-Newtonian, normal-scale effects. This stuff is not merely the dream of a mad scientist in some future possible world. No, it's being done today.

Split-mirror experiments building on the Aspect experiment and others of the 1990s have not only demonstrated quantum teleportation, they are being duplicated and expanded upon constantly. We can make quantum weirdness happen right before our eyes.

There's more. Superconducting quantum-interference devices have long been used to measure vanishingly weak magnetic fields. But the most interesting application for SQUIDS may await. A SQUID is a superconductor made into a ring about half a centimeter across (big enough to see; big enough to handle) with a constriction narrowing down in the loop to about one ten millionth square centimeter. The constriction acts as a Josephson junction, an area where various quantum effects are produced.

What's so great about that? This: the SQUID acts as a kind of magnifier, a bullhorn (or organ pipe, if you like) that transmits the quantum effects occurring at the junction to the whole structure.

In other words, a SQUID behaves as a single subatomic particle. All quantum mechanics, all the time.

What happens at the subatomic level that might be interesting to us up here in the world of Big Matter? For one thing, particles teleport from place to place instantaneously. They make quantum leaps. One of the more interesting of quantum leaps is the leap of a photon across the Planck distance, the so-called quantum foam, of space-time. If this instantaneous leap could be magnified, transmitted to entire conglomerations of matter...

To a spaceship, say...

You're talking faster-than-light travel.

Actually, you're talking *instantaneous* travel.

And how might this magnification be accomplished? Well, that's what SQUIDs do *now*. If SQUIDs could be refined, perhaps networked...

A SQUID of SQUIDs?

Might we not be able to make instantaneous leaps over distances far greater than the smallest distance possible, the Planck length? Miles. Astronomical units. Light-years.

Anyway, that's the idea behind the FTL in *Guardian of Night*. Possible? We may find out sooner rather than later.

And speaking of which: The craft suture movements and quantum-wake effects? Let's just say my goal was to stay *plausible*— which is all a poor science fiction writer can ever really hope for when exploring the outer reaches of a particular idea. If one is going to tell stories of space naval maneuvers involving quantum effects, one should be allowed a few wild-ass guesses!

COMMUNICATION

The beta, the communication system used by the Guardians (and adopted by humans), is also the extrapolated product of a quantum effect. Quantum teleportation of coded and meaningful information has not been accomplished yet, so far as we know. Some have declared it theoretically impossible. Quantum teleportation of known information *has*. If you create a pair of electrons or photons in the same subatomic process, their quantum states—their electrical spin properties, their quarky color properties, etc.— become causally entangled. If you do an experiment to determine what the spin of one particle might be, you immediately make its entangled twin take on the opposite spin. It's as if neither particle has decided which way to swing until one of them is hit on in the Rick's Café Americain of physics. At that point, the particle, merely from being observed, will resolve into one or the other spin state. You can't be an electromagnetically bi electron in *this* observable universe. And that particle's entangled twin, even if the twin is across the room or even across the galaxy, will also resolve into a determined value—and that resolution will occur not at the speed of light, not faster than light, but instantly. How could it be otherwise? Nonlocality is fundamental to quantum mechanics.

If this resolution of entanglement could be used to convey information, you'd have yourself an instantaneous radio system.

What I do herein is to posit that such instantaneous communication has been achieved, but over a limited distance due to the fact that particles are damn hard to retain unentangled—and finding which particle might be entangled with another a few parsecs distance away might be a bit difficult to accomplish.

LANGUAGE

What about the sceeve language? Well, this is very much an invention. My science fiction influence in the matter, however, is rock solid. Back in the 1980s I discovered, somewhat to my own chagrin, that I wasn't going to be a brain surgeon or rocket engineer, but that, due to the roll of the dice that resulted in my peculiar brain structure, the writing life was for me whether I wanted it or not. At about that time, I came across an amazing novella by Greg Bear. It was called "Hardfought," and it changed my world, so far as storytelling was concerned.

In "Hardfought," humanity is fighting aliens so completely, well, *alien* that we essentially cannot experience reality in the same manner as they do. We (that is, us real live humans today) live in the third generation of star production in our universe. Population III stars, the first stars in the universe, were hydrogen monsters. They are the stars that began baking the heavier elements in their ovenlike hearts. The universe suddenly had the lighter gases. From the exploded nebula formed by these stars were born Population II stars.

These stars made metal.

And heavier elements still.

And so the universal epoch of metalicity dawned—or, as you might like to call that epoch, the Age of Heavy Metal. From the deaths of Population II stars emerged Population I stars such as the Sun, and rocky, element-rich planets such as our own.

Greg Bear's genius was to extrapolate on the sort of life that might have evolved under the light of a Population II star. And thus were born the Senexi of "Hardfought."

Very creepy and cool aliens, indeed.

So brilliant was the entire concept, and Bear's execution of it, that I decided then and there that to become a science fiction writer might be the coolest damn thing I could possibly do as a writer. To attempt to approximate the greatness of a story like "Hardfought" myself would be incredibly *fun.*

And, over the years, trying to do so has been exactly that.

So thank you, Greg Bear.

But back to the Senexi. Bear's aliens communicated by chemical transfer—by, essentially, smell. Life on Earth does the same, of course. In fact, chemical communication is far more common than visual signal or audible yack in nature. Why wouldn't a sentient alien species, particularly one that evolved in airless space, also make use of it? Seems like a no-brainer to me.

But how to describe such communication? How to make it *plausible*? There's the rub. And the fun part. You can judge whether or not I succeeded, but I can tell you for sure I had a blast attempting to work out the implications.

So thank you again, Greg Bear.

TECHNOLOGY

Technology progresses because people want it to progress. In my opinion, there is no such thing as "culture"—at least in the sense of some supra-human thoughtweb that transcends the individual. Like DNA in cells, culture comes in one size and one size only: the human being.

This is why freedom is essential for survival and why totalitarian societies are ultimately doomed. It isn't really a moral question— or, at least, it isn't *only* a moral question—at all. Freedom is logically necessary for sentience to develop and to prosper. It is, as certain old dead dudes once put it, a self-evident conclusion concerning life.

Technology is the knife edge of culture. When we are hard-pressed as a species, it progresses more quickly. Nothing presses us so hard as war.

So, do I think it unlikely that we will see such advances as depicted in the book in a relative blink of the galactic eye?

No way. It'll be even weirder. I think I've erred on the conservative side as far as the extent of change to come is concerned. Whether I've guessed the right direction is another matter entirely, however. Therein lies the danger and fun of writing science fiction.

Anyway, I've never bought the "humanity disappears into its own navel" idea that we are destined (or *doomed*) for a virtual existence in a virtual world. On the contrary, virtual reality as we currently experience it is *real* reality that augments our current senses, experiences, and thinking processes. Will a futuristic virtual reality alter us? Absolutely. Will it make us somehow less than human? Hardly likely.

The chroma and salt in the book are my idea for such a virtual reality. Life is *not* an app. We are always going to remain in this beautiful, dangerous material universe. But, like the weather guy on the evening news, our virtual overlays will give us current readings and, more importantly, the *extended forecast.*

Why not take the analogy literally and extend our senses with the special effects of the television weather forcaster or the film-maker? If you could make a portion of observed reality as it falls on your corneas (say, a less used bandwidth of light) into something like the green screen the weatherman is physically standing in front of in his studio, you might then be able to filter in (using those same excluded wavelengths) helpful new material before those images landed on your retina. Now apply the same principle to your other senses....

That's the idea behind the chroma. Not particularly mind-shattering as a concept. The fun part was positing it in mid-development. Like the original television with antennas you sometimes had to bend into heiroglyphics in order to get good reception, it seemed like it would be fun to extrapolate an idea of true virtual reality, but VR in a clunky, earlier stage of development where all the kinks haven't been worked out.

And those are some of the ideas that animated me while writing *Guardian of Night*. I hope you liked the book.

—Tony Daniel

ACKNOWLEDGEMENTS

Lucas Johnson, Lauren Dixon, Sean Sutherlin, Olivia White, Matthew Bynum, Abigail Manuel, David Afsharirad, John Gonzales, Justin Boyd and V.J. Boyd make up Junto, my writing group (we're named after Ben Franklin's group and you say it with a *j* and not an *h* sound). They put hours into reading the book in draft and gave me notes, notes, notes. My best friend Michael Taylor, scriptwriter of many a *Star Trek* and *Battlestar Galactica* episode, has pitched ideas back and forth with me for years and was a great help. Finally, my wife Rika read the book aloud and gave me suggestions—and my kids, Cokie and Hans, kept getting hungry again with each sunrise and drove dad onward to THE END.